Sette e Mezzo

Francesco II and Maria Sophia of the Two Siciles

Sette e Mezzo

SEVEN AND A HALF:
THE PALERMO REVOLT OF 1866

Giuseppe Maggiore

Translated by
FREDERICK HAMMOND

with the collaboration of
MARIA CARLA MARTINO

Epigraph Books
Rhinebeck, New York

Paperback ISBN: 978-1-954744-72-1

Library of Congress Control Number: 2022905936

Book design by Colin Rolfe
Cover image: The Genius of Palermo, Fieravecchia, Palermo

Epigraph Books
22 East Market Street, Suite 304
Rhinebeck, NY 12572
(845) 876-4861
epigraphps.com

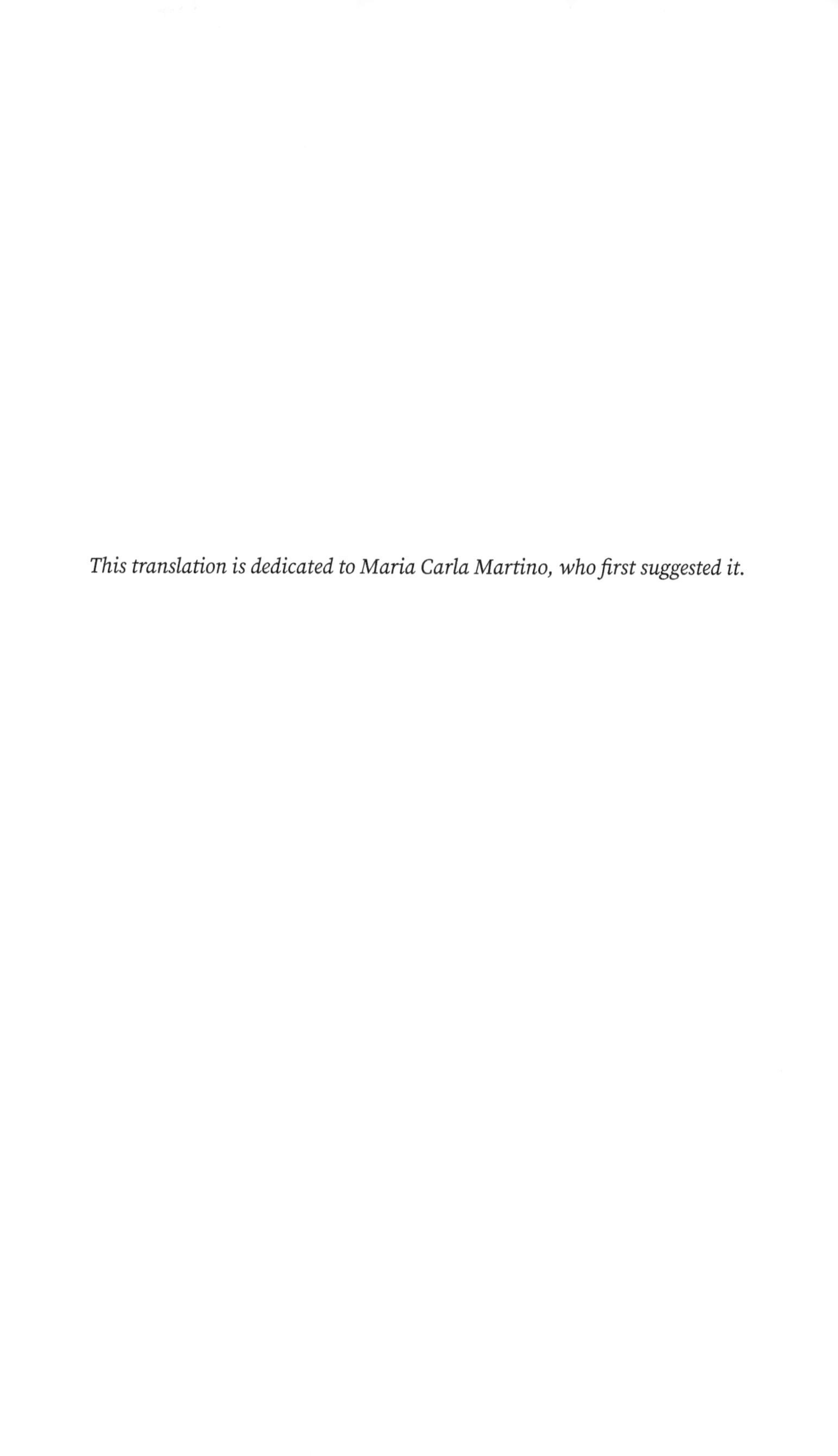

This translation is dedicated to Maria Carla Martino, who first suggested it.

PART I

Chapter 1

THE CALENDAR indicated 16 January. The year was understood. It is the custom of almanacs to record only once, on the first page, that another cycle of our life has slid down into Nothingness. Then begins the smaller accounting of the months and days: February, March, April...Tuesday, Wednesday, Thursday...All of them the same. *Sufficit enim diei malitia sua,* Sufficient unto the day is the evil thereof, the Gospel says.

In 1864 the official birthday of His Bourbonic Majesty Francesco II, King of the Two Sicilies, fell on that January 16. A king without a kingdom. Francesco had been dethroned for four years. Dethroned by whom? By Providence? By History? Unimaginable. Only by brute force allied with crime and betrayal. If History, poisoned by the over-strong wine of perverse ideologies, had surrendered herself to a half-witted course by overturning the Bourbons, Justice and Nemesis would have made her reverse, as you turn a demented clock back to the right time. It is not true that History is irreversible, that it marches in only one direction. Everything waits until God gives the signal. Did the Bourbons of France not remount the throne of the Capets after the cataclysm of the Revolution? And had not the golden lilies on a white field of the Bourbons swept away the revolutionary tricolor, the symbol of Sin and Rage? And had not the well-beloved Ferdinando I, ancestor of the unhappy Francesco II, been restored to power twice, once after the sad episode of the Neapolitan Republic and once after the Napoleonic usurpation?

Thoughts of this type, filled with resentments and regrets, parti-colored with nostalgia and hopes, buzzed around in the head of marchese don Fabrizio Cortada as it lay on his pillow. Those thoughts, customary denizens of a mind incapable of change, danced and whirled in a mad tumult on the morning of 16 January 1864. Finally his thoughts knelt, with a mixture of tenderness and devotion, before the image of the best—the last—of the three reigns that the marchese had faithfully served, Francesco I, Ferdinando II, Francesco II.

Ecco. There it is, complete with a fulsome autograph dedication, the photograph of the august royal couple. On the night table, within reach of eye and hand. Two figures joined by their linked arms, like the two talons of a capital *X*. He in the long double-breasted tunic of a colonel of the line, cinched at the waist by a gun belt of black leather with a gilded buckle, his slender neck planted in the middle of his upright collar like a flower stem in a vase, his cap under his arm, his feminine hand on the hilt of his saber. A sharp face, adolescent whiskers on his rabbity lips, gentle and thoughtful eyes under the firmly parted hair. She, enclosed in a vast crinoline with three rows of ruffles, her corset rigid, her sleeves puffed out, her fan clutched like a scepter in her nervous hand, experienced and wilful: small eyes of an almost aggressive astuteness under two cutting eyebrows declining toward the bridge of her nose. Who said that in the photograph, weighed down by subjection, he seems to stand a step behind his wife? Who seemed to surprise in the slightly bewildered glance of the last Bourbon the unctuousness of a religious novice? Study him well. Under that modest appearance there is none other than a king. If they had allowed him to rule they would have seen that he could have become the leader of all Italy.

So thought don Fabrizio on first awakening, caressing with his glance the image of *his* sovereign, set like a jewel in a frame of gold and tortoise shell.

His sixty-five years notwithstanding, don Fabrizio was still in perfect form. A bull-like torso pitched on two rather short legs, a fine head with a thick weight of steel-colored hair, mingling from his temples down into the collar of his beard, which was a faithful copy of king Ferdinand's. A blue gaze under two cornices of black hair which flickered and sometimes joined like two earthworms; something resolute, firm, and bitter in his expression, not unconnected with an hereditary sense of nobility and rectitude. Only two pouches, tending toward violet, under his eyes provided a false note in his face, making it appear withered without being droopy, flabby without being weak.

Don Fabrizio opened a crack in the curtains of the heavy bed canopy, made sure that it was daylight, no matter that the sun was slow to dissolve the coils of winter haze. Grasping the little bell with the Cortada family arms, he shook it with youthful energy. If he had not rung it loudly it was possible that the faithful Marco, the majordomo inherited from the late don Alfonso, the marchese's father, would have paid no attention: old Marco was deaf as a post. A discreet tap at the door. A light creak of the handle. There, on the threshold, Marco, bald, smooth except for a brow furrowed by some wrinkles, with two rosy cheeks above his snowy mutton-chop whiskers.

—*Eccellenza benedica*—the old man greeted, bowing low enough to graze with the tip of his nose the silver tray he held in both hands, bearing the coffee service and the morning's mail.

—I knew you were deaf. Now you're starting to go blind too, old boy. Don't you see that the table is covered with books?—cried don Fabrizio, seeing that the butler was struggling to arrange the tray on the bedside table.

Various volumes were piled up on the marble. On top of them all stood out, still open, the work of Antonio Capece Minutolo, *The utility of the Catholic religion for the tranquility and peace of the people and of the princes*, printed in Naples in 1825. This was the book on a few of whose pages the marchese meditated very evening before going to sleep, mixing it with his equally customary reading of the writings of Haller and Giuseppe De Maistre, champions of legitimism. With those three evangelists of sane politics, he—who would be the fourth, when he had finished the work which for some time had been buzzing about his mind—felt in good company, indeed in an iron vessel, to bring into port the undertaking of the holy restoration, in which he was employed in the sight of God and man.

The coffee smoked in the cup with a delicious fragrance.

—So, are we ready, Marco?

—Everything is in order.

—Have the invitations been sent out?

—All of them, just as Your Excellency instructed.

—I can't imagine that you sent them by post. Under this government not one public service functions.

—No post. Didn't Your Excellency order them to be delivered by hand?

—So I ordered.

—They have been delivered by the second footman.

—Always under your responsibility, of course.

—Whatever are you saying, signor marchese? Of course I am responsible.

—The gallery is in order?

—Yes, Excellency. Since yesterday.

—The portraits of Their Majesties, God save them?

—They are there, in the place of honor. The flowers will arrive during the morning, so as to be fresher. I agreed with the gardener. The green plants are already arranged along the stairway, the entrance, and around the gallery.

—Bravo, Marco! You will have a gift in honor of His Majesty.

—What are you saying, signor marchese? I have lived within these walls for fifty years. I was a boy when the late marchese Alfonso took me into his service.

—I know. You are a veteran. So it is not necessary to recommend prudence and silence about what happens in this house. We are surrounded by enemies, by spies. The liberals, the government toadies, the revolutionaries are all at our heels. They are on the lookout everywhere, always ready to shout: 'give it to the *rats!*' I don't like to say it, but, if they were cats they would have devoured us a long while ago.

—But I wager, Excellency, that in a little while the rats will make a tidbit of the cats.

—Why not?—don Fabrizio smiled, pleased.—Now help me dress.

The marchese made the sign of the Cross, dangled his hairy legs over the bedside, putting on the slippers that Marco held out to him, slipped into a soft velvet dressing gown, stretching his arms with satisfaction at being alive, and went with a firm step to his work table, a disk of red marble gracefully resting on the slender necks of three bronze swans impatient to take flight. The marble was so shiny that the head of the marchese was reflected like that of the Baptist on the platter of the dancer Salome.

The whole room, orchestrated in the purest Empire style, mingled in a peaceful harmony the dark blond of the mahogany, the faded blue of the damasks, the glimmer of gold, and the somber and varied tones of the tortoise shell that framed rare engravings by French and English burins.

Don Fabrizio started to leaf through his mail. A sacred notice from the Confraternity of the Dying, where he was prior; an invitation for a meeting of the Academy of Sciences, Letters, and Arts, which was honored to number him among its members; a number of 'Il Presente,' the reactionary sheet directed by the little duke of Acquaviva; an account balance from the Bank of Sicily; and at the end a yellow envelope, rather dirty and adorned with greasy fingerprints.

The address, penned in faded sepia ink by a hand really or seemingly inexpert at writing, read in Sicilian, 'marchisi Don Fabrizu—at the Addauru [Via dell'Alloro]—City.'

C'é cu vi chiama gran riazionariu/pirchì tiniti manu a lu burbuni; / io ci giuru ch'é tuttu lu cuntrariu: / chiuttostu aviti' a testa a pinnuluni. / Vui priparati la rivuluzioni / circannu a lu cuvernu dari 'mmastu. / Chiù saggia la marchisa, pi riazioni / vi metti nna lu stemma un beddu crastu. / Siti lu capu di legittimisti / e spirdati vidennu un liberali: / Lu liberalismu, nun c'è Cristi, / è 'n casa vostra, o marchesi minnali.

Some call you a great reactionary/because you support the Bourbons,/I swear that it's quite the opposite/instead your head is dangling. /You prepared the revolution/seeking to give trouble to the government. Your wife is wiser, by reaction/she puts a fine sheep on your coat of arms./You are the head of the legitimists / and stare in horror at seeing a liberal: /There is no doubt / liberalism is in your house/, slow-witted marchese.

The first reaction of the reader was dignified anger. Who dared to besmirch the spotless and fearless blason of one of the noblest houses of Palermo with even a breath of suspicion? Who was the infidel pig who dared to stick his nose into the sanctuary of his family, violating its inmost intimacy?

Don Fabrizio, an aristocrat of Catalan blood with four quarterings of nobility and more than one viceroy in his ancestry, could not admit that donna Teodora, his lawful wife in the sight of God and man, had let some drop of ink stain the purity of her marriage contract, whether inadvertently or not. He must not admit it. And then... It was not the first time that wretched anonymous letters, if not precisely of this kind, letters breathing threats and outrages, had been directed to him by the rabble, who distrusted his agitation for the cause of legitimism and bore a grudge against his house as a second Coblenz, a haven for secret plots and shadowy conspiracies. As if the pricks and the poisonous bites of so many cheap liberal, Jacobin, and Masonic newspapers were not enough, mysterious anonymous letters, sometimes illustrated with skulls and daggers, had rained down on his house to intimidate him and put him *hors de combat*. Infinite and torturous are the ways of evil. Because he stood like a man, supported by two pillars of the Christian life, the throne and the altar, he could not prevent the forces of the devil from descending to do battle against him. It is ever thus in this world, the sons of Darkness against the sons of Light.

The metaphor pleased don Fabrizio, who had developed a taste for certain literary delicacies through his frequent readings. And the tidbit that pleased him the most was the personification of the revolution as a monster with seven heads—seven for the mortal sins—each head bristling with slimy and disgusting serpents. From the time that he had seen the famous head of Medusa at the Uffizi in Florence he had privately selected that poetic representation as the symbol of revolution. Now it seemed to him that the same tangle of reptiles writhed, slimy and filty, in his own hands, which still clutched the anonymous letter. He felt a spasm of disgust. He crushed the paper, rolled it into a ball, and threw it to the gound, planting his foot on it, as if it were indeed a knot of vipers.

His burst of rage lasted only a few seconds. It was sufficient for him to get up from his seat and to take a few steps up and down the room for his anger to cool down and for contempt to calm it like ashes over a fire. Reflection had leaned into his ear to say, 'It's all very well to despise a document like that, but preserving it is better.' So he picked up the sheet, unfolded it as best he could, smoothing out the creases, put it back in the envelope, and threw it into the bottom of the drawer.

—The Revolution is an idea of the devil—he declared in a firm voice—and Teodora is an angel.

He continued to brood to himself,—certainly even the angels are subject to temptations. Although they are made of unearthly substance, they have their own fragility. One of them even fell, and it was the one who shone the brightest. But there are those who fluctuate, who waver like the needle of a magnet. Them we must save from this dangerous wavering, we must hold back their falling instead of hastening it with our suspicions.

That the behavior of Teodora for some time had been (how to say it?) inlaid with strangeness there was no doubt. Frequent migraines, long silences, unexpected outbursts, unusual pallor, fevers of worldliness alternating with languors of solitude: in a word, so many symptoms worth being watched. Studied, yes. Not interrogated. Was he, marchese Cortada, descendant of proud knights, grand-nephew of viceroys, descendant of conquistadors, was he the stuff of a police examining magistrate? Heaven forbid, *Potius mori quam foedari*—Better to die than to rot. A Cortada would never sink to mounting guard over the chastity of his wife. In his family there shone men of the scepter, of the sword, of the law-gown, of the cloister, there were counted high civil and military authorities, dignitaries, judges, penitents, blesseds and venerables: never jailers. No one would have lowered himself to shadow or spy on a woman, a participant of the name and dignity of the family. Could he now become a police spy like Salvatore Maniscalco, he, don Fabrizio Corada, a marchese with four quarters of nobility, Gentleman of the Bedchamber with the favor and the golden key of the most loyal and chivalrous of kings?

Such thoughts, now lazy, now violent, floated around within the soul of the marchese without reaching an outlet. He found only one way to divert them, by immersing himself in the Bourbonist newspaper which had arrived that morning.

The gurgle of a little bell—a liquid silver note—throughout the palace. The prolonged trill draws closer, moves farther off from stairway to stairway, from loggia to loggia, from room to room, finally to die away in the quadriportico of the courtyard. It is the mass, the mass...

—Can it already be nine o'clock?—don Fabrizio wonders, shaking himself awake from his timeless soliloquy.

The gilded clock pendulum, an Adonis wounded and lying in the arms of Venus, sounded nine metallic strokes from atop the console table.

The tenth was struck on the door by the woody knuckles of Marco.

—Signor marchese, the mass is ready.

—Already?

—It is nine o'clock.

Time has its own truth, which often is not ours. Nothing is more true and more unreasonable than its passage.

—The marchesa has been informed?

—Yes, Excellency. She is coming down the stairs. We await the senior marchesa and Your Excellency.

—The priest is already vested?

—He is just finishing donning the sacred garments.

—Give me my tailcoat and the golden key, the marchese ordered.

—Here it is. I know my duty. And today is a great day. The king's day.

—The holy mass is dedicated to him.

Having given the last touch to the large cravat wound several times around his starched collar and secured the knot with a golden pin, Don Fabrizio held his arms out to the butler, who inserted him into his green tailcoat. Then the marchese draped around his neck the heavy chain from which hung a golden key inscribed with the august initials V.R.S. (*Vitæ Regis Securitas*).

The chapel was on the ground floor of the palace with an entrance on the courtyard, as was customary in many noble palaces in order to allow the servants and the neighborhood people living in the shadow of a great feudal house to assist easily at the sacred functions. A Baroque with overlays of *Rocaille*. More sculpture and decoration than architecture. Something muscular and bold suffocated by stucco, gold, and porcelain. A sumptuous triumph lightened by the coquettish and simpering graces of the century of the powdered wig. Festoons, cornets, volutes, cartouches, little garlands of flowers and fruit surmounted by dances and flights of cupids. A play of light and dust motes. The enamored sun caressed the animated whiteness of the figures. Dust drowsed in the niches of the trabeations, in the embroderies of the friezes, in the folds of the draperies, in the dimples of of the little angels' cheeks, in the whorls of their hair. It played over their outlines, softened the rays of the light, robing the stuccoes in a suffused flesh-like pallor. On the vault, panels, ceiling panels, and lunettes painted by Vito d'Anna: sacred coloristic fantasies governed by a severe design.

The chapel was dedicated to Sant'Oliva, a name borne by more than one woman in the ancestry of the Cortadas. In the icon, upright on the altar—a work from the brush of the painter of Monreale—the Palermitan saint could be admired appearing in a dream to the monks of San Francesco di Paola, revealing the secret place of her burial.

To the right of the altar, *in cornu epistolæ,* were enthroned the oil portraits of Their Majesties Francesco II and Maria Sofia Amalia of Bavaria, draped in the folds of the Bourbon banner atop a background of flowers.

Donna Teodora, the wife, and donna Ortensia, the dowager marchesa, entered first, followed by a footman with a pile of books of devotion under his arm. They take their places on two gilded armchairs in the first row, in front of the *prie-dieu*. Behind them several rows of benches for guests are lined up. At the back the full staff of servants is standing.

The celebrant, don Assardi, is waiting stiffly in front of the altar, shining in red vestments; he descends from the footpace and intones the preparatory psalm, the *Introibo*.

The mutter of the Latin words wavers, clearer or less clear, like the flames of the tapers.

Donna Ortensia. Grace and Irony. Two magic symbols that render her old age invisible. Time, the conqueror of her hair, once blond but now white, is defeated by her eyes sparkling with a youth which neither wishes nor knows how to die. Her small hands, half covered by the inevitable *mitaines*, play distractedly with the prayer book which remains closed on her knees. Her impassive mask stretched by a white skin still innocent of wrinkles breaks from time to time into a sardonic grimace, which her innate gentility prevents from widening into a smile. She thinks, The Christian God is a melancholy one, and it is not good to laugh in his house.

In the palace and outside of it she has the reputation of being a non-devout, perhaps even an irreligious woman, but a woman of an elegant and polite irreligiosity, such as casts no shadow even on pious souls. Is it her fault that the the little priest, almost a dwarf and bald, with a bit of red perspiration on his pate, fidgets clumsily and hops around the predella, prompting her to irresistible laughter?

The irony of Ortensia is contrasted by the impeccable composure of Teodora. Her head covered by a light black veil which does not extinguish the reflections in her beautiful black hair; dressed and gloved in black, from her face outward she seems like an ebony statue. Immobile, her hands supporting her mass book, her eyes with their long lashes resting on the page gilded by the light of the candles, she follows the ceremony on her knees. She might seem more than just absorbed in prayer, she might seem transformed into prayer itself, if her green eyes did not look around from time to time as if to reconnect her with some earthly interest. A matter of a moment, then heaven receives her back into the music of its spheres. No one is surprised. Everyone in the palace knows that she is an otherworldly woman, while the old lady is an impenitent worldling. They say that some archangel mounts guard around Teodora, while the devil, more or less, buzzes around the shoulders of her mother-in-law. A fine woman, but her unbelief...

Don Fabrizio, who does not fall within the field of vision of the green glances of his lady, loses none of her movements. He studies her. She is beautiful and she is young. And then she has so honest a way of praying. Is it possible that she is sinful? His conscience throws the question back on him: Are *you* completely without sin toward this woman?

In his mind he retraces his history. His first fault: marrying too young a woman. He, a widower, rather elderly, had linked his fate with a woman younger by at least twenty-five years. He had brought her into an old house. Not one happy with parties and amusements, but one overshadowed by gloom, leaving her alone among the witticisms of her mother-in-law and the unpleasant company of some old mummies.

For ten long years Teodora had been an irreproachable, not to say unblemished creature. She had passed through the hidden dangers of the world wirh a gravity worthy of the noble house which she had entered and of which she had become a part. If in some moment of frailty she had given way to an impure desire, if she had consented to the blandishments of the noonday devil, if she were pushed to the edge of sin (a sinful *thought*, you understand), did he, don Fabrizio, have the right to judge her? No. And what would he have done if by chance he had discovered that she was guilty? Only one thing, a voice from on high commanded him, while the priest spread his hands in the final *Dominus vobiscum*: 'Pardon!'

His soul having reached this decision, Fabrizio felt reconciled and lightened. As soon as the priest had descended from the footpace carrying the covered chalice, the marchese approached his wife, bowed, and offering her his arm with aristocratic gallantry went off with her toward the staircase.

Late afternoon. Unusual animation in via dell'Alloro. Gangs of delinquents romping in the circles of light pouring from the oil lamps. The rumble of carriages on the rainy pavement. Contrasts of nobility and poverty. Sumptuous buildings interspersed with a clutch of plebeian huts. Heaps of garbage and carrion of dead cats mixed with mud, sweaty rags stretched in front of little doors that exude filth. Smelly clouds of *stigliole,* lambs' innards, frying on grills, while the rain pelts down from the heavens, from the tiles, from the overflowing old gutters, circling in little swirls on the street. The garbage, covered in mud, is released with a sound like a flock of sparrows.

Via dell'Alloro no longer breathes forth its air of the lovely eighteenth century. It is going downhill. Little more than a half-century has been sufficient to dethrone its royalty. The palaces that line it, with their baroque masses, their frequent balconies whose railings swell like female breasts, supported by heavy consoles of sculptured stone; their wide portals surmounted by family coats of arms; their shady courtyards, where grotesque masks spout a thread of water into fountains lined with moss, are still there, but they have lost their enchantment and their illusions. Life no longer pulses within and without the noble houses with the same rhythm, with the same gilded nonchalance as in the times of the poet Giovanni Meli. The splendid sedan-chairs no longer wait in the entrance halls where the incendiary smiles of powdered ladies dazzle among the bows and hand-kisses of mincing cicisbei. On the stairways of red marble the *va-et-vient* of little bewigged and decked-out abbés, dancing masters, sybarites and parasites greedy for Trimalchian meals is silent, and the buzz of the many liveried and gold-braided waiters, grooms, and lackeys grows dimmer. Already in the middle of the nineteenth century the aristocracy has started to become middle class, it has trimmed away the splendors of the *ancien régime* and weakened the virility of the Empire style.

Nonetheless via Alloro still exudes its fascination, composed of harmonies torn by dissonances and contrasts. Its decaying eighteenth century grace is ensconced between two presences, a power that is declining and a force that is rising. There, on the left of the old throughway, narrow and torturous, nourished by the purest blue blood, rises battlemented and iron-grey the prison of the Steri: the emblem of feudal power, the fortress of the Chiaramonte, who dictated laws even to kings. Hanging from its façade, to the terror of rebels, are iron cages with the skulls of the executed. Here, on the right, beyond a maze of little streets there opens the plain of the Kalsa, an extension of one of the most popular quarters of the city. In its meanders circulate rough toilers of the sea, whose women bend over their looms intent on the business of weaving: a strong plebeian race, perhaps mixed with Arab blood, quarrelsome, violent, rebellious, swollen with class hatred. Via Alloro might resemble a Parisian street in 1789, between the Bastille and the Faubourg Saint-Antoine. On one side the plain of the Marina with the tribunals and the *Vicaria,* the ancient prison, now palazzo delle Finanze, with its dungeons, whence there issued forth the gloomy processions of those condemned to death. On the other side, one of the most proletarian quarters where rage and rebellion smoulder along with poverty, contrasts which today are softened by the shortening of distances. Around 1860 the stone pavements still remained as a witness to the ancient conditions. Today even those pavements, smashed by American bombardments, are nothing but ruins and dust. The end of a civilization. Like mankind, Time gazes impassively and passes on.

It is raining. The coaches arrive one by one. Lumps of mud splash between the legs of the horses which pull up by a jerk of the bit in front of palazzo Cortada. The coachmen do not lose their dignity even though streams of water are pouring past their noses from the brims of their top hats. The grooms jump down from the boxes, remove their hats, open the doors, bow deeply before the *signori* descending from the carriages. Velvet cloaks, flowered coiffures, silken crinolines inflated like lampshades, sparkles of gold and jewels, shovel hats, frock coats and greatcoats, sticks with gold handles, canary-colored gloves. The best society swarms from the entrance hall toward the wide staircase set off by a dark red carpet rising between two green hedges.

Don Fabrizio does the honors of his house from the entrance to the portrait gallery. A crowd of ancestors, looking down from three centuries, is present at the procession. There are viceroys, commanders, bishops, abbots, abbesses, ambassadors, men of laws, gentlewomen; a great display of batons of command, swords, helmets, croziers, books, fans, handkerchiefs, cuirasses, ermine, cassocks, judges' robes, crisp and starched neck ruffs. In many of the portraits the twisted nose and the fleshy lower lip of the Cortadas testify in their continuity to the uncorrupted purity of the race. They look down angry and impotent from their frames, which are moldering and losing their gilt here and there. They gaze at that Vanity Fair, at that empty flaunting of pride, self-interest, and passions, and if they were not glued to their smoky old canvases they would happily escape from their prison.

As the guests cross the threshold, with a great abundance of bows the majordomo announces: the prince of Torrebruna, the prince of Fitalia, the marchese Mortillaro, the prince of Galati, the marchese Arezzo, monsignor Turano, canon Sanfilippo...

The arrivals spread out in the vast gallery like a multicolored fluid. The buzz of conversation weaves webs of sound from one end to the other of the hall. Rays of light and little cascades spray from the faceted crystals of the chandeliers. From the soft surface of the tapestries curious heraldic monsters stick out their heads and widen their eyes, almost as if to espy the invisible legs of the ladies among diabolical intricacies of lace, under their trains and billowing bells of silk. In an ever-changing whirl of frivolities, passions, interests, and calculations, more or less harmonious clusters and groups are formed.

—Have all the *Scioani* arrived?—donna Ortensia asks Marco sharply, from behind the scenes.

The *Scioani* is the nickname she gives the legitimist Bourbon society which frequents the palace, just as the Jacobins nicknamed the faithful of king and Church the *Vendéens*. The witty soubriquet is derived from the *Chat-huant* or nighthawk, the name given to Jean Cottereau the arch-anti-revolutionary leader, who in his earlier profession of smuggler employed the cry of the lugubrious nocturnal bird as a password. The old lady calls her son 'barbaggiano,' 'nighthawk,' when she is in a bad mood.

The amiable donna Ortensia makes her entrance with a light little step. Sparkling with an almost immature sprit of youth, her seventy and more years glide off onto the carpet. In a period when the most elegant women are beginning to squeeze themselves into less ample garments she ostentatiously wears the crinoline, because this is the costume of the Second Empire, and the Empire for her is always the continuation of the Revolution. On her shoulders she has a rich black *cachemir*, with changing lights of green and old gold; in her white hair, powdered with blue following the fashion of the time, a rust-colored rose. Everyone crowds around to compliment her. Each of then hopes to blunt with exaggerated displays of affection the arrows that are ever-ready to strike from her corrosive mouth.

—I see the fine flower of our crowd—says monsignor Turano to don Fabrizio, who is surrounded by his most faithful adherents—you have assembled all that is best in our ranks. It is a beautiful display, after the daring challenge of the liberals on January twelfth. It takes a lot of presumption to celebrate the revolution of 1848, now that our island groans under the tyranny of the Piedmontese. It goes without saying, these liberals are ignorant and ridiculous.

—Yes—commented the marchese of Mortillaro devilishly—processions, flag waving, speechifying, illuminations, the usual cries of 'down with the Bourbons'... What a splendid celebration!

—Really?—exclaimed don Fabrizio, seeming to tumble from the clouds.—I assure you I knew nothing about it. I ignore such patriotic boasting, I am blind and deaf. They told me that the procession marched from piazza Fieravecchia to the church of the Gancia, in order to lay garlands on the famous 'hole of salvation,' where the two revolutionaries escaped.

—So it passed under your house?

—Precisely for that reason I didn't see it. I made them bolt the doors and the windows (here he winked). Even the flies were forbidden to look out!

—I think it is better to see certain spectacles, in order to aggravate oneself into reacting—marchese Mortillaro disagreed bitterly.—You shouldn't behave like the ostrich, who in the presence of danger sticks its head in the sand, hoping to save itself that way.

—Gentlemen, allow me—said marchese Arezzo, conciliatory—I'm all for making distinctions. It's not necessary to make a mountain out of every molehill. I don't think there's anything wrong in celebrating the '48.

It is a great date in the history of Sicilian independence, like the '20, like the '12, and it is perhaps the most illustrious of all. For the '60, I agree with you: a mistake, a foolishness. That's when this frenzy for unification started.

—Unity has failed Italy in every period. The idea of unity puts a curse on our history. A pernicious phantom of pagan Rome! Think: if Rome, instead of defeating the Etruscans, had been contained by them and had been obliged to follow their system, the peninsula would have been obliged to a federation from the beginning. How many wars of conquest, how many disasters, how much blood would have been spared! Those two gentlemen Mazzini and Garibaldi would not be splitting our eardrums with their raucous and unholy cry, 'Rome or death.'

—Rome is the symbol of unity in one sense only: as the center of Catholicism and the seat of the pontificate. As the capital of the Kingdom it is laughable. Either it is the *Caput mundi* of the religious world, or it is nothing—asserted the abbé Galeotti.—There are so many capital cities, one for evey region, and every region lives in a perfect geographical and historical autonomy.

—In short, Italy is made for regionalism and regionalism for Italy. A geography made to measure, it is enough to think of its shape, an oblong enclosed in a rosary of islands. An observation of Giuseppe Ferrari, if I'm not mistaken,—commented professor Errante.

—What does regionalism mean?

—It's simple: Sicily must do it by herself. It seems to me a very sensible and concrete case of Victor Emmanuel's famous saying, 'Italy will do it by herself.' Sicily, an island which for seven centuries had its own parliament, which dictated its own laws, administered its own riches, can well do without Italy...

Don Fabrizio admonished bluntly—Alone with Naples, single and double. Two Sicilies under one dynasty by divine right: the house of Bourbon, God save it. Remember that.

—Never—protested the marchese of Roccaforte, one of those excluded from the amnesty of the '48.—I always keep in my pocket the *Political catechism of Sicily* of the great historian Niccolò Palmieri, where it is written that any union with the kingdom of Naples is fatal to the independence of Sicily. That cannot depend on foreign princes and nations.

—Gentlemen—intervened cavaliere Pellegrinetto, the wild man of the company—at this point you must come to an agreement. You are all antiunitarians, indeed anfusionists. But what sauce is Sicily to cook in? If I were the emperor Vitellius, I would convoke the senate to hear their opinion. Assume that our island is a fish. It seems to me that here you are giving voice to a triple alternative: the island completely independent, the island united with the kingdom of Naples, the island autonomous but a member at the same time of an Italian league or confederation, with or without the pope presiding. I propose that the three solutions be put to a vote.

—Enough of your jokes—don Fabrizio decreed, rough and peremptory—there is no voting in my house. Whoever has democratic ambitions should leave them at the door before entering. We've had all too many infamous plebiscites that ended by handing our nation over to Piedmont.

—We are all for the federation—a voice shouted.

—What is a confederation?—asked the duchess Abatellis.

—It is that association of States with a head and without a head, where everyone commands and no one obeys, a decentralized or invertebrate unity, something like a marriage of three and more persons, where adultery is not a sin and divorce is at the will of the contracting parties...

—Then hurrah for the confederation—laughed the duchess, shaking her curls and her bosoms, which were undisciplined despite the constriction of her garments.

—After all, what do they want,?—one of the federalists present explained in the form of a question.—Nothing other than a second Switzerland, a second starry republic, like the United States of America. Two great living examples stand before us.

—And the Etruscans? Why not imitate them, who lived so happily? I adore them, said the duchess in fluty tones.

—We'll go back to the rule of the *lucumoni,* the Etruscan kings.

—What are these lucumoni...or lumaconi, if I have understood correctly?

—The best thing is to ask professor Emerico Amari about it. He is the only authority on the subject. He was here a moment ago.

They looked for him. He had in fact been seen a moment before—tall, closed in his black redingote, with his almost white beard open on his chin, his straight nose, his mobile eyes made blue by his eyeglasses. Still and solitary like a cypress, in contemplation before a picture by Salvatore Lo Forte, unheeding of the chattering that surged around him. He was no longer there.

—He's taken English leave—said one of the bystanders.

—I have nothing in common with the English...even when I leave—thundered the illustrious man, just visible in the door opening—they are the traitors of the '12 and of always.

—The Russians will help us—continued marchese Fabrizio, almost haranguing the little group of the faithful, who made a circle around him.—Many of you will recall with me a memorable episode. In the spring of 1846, when the tsarina Alexandra of all the Russias left Palermo with her court, leaning out from the launch that brought her back on board her splendid warship, she dipped her handkerchief in our sea and called out, kissing it, 'We shall return.' Russia represented the Holy Alliance. Who has ears, let him understand. And now let us go to render homage to our beloved sovereigns.

Followed by his guests, don Fabrizio marched at a theatrical pace down to the end of the gallery. Under a canopy of crimson velvet, draped among flags with the golden lilies on a white ground, surrounded by garlands of lights, glowed the effigies of Their Majesties Francesco and Maria Sofia.

Don Assardi read the ritual prayer for the safety of the August Sovereigns.

The bystanders bent the knee.

—For our legitimate Sovereigns: three cheerss!—ordered the marchese.

—Hip, hip, hurrah!—they responded in unison.

—May they soon return to the throne!—someone shouted.

—They have never ceased to reign—corrected don Fabrizio.

Chapter 2

NO PORTRAIT of donna Ortensia exists in the house. When she is dead the gallery of the ancestors will be deprived of a picture with an enchanting female figure. At night, when the chatter of the living is silent and the images hold council, it is not impossible that the painted brigade of ancestors—in arms, in surplice, in law gown, in monastic habit—relieve themselves by abusing the absent one, accusing her of pride. She had always refused to have herself depicted in marble, in bronze, in wood, or canvas, for fear that the copy would not come up to the original.

—No, my dear colleagues—answers donna Ortensia, laughing her most ambiguous feline smile—the reason for my iconophobia is a different one. I think that in general our portraits resemble us less than we resemble them. Let me explain. When you make a portrait—all the better if it is, as they say, 'successful'—this curious phenomenon occurs. By a series of little steps, knowingly or unknowingly, you end by imitating your image, so that you become the copy and the image becomes the original. Your real personality finally becomes the echo of a picture, of a statue, of a medallion. Now, I want to be myself, an original, not a copy. I would feel crippled in my freedom if I always had before my eyes an image of myself that would remain forever the same while I changed continuously. Let me change and transform myself freely, like nature, without being chained to the immobility of art. Not that I despise art, for heaven's sake! On the contrary, I admire its power. It is so powerful as to transfigure nature. I believe that not only do the men and women of a given date think, pose, and act like the characters of the pictures, the novels, and the plays most in fashion, but that even landscapes end by resembling those described or depicted. This is an arrogance, an act of brutality. After I am dead, if someone wants to paint me, feel free. They will write my name under a stuffed animal and will say, This was Ortensia. And I will laugh at it from the other world.

Donna Ortensia dialogued with the dead in this manner. With the living she held a different discourse, if we are to believe certain notes of hers banished to the bottom of a drawer.

'I am a daughter of the eigteenth century lost in the nineteenth, an *esprit fort* with some romantic frailties. My romanticism is no more than a clover-leaf stuck to your shoe, when you leap impulsively from the high road onto a grassy verge. My first teacher was Rousseau, corrected by Voltaire, the second is Stendhal. Two romantics, one in the weak style, one in the strong. If I had to follow the latter, who had them inscribe on his tombstone, "Arrigo Beyle *milanese,*" I ought to call myself *palermitana* out of respect for the country of my adoption. Instead, after sixty years of life in Palermo, I have unfortunately remained French, even more so than when I was born. I wager that if another Sicilian Vespers broke out and they asked me to say *ciciri* to reveal my nationality, I would pronounce it *sisirì* and would get myself slaughtered. My name is Duplessis, and I know that my family has always proudly boasted descent from the loins of Armand Duplessis, cardinal duc de Richelieu. My successors will judge whether something still clings to me from my kinship with so illustrious a personage. Armand was a politician of great *envergure,* a warrior wrapped by chance in the scarlet of a cardinal, an armed man who by mistake had traded his steel helmet for a cardinal's hat. I am an adventuress of the spirit, a revolutionary of the intelligence, fallen to the rank of mother of a family, that is to say a brood mare, in the most conservative and traditionalist house in all Sicily.

'Even before 1789 the Duplessis family were progressive and forward-looking in their ideas. They pulled pigtails and shook the powder off their wigs, they ridiculed the privileges of the nobility, they played at *libertinage.* They displayed an easygoing tolerance, they read without concealment the *Lettres persanes* of Montequieu, they consulted Voltaire's *Dictionnaire philosophique* as if it were a gospel, they slept with Rousseau's *Contrat social* under their pillows. The Duplessis family applauded the

States General, along with the other nobles they generously gave up their feudal rights, perhaps they jeered at the king when he was brought back from Varennes as a prisoner... Nonetheless, this did not save them from the wrath of the Jacobins. By pure miracle, as the Terror raged, they succeeded in keeping their necks out of the guillotine by taking refuge in Italy. Here we remained for four years, until when things got better under the Directoire we were able to return to France. I was at the happy age of sixteen.

'The lovely sky of Italy, who could forget it? I should rather say "the skies," since they are many, and they differ according to their cities. The sky of Lombardy, in my memory, is low, metallic, and dark like burnished armor; that of Venice is pearly, untouchable and lightly gilded by the reflections of the bell towners mirrored in the laguna; that of Florence, distant, spiritual, and lyrical. The air over Umbria is drenched in green; over Naples the atmosphere sings passionate sky-blue songs; in Palermo the sky is violent and a thief, it steals the cobalt blue from the sea and does not restore it except on some rare winter days.

'It was the first year of the Consulate, 1799. It was the will of destiny that in Florence I stumbled over (that is how they express it in that well-spoken city) the man who later became my husband. Proud of my freedom as I have always been, I do not believe in fate, but I swear to you that it exists. It was decreed that I should fall in love with a Sicilian, in an Etruscan city, under the gaze of a Greek statue. The scene of the crime was the Uffizi Gallery where an April afternoon, loaded with pollen, drew a mantle of rosy light over the nudity of the Medici Venus. As if by a mysterious *rendez-vous,* under the marble I happened to meet with a handsome strong young man, pale, with two great Mediterranean eyes under his black hair. He seemed very admiring but disconcerted that a woman, even one of Parian marble, was clothed only in her hands, one to the north and one to the south. He thought emphatically, "Beautiful, yes, but audacious."

'I remembered, indeed out loud, the words of Marat, *De l'audace, encore de l'audace, toujours de l'audace.*

'He looked at me as if he wanted to ask me something. I understood that he was asking me for the definition of modesty, and I said the first thing that popped into my head.

'—*La pudeur est la crainte de montrer un corps mal fait.* Modesty is the fear of showing an ill-made body.

'The statue smiled, satisfied that I had come to her defence. The unknown young man became serious. A shadow touched his noble brow, the shadow of a likeable provincial chastity.

'The following days we met again in the Gallery, and our admiring pauses were always before fully clothed works of art. Perhaps the story of naked Amor is nothing more than a myth. My Directoire *toilettes* enchanted the unknown young man with the fascination of French fashions. Our meetings moved out from the museums into the gardens and the villas, our walks became ever longer and ended in a ... wedding march.

'My marriage with the young marchese Alfonso Cortada was not without conflicts, coming more from his family than from mine. I was a foreigner and a Frenchwoman, two black marks. The first objection was overcome with relative ease. The second obstacle, my nationality, was more difficult to overcome. My fiancé's relatives viewed the French like a thorn in the eye, not only as Sicilians, but as Bourbonists. The kings of this dynasty had lost their scepter twice through our fault. The first time in 1798, when the Parthenopean Republic was proclaimed after the invasion of Naples by Championnet, the second in 1806 when the kingdom of Naples was assigned by the emperor Napoleon to his brother-in-law Murat. Both times the dethroned sovereigns came to take a Sicilian holiday on the Conca d'Oro. How could my in-laws, bigwigs at court, have ever found a French daughter-in-law pleasing? If only I were English! Or at least Spanish! So thought my fiancé's kinfolk. But he was so smitten with me that he would have married me even if I had been black. Instead, I was very blond, I was twenty-two, with a bright blue smile, a keen spirit seasoned with grace, and as soon as I had disembarked I conquered Sicily like a Norman.'

Here the autobiography of donna Ortensia ends, and here her biography might begin. It would be too long a story—or a very short one, if you considered only what was essential. In fact the lives of every human being reduce themselves to a few sentences and a few deeds, the quintessence of their personalities, everything else is useless nonsense. Human value consists in the inequality of one being with respect to other beings. Therefore egalitarian ideals have no other effect than to brutalize mankind. The merit of the soul consists in emerging and in distinguishing itself, not in flattening and confusing itself. The ancient judgment of Terence, 'I am human and I consider nothing human alien to me' should be corrected to, 'I am human, insmuch as I feel estranged from common humanity.' The salt of the earth is concentrated in the saints, the geniuses, the half-wits, the madmen, the extravagant spirits. The rest is dullness and inanity.

Judging from her words and deeds, perhaps this was the philosophy of donna Ortensia.

Questioned by the usual bores as to how she, a Frenchwoman, had decided to give her hand to a Sicilian, she answered impassively, Because he is a countryman of count Cagliostro.

Some of them were scandalized, some made witty remarks, some made the sign of the Cross. They were certainly unaware that Giuseppe Balsamo, the so-called count Cagliostro, the follower of Casanova, had enjoyed a resounding celebrity in Paris during Ortensia's adolescence. Cagliostro, the successor of the magnetist Mesmer, implicated in the 'affair of the diamond necklace,' idolized as a wizard, the benefactor of humanity and the hero of freedom of thought, had enjoyed a fame that bordered on fanaticism. The Olympian Wolfgang Goethe, although reluctant to mix in mundane matters, when he came to Palermo in 1787 had thought it his duty to call on the adventurer's family, who were living in great poverty in the street called 'The land of the flies.' Was it any wonder that Ortensia kept in her *boudoir* a copy of the bust of Cagliostro sculpted by Houdon, beside the images of the two patron saints of occult studies, the counts of Saint-Germain and Saint-Martin? It was a sign of the times. Donna Ortensia was an unbeliever with elegance, which consisted in tolerating everything and being surprised by nothing. She said these two virtues constituted her humanity. On her mass-book, which she kept for show and never read, she had written the words of Voltaire: *La tolérance c'est l'apanage de l'humanité. Nous sommes tous pétris de faiblesse et d'erreurs: pardonnons nous réciproquement nos sottises, c'est la première loi de la nature.* Tolerance is the privilege of humanity. We are all riddled with weakness and errors. Let us pardon one another's foolishnesses, that is the first law of nature.

In reality she pardoned little, and her greatest tolerance was only for the wit by which she choked off her interlocutors with the most exquisite grace.

Accustomed to the greatest frankness for her fanatic love of the truth, she detested two-faced peeople. Therefore, although she admired Giovanni Meli as a poet, she no longer esteemed him as a man because of his clever political dissimulation. Meli played the progressive in theory and the reactionary in practice. According to opportunity, he was a revolutionary or a powdered wig. He became inflamed for the rights of the people and kowtowed to the rich and the nobility, climbing their stairs to humble himself in oily prostrations. At a party the poet once came to pay Ortensia his respects, surrounded by a swarm of 'talkative and lascivious little maidens.' She complimented him on his light-hearted company.

—*Unni c'e meli, su' l'api,* Where the honey is, there the bees are—said the author of the *Ditirambo,* punning on his own name—*Si c'è lu meli, ci avi ad essiri la rosa,* If there's honey, there the rose should be also.

—Where is this rose?

—Here she is—said the poet gallantly, pointing to her with a courtly gesture.

—The sunflower overtops the rose—donna Ortensia noted somewhat acidly.—A pity that it changes faces several times a day.

—*Eccu 'na nova qualità di rosi. Si cunusci da li spini,* This a new characteristic of roses, they are recognized by their thorns.

When the famous abbé Giuseppe Pitré, who discovered the planet *Ceres* in 1801, was presented to Ortensia at a reception in the Royal Palace, she surprised the scientist's lynx-like gaze intently peering into the shadowy cleavage of her *décolltage.*

—Sir—she smiled, after greeting him—you discover planets, but I see that you also have a weakness for the milky way.

The humor of the new marchesa was unscrupulous, biting, and capricious. And there were some who, to avoid scolding her for impropriety, would have wished her to be more reasonable. She answered composedly that unreasonable minds are the only ones that do not become boring, and that she loved the Sicilians for their lack of reason.

—The Frenchman is to the Sicilian as good sense is to its opposite. Show me a single race—she enumerated—that uses the word 'to tire onself' for 'rest,' 'to move' for 'standing still,' 'tasty' for 'attractive,''beautiful' (speaking of food) for 'tasty.' A boldness unknown even to our own language, which in matters of verbal inventiveness knows no fears.

With the collaboration of don Alfonso, Ortensia had given three sons to Sicily: Fabrizio, Federico, and Ramiro. Three types, she said, so different that they seemed the sons of three different fathers and mothers.

Made of differing clay, the boys had grown up as God—or rather nature—willed, without their mother wasting too much time on transforming their basic characters. Faithful to the principles of Rousseau, she said, 'There is nothing worse than combating or violating nature: instead of men, you create monsters. Every man is a sponge, or rather a porous body which absorbs what it needs from the liquid in which it is immersed. Immerse the man in a healthy liquid and let happen what must.' The liquid, that is the surroundings into which the three young men had had been immersed from birth, was that of an ancient feudal Sicilian family: upright, religious, conservative, firm in its sentiments of honesty and of honor. Each son had absorbed it in his own way.

Fabrizio had remained the perfect type of the old feudal gentleman: honorable and proud, generous and authoritarian, practical but traditionalist, stubborn without deviousness or deceit. Tied to the past, the guardian of his family's prestige, devoted to the Church and to the regime of noble privileges which had been foolishly abdicated by the aristocracy in 1812, in his every action he seemed to say, Although the times change, I do not change. Whence his fanatical attachment to the Bourbon dynasty, which the '48 showed to be in decline and the '60 unseated once for all. Looking at her son's head, massive as a rock, all descending planes and hard corners, Donna Ortensia sometimes said, He is a fine boulder, a pity that he lacks *l'esprit de finesse*, without which neither brain nor heart exists.

Federico possesed what was lacking in his brother. He swung back and forth like a pendulum, between outward sensitivity and daydreams. And this continous wavering rendered him irresolute and changeable. He was good and therefore indecisive, because—Ortensia philosophised—decisiveness is, unfortunately, the art of being cruel when necessary. Not content with being good in himself, he wanted to make others good. And what is worse, he deceived himself that benefiting humanity made it happy. The only effect that he achieved was to render humanity neither good nor happy, since it appears that the two are irreconcilable. His fixation was 'philanthropy.' Donna Ortensia knew well this terrifying virtue, the obsession and the illness of the eighteenth century, but she limited herself to observing when she saw Federico busying himself about good works as a boy, 'This son of mine worries me. He's playing with fire and one day he will burn himself. Let's hope that he doesn't set the whole house in flames.'

The thirdborn, Ramiro, was believed to be a reckless daredevil. We will say more of him later on.

Of the three brothers only one, as they said then with the most inelegant and crude of metaphors, had 'tied the knot' in the right kind of marriage: Fabrizio. Even if he had had celibate temptations, he would never have been able to escape the necessity of marrying. For the firstborn of noble blood this was a kind of public duty, motivated by the necessity of not leaving his family without a continuation. The Verdian 'croce o delizia' ('cross or delight,' according to your taste) of celibacy was reserved, in conformity with the severe laws of primogeniture, to the younger sons destined *de jure* to military or ecclesiastical careers, even if they had absolutely no wish either to kill or to pray. But laws are made like that: they have their own logic, which is very rarely that of the heart. And so it happened that don Fabrizio, who had barely attained his majority, found himself married to an aristocratic girl who had all her cards in order for being an excellent consort: nobility, riches, goodness, minus one—health. And in fact, striken by consumption, she silently left this world without having given him an heir.

When a spouse dies everyone surrounds the survivor to induce him to consider a makeup exam, if he does not think of it by himself. Indeed, don Fabrizio was a thousand miles from thinking of it. He was not so much in love with his wife as to feel the immediate urgency of a second marriage, and having lost his first wife he became a misogynist. Instead of a woman, he married himself to books and politics, which have no gender, or only a symbolic one. Having lived between two revolutions, which had shaken the legitimate throne of his beloved sovereigns on its pedestal, he had immersed himself in the study of politics in order to investigate, with the help of the classics, that phenomenon of madness which is a revolt of the people, so as to devise the means of saving humanity from similar calamaties. It seemed to him that he was close to finding the remedy for rendering the people quiet and happy when the '60 struck like a lightning-bolt which shattered in an instant the throne, the dynasty, and the absolute and paternal reign of the crowned despots whom he and his family had served faithfully for more than a century. Was everything therefore lost? Not at all. His hope had remained standing. The Bourbons, against everything and against everyone, would one day ascend their throne again. He would battle *contra spem in spe,* in hope against hope. The Idea does not die. The legitimist idea would unite around itself such and so many forces, sharpened and pointed such a store of talents and wills, as to prepare the outbreak of the Counter-revolution, which was not long off. God was on its side, because God is a legitimist. And if God be for us, who can be against us?

Obsessed by his passion for politics, don Fabrizio had already stretched one leg over the threshold of fifty but still remained unthreatened by every matrimonial temptation. But his destiny awaited him on another threshold. On the stairway of the church of the Gancia, as he was coming out from a Lenten service, the blue eyes of don Fabrizio met a pair of green eyes, feminine and anonymous. Green mixed with blue gives the color of the sea, and the sea is the primal seat of life if we are to believe the scientists.

With what enchantment does the sea sparkle, if one discovers it unexpectedly at the foot of via Alloro, from between the stage flats of the old palaces darkened by the patina of time! The joy of a sapphire set in a heavy necklace of black silver. In that moment the vision of the sea, surrounded by a constellation of poetic symbols, smiled on the aged marchese. They say that it is the privilege of poets to discern in the bosom and on the surface of the waters fanciful nereids, foraging undines, and playful sirens, instead of sardines, hake, and crabs. On that morning all shining with spring, what kind of wonderful divinity of the oceans had emerged from the sea?

The emerald eyes, edged with thick lashes, flashed in a pale face, which was rather long, cut by the horizontal line of a wide mouth gracefully sketched upon pure white teeth. From under the folds of her plumed hat thick masses of night-black hair, struck by turquoise glints from the reflection of the sky, fell on her temples. Alcaeus saw something like that when he described Sappho as crowned with violets. Her slender and upright figure, of a slightly stiff haughtiness, showed the thighs of a horsewoman and a noble and strong frame, despite her voluminous garments. Masculine nuances in her voice, which was varied in the lower notes by tones of velvet. Altogether, a strong-willed and dignified personality with flashes of wildness and restlessness. A flower which has finally opened and which is developing its ripe perfume, tempting, dizzying, and perhaps a bit perverse. Such was Teodora.

The only child and rich heiress of a baron of the Kingdom of Naples, well brought up but without any cultural refinements. Imperious, melancholy, proud as a queen in exile, Teodora was known as an indomitable horsewoman. A bold and fearless rider, she was often seen riding fiery chargers, and those who knew her were more afraid for the animal than for her. Perhaps these fine sporting qualities (equitation was then the only sport permitted to a lady) had discouraged men from seeking her hand, and so she had cleared the bar of thirty by a bit, still a virgin like the Amazon queen Penthesilea.

For the first time in his life, don Fabrizio, armored against the fortunes of politics but weak-hearted against *femmes fatales* by lack of experience and perhaps by nature, suffered a *coup de foudre*. The dark horsewoman with the green eyes drew him out of his solitude and confronted him anew with the problem of matrimony, which until then had been on the Index of Forbidden Things. He decided to marry her. Donna Ortensia, faithful to her creed of tolerance for herself and freedom for others, neither approved nor disapproved. But she was not pleased. Above all, the young woman was not physically 'her type' (I don't like bottles of ink, she said, proud of her delicate Norman blondness). In the second place, she considered the mixture of her son's four quarters of noblity with the tired little blason of a provincial baron to be a *mésalliance*. But she knew well that the obstacles raised by parents to the marriages of their children end by reinforcing what had previously been only a wavering determination. 'If an heir is necessary for a family of noble lineage, then welcome even to a branch with green eyes and black hair. I would have preferred a grandchild with straw-colored hair.'

But it was in fact the will of Fate, often the unwilling accomplice of our desires, that the last of the Cortadas should be a boy with golden hair.

Chapter 3

BETWEEN TWO marriages don Fabrizio had remained without issue.

The Cortada fanily tree, formerly so prolific in branches and leaves, risked drying up in its principal trunk and dying: an infected tree, which sees ants and snails crawling on its budless bark and no longer feels the force to rebel. Three years had already elapsed from the marchese's second marriage. Hopes and fears, illusions and disappointments, counting on fingers and calculating by months, dreams of first cries and cradles, consultations with midwives and discussions with doctors, precious vows to the saints and to all the Madonnas most favorable to childbearing—only wisps of smoke that vanished into nothingness.

One unfortunate day science decrees that the womb of the lovely Teodora is resistent to the validating seal of maternity. A sad message in an aristocratic family which, like a ruling house that has decided not to die, counts on its descendants. Don Fabrizio is inconsolable. But his silent discouragement, mitigated by his religiosity, bit by bit rises to God in resignation like an incense. Donna Ortensia, whose soul is divided as her tongue is forked, is balanced between two arguments. From one point of view, which she calls 'absolute,' she is content. She has so low an idea of the human race that it would not displease her to see it sicken and die on the earth like a lizard which is being fried and dying for lack of oil. From another point of view, let us say 'relative,' all the same it seems unfortunate that a family with a great past has to hand in its resignation from the future through the fault of a woman whose duty should be to sprout branches for the man who legitimately expects them.

However, some doctors (by agreement with the bride?) observe that it takes two to make a child, and that according to the science of genetics there also exists a masculine form of sterility.

—If they made the test—donna Ortensia suggests—they would see which side the fault lies on.

It is a pity that don Fabrizio, terrified by the abyss of sin, is unwilling to lend himself to such a proof and confirmation. The intention might be honest, but the fact remains what it is. And the road to Hell is paved with good intentions.

To stifle the mother-in-law's complaints, the priests advise patience. The last word is never spoken. Infinite are the ways of the Lord. Sarah was ninety years old when she presented her bald husband, Abraham, with a fine little boy, Isaac.

—Miracle for miracle—donna Ortensia answers—it would be easier for me to have a baby at almost seventy than my daughter-in-law at thirty-five.

Conversing with her melancholy image in the mirror, Teodora sighs, 'Sad is the fate of an honest woman.' Then, clenching her hairpin between her teeth and knotting her solid black tresses over her head, she looks at her rosy elbows contrasting with her heavily-shadowed armpits and exclaims with malice, like a Sicilian, 'Gnaw your elbows; whether you like it or not, I am still a desirable woman.'

What is happening that day in the palace? It seems that the heavy blanket of fog that oppresses it moves aside to let a pale ray of sun pass through. It is a sickly sun, a pale winter sun, but light is always a joy for the universe.

—So, tomorrow don Ramiro's boy arrives from Malta?

The news runs through the palace, echoes joyfully from the galleries to the kitchens, from the stairways to the dormers, from the chapel to the stables, carried from mouth to mouth by friends, administrators, servants, the curious, like the merry jingle of a bell-collar.

Don Fabrizio does not know what expression to assume. In order not to contradict his character, it ought to be surly. But it is a skin-deep surliness which does not go beyond the wrinkles of his brow. Deep inside, he gloats, he trembles with pleasure. His immaculate house is about to welcome a child of sin. A sin with a trail as long as the tail of the Devil:

scandal. This is very true, but the guilt of others must not fall on the innocent. The dew of charity rains both on immaculate flowers and poisonous weeds. *Charitatem habete quia est vinculum perfectionis,* says the Apostle, Have charity, for it is the bond of perfection.

But that 'scoundrel,' Ramiro, why could he not have put together for himself a modest family, at peace with Holy Mother Church, instead of hunkering down with some nameless woman and fathering a little bastard...a miserable brat sprung up like a wild thistle, without God or fatherland, in that sort of Devil's Island which is Malta, the refuge of con men and castouts. And then 'Goffredo'—why this bombastic and melodramatic name? Wern't there enough good family names without borrowing one from *Gerusalemme liberata*? When someone is thoughtless, it's all along the line, there's nothing to say.

—As a Catholic, you should be pleased with a name that recalls the man who freed the supulcher of Christ.

—Yes, but he remains a bastard.

—Who? Goffrey de Bouillon?—asked donna Ortensia.

—The one who bears his name.

—Foolishness, lies! If you start looking, we are all bastards. If you go back to the farthest branches of our family trees you always find a *faux-menage*. The good Lord himself assigned to our mother Eve *un mari sans la banalité de la mairie,* a husband without the platitude of the registry-office.

—Mamma, I beg you not to joke about certain subjects—don Fabrizio cut her off, aware that on the subject of religion his mother knew no bounds.

—When push comes to shove—the old lady continued—your ancestors, a race of soldiers and conquistadores, would be proud to give a place in their midst to the son of one ...who died on the field of honor.

—Our ancestors fought for King and Church, not for the revolution. They were Christian knights, not troublemakers.

—And was Christianity itself not a revolution? Was it not Christianity that overturned the pagan world? The Nazarene said that he had come to bring to the world not peace but a sword.

It must be said that don Fabrizio was arguing without conviction. Usually so duplicitous, dialetical, and sophisticated in debating, always reluctant to disarm, always obstinate to overcome, he now let his mother wrap herself in the fantastic coil of her eccentricities, objecting weakly or finding nothing to answer. A new feeling like a sweet sap flowed through his veins and reconciled him to life. At the unaccustomed warmth that spread in the twists and turns of his soul, often hard and dry as a stone, many knots untied, many harshnesses softened. A kind of unprecedented lightness loosened his joints, shook the laziness out of the play of his articulations, bathed his mind with a splash of invigorating optimism. Finally to be a father! Not to die! To have someone to whom to transmit his own ideas, his riches, a fearless name, a task and a mission... in a word, life! A sublime thing, inmmortality! In pronouncing this word don Fabrizio felt guilty. Had not religion taught him that the only immortality is that of the personal soul, that in the next world the soul will see God face to face, as absolute truth, and no longer through a glass darkly? Is it not a blasphemy to conceive immortality as the continuation of oneself in one's own sons, prolonging oneself in future generations? No, the Lord cannot have condemned our anxiety about this other type of immortality: the longing not to die, of outliving others, of fighting against death for earthly life, of being reborn in a new being who resembles and perpetuates us. By living in others and for others one also obeys the divine precept, 'Who loses his life will save it.' In the meantime it was urgent to save the boy, an abandoned adolescent who, above all, bore in his veins some drops of Fabrizio's own blood. What more noble task than to straighten a tender shoot grown in an unhealthy air and among parasitical vegetation, to make of it a strong tree which tomorrow will bring forth promising flowers and delicious fruit. To educate is not only a good work but also a religious duty.

Don Fabrizio had his own ideas about education, which differed considerably from those of his mother. It was not a question of bringing man back to nature, of restoring him to a primitive innocence, of drawing him out of society and making him a gentle savage opposed to all forms of civilised living. It was necessary, instead, to infuse into the pupil a more aware and mature spirituality, to instill in him the feeling of duty, helping him to ascend from the level of nature to that of Grace. Without doubt Ramiro would have grown up into a different man if, instead of being left a prey to the storms of his temperament, he had beeen tamed in his instincts, correcrted in his unruly passions, torn away from his evil companions as an healthy fruit is separated from rotting ones. A bit of caution and energy would have been sufficient to preserve him from the contagion of the revolution. Some providential slap administered at the right time would have kept him from embarking with that gang of madmen who gave Sicily the '48 and the '60. Miserable man! In His infinite mercy the Lord will have pardoned him his dissolute recklessness, so Fabrizio also pardoned him. And to offer tangible proof of his forgiveness, he opened the hospitable doors of his palace to welcome Goffredo as if he were his own son.

The heavy velvet drapery of donna Ortensia's *boudoir* ripples, sways. The wind? Someone wants to enter?

From the folds of the curtain has burst a big boy with square shoulders, an unruly mop of blond hair, and an air halfway between nervous and frightened, like a young deer caught in a trap. He advances slowly, stops, looks around, clutching a bundle under his arm.

—Goffredo!—cries the old woman, leaping up from her chair as if she were twenty again.

No, she did not expect this sudden apparition. The boy's arrival had no precise date. Who wanted give her this surprise? Perhaps the servants had arranged things to let him slip unexpectedly into her little salon without her suspecting. What tricks! Don't you feel that her heart is pulsing strongly in her throat?

—Is it really you, my child?—And the old woman disappears into the arms of her nephew, who overtops her by a head and more.—Fabrizio! Teodora! Come!

Don Fabrizio enters with his arms hanging down and a heavy step, he stops, scrutinizes the youth from the tips of his tattered shoes to the top of his head, hesitates, then draws the boy to him. Tenderness has won. It seems that two epochs and two mentalities have made peace.

Teodora, the last to arrive, holds her long ringless hand out to the boy and fixes him with her cold malachite eyes, marbled with shades of curiosity and distrust. Perhaps with jealousy (since women are not jealous only of other women). She seems to be thinking, Here is youth in flower, entering to overshadow my approaching autumn. And is not this new being, happy to grow like a young sprig even if the son of an unknown mother, a reproach to her own unfruitfulness? Yes, he is blond, of a calm and ashy blondness, which has something of the Nordic about it.

—He has my hair—says his grandmother proudly, and she strokes her hair, as if her touch had the power to turn the snow back into gold.

Teodora almost blushes at the irremediable black of her hair. She cannot take any more of this constant praise of blonde hair, of seraphim, cherubim, and similar heavenly beings. She doesn't know where, but she has read that in certain religions of the far East the devils are golden-haired and the angels black as coal. If she could only rid herself of the wish to tell her mother-in-law certain things! But even silence is golden. Accursed metal!

In don Fabrizio's study Goffredo is bombarded with questions. He responds with simplicity. Sometimes he blushes and answers confusedly. Only lies are definite and unchanging. The truth, which almost always trusts to memory, has unfocused and imprecise outlines. How many things are confused in the boy's mind! He was born on Malta and has always remained there. He came to Sicily only once, with his mother. He has only faded memories of the trip. His mother died young, she left him when he was six. From then on he always lived in the houses of strangers, acquaintances of his father, because his father disappeared from time to time and was absent for long stretches. Nothing was known of his father's travels. There often came to the house people, like displaced persons, who spoke cautiously and gathered some news from him (here don Fabrizio lowered his head with visible signs of indignation). Studies? Very little. A few years in a school kept by an exile, then he had done it by himself. Not much, because he had to earn his living after the death of his father. But working as a type-setter you learn something. The art of a compositor is a noble one. Added all up, a life of hardships.

Don Fabrizio is moved and becomes angry.

—A descendant of the Cortadas who ends up working as a type-setter! Oh Ramiro, Ramiro, just look where your life of sin leads! *Abyssus abyssum invocat,* The abyss calls to the abyss., and evil overwhelms even the innocent.

Now he has decided to draw a veil over the past. What has been, has been. Ramiro no longer exists. Let's assume that he never existed. Fabrizio's own method of educating his nephew will consist in severing bit by bit all the strands that tie him to the past, in cancelling from his nephew's heart the image of his father. Certainly, Ramiro never existed.

When Goffredo says that he has some souvenirs, some relics of his father to give to his grandmother, his uncle interrupts him, grumbling:

—Relics are only for the saints.

Then, rearranging his ugly expression, he questions his nephew about his projects, his vocation, his ideas for the future.

So. If he had to choose a career, Goffredo would go into the navy. He has read books of travel, of explorations, of adventures...He has a great passion for the sea. His knowledge is limited to two islands, Malta and Sicily, and of the latter only Palermo. He would at least like to see Italy and its beauties close up. It is a duty to know one's fatherland.

—Your fatherland is Sicily, and the Conca d'Oro is the most beautiful place in the world—don Fabrizio observed peremptorily.—What is Italy? A group of many States, of which the most important is the Kingdom of the Two Sicilies governed by His Majesty Francesco II by the grace of God.

—I don't have a clear idea even of Sicily. I only landed here for a few days. I remember that on very clear days, standing on a bench I often strained to make out the shores of our island across the sea.

—You will see everything. But first you must study. We will speak seriously of your studies and your education later.

When donna Ortensia is alone with her grandson she says:

—Your uncle Fabrizio is jealous about your education. Anyway, it is for your own good. I advise you to satisfy him, not to contradict him. He has his whims.

He wants to raise you to the height of the customs and traditions of our family. 'Elegant' manners, as he says when he wants to speak affectedly. You are, how to say it?, a bit savage, *nature*... Here democracy is looked at askance, like a dog in church. For example, your uncle saw you shake hands with the majordomo and he was horrified.

—Really?

—Indeed. Here everything is blue. From the blood that runs through our veins to the damask of the wall hangings and the tapestries, from the majolica plates to the floor tiles, from the caparisons of our horses to our bedroom slippers. A question of taste. Not my taste, you understand, but the taste of the ancestors who mount guard from their musty pictures. Always be sure to wear blue eyeglasses. And sometimes ones of very dark glass, because we are, above all, black aristocracy, the blackest, like Teodora's hair. Here, anyone who doesn't go along with the priests is a Freemason and is excommunicated, whoever does not shout 'long live King Franceschiello' is a Jacobin. What difference does it make? Who knows (I whisper it in your ear) whether your grandmother isn't also a Jacobin?

—You?

—Yes, Jacobin, sansculotte, even Robespierrean. I represent the holy... devil, while all the others in this house are authentic saints, plaster saints stuck up on the wall.

—I was aware of it.

—Already? You're a monster of intelligence, my little grandson, a real Duplessis. Come here, plant a kiss on my left cheek.

—Why on the left?

—Above all, because it is cheek on the side of the heart. Because it combats the evil eye. Who knows? I don't. But it might be right that such a thing should exist...for certain persons who deserve it. How full the world is of many invisible things that we do not know. Cagliostro tore the veil off a fourth dimension of the world, whose beings are so subtle and light that they escape our perception. The truth is perhaps there. He showed the severed head of Marie Antoinette in a bottle when the poor queen saw before her nothing but a long and happy life, so happy that often the vertigo of boredom went to her head. The price of happiness is in fact that it is boring.

—For that reason I am never bored, grandma.

—Nor was your father—she said sadly.

—About that, grandmamma. I still haven't handed over some souvenirs of him.

The young man hurried to his room in two skips and returned with a little package. He undid the waxed wrapping and dropped on the table a portrait, a medallion, a document, and a red shirt. On the front of the shirt at the height of the right ribs one could see a hole with scorched edges, still crusted with blood.

—That's all—said Goffredo.

His grandmother raised her tearless eyes to her grandson, lowered them to the poor but glorious remains, took them with her trembling fingers, and brought them to her lips.

Then she lowered her head until her chin touched her heaving breast.

Silence.

Ramiro. Adorable crazy boy. The scandal, the abomination of the house. The despair of don Alfonso. The complete reprobate, with every defect except a great heart. At seventeen he had escaped from the military school of the Nunziatella in Naples and had embarked secretly on a boat that carried him to South America. There he had fought for the freedom of Bolivia. Migrating to Uruguay, he had encountered the exiled Giuseppe Garibaldi and had fought under his banner. Returning to Italy just before the '48, he had conspired with the carbonari, taken part in several subversive episodes, and hounded by the police of various States, he had fled through the peninsula, surviving by a miracle. On the dawn of January 12, somehow back in Palermo, he was among the first to raise the flag of revolt on the Baroque statue of 'Old Palermo' in the Fieravecchia. When the Bourbons, trampling the Constitution underfoot, began the reconquest of the island, he fought below the fortress of Messina against the troops of General Satriano. When the freedom of Sicily was extinguished after a bloody repression, he fled with other exiles to Malta, where he remained except for occasional and mysterious journeys until the eve of the '60. He was present when Garibaldi landed at Marsala, and although he was over forty he managed to enroll as a simple legionnaire in the column commanded by Giacinto Carini. Seriously wounded in a bayonet charge, he was carried off to the house of some fishermen and died without a word of complaint, proud of having served the cause of liberty. A letter written to his mother before he joined the campaign begged her that in the case of his death she would look after a child he had fathered on a woman who had predeceased him, a boy who was kept in the home of a friendly family at La Valletta. With his prayer he asked pardon for all the sorrow he had caused his family and begged them to blame his scatterbrained head rather than his heart.

With her eyes closed donna Ortensia relived the anxieties, the heartbreak, and the anguish she had suffered through that son. But her renewed sorrow was not without pride. After all, he had been a brave and selfless man, and certainly the most generous one of his family.

Slowly she retied the package of relics, kissed it, and with a slightly dragging step put everything into a drawer of her night table.

—When I have closed my eyes—she said sweetly, turning to Goffredo—know that here is the best of my life.

Chapter 4

CURIOSITY AND distrust. Feline virtues. There is nothing else in Teodora's green eyes. From the moment that Goffredo entered the palace she both flees from him and stalks him, like the cat who rules a house when there arrives a stranger kitten that everyone makes a fuss over. With an air of friend-enemy, unnoticing and suspicious, nonchalant and sly, she circles around and around as if courting him, she looks at him with one eye open and the other closed, with one paw in the air like a question mark. What is she doing? Does she love him? Hate him? Fear him? Is she spying on him? Nothing. She is only studying him. Hers is the abstract interest aroused in us whenever a mysterious event occurs nearby.

Now, in the tenth year of her marriage, Teodora has made for herself the mask of a woman without emotions. Inert, marble-like, silent, with something enigmatic and crystalline in her cold malachite eyes, you would say that she was a Monna Lisa del Giocondo, without the fascination of the smile. Her own smile, suddenly lit up, dies on her lips in an unchanging shadow of melancholy. An expression of decided seriousness dominates the trembling impatience of her body, an impatience barely visible in the passing excitements of her blood, which flush the tender pallor of her flesh.

In society, some call her 'the beautiful melancholic,' some pin on her the name 'the statue of ice.' All except donna Ortensia agree on the frigidity of Teodora, who resembles more a symbol than a woman, more an allegory than a living creature. She moves through the world always remote and far off. Closed in a shell of indifference without even a small chink through which she can be wounded, she passes as if no one else existed.

One who has never existed for Teodora is her husband, marchese don Fabrizio. You can't say that she had loved or had not loved him, esteemed or despised him, held him in sympathy or in dislike. And you can swear the she has never betrayed him—so far. Not out of virtue or devotion to duty, but simply because there is no taste of pleasure in betraying someone who does not exist. And Teodora is a woman of taste.

Which does not keep the two spouses from representing two dignities, the dignity of two equal and contrasting symbols which compose that unit or institution which is called an aristocratic family of the nineteenth century? He, punctilious, courteous, chivalrous ('*O gran bontà dei cavalieri antichi!*, Great goodness of the knights of olden time!'), she docile, smiling, respectful. Don Fabrizio never speaks to his wife without bowing deeply from the waist, he gallantly kisses her hand morning and evening, he never mentions her without calling her 'marchesa.' Teodora lets her hand be kissed with tender pride, forcing her mouth into a grimace of pleased happiness while he speaks. It seems as if she were reciting, although with the air of a benign goddess, the ejaculatory prayer, 'If so it pleases my Lord...'

—An exemplary couple—many comment, with edification.

—A true mirror of the Gospel's words, 'You two shall be one flesh'—add others, with unctuous religiosity.

—That they are two, there is no doubt— someone insinuates more cautiously.—As to one flesh, it is better not to make hasty judgments. God save us from rash judgments!

In short, the life between the two spouses has run on for ten long years with the monotonous tranquillity of a clock which has no need of the repairman. Two clock hands which meet more and more often during the day, without ever stopping at the same time, therefore in perfect harnony.

But one evening there was a novelty. Teodora, the silent one, spoke at table.

—Have you heard that Goffredo plays like an angel?

Nothing simpler. We know that the angels are always playing. If their invisible orechestra did not exist in this world of dissonances and conflicts we would be surprised. But the question in the mouth of the usually silent woman aroused something like a buzz of amazement. Donna Ortensia, who did not believe in angels, and don Fabrizio, who believed in them all too much, looked at her dumbfounded. That the heavenly Cherubim and Seraphim had performed a concert just for Teodora—go on!—seemed to them quite unlikely. But that she was speaking positively about Goffredo for the first time was one of the Joyful Mysteries, which filled them with sweet amazement. Finally (and it was about time) Teodora was abandoning her attitude of polite dislike toward the young man.

It had happened like this. One night the invisible threads that were stretched in the old palace like spider webs vibrated in its silence with unaccustomed chords. They were guitar chords, accompanied by a muted voice, to which it would have been difficult to assign a gender. An androgynous voice: masculine in the bass, feminine in the high notes, dark and heavenly, passionate and innocent. Who was singing? who dared to disturb the stillness of those ancient walls which in the first hour of night were usually already plunged in sleep and silence? As the mysterious concert was repeated it finally aroused the curiosity of everyone, especially among the servant population. Who is it, who isn't it? Whence come these sounds, always at the same hour? Conjectures overlapped, multiplied, there were even some who blamed the spirits.

For Teodora the mystery had lasted but a short time. On the second night, as soon as the notes of the guitar tickled her ears, in her nightdress she had glided on her pink silk slippers to the door of the young man's room and had set herself to eavesdrop with a curiosity intoxicated by pleasure. How she loved the Oriental laments that the young man was singing softly to the strumming of the harmonious strings! How bold in tone were certain passages and how passionate some of the cadences! And what expression in his voice! Whoever had seen her white figure leaning against the lonely door, almost glued to it, in the heart of the night, would have raised an hymn to music as the pledge of solidarity among humanity. Perhaps from that moment the veil of ice that separated the woman from the unwanted youth had dissolved, and some sweetness had glided into the void between their two souls.

—You play?—asked don Fabrizio, looking at his nephew with surprise.—And, if you please, what instrument?

—The guitar—said the young man, blushing.

—Who taught you?

—No one. Papà played it and I leaarned by listening to him. By ear, naturally.

—The guitar, I might have known!—exclaimed the marchese, dropping on his plate the skin of a pear which he was unwinding in a spiral along his knife blade.—I don't like it. An instrument for barbers.

—I love barbers—interrupted donna Ortensia—if only because they know how to cut people down to size.—Music is always something divine, Teodora agreed.

—So divine—said don Fabrizio ironically—that since the time we have had a pianoforte in the house no one plays it any more.

It was true. Soon after his marriage the marchese had had one of the ealiest fortepianos, the successor of the glorious harpsichord, sent from France, as a present to his wife for her name-day. But the magnificent *Erard* had remained firmly closed once the first enthusiasm for its novelty had cooled down. Without being a professional, Teodora as a girl had played the harpsichord with considerable virtuosity and accompanied herself in the Italian *romanze* that she sang in her velvety contralto voice. But, as happens to all young brides, from the day after her wedding she had lost her taste for music bit by bit.

But all rules have their exceptions. And the next day after the unexpected dinner-table conversation marchesa Teodora opened her *Erard* and sent for her old music teacher Geraci, to return to the study of singing and the piano.

Like Sleeping Beauty, the old palace woke up suddenly and began to sing. After years and years of silence, the rooms began to echo again with scales and arpeggios, octaves, trills, cadenzas, vocalises. A *carillon* of youth and joy seemed to ring out from the heart of all beings, animate and inanimate. They all smiled—the little cherubs frescoed on the ceilings, the figures in the tapestries, the porcelain statuettes and the miniatures on the fans displayed in the glass cases.

Only old Ortensia complained, without anyone listening to her:

—What in the world is happening? Are the frogs singing in the daytime?

But when she encountered her daughter-in-law, with the friendliest of smiles and with that ability to dissimulate proper to gentlewomen of breeding, she said:

—You do well to return to music, my daughter. If art does not succeed in imitating life, life must imitate art. There will aways be something to gain, because life is ugly, art is beautiful. And music is the most beautiful of the arts because it imitates nothing, it expresses only itself.

Repaying the friendly little speech with her rarest smile, Teodora thought:

—This is the first time that my mother-in-law understands me. I have never felt myself so far removed from daily life as in this moment. I seem finally to be sailing toward a dream of beauty...

Several days passed. One afternoon, coming out of the dining room, Teodora approached Goffredo. It was the first time that she had spoken to him for reasons other than strict necessity:

—Are you free today?

—I'm always free.

—I mean, do you have any engagements?

—No, aunt.

—Well, if it doesn't bore you to stay home...we'll make some music. I'll perform for you some romanzas that you will like. Old or modern?

—All the same. I like all music.

—We'll meet in the music room at five, then. Until then.

When Goffredo turned the door handle of the room at the appointed hour, he felt caressed by a soft silence and a half light in which he moved lightly as in a warm bath. Through the blue-green curtains the spring day languished like the water of a pond reflecting the leafage of thick trees, interrupted here and there by broad patches of sky. A large bunch of roses, whose spent perfume lay over everything, was dying in a crystal vase. In her long clinging white dress, the Botticellian figure of Teodora, seated on a low stool like a swan ready to plunge her neck into the stream, was leaning over leafing through sheets of music.

—Can I help you, aunt?—and he bent to rummage among the sheets—Rossini... Bellini...Haendel... Mozart... Pergolesi... Paisiello...

—Here, this one: *Nina pazza per amore.*

—Is that enough?

—No. Also take the *Capuletti e i Montecchi* of Bellini. I want you to hear the famous romanza, 'Oh quante volte, oh quante!'

—I think I've found it. Here it is.

—How clever you are! We'll begin with that one. And will you kindly lower the piano stool?

—How tall you are.

—You only realize it now?—she said coquettishly.—There, that's enough. Thanks.

She sat down, throwing back the short train of her skirt to free her feet for the pedals. The varnish of the piano reflected her white and slender image among the gold of the finely carved candelabra. A sidelong glance at her silent listener, a few lazy chords drawn from the ivories of the white keyboard.

The song, flying over the ever-changing waves of the arpeggios, was master of the room. 'Oh how many times, how many, I begged heaven weeping.' In the loving memory of Juliet, eroticism purified by the vision of death, passion which hovers on the edge of madness, the shipwreck of the individual being in endless desire—all these passed and repassed, arose and descended the ladder of her voice: the warm and mellow mezzo soprano, with its dark and velvety tones filled with restrained passion. When the aria paused for the recitative, 'Romeo, where art thou? In what land are you traveling? where am I to send you my sighs?,' the voice of the singer trembled as if struck by a sobs, there was such grief in those simple words.

With the sigh of the last note, Teodora dropped her hands into her lap.

Neither of the two spoke.

—So, what do you think?—she asked after a bit, still possessed by the ecstasy of singing.

—Stupendous.

—Don't you feel yourself a bit ravished... off to heaven?

—Could be. I have no idea of heaven. I'm not dead yet—smiled the young man.

—And do you think one must be dead to have an idea of heaven?—said the woman in a dark voice, with the loveliest timbre of her golden 'basses.'—Everyone can create his own corner of paradise in this world... if he only wishes it. There is always time to die.

—Luckily we're both alive, the two of us.

—Yes—continued Teodora, ingratiatingly.—But life is not what counts.

—No?

—What counts it not life in itself, but its intensity—do you understand?—its vibration… Do you see this key? As long as it remains still it is as if it did not exist. If I touch it—and she pressed the ivory with her nervous finger—the string inside begins to vibrate. You don't love the intense life, it seems—she smiled with some hint of biterness.

—On the contrary, aunt. You know that my father's blood runs in my veins, dark and harsh blood.

—I understand: the passion for politics, patriotism… And nothing more?

She waited for an answer, which was not forthcoming.

From outside, the change in the weather, which became brighter as the clouds cleared unexpectedly, was reflected within the room, detaching its rounded forms from the opaque covering of the shadows.

In the new light the woman's face appeared more pale.

Annoyed, almost angry, as if reacting to a personal injury, she said—then I'll sing you something…more touching.

'For three days Nina.. Nina…has remained in bed.' The elegy ripples like a sad *berceuse*. It seems a lament made peaceful by its resignation to death. No, love cannot accept the end. It is not death itself, only a dream, a sweet dream, from which one can awaken. Harmonies of life, arouse her! 'Fifes, cymbals, drums, wake Ninetta.' Hear the appeal of hope and despair. It is the Bacchic exaltation of the resurrection. She is rising again, she *will* rise again. Illusion, madness, this is love. Life is nothing but madness. Weeping and smiling, smiling and weeping, this is love.

The wonder of the music had passed into the soul of the singer, who stood up disturbed and disconnected. When she looked at Goffredo her eyes were immense. The emerald irises completely devoured the whites edged by their long dark lashes.

—It's like that—she whispered, overcome.

—What do you mean?

—Which of the two pleases you more?—Her voice had an artificially distracted air.

—I don't know. I'm not a musician. I don't even know the notes.

—It's not a question of notes. Only of feeling, of the heart. It is true that some people have a piece of unresponsive clay instead of a heart.

—Could that be me?—Goffredo asked childishly.

—Not you. But a person close to you.

The boy looked at her, puzzled.

—For example, your uncle—she continued, after an hesitation.

—My uncle?

—Isn't he the one who opposes your studying music?

—I don't study. I play, I strum as best I can.

—It's a pity. You should study. You have talent.

—Imagine if my uncle would let me study!

—It doesn't matter. I could give you a few lessons myself. You know, in my youth I studied, and a lot.

—I have heard that one has to start very early to study the piano. Later your hand no longer obeys you.

—I know. But it is not a rule that you have to begin at age five. Above all, you are still so young. And then it is a question of talent, of sensitivity. And also of much patience. Give me your hand.

She took the youth's hand between her own. She spread it out, tried the wrist joint, uncurled the fingers, joined them together, separated them, then she opened his palm almost like a fan to measure the greatest diatance between the little finger and the thumb, she stroked his fingertips.

—A beautiful hand—she said, darting her eyes into his—the hand of a pianist. If only you wished...

Goffredo's hand had remained imprisoned between those of Teodora, under her soft caress, when there was a knock at the door.

It was Marco, asking for the signora marchesa.

She collected herself, stood up, attempted a step. The bunch of roses, grazed by her thigh, fell apart with a soft rustle, strewing the carpet with petals.

Geometry teaches us that between two circles there can exist one and only one point of contact. But human beings are not circles. So Teodora discovered without much effort that there was more than one tangent between herself and her nephew. At least two: in addition to a passion for music, a passion for horses.

Teodora was like a horsewoman of the Amazon kingdom of Pontus, except for her virginity, which gave rise to malicious remarks. Goffredo could arouse the envy of a *búttero,* a cowboy of the Roman campagna, or even better, a *gaucho* of the Argentine pampas. Without formal training, he was almost by instinct and by nature an undaunted horseman. He fearlessly mounted any horse, saddled or bareback, he jumped any obstacle, he did trick riding, he danced on the animal's back like a circus acrobat. Teodora, on the other hand, was a horsewoman of *haute école,* dressage. A regular attendant at all the meets, a contestant in all the horse shows, the winner of many prizes, tireless in hunting the fox, she was known for her skill and her boldness, disciplined by a prudent elegance. In the trot, in the gallop, in the obstacle course, in fording rivers, she was reputed to be unbeatable. No horse could withstand her will and her whims.

That morning Goffredo brought out of the stables his young bay, already saddled, dancing on three hooves, shining like a block of varnished mahogany, with a lively eye and flaring nostrils. Because the horse, well fed and bored by his long rest, was showing signs of impatience, Goffredo gave him a pat.

—Calm down, Lince, now we're going for a good gallop.

Then with a leap he was in the saddle. The horse shied and broke into in a nervous pirouette.

—Goffredo, be careful—cried his grandmother, leaning out from the railing of the loggia.

The young man glanced upward, calm.

—Grandmamma, do you want to mount? We'll go for a ride.

—I've been astride for quite some time, my child. Astride between two centuries. I am racing with death on my back. Go on, you won't catch me.

—On the contrary, death will flee ahead of us, like a terrified fox.

A groom moved into the middle of the courtyard, leading by the bridle Astrea, the half-blood black mare of the younger marchesa, who at that moment was descending the last steps of the stairway: her Amazonian thighs enclosed in a dark green riding habit, her head upright, with a little plumed hat on her night-black hair, her right hand on the handle of her whip.

Astrea, who was a noble beast as her pedigree showed, had a special sensitivity. She shared her owner's feelings, and therefore when the woman was bored her horse felt it her duty to be bored also. But that morning Astrea was beside herself with joy and showed a festive impatience.

Her eyes shuddered with happiness when her mistress slid into her mouth a lump of sugar, which her white teeth crunched up in a flash.

—I'm at your orders, aunt—said Goffredo, bowing. It's just striking seven.

—Thanks. You're frighteningly punctual.

—Where are we going?

—To the park of the Favorita. I don't believe there is anything more beautiful than trotting early on those lanes bordered with green, among the songs of the birds.

She mounted with a single leap, springing from the young man's hands, which he had cupped under her foot. She straightened her skirt, making sure that it draped well over her legs, took the reins, and gave a last pat to Astrea, who turned her head around, as if to enjoy the elegance of her mistress.

Goffredo, astride his bay horse, placed himself at her left.

Amid the bows and scrapes of the servants, the couple rode out of the courtyard.

The horses pawed with spirit, barely restrained by their harsh bits.

—Are you happy, Goffredo?—asked the dark horsewoman, smiling at her companion under her hat plume, which fluttered in the wind.

—How could I not be?

—I am, very much. It's the first time we have gone out together. A morning's ride is a good massage for the muscles. As soon as I'm in the saddle I feel lighter, free from every chain, every constraint. A strange sensation. I become one with the earth that I tread, with the trees that rush past beside me, the sky... It's like living several lives in a single one. And you?

—I don't know. I forget everything.

—Even life?

—Why not?

—So you don't love life? One doesn't forget what one loves.

—I've never asked myself such a question. I'd like to know what you think.

—Well... I love life.

—You mean, on horseback.

—I mean, in company. Not with only the horse. Loneliness upsets me. Sometimes it frightens me.

—And yet the proverb says, Better alone than in bad company, joked Goffredo..

—Yes. But when you're in bad company you can't even say you're in company. It is loneliness for two, which is the most painful.

—Are we one or two now?

—Two, if you like. But confess it, in this moment you would like it better if a girl of sixteen or eighteen were riding beside you... instead of me.

—I told you that when I ride I don't think of anything, not even girls.

—Then you do think of them when you're on foot?

—Maybe never—the young man answered, blushing—I walk too quickly to think about women.

-Which doesn't keep women from thinking about you. You're a handsome boy, and women are never in a hurry when they like a man. They play with time, they lead him around like a dog on a leash, taking him where they like. Sooner or later they get where they want to go.

—In fact, here we are at the gate of the Favorita—said Goffredo, blushing more than ever.

As soon as they had passed the squat pilasters of the entrance, a simultaneous twitch of the bridle sent both horses from a walk into a jog trot. Then they dashed off at a full gallop straight along the viale of Diana, so called from the damaged image of the goddess of the hunt, beyond which the *allée* loses itself among the slopes of Monte Pellegrino. The road, inclining lightly upward among the thick colonnades of oaks and plane trees, rose to meet the horses, who dragged their violet shadows along behind them. In the morning hour, the concert of the sounds and songs of the countryside was silent under the quadruple thud of the horses' hooves. In the tangled branches the horizontal rays of the rising sun pricked out golden embroideries on the habits of the two riders.

When they reached the end of the viale, where it rests in a short plateau at the western outcropping of the mountain, the two dismounted. Leading their horses by the bridle, they ascended the grassy ramp toward the rotunda where the marble shrine of the goddess rises. On the background of an unchanging green, the mutilated and seminude Diana stood out in the full beauty of the morning light. Her blond thighs were draped chastely near the pubic zone by a veil of stone. The marble of the ancient pedestal was softened by light mosses. The sun, in triumphal ascent on the horizon, drew changing reflections from the sweat-soaked coats of the horses, who were tethered to the rocky base of an oak.

—A splendid ride!—exclaimed Teodora, inhaling with large breaths the balsamic air of the resinous conifers and the perfumes of the wild herbs.

—Do you feel tired?

—I have never been so happy. Now we can rest in some shady corner... where the sun cannot enter without asking permission. There, for example.—And she indicated a small clearing in the shelter of a some shrubbery, among the velvety masses of ferns and sedum.

She drew off her long gloves, removed her hat, and relaxed on the grass, wreathing her head in her arms with the waves of her hair still disarranged. Her limbs abandoned themselves to a lazy pose, a delicious lethargy.

Still standing, curious, Goffredo wandered around among the clumps of yellow-spattered broom, amusing himself by stirring the plants and poking at the sleeping stones with the end of his whip. Experienced in the countryside as he was, he named the insects, the grasses, the ornamental plants, the medicinal ones, the poisonous ones, as he uncovered them one by one.

—That one—he said, pointing to it—is a poisonous mushroom.

At the feet of a monumental oak a gold-colored *agarico sulfuro* flaunted itself among lichens and moss, and farther off glowed a *boleto melefico* with its convex flambuoyant red cap.

—How do you get to know so many things? Are you a botanist?

—On Malta I lived in the country. It's true that down there they have a flora somewhat different from ours. They're almost in Africa...Nature is so various and so interesting everywhere.

—It's so beautiful here too. Let's enjoy it. Why don't you rest too?

She lowered her eyes, in whose pupils all the green of the woods seemed gathered.

—Doesn't it seem to you that there is a bad smell?—she asked after a bit, reopening her eyes.

—Yes, something rotten.

—It's coming in waves. Now it's unbearable—she continued, flaring her nostrils.

Goffredo went to explore, rummaging around in the hedges, in the underbrush, under the rocks. Suddenly he drew back with a gesture of disgust.

—What did you see?—cried Teodora, leaping to her feet.

—Nothing. A dead animal.

In the midst of the scrub, the corpse of a cat. The only lively thing: two enormous eyes of green glass wide open with terror. The half-decayed paws showed their bones, the back partially unskinned, the belly reduced to a bloody hole swarming with wasps: so many that from the crawling of the little black and yellow bodies it seemed that the unclean carcass was rolling about on the ground. A thick buzz cradled the woodland silence like a funereal lament.

—How horrible! A black cat—bad luck. Let's escape! Let's go, please—pleaded Teodora.

The little animal must have been chewed by some dog. The rodents and the wasps had done the rest.

As the cloud of insects grew thicker, crowded by those who were gathering from every direction, Goffredo threw himself on them, stamping underfoot as many as he could.

—No, Goffredo, don't make them angry, for heaven's sake. They'll fight back!

A more aggressive buzzing rose from the surviving swarm. The scattered insects regrouped themselves. With all the others who had immediately rushed in, they formed a sort of vortex on the head of their persecutor.

—Let's get away, please—she said again, and gathering her long habit about her, she fled hurriedly.

Suddenly changing target, the wasps became enraged against the fleeing woman. She shielded her face with the palms of her hands but she could not stop part of the swarm from throwing itself angrily on her legs, penetrating under her disheveled garments.

—Help! Help!—she implored.

Goffredo had removed his jacket. Wrapping it around her, he frightened and drove away the poisonous wasps.

Now carried out of the enraged swarm, Teodora collapsed on a grassy bank, weeping.

—Did they sting you?

—Yes, on the legs. What torture! I feels like my flesh is on fire.

Pale, terrified, she lifted her long heavy skirt. Above her black stockings there shone a circle of shining flesh. Freed from the garter, her stocking slid to the ankle of her right leg, which was the worst afflicted. The golden nudity swarmed with little red spots.

—Here, how it burns!

The young man leaned over, examined, kneaded the wounded flesh.

—Let me do it—he said—once the stingers are out you won't feel anything. It's not the first time that I have been the surgeon for such things.

When he had finished his patient work, he said:

—Now we need water to wash it.

He looked around. In the clearing he discovered a small shepherd tending a little flock of sheep. He reached him in a trice. Shepherds carry water to relieve their thirst. The boy offered a terracotta jar that sweated hunidity from its pores. The water poured by Goffredo's hands fell on Teodora's wounds. A handkerchief served to bind her calf, where the stings were thickest.

She felt a sense of relief. Then, with a swift movement she rearranged her clothes over her naked knees, leaving only the lower part of her legs uncovered.

—Does the sun bother you?

—No. It actually restores me.

—How do you feel?

—Better, much better. But I need peace, so much peace. Sit by me, while I stretch out a bit on the grass. Do you know I'm very grateful to you?

—For what?

—For what you did.

—Anyone would have done the same thing, in my place.

—And if I had been alone?

—I can't accept that. I know that you never go out alone when you ride.

Whoever had accompanied you would have given exactly the same help that I offered.

—It isn't the same thing. All men are not the same. And you, Goffredo, you are not...just a being, like all the others.

The young man started to get up.

—No. Don't go away—she begged—stay here a bit longer. Give me your hand. My head is burning. Feel—and she brought his hand to her forehead, sliding it up under the edge of her hair. I have a buzzing in my head...the buzz of the wasps. As if I had a fever.

—It's nothing. Nothing but a little upset. Calm yourself, aunt.

—Why 'aunt'?—she said, without letting go of his hand, in a tone of sweet reproach. — I am ...Teodora.

Her eyes had never been so green, so magnificently dark.

—Isn't it time—she continued in an ingratiating tone—that you addressed me as 'tu,' that you called me simply Teodora... Don't you think so?

A grasshopper chirped. Some birds descended to peck around on the grass, immediately taking to flight again. Humming, shivers, whispers moved between the earth and heaven. They seemed to hear the the sap rising secreetly up through the tree trunks to moisten the buds and the leaves, which drank light and air in their mysterious union with the birds. As noon approached, the life of all beings, of the myriad of creeping and winged creatures, visible and invisible, became intense and feverish, mingled in a insistent symphony that heated the blood in their veins ever more intensely.

Goffredo was silent.

—You, *tu,* also have a sting on your hand. Didn't you realize it? See, here. Does it hurt? Let me treat your wound.

And she placed her warm and moist lips on his hand, holding them there for a long time.

—How do you feel? Are you still suffering?—he asked.

—A bit, yes. But I am happy. When one is happy there is a certain... pleasure even in suffering.

In fact she seemed, more than a person who *is* happy, like someone who is *about to be* happy. A single word from him, the word she waited for, would have been enough to transform her desire into fact.

He said simply:

—Do you think you can make the trip back home? It's already late.

Teodora only bowed her head, darkly. And she was immediately on her feet, with a sorrowful twist of her lovely mouth, as if the sting of her wounds had suddenly reawakened.

The silence of their return was broken only by the rhythmic tread of their horses' hooves.

Chapter 5

A JINGLE of bells rebounded from one corner of the courtyard to the other, setting to flight some chilled little sparrows who were pecking between the stones of the pavement in delicate skips.

It was the signal that someone was comng to the palace, where no one could enter without being checked out by the concierge, don Ciccio Sacco. He was, if not a professional, at least an amateur of the mafia, nicknamed 'the Corsican hound' in the whole quarter of the Vetrereia by reason of his flat nose squashed over an ever-drooling mouth.

This time the arrival was don Bastiano Assardi, coadjutor priest of the parish of S. Maria della Catena, as well as private chaplain and great friend of the marchional house of Cortada. He was recognizable at a distance of an hundred meters and more by his Lilliputian stature, his shabby hat, and the eternal *rictus sardonicus* on his lips and his yellow teeeth.

—*Voscenza benedica*—said don Ciccio, bringing his hand to his gold-braided cap.

—God bless you, and also bless your belly full of secrets and lasagna—joked don Assardi, making the gesture of boring the little round cheek of the concierge with his finger.

—Secrets yes, lasagna no, dear father. One eats only to keep from dying. Life is so expensive that you can't even put a pot on the stove. Believe me, as God is my witness.

—Let's start by not taking the name of God in vain! For the rest, let's thank the *re befé, viscottu e minné*—roast beef, biscotti, and cassata. You remember, don Ciccio, that when our king still reigned an entire family could manage on three *tari* a day. Wonderful times! Now we have freedom, which Victor Emmanuel has brought us! We are free and enlightened. They have lightened everything, even our pockets—and saying that he turned a grey and sweaty pocket inside out from his cassock.—Long live united Italy!

—Your reverence may go up—and don Ciccio pointed to the grand stairway, striped by a red runner carpet.—The marchese is expecting you.

—Never, never—protested the little priest, with an air of scandalized modesty—that's where the bigwigs go up. I am a very humble servant of God.

And he slipped into the service stair, humming.

Don Assardi wore a pair of shoes too wide, so it seemed that they must slop away from under his feet at any moment. His bullet-shaped body was balanced on those awful shoes, surmounted by a large mangy head like that of a vulture. Something unpleasant exuded from his appearance: his ill-shaven cheeks always flecked with little red hairs, his small pig-like eyes, and his grating, soapy voice. What made him interesting, on the other hand, was an inexhaustible way with words punctuated by jokes and wisecracks and a wealth of gestures that bordered on the comic.

Without comparison, don Assardi was the greatest busybody and intriguer of all the priests, not only of his quarter, but absolutely of the whole city. Always completely informed about all public and private business, he buttonholed anyone whom he happened to meet. He had a world of acquaintances in every level of society. He frequented numerous houses, from the most plebeian to the most aristocratic. He stuck his nose into any number of businesses, he arranged and dissolved marriages, he was a link of union and disunion between the political parties. More out of amusement than malice, he made peace and sometimes war as well between families, by turns poking up and damping down the flames. For his extraordinary versatility, leaning more toward amiability than toward malice, he had earned the popular nickname, ''*a cucchiara di tutti i pignat,*' 'a spoon for every pot.' And although everyone grumbled and spoke ill of him, no one was more popular in the city than that comic little man, nor was there any house that did not feel honored in opening its doors to him.

Don Assardi did not have a good press even in the archbishop's Curia. Some of them called him an ass. Some accused him of low flattery of his superiors, combined with downright cunning, some dismissed him as a busybody and a daydreamer: but they all feared him. He said to those who informed him of these humors, 'I know it, in the world of the Church everything is pardoned except intelligence,' and he resigned himself to persecution, sure in holding both keys of the archbishop's heart.—There's room in the world for everybody—he repeated without bitterness;—what harm do I if I know how to choose the best little place for myself?

When he had reached the presence of don Fabrizio, the priest bent in a deep bow, so deep that he would have lost his balance without the help of his enormous shoes, like those of a circus clown.

—At your orders, signor marchese.

—My humblest prayers, father. And forgive me if I have made you come so early, but the morning is the best moment to talk with ease. Later one is never alone.

—Solitude is salvation, union is perdition—said the priest unctuously, rubbing his hands as if washing them with imaginary soap.

—That's right. But the trouble is that in politics one can never work alone.

—You remind me of the man—replied don Assardi—who being challenged to a duel told his opponent, Fine, I will name my seconds, in the meantime you start by yourself.

—Exactly—approved the marchese, also laughing,—politics is a duel... the only one allowed without sin to us Christians.

—A duel? If only it were! But this is a Tower of Babel. We speak and do not understand, this one wants it hot and that one cold, this one says white and that one black...—and the priest ran his hands through his non-existent hair.

—In the meantime, padre, some friends of Sicily, from down here and up there, are asking me what point we're at, if we're working, if we're pulling our forces together, if we're preparing for this restoration. You understand, it is more than four years since our legitimate sovereigns lost their kingdom and it is our sacred task to put them back in the saddle. Time is burning up.

—One word: put them back in the saddle. If it were only this, your rider would be enough. But today we find ourselves in the presence of a constituted authority, of a kingdom that cannot be overthrown except with a revolution. That is the revolution which must be made.

—I too know this. But when?

—Not a minute before nor a minute after when it *will* be made.

—The soonest possible.

—You know the saying? *Festina lente,* Make haste slowly. Everyone is talking about doing, about acting. To do a thing is easy, the difficult thing is to think. To do something without having thought it out well is madness. Every madman is good for doing and also for overdoing. But we're not madmen, my dear marchese. Since politics is not made by individuals, we must take account of the forces that we have with us and against us, friends and enemies.

—Even enemies?

—Certainly! You know that in politics everything is relative. Today's friends can become tomorrow's enemies, and viceversa. Sometimes our enemies can be more useful than our friends. Everything lies in knowing how to manoever them. Sometimes nothing is more true than the motto, *Salus ex inimicis,* Salvation comes from your enemies.

—To know the situtation of the contending parties, all you have to do is read the newspapers.

—Newspapers, journalists!—sneered don Assardi scornfully.—The journalist, like the orator, is someone who possesses the art of speaking without saying anything. Pay no attention to them. They don't say what they know, and they write what they don't know. Better to trust what your most humble servant tells you.

—I'm listening.

—Well? Do you want to know the situation of the political parties? I will make you a photograph. I'm not saying that I will be one hundred per cent impartial. But is a photograph? How often do we complain about a portrait that has enlarged our nose or loosened our mouth? Even the sun has its sins and its spots. Anyway, I will try to be as objective as possible. Listen. Let's begin with the so-called *moderates* or *conservatives.* No need to fear. They are moderate in everything except their appetite. They want to eat, whatever the trough. They ate under the Bourbons, today they are gorging in the service of the house of Savoy. They call themselves *pro-government,* the people call them *time-servers*. Yesterday they were shouting, 'Long live Ferdinando and Francesco,' today they scream, 'Long live Victor Emmanuel,' tomorrow they will once again acclaim the Bourbons if they return.

Next comes the *party of action*. Here we must keep our eyes open. They are restless people, always in contorsions. You understand: they want to eat, while the others have already eaten. They are complainers, dishonest, jealous, ambitious. Who is more ambitious than Franesco Crispi? They could be dangerous. They will not be if we know how to use them for our own ends. We disagree with them in everything, except one thing. They want the revolution as much as we do, with this difference: they want the revolution for the revolution, we want it for the restoration. We'll see who is more cunning. For the moment we are swimming together. At the right moment we'll sink them. Have I explained myself, dear marchese?

In third place I put the *separatists* or *regionalists*, as they like to call themselves. Harmless people. Idealists, visioraries, cloud-catchers.

—There are eminent men in the party, without doubt: D'Ondes Reggio, Ferrara, the Amari, Peranni, Perez, but… interrupted don Fabrizio.

—Even intelligent men can say and do foolish things in politics—the priest continued—and when they put their mind to it they are crazier than all the others. 'Independent Sicily' makes me think of a top which doesn't spin unless someone pulls the string.

—And this is precisely my idea—replied the marchese.—I do not admit any other future arrangement for our island than the reconstitution of the Kingdom of the Two Sicilies. A great southern kingdom under a single dynasty. Francesco I came out of the Congress of Vienna with the title of 'King of the Realm of the Two Sicilies.' Italy must remain as it was constituted by that Congress, which liquidated all sinful revolutionary fears. Neither unity, nor federation.

—A real mess, the federation!—commented don Assardi—Let's leave Switzerland as it is. We Italians have a rage for imitations, for copies. And we only succeed in making bad copies.

—Switzerland serves only one purpose, to furnish troops faithful to our Majesty the king.

—Which does not alter the fact that even separatism can be useful to our cause, at least for now, if we know how to exploit it. It is a motive for discontent, a disunifying force to keep in mind.

—And our forces? Our party?

—I'll tell you right away. The clergy, secular and regular, are almost all with us. A fine force! The few who since '48 had flung themselves into liberalism, crying 'long live Pius IX,' changed their minds as soon as that good pope, realising the ugly trick that the Masons were playing on him, changed course. Now they say 'to hell with the liberals.' True, there remain some little priests or crazy excommunicated old friars, like fra Pantaleo, who still follow Garibaldi. But that doesn't count. One swallow doesn't make a springtime. And those ones are not swallows, but carrion crows of ill-omen.

—There remains the mafia—don Fabrizio said, as if to himself, darkly.

—So?

—The mafia is always linked with the government. In their hands it can become a force against us...

—Yes. The mafia is always with the government...The mafia is always with the strongest. But if the strongest is us, we'll see them come over to our side all at once. History teaches us that the mercenaries always follow the strongest lords, the ones who pay best. Today we are the strongest.

—Are you sure?

—Remember, the strongest are always the discontented. It is they who make wars, uprisings, revolutions. Whoever is doing well is always a conservative. It is the poor, the humiliated, the offended, the disappointed, the oppressed, that move the world. The cream of the jest is that today in our Italy, this *great* Italy (and the priest underlined his last words with a mocking smile) they are *all* discontented: the liberals, the moderates, the unitarians, the federalists, the municipalists, and even the Garibaldini.

—You have forgotten the Bourbonists—don Fabrizio observed.

—On the contrary, we are quite content. Content with the general discontent. We can rejoice like fishermen after a good catch. After all, what does politics boil down to? Fishing in troubled waters.

—And now—the marchese cut him off as if giving way all of a sudden to a tormenting thought—let's talk about serious things.

—My goodness! What have we been talking about up till now? Or perhaps you're right, my friend. Today the only serious things are those that make us laugh, while that which moves us to laugh is dying of seriousness.

—Unfortunately, there is nothing humorous in what I'm about to tell you—don Fabrizio replied, with the severe expression he reserved for great occasions. —Do you wish to hear me?

—I'm all ears.

The marchese arose, approached the cabinet, drew from the drawer a crumpled sheet of paper, and held it out to the priest.

—Read it.

Don Assari rummaged in his pocket, pulled out a leprous cardboard container from which he slid his eyeglasses, and putting them on he started to read rapidly with a cantilena, alternating high and low notes, exactly like a priest reciting his office.

When he had reached the end, he exclaimed with a little smile almost of satisfaction:

—Ah! An anonymous! I expected to find a signature.

—That doesn't change things.—said don Fabrizio darkly.

—No, rather it has great value. You mustn't believe anonymous letters. Whoever uses them is either a coward or a villain.

—That doesn't mean that it can't tell the truth.

—The truth is an act of courage. From villains you cannot expect anything but lies. Shame! Shame! The marchesa is a pious and God-fearing woman, above any suspicion, believe me. I see here the diabolical work of some enemy of yours, of ours—concluded don Assardi.

—I did not suppose that I had so malicious an enemy.

—Don't underestimate yourself to the point of maintaining you have no enemies. A person of your rank *must* have enemies, and unknown enemies are always more dangerous than known ones. You are nothing less than the head of the legitimist party. You are a force and a symbol. Would you claim not to have the honor of some enemies, either in plain sight or hidden in the shadows? Since your name makes you unassailable in public, you are assaulted in your peace, in your personal affections. That's all. For goodness' sake! All we need is for you to lend yourself to their game. Assume that you have never received that contemptible letter, as would any gentleman without stain and without fear.

—Fear? Me?—said don Fabrizio, proudly rising to his full manly height.—To prove it to you, I will tear up this foul paper.

—Easy,—the priest observed smoothly—don't tear up anything. Even an anonymous letter is a document. And documents are not to be destroyed. What is obscure today could be made clear tomorrow.

—So...you might have doubts about my wife?

—For the love of God, I'm not saying that. No, a thousand times no to anything like that! I am only saying that the document might serve tomorrow to identify its writer. And it might set us on the way to something interesting. Think: it is an enemy who has written down this filth. In private life one can be as generous as one wishes. In politics one must be prudent and shrewd. As a Christian I cannot advise you, like the Greek philosopher, to do the greatest good to your friends and the greatest harm to your enemies. But to be watchful and to defend yourself, yes, that I can advise you. That is your duty.

Chapter 6

WHAT DO you think of Goffredo?—don Fabrizio asked his mother, smoothing the collar of his beard under the curve of his chin with a disdainful air, like a cat grooming herself in the sun.

—Why do you ask?

—Because it seems to me that he is finally on his way to becoming a respectable young man. *Our* training has made him another person.

—Was he a criminal then, when he entered this house?—donna Ortensia answered angrily.

—Let's not dramatize things, mamma. I'm only saying that certain whims...certain fancies that his father must have put into his head have passed...

—Which fancies? Is he perhaps a glutton, a gambler, a womanizer?

—As for women, we must be fair, he doesn't resemble his father. He doesn't bother himself with them, he doesn't even look at them.

—Too bad.

—Purity of conduct is bad, then?

—No. But when you don't love women at age twenty, at thirty you hate life. Woman works on the man like emery on hard stones, she forms his character.

—Or his bad character.

—Perhaps. *Quand on a du caractère, on l'a toujours mauvais,* When one has character it's always bad.

—And yet—don Fabrizio continued, unspooling the thread of his secret thoughts—I would prefer that Goffredo had amorous fancies, rather than political bees in his bonnet.

—Let's not offend the bees. They are merry little beasts, which buzz around without doing harm to anyone. What I fear is the bee-mole, which borrows underground and gnaws plants at their roots.

—What do you mean?

—I fear the priests that you surround him with.

—You're always a priest-hater, mamma. Be careful. Remember the proverb: *Qui mange du pape, en meurt.*—Who eats the pope dies of it.

—I'll never eat a pope, don't worry. Imagine if I could swallow a Boniface VIII, a Julius II, or an Alexander VI! It's is rather they who are gnawing at our house.

—Today the Church is the only antidote that can be oppposed to the poison of Garibaldi.

—Forget about Garibaldi, who is quietly farming at Caprera.

—Poor litttle man, he plants potatoes and carrots! He went down there, their newspapers say, with a sack of seeds, a hoe, and a barrel of salt fish. Everybody knows the sack contained a nice hoard of gold coins.

—Garibaldi is poor, as poverty-stricken as Mazzini.

—They're all Franciscans, these leaders of the people—sneered the marchese.

—They don't resemble your General Landi, who pocketed four thousand ducats for handing Sicily over without a fight.

—He didn't pocket anything, because signor Garibaldi paid him with a bad check—don Fabrizio, green with bile, shot back.—That was the scoundrel's greatest American-style fraud. Now the troublemaker is playing Cincinnatus on the rock of Caprera. No, there's something that doesn't smell right. He plays dead, and in the meantime he's preparing one of his usual tricks. First he was screaming, 'Death to the Bourbons,' now he's shouting, 'Rome or death.' Robbery upon robbery. Having torn Sicily away from its legitimate sovereigns, he turns his rapacious eyes on Venice and the Papal States. But there he will find grist for his mill. Franz Joseph will never allow Venice to be amputated from his kingdom, and Louis Napoleon is watching with his forces on guard to see that not a hair of the pope's head is touched.

—My son, even the hairs of the pope are numbered. And he has so few of them. We are at a standstill, history marches on.

—The truth is that there are restless, frenetic men, disturbers of the world, as the English defined Napoleon I. For such men there is only perpetual exile to an island or the strait-jacket.

—The English call anyone who gets in the way of their dreams of domination 'disturbers of the world.'

—You know what I'd do with Garibaldi? Instead of letting him plant carrots on Caprera, I'd exile him for life to a second Saint Elena or Devil's Island.

—And if I told you that Garibaldi is not longer on Caprera?

—What are you saying, mamma? Who is circulating such nonsense?

—I am. For several days Garibaldi has been traipsing around Lombardy with the excuse of treating his old wounds at the Trescore spa. He lets everyone believe that he has gone up there for one reason, official, let us say: to inaugurate a local branch of his national marksmanship program. In reality, he is waiting to recruit volunteers for his next enterprise. Enthusiastic welcomes everywhere, frenzied crowds. The young carry him in triumph. Even Alessandro Manzoni went to pay his respects.

—Manzoni? A Catholic!

—Do you believe that all Catholics are like you, milksops with no blood in their veins?

—A Catholic cannot side with those who believe neither in God nor in the saints.

—Imbecilities! I can reassure you that Manzoni too is a believer. Do you think you have a monopoly on God?

—People of that ilk have no god but the devil. But tell me, please, who gave you such news?

—Beelzebub, naturally. I have a direct line to him.

In fact, the informers of donna Ortensia were neither Beelzebub nor Belfagor nor Barbariccia nor Calabrina, nor any other representative of the infernal world, simply Goffredo. He maintained contact with the party of action, with the exponents of Garibaldism and Mazzinianism. Before the newspapers reported the news he was completely up to date about the numerous threads that the patriots were weaving from one end of the peninsula to the other in order to keep the feeling for unity alive and to prepare the annexation of Venice and Rome.

The morning of 28 June 1862. Goffredo plummets like a stone from a catapult into donna Ortensia's bedroom.

The old lady, who is giving the final touches to her coiffure in front of the mirror, turns, halfway between annoyance and resentment. What an impropriety to surprise a woman, even one past her seventieth year, at her toilet.

—A nice new idea—she says—to barge in without asking permission.

—Sorry, grandmother. You don't know the great news?

—What news?

—Garibaldi has landed.

—Where?

—Here, at the marina.

—Well, let him land.

—But granny, isn't the blood boiling in your veins, don't you too feel rejuvenated?—And he throws himself on the old lady, besieging her with kisses.

—I'm always young. But that's no reason that you have to strangle me just because of Garibaldi. Not to mention completely messing up my hairdo.

—You're more beautiful unkempt.

—Flatterer!—said donna Ortensia, with an air of satisfied self-respect.—But sit down like a good boy and tell me everything.

—I can't sit, I've got ants in my pants. Don't you hear all this noise outside? It's the crowd running down to the Foro Italico.

—The 'Foro Borbonico,' your uncle would correct you. But fire away.

—You can hear the music starting. See, the flags are beginning to fly at the windows.

—And now, what do you want to do?

—It's simple. I'm going along with the crowd.

—But be careful! No tricks!

—If there is rejoicing for everyone, there may be some for me too.

—For you young people everything is joy. 'Pace e gioia il cuor vi dia' ('May your heart give you peace and joy,' and the old lady starts to croon don Basilio's aria from *The Barber of Seville*). All things considered—she continued, almost to herself—that dear man would have done better to stay on Caprera to plant potatoes. From joys new sorrows often sprout.

—What do you mean, grandmother?

—I mean that now we are tired of wars, of tumults, of revolutions. A bit of quiet wouldn't hurt anyone. We have been dancing for more than half a century. Humanity has St. Vitus' dance.

—I no longer recognize you, grandmother. Aren't you still a revolutionary? One can see you'e getting older.

—The only rebellion I would like to make is against my seventy-five years, against the infirmities of old age. What would you have, my boy? The calendar makes conservatives of us all.

—What would you want to conserve? Venice for Austria, Rome for the pope and his vicar Napoleon, or Sicily for the Bourbons?

—That, never. *Jamais.* With *Napoléon le petit, sapristi, jamais!* I am a republican, by God, and I hate tyrants, especially bigots and hypocrites.

—Then you must shout with me, 'Rome or death!' This is the watchword that Garibaldi brings us.

—Death to the false Napoleon! Long live the French republic and even the *Repubblica Romana*!—cried the old lady, clapping her hands.—I'd like to be a half century younger to dance the Carmagnole. *Ça ira*!

—Pretend you *are* a half century younger and let's dance anyway—exclaimed Goffredo, and seizing his grandmother in his strong arms, he dragged her into a mad whirl.

Don Fabrizio appeared at table with a face like a first-class funeral. The hairs of his thick eyebrows were erect like insect antennas, his lips were composed in a tragic grimace, his eyes darted here and there as if they had decided not to look fixedly at anything.

Storm warnings. Teodora, as usual, taciturn and self-contained. Goffredo, as if he wore a muzzle, was trying to eat what the servant put on his plate.

—Tomorrow, the 29th, is St. Peter's—said donna Ortensia to break the ice—have you thought about good wishes for your friends who are celebrating their name day?

—The celebration is today—don Fabrizio grumbled in a muffled voice—a celebration for everybody, universal rejoicing, happiness, great joy...The Leader has landed, the Leader of the Thousand...of the Thousand and One Nights. Not in Marsala, this time, as in '60, but in the city of the Vespers. What an honor!

—Garibaldi?—said the elder marchesa—with an assumed air of surprise.

—Yes, *Carrubardi,* and with him the little clown prince, the son of the excommunicated Savoia king. Bravo, Umbertino, you're beginning to make a career too! Go on, you bells, ring in glory! Let everybody drop dead with happiness.

—Landed to do what?—insisted donna Ortensia, playing the innocent.

—To inaugurate the new shooting range—Goffredo answered timidly.

—You, be quiet—ordered the marchese, striking his nephew with a terrible glance.—Don't repeat the nonsense of the devil's newspapers. It's the same 'shooting range' that was used to cover up the expedition into the Tyrol, the miserable expedition that ended with a general fit of the shakes. A sneeze from Franz Josef would have been enough to make Garibaldi slope off into oblivion.

—They're saying that he is coming—Ortensia continued—to head the separatist movement, proudly reattempted by Mazzini.

—The separatist movement!—don Fabrizio interrupted in a teasing tone.—Four cats, four crazy fanatics, who would like to detach Sicily from the Kingdom of the Two Sicilies, like you pick a fig off a branch, to make it a little independent state of deadbeats incapable of self-sufficiency.

—And the Bourbons weren't foreigners?

—When a dynasty governs a State for more than a hundred years and rules it by the grace of God, it is no longer foreign. The Normans, the Swabians, the Aragonese were also foreigners. That doesn't change the fact that they were kings of Sicily.

—Go on, all conquerors keep God under orders, and when they have made themselves masters of a territory they force him to bless their thefts.

—These are blasphemies—deplored don Fabrizio, frowning. —We have God, what do you have?

—The people.

—The rabble. The ones who today are cheering the scoundrel Garibaldi.

—The ones whom your sovereigns governed with the three F's: *feste, forca, farin*a—shows, gallows, bread.

—It's what your sovereign people needs—grumbled don Fabrizio, rising from the table.

That evening, don Fabrizio—almost as if to justify his catastrophic predictions and the angry impulses to which he had given way at dinner—approached his mother as she was entering her bedroom and held out to her the *Precursore,* the house newspaper of Francesco Crispi.

—Read—he invited her, green with bile—you who say, 'enough of wars,' read the speech of the scoundrel at the Foro Borbonico and tell me if he isn't about to plunge us into the horrors of a new war.

The old lady sat down on a sofa, put on her eyeglasses, and moving as close as possible to the weak light of the oil lamp, she read: 'Yes, we must free our enslaved brothers in Rome and in Venice, but to achieve this we need deeds and not words. With deeds and not words we will drive Bonaparte from our Rome. He is not there to defend the interests of our Rome and the interests of the religion of Christ represented by the pope ('excellent,' commented the old lady, while her son paced the drawing room). Lies! Lies! The man of the December 2 *coup d'état* remains there for his own low interests, for his uncontrollable desire of dominion. Stained with the blood of the people of Paris, he remains there because he is a tyrant, because his cause is the same as that of the pope-king: the ruin of Italy ('I like it,' the old lady interpolated once more). He stays there to maintain the brigandage by which he makes himself head of the assassins of Italy. Deeds and not words and not vain protests. To drive Bonaparte from Rome we must speak the language of the Vespers, the language that you the people spoke in 1848 and 1860...'

—Unheard of—snarled don Fabrizio.

—Let me finish, please. 'In Rome—donna Ortensia continued—we will join you, but with arms, with the holy program with which we crossed the Ticino and defeated the Austrians, with which we landed in Marsala and came here to decide your fate, brave people of Palermo...'

—And a prefect has allowed him to pronounce such words, slanderous to a friendly nation, in public, before thousands of people!

—Not slanderous to a nation, but to a despotic usurper, who represents it badly.

—But Napoleon is France.

—France? Not at all. He is a toy in the hands of a foreign woman, the most depraved of all bigots, Eugenia Montijo.

—A prefect incapable of silencing a madman who is about to create a *casus belli,* it's horrible, it's simply comic.

—Do you know what is really comic, my son? That you, an Italian, defend the Frnch, while I, a Frenchwoman, line up with the Italians.

—Who told you I am Italian?—don Fabrizio protested disdainfully. —I am Sicilian born and bred.

—So you are with the separatists?

—No separatism. My party is the Bourbons and I am proud of it.

While don Fabrizio choked down fresh drops of bile every day, news arrived about Garibaldi's travels in Sicily, news ever more exciting or depressing according to the tastes of the various parties.

On July 19 the hero reached Marsala with his son Menotti, together with Giuseppe Missori, Giuseppe Guerzoni, Giacinto Bruzzesi, and other survivors of the Thousand. Fervid welcome. In the principal church of the city, jammed with a frenzied crowd, up in the pulpit father Giuseppe Martinciglio improvised an oration justifying the Condottiere. Garibaldi ran to embrace him and kiss him on the brow, calling him 'a true priest of the Gospel.' The day after, in the presence of Garibaldi, the Franciscan fra Pantaleo celebrated mass in the Cathedral and pronounced a fiery discourse, inviting the Hero and the people to swear 'Rome or death.' And Garibaldi, his hand stretched out on the altar, repeated the fateful words in his ringing voice.

A bit later he exhorted the populace from the town hall: 'There is no longer time to suffer the foreigner on Italian soil and the slavery of a part of our brothers. This lie can no longer be tolerated. It is a disgrace for twenty-five millions of Italians, and this must cease, and within a few days it *will* cease. Yes, Rome is ours. From Marsala went forth the cry of liberty, and now rises the cry, *Rome or death.* And this cry will resound not only on the peninsula, but will find an echo in all Europe, wherever the name of liberty has not been profaned. We do not want the goods of others, but we are taking what is ours, yes, ours. Rome is ours. Rome or death.' And the cry resounded in the billowing sea of people.

The echoes of the Sicilian frenzy had not yet died away when don Fabrizio appeared at table one day with a slightly more Christian look on his face.

—God doesn't wait for Saturday to pay—he pontificated, tucking his napkin into his collar.—The famous prefect Pallavicini, the great patriot, the prisoner (he says) of the Spielberg, was sent home like a servant. Fired by telegraph. That spineless Ricasoli, for once, is showing a burst of energy. No government could have tolerated the outrage of one of its representatives, all the more a prefect, who publicly vilifies the pope and the Catholic nation that protects him.

—*C'est le ressac, c'est la vie,* It's the backwash, it's life—donna Ortensia noted with her aristocratic serenity.—One prefect comes and another goes, and one is worth the same as the other.

—We need a courageous prefect, one who will make the government understand the real state of soul of the of the Sicilians. We are tired of these continual blusterings and clownish antics in red shirts, which disturb the public tranquillity and keep the populace in turmoil. A handful of impostors and profiteers: the men of the first and second wave of debarkations, the Sicilians and the continentals, the living and the dead...

—The dead, no. At least respect the dead. There was my father—an uncontrollable voice rang out.

Goffredo had risen to his feet in a gesture of defiance, ready for anything.

—Your father is among that number, as you know. Wretched, him and you!

Donna Ortensia and Teodora held their breath. It was the first time that any one of the family had dared to contradict the marchese openly, confronting him face to face. The feudal authority of the head of the family, who had reigned for many centuries within the walls of the ancient palace, had never bent under so mortal a blow.

—Papà was a Garabaldino and a man of honor.

—Honor, honor!—the marchese sneered diabolically, turning purple, with the tendons of his neck looking as if they must explode.—It is he who has dishonored his family, who has flung a fistful of mud on our name, your name... which you are unworthy to bear...Get out, out from under my feet...Remove that infamous...O God, I'm strangling, strangling...

Flushed, apoplectic, the marchese threw himself back onto his chair, while his purple hands scrabbled unsuccessfully to undo his neckerchief.

Night. The scratch of fingernails on the door. A hand slides along the doorframe looking for the lock. No. The door is not closed. It gives way to a light pressure.

She is there, on the threshold, like a statue, ecstatic, with her immense eyes like those of a sleepwalker. Now she has glided into the middle of the room and Goffredo has not realized it. The dark kingdom of the shadows. Only a circle of green light from the oil lamp makes his hands hesitate, searching in the bottom of a drawer. From time to time some white sheet of paper, spred out under the light to be read, brightens the opacity of the room by a new reflection. Now that she has come forward, the transparent wings of the light beat on a nightdress which barely conceals nakednesses.

—Goffredo—rustles a voice like a pale sigh.

The young man, surprised by the invisible specter, starts to spring up. But a strong and sweet force holds him fastened to his chair.

—Don't move, don't turn around. It's Teodora. I don't want to be seen. I am in *déshabillé.*

—But then how can we talk?—says Goffredo, still trying to free himself from her grip.

—I said that I don't want to be seen. Do we have to look each other in the face in order to talk? Be a good boy, then. I should not have come—she continued, with a captivating voice—at this hour, here. I have done wrong. But I felt something serious, perhaps irreparable, in the air that called for my intervention. I have not acted on impulse. I have thought about it a great deal. I have done nothing but think about it. For many hours, since that...disgusting scene. Finally, I have come. To do what? Above all to tell you...that you are not alone. You must not feel alone.

—Are you still thinking about that business, aunt? I almost no longer remember it. Maybe I have forgotten it, or I'm on the way to forgetting. I never dwell too much on the past. I haven't this time. Better, I look toward the future.

—You are so young.

—It's not a question of youth, but of habit, perhaps of upbringing, I don't know. My father used to say, Only weak spirits brood over the past, to grieve about it; strong souls think about the future, to make decisions. Deciding is everything.

—What do you want to do?—she asked with a tremor that distorted her face.

Goffredo felt the tremor, and instinctively turned his head to meet her eyes.

—No, don't turn around, I am...not to be looked at. Pretend that you are talking from another room, from another world. Can't you see the people who are speaking from another world?

—You're here now.

—I know. And I myself don't know why I have come. It would have been better for me to go to bed. But a powerful force ordered me to come. I heard a voice that said, 'Go, you must not leave him alone with his bitterness.' Who cares about you in this house, except me?

—My grandmother. She understands me.

—Yes, your grandmother. But that's something different. You are the son of her son, it's natural. Of a son whom she loved more than any other. But who can understand you better than Teodora? When they have a common fate, people truly understand each other. What are we in this house, you and I? Two prisoners. Nothing more.

—No one says you can't escape from prison.

—You, perhaps, yes. I, no. There are no bars, no chains in this palace, but the heavy velvet drapes, the silent doors padded with leather, the very railings of the balconies...they all suffocate me like a prison. What oppression! Freedom is a lovely thing.

—Freedom is within us. It is never lost when you don't want to lose it. I already feel free.

—Why 'already'?

—For some time. More than ever, for some hours...

—So you want to...?

—Who can stop me from leaving?

A long thoughtful moment of silcnce passed between the two.

—Is anyone ever completely free?—she said, withdrawn, as if talking to herself.—We are always the slaves of something, if only of our own feelings. These cannot be commanded. On the contrary! We swear to be alone, we grow to love our own loneliness, we make a kind of religion of it...and yet we become attached to something, always. We propose to build ourselves a strong life made of independence and indifference, and we end up by being the slaves of our own weakness, of our own fragility. To live is basically to bind oneself. That is, to die to oneself. You know that I am fond of you...

Goffredo nodded his head.

...like a mother. Age lies between us. Believe me that I have no longer felt that I am alone since you have been in this house. Within me something has died, something has been born.

Her hands are now disengaged from the shoulders of the young man and they rise along his cheeks to his hair, in a soft caress. There is something like a sweet lassitude in her body that makes it adhere with all its weight to his.

—And you?

—I too feel myself less alone, aunt.

—Why always 'aunt'? I am Teodora. Isn't it a nice name, Teodora? You can always trust me, near or far. But I hope you will always stay here, won't you?

—In this house I'm just in the way.

—For whom? Maybe for 'him.' But what does it matter if the whole world hates us, if even one single being loves us. And I love you. So very much.

Her voice trembles. But at the same time it is a velvety caress. And a feverish voice. Goffredo has risen to his feet. She has turned white with a deadly pallor, whiter than her nightdress, which increases her staturesque form. Then her arms wind around his neck, her lips seek his lips, savagely.

And that is all.

—Let me go now—she says, out of breath.—I'm leaving. I am afraid. But I am happy.

The door has remained half open. She has disappeared, vanished, without the sound of a step, without a trace, like a fleeting shadow.

Chapter 7

DONNA ORTENSIA insisted that she did not want to celebrate her birthday. She maintained that 1862 would be an unlucky year. The sum of the two numbers in fact adds up to seventeen, the number of disaster.

Aside from the ill-omen of the number seventeen, in reality 1862 appeared unclear. To judge from the many stormy petrels flying low among the cloud-mass of events, every prophet of doom would have been justified in pronouncing dark predictions.

The unity of Italy, patched together barely two years before, creaked and cracked from every side. Venice awaited its release; the Roman question, like a wound, festered ever more instead of closing; the regions that were the heirs of the ancient States were seething with selfish and centrifugal tendencies. Parties and sects grew more embittered in skirmishes that were as virulent as they were sterile, personal ambitions prevailed over national interests.

A deaf disquiet, an ill-repressed anger was curling around Sicily like a fog which creeps and thickens visibly at the bottom of a valley. The island, which had given the first impulse to the revolution, was now straitjacketed by French-style centralization. It was humiliated by the bureaucrats that poured down from Piedmont; it was offended by obligatory conscription, from which it had always been exempt; oppressed by the increase of new taxes; alarmed by the possible suppression of the religious orders; devastated by factions and parties. Sicily showed signs of uneasiness like a volcano which conceals an imminent eruption in its bowels.

Finally, the unexpected arrival of Garibaldi had acted like an electric current which breaks down a substance and frees its constituent elements, from which a new chemical combination emerges in an explosion The dreams of the legitimists and the reactionaries, the tantrums of the separatists, the proposals of the liberals, the ambitions of the republicans, which previously had co-existed in an occasional compromise, now being unchained and unrestrained had become the preconditions for anarchy and inevitable disorders.

Not even the house of Cortada could escape this general state of tension. Its internal peace had ceased to exist after the breach between uncle and nephew, although it was followed by an apparent reconciliation.

All this would have been enough to postpone the celebration of donna Ortensia's birthday, as she ardently desired. But don Fabrizio did not wish to interrupt a family tradition. He did not want it said that in 1862 they failed to celebrate a solemnity that had been observed even in 1860, the most disastrous date in Sicilian history. Would the presence of Garibaldi cause even more fear and uneasiness today than in 1860? The celebration would take place all the same, with the customary ceremonial: the holy mass of thanksgiving in the morning, followed by the good wishes of the assembled family and servants; the visits of friends in the afternoon; and in the evening the dinner, in which the dearest and most intimate persons took part.

That evening the gathering, 'allegro ma non troppo,' was set in the large windowed drawing room giving onto the cortile. The heat beat down, even on an inside room, since he sun was about to cross from the Constellation of Cancer to that of the Lion. But don Fabrizio was concerned to preserve as much as possible the incognito of the celebration to avoid its being interpreted as an expression of joy (and Palermo was full of such expressions) at Garibaldi's presence on the island. That was all they needed, for the public to attach a meaning of political rejoicing to a purely private family party! Therefore the marchese had given orders that the dinner was not to take place in the usual luxurious room overlooking via Alloro.

In addition to some of the most conspicuous titled members of the black aristocracy, the invited guests were the acting attorney general, don Prospero Camarda, a constant friend of the family, the retired Borurbon general don Pietro Cacioppoli, don Fulgenzio Errante, docent of history at the University, not to mention the omnipresent and irreplaceable father Assardi.

Donna Ortensia sat in the place of honor with the prince of Fitalia on her right and her son on her left. Facing her, donna Teodora was flanked by the attorney general and the duke of Amalfi. As the centerpiece of the table a group of Romans of gladitorial musculature clutched two or three recalcitrant Sabines who wreathed their arms together to protect their little porcelain breasts, unauthentic and all the same desirable. It was a triumph of Sévres of inestimable value, given by Charles III to the marchese Blasco, grandfather of don Fabrizio, in commemoration of his services to his Most Serene sovereign. A row of candelabra in finely chiseled gilt bronze, like trees loaded with luminous fruit, was interspersed among the tableware.

The master of the house rose—imitated by all the guests, except his mother, who was excused owing to her advanced age—made the sign of the Cross, and implored the blessing of Heaven on the banquet. At the master's order, servants in impeccable livery began to serve the meal.

The general gaiety flowered in smiles, in winks, in witticisms, in animated conversations woven like golden threads from one end of the table to the other.

Only the cavalier Salina—famuous for gorging himself at every gathering and a sycophant of all the noble houses, always present where there was anything to chew on—gobbled in silence. His plate was always empty, while the other guests toyed genteelly with the entrées. At every new course the cavalier unpeeled his eyes, round as chestnuts, drilling his cheek with a finger, to mean, What an exquisite thing!

—If you please—said don Assardi, who was seated next to him—I know only one man who has stronger jaws than yours, general Garibaldi.

—He gorges on gold ducats, I do it modestly with pasta—blubbered the cavaliere, with his cheeks inflated like those of a bagpipe player.

—Gentlemen—the authoritarian master of the house interrupted—today we have agreed not to talk about politics. Why ruin the dinner?

—Even when we all hold the same opinion?—asked the priest, accustomed to the '*distinguo*' of Scholastic philosophy.

—In politics you're never more disunited than when you seem most united, just as in marriage—observed donna Ortensia.

—Even in England and America, the greatest and most complicated political questions are resolved at table.

—Therefore England is gobbling the world up, as if it were a pie, commented professor Errante.

—All things considered, it's better not to concern ourselves with politics, are we agreed?don Fabrizio insisted.

—Unfortunately—his mother resumed—*Vous avez beau ne vous occuper de politique, la politique s'occupera de vous tout de même*—It's all very well for you not to concern yourself with politics, politics will concern itself with you all the same. Nonetheless I am of the same opinion as that lady, who when she heard political discussions heating up at her dinners, dropped and broke a piece of china in order to choke off the dangerous conversation.

—Alas, today you would have to smash the table services of an entire household to put a damper on this subject. And it wouldn't be enough. Everybody is insane and they only talk about one subject—the prince of Fitalia noted with aristocratic composure.

—I would propose talking of love, as in the fine gatherings of the Renaissance where the best humanists participated—suggested the attorney general, who was playing the cup-bearer to the marchesa Teodora, fixing her lustfully with a glance that moved from part to part of her body as if it were as transparent as glass.

—Provided it is conjugal love—objected don Assardi—if you don't want to end up in the Inferno.

—Is it true that you there is no love in the Inferno?—intoned the duchess of Villafiorita in her pathetic voice.

—Where hatred rules there is no place for love. That is clear.

—And yet there is no love without a little bit of hate. If there were not something in common between the two sentiments we could not pass so easily from love to hate and viceversa.

—Now I understand why I have a great fear of going to hell—said don Prospero Camarda to Teodora.—Because love does not exist down there. What does donna Ortensia say about it?

—I say that love is a mixture of curiosity and memory. For that reason after the first blaze there barely remains a fistful of ashes.

—What pessimism!

—I didn't say that nothing at all remains. Even ashes are something. And the ashes of love are composed of the memory of curiosity and the curiosity of memory.

A general laugh sounded, like the unstringing of a pearl necklace into a crystal chalice.

—Since we are on this subject, satisfy a curiosity for me—the prince of Torrabruna askd the attorney general.—However can a public prosecutor like you, who lives in the midst of hatred, talk of love?

—Whatever are you saying, prince?

—I'm saying that by your profession you are always hating, either the crime or the criminal. How can you even conceive of love?

—First of all I could answer you that we *do* love...Justice.

—A nice effort! Justice is something ethereal, elusive—and the marchesa suggested the flight of a bird with her lovely ringed hands—not a created being.

—In second place, I want you to realize that we magistrates have a double life. We are terrifying, implacable in the exercise of our work, and tender and affectionate in private. When we investigate and condemn we are austere priests, when we love we are capable of delicacy like the most sensitive of men—and the magistrate, satisfied, looked off toward the wall, as if to follow the shadow of his fine phrase.

—God preserve me from the benevolence of a magistrate!—chirped don Assardi, winking an eye bright with cunning.—It is the affection that the cat feels for the rat. How the cat caresses the rat before making a mouthful of him!

—So you think that a magistrate has no heart?

—He has a heart that rejoices in another's ill—proclaimed general Cacioppoli, inserting himself into the conversation.

—A good Christian is happy when he can pardon, a judge is overjoyed if he can punish, that is, if he can inflict harm on his neighbor.

—In a minute you'll make the magistrate a criminal for sure—don Prospero agreed with all the wrinkles of his monkey-like face.

—Do you want to hear my opinion?—pursued the general.—If I had a son with vindictive, perverse, bloody instincts, I would make him a priest of Themis, of the Law. Thus I would give him a way to vent to his nature honestly while remaining at peace with his conscience and with the law. He could commit evil, sitting with dignity on his bench. He could work harm with elegance and with the satisfaction of doing his duty.

—We dictate sentences—retorted the attorney general—but you make war, which is a more terrible thing. We send some scoundrel to solitary confinement or to the guillotine, you cause the butchery of thousands of men, you sow the world with mourning and slaughter.

—There's quite a difference, my friend. We fight openly, risking our lives against an enemy who can defend himself. You fight under cover, smiling and often sleeping, against a helpless enemy, already defeated, who is placed so he cannot retaliate. And war is the training ground of nobility, the school of heroism. The national heroes whom we all revere are born of war. That is why the declaration of a just war arouses enthusiasm, while the execution of a sentence of death is a shameful and demoralizing spectacle.

—And isn't war a condemnation to death, the condemning to death of an endless number of often innocent persons? Is it not unjust to force men who are naturally peaceful to submit to death and to deal it out?

—But no one calls the soldier a murderer, while everyone agrees in calling the carrying out of an unjust sentence a legal murder. Wasn't the execution of the duke of Enghien blamed on Napoleon I as a crime?

—Please—joked marchese Fabrizio—don't upset mamma. Don't touch her Napoleon.

—Let's clear things up—donna Ortensia protested with elegance.—I am not a bonapartist. If I were I would have to be a partisan of this Napoleon, of the man of the *coup* of the second of December, of the man who massacred the people of Paris, of the unmanly and bedizened husband of Eugénie, who today makes rain and good weather...or rather, bad weather, for our Italy. I have no fondness for this degenerate Bonaparte. Instead I worship the first Napoleon because I am French, republican and also... revolutionary, say the spiteful, and some of my most intimate enemies repeat it.

—I bow to your opinion—said professor Errante.—But, with the greatest respect, may I point out to you that Napoleon was in fact the destroyer, the liquidator of the revolution.

—Liquidator?—said don Fabrizio, amazed.—But has he not been called, I think by the philosopher Hegel, the revolution on horseback? He incarnated the dangerous principles of 1789 with his wars and his codes, his intrigues and his falsehoods, he annulled the freedom of the Church, and undid the centuries-old constructive work of the Monarchy.

—Excellent!—agreed marchese Mortillaro.—His greatest stroke was to destroy the genuine aristocracy of birth to create a gang of parvenus, lavishing titles and coats of arms on enriched bourgeois and jumped-up peasants, starting with his own relatives. How many *papier-mâché* kings, princes, and counts!

—And I will never pardon him his satyrlike licentiousness—declared in clarinet tones the duchess of Amalfi, who in the springtime of her years had been a beautiful sinner and was now converted to chastity in her ripe autumn.—He made a hecatomb of womsn's hearts! Shame! One can pardon everything to a head of State except having mistresses.

—That's why the duchess never wanted to be a head of state—whispered don Assardi to his neighbor.—*Megghiu cuda di cicreddu ca testa di pisci spata*—Better the tail of a whitebait than the head of a swordfish.

—And now that you have relieved your feelings—said donna Ortensia—allow me to tell you my own thoughts. You can understand nothing of Napoleon if you do not recognize in him a poet, the poet of action. He thought as a poet and he acted as a poet, just read his war bulletins, his letters, his memoirs from St. Elena. Perhaps because of this privilege, the material of common life remained out of reach, eluded him, and finally it took its revenge on him. Like a poet, he often aimed his gaze too high and too far off, and he did not see the pit that his wretched contemporaries were digging under his feet.

—But a poet of what, after all?—crowed a voice from the end of the table.

—Of France—donna Ortensia exclaimed solemnly. —If we are proud to call ourtselves French, it is because of this great Italian.

A burst of applause thundered from one end of the table to the other.

—When a speaker is applauded it's a sign that he has said something foolish—said the guest of honor, with the most ironic yet most amiable of smiles.

—You have spoken excellently, marchesa, as always—profesor Errante observed in honeyed tones.—But resolve a doubt for me. How can you reconcile in Napoleon two loves: a love of despotism and a love of freedom, a love of the revolution and a love of democracy? You know that Napoleon was antidemocratic, that he wanted the people prostrate at his feet. You inform me that when poor Louis XVI appeared trembling on the loggia of the Tuilleries with the Phrygian cap on his head, the little lieutenant Bonaparte, in the midst of the crowd, said to an officer friend of his, 'What a coward! it would take me just two cannon-shots to sweep away this rabble.'

—I insist in saying that he was the truest and the greatest democrat. Democracy consists in elevating and educating the people, in raising them from poverty and ignorance, in not handing them over to the righteous, who serve only to let them be exploited by the intriguers, the demagogues. These are the real rabble. Democracy must not be a rabbleocracy.

—Let's leave the name of rabble to Robespierre—the professor concluded.

—Indeed—continued the old lady—but in any case I prefer a single rabble to a collective mass of rabble. Robespierre was a monster, but also a monster of purity. They call him the Incorruptible deservedly. He was cruel without baseness. No one could accuse him of having appropriated a single cent of the public money. He was cruel with the sole aim of controlling the anarchy of the parties. Right, Center, Left, Feuillants, Jacobins, Girondins, Monagnards all did their best to sabotage the revolution with their quarreling and their disruptions. Every party hungry for power, for riches, cried, 'Long live me and to hell with the country.' Robespierre wanted to strangle anarchy, and instead he unchained the Terror. He was mistaken in his measures, but his basic proposal was good: he was obsessed with founding the reign of Virtue. He was undoubtedly a pitiless dictator. But better the dictatorship of one than the dictaorship of everyone.

—But in fact, profesor Errante commented *sotto voce*—after the death of the Incorruptible they discovered precious silver with the royal seal of the Capets hidden under his mattresses.

—If it's like that, mamma—observed don Fabrizio—I don't see why you are opposed to the Bourbons and their absolutism. In substance, what was the Bourbon monarchy except a beneficent dictatorship against the excesses of liberalism, a heaven-sent bulwark against the overflow of revolutionary ideas?

—I defend the dictatorship of the great ideas, not of the mean little thoughts, therefore I am Napoleonic. Napoleon obeyed a generous inspiration, he wanted a great France in a unified Europe. He lived and died with the dream of unifying a Europe which was torn apart by the various nationalisms that one day will provoke her ruin. The Bourbons, once they had entered the orbit of Metternich's blind politics, did not have one single generous idea. The kingdom of the Two Sicilies, the largest, the most populous, the strongest kingdom of the peninsula, could have placed itself at the head of a national movement, could have done what tiny Piedmont—against whom you are all now hurling yourselves—dared to do, but with more authority. Instead it followed a servile policy and played the game of its masters, Austria and England. People say they lacked a Cavour. I maintain that what they lacked was a heart and a head in the dynasty that governed them. What was the only territorial enlargement of the Siculo-Neapolitan State in one hundred and nineteen years of rule? The acquisition of the Isola Ferdinandea, a few miles of land, which a tidal wave brought to the surface in June of 1813 between Sciacca and Pantelleria and another tidal wave swallowed up six months later. And now, my friends, let's make an end of politics if you don't want to ruin my party. Remember it was I who advised you, no politics at table. My dear old Voltaire is right: *Le matin je fais des projets, Et le long des jours des sottises*—In the morning I make projects, And throughout the days I commit follies.

At that moment the butler entered bearing in both hands an enormous cake smoking with seventy-five little lighted candles, as many as the years of the lady of the house.

Everyone rose to applaud.

—*Ad multos annos*!—cried don Assardi, as if it were the birthday of the pope.

—My friends, I thank you—smiled the old lady—but believe me, *Le jeu ne vaut pas la chandelle*—The game isn't worth the candle.

The good wishes, the embraces, the kisses came thick and fast. Donna Ortensia was moved and her eyes became moist when Goffredo clasped her tightly, putting his lips for a long moment on her cheeks.

The silence of the young man throughout the dinner had been noticed by everyone.

Chapter 8

EARLY THE next morning don Fabrizo ordered Marco:—Go to don Goffredo and tell him that I'm waiting for him here.

He was almost in a good humor. You might have said that the party in honor of his mother had worked on his gloomy spirit like a beneficent breeze which banishes a dim veil of fog from the suddenly rejuvenated heavens. The first to notice the unexpected change of weather was his barber, monsù Carmin Ballarò, while shaving that face innocent of wrinkles. As a good psychologist, like all barbers, he believed that the skin is the sentry of the spirit. When the spirit is cheerful, the blood sings in the veins, the skin is taut and velvety and the razor skims over it through the lacy soap, a delight. When the spirit is wrinkled, the skin is also flabby and sagging, and the razor labors with visible effort, as if it were sawing wood instead of hair.

This morning the marchese's skin had offered itself to the razor smooth as silk. A happy indication—according to don Carmine—confirmed by the conversation of his illustrious patient, which had been sparkling and fluent, as rarely occurred. Don Carmine took advantage of such moments to become the confidant and the confessor of his clients. Without revealing himself, without compromising himself, he waited for them to bare their souls as one turns the sleeve of a garment. A good barber—he thought philosophically—must behave like Socrates. Let everyone bring forth his own truth by himself, in the course of things, without undergoing the inquisitorial arrogance of the interrogator, almost without even being aware of the presence of an interlocutor. A high-class Figaro, so to speak, must be as impartial as a judge, discreet as a diplomat, patient as a confessor. Don Carmine had synthesized a similar program in a sign placed near the front of his barbershop: 'I shave the skin and cut Bourbonists and anti-Bourbonists down to size, I trim the beards, the stubble, and the pompadours of the Garibaldians and the Mazarinists, I apply leeches to the unitarians, the separatists, to priests and monks, I pull teeth for everybody with small expense and no pain.' Faithful to these principles of absolute equanimity, which in so stormy a moment placed him above the melee as well as accumulating a copious clientele, he had succeeded in acquiring genuine popularity in his neighborhood and beyond. And when he warbled Figaro's aria, 'They all seek me, they all call for me,' you could wager that he was not merely boasting.

Don Fabrzio, following in the mirror the work of his barber, who having duly shaved him, was rounding off the curve of beard under his chin with the point of his scissors, thought over *sine ira* the happenings of recent days. The scene between him and his nephew, immediately after the landing of Garibaldi, returned to his mind in a light of dispassionate calm. Good-natured and deeply upright as in his soul he basically was, he realized that on that occasion he had not behaved nobly. Goffredo was a rough scatterbrained boy, thoughtless more than dissolute. He had shown himself to be disrespectful, not to say downright rebellious. But in the last analysis did not the blame all go to him, don Fabrizio? Or rather was the blame dispersed in the torbid gutters of the upbringing which Goffredo had received in his earliest years, in the unhealthy suroundings where he had been brought up? In questions of responsibility one should not yield to rash judgments. That would be a lack of Christian charity. The boy was not really bad. And if he had not grown up with a father who was certifiably insane and a mother from who knows what level of society (better to draw a pitying veil over that question), perhaps he would even have been a good son: the rose often flowers from the thorn. Of an open character, a somewhat rough sincerity, more impulsive than reflective, without doubt Goffredo had the merits of uncommon honesty and seriousness, and he made himself loved for an openness that was not common among young men of his age and condition. He was a soul which, treated with affection, would respond with even greater affection. And here don Fabrizio did not hesitate to recognize his own wrongs. Although he had welcomed Goffredo tenderly into his house, he could have shown himself less harsh, less authoritarian and bad-tempered with his nephew. He should have closed the gap between himself and the boy, instead of widening it by a mistaken adherence to an old-fashioned code of manners. A wrong, certainly, if not completely his. He himself, don Fabrizio, would have been better if he had not lived between a mother, intelligent but shrewish, witty, and ironic without pity, and a wife as cold as a frozen statue, without tenderness and understanding; and if the politics on which he had embarked, with its suspicions, its deceptions, and its forced compromises, had not reduced him to shutting himself up in a rough and thorny shell more conducive to friction than to mutual affection. Finally, what remained to him of his life, now nearing its sunset? Perhaps nothing more than the youth and the affection of his nephew, if he had known how to cultivate them, instead of neglecting and rejecting them as useless. After all, Goffredo was a being who bore his name and his blood, however slightly polluted by its plebian admixture. On him could be reconstructed the future of the Cortada family, which was about to become extinct by failure of heirs in the male line. Without sons of his own, did he not now have his brother's son, who by divine and human law was the one called to carry on his family? A son, a son!

At this thought don Fabrizio was overcome by a feeling of tenderness, to which was joined a not less bitter sense of pain. The memory of his nephew at the celebration of the previous evening crossed his soul: the boy off by himself in a corner of the joyous table, alone, silent, crestfallen, forgotten, almost non-existent. No one paid any attention to him, no one spoke to him...He, don Fabrizio, had more than once glanced at him in passing, and he perceived in contemplating that loneliness a sense of grief, almost of remorse...No, even if the boy had been unsatisfactory, his punishment was becoming too harsh and pitiless...it couldn't go on like this. It would have been too unjust.

During the night such thoughts had been transformed into a desire for pardon, for real reconciliation, into the will to begin a new life where there would be room only for love and tenderness. So he had decided within himself to break the ice and to have with his nephew an open-hearted dialogue which would finally begin a new existence.

While the thoughts of don Fabrizio—he had just emerged from the hands of his barber—were flowing like a crystal stream between banks flowery with exquisite sentiments, Marco entered with a distraught face.

—Signor marchese, the *signorino* Goffredo's room is empty.

—What are you saying? He must just have gone out for a minute...earlier than usual.

After hesitating for a moment Marco added:

—*Voscenza,* no. His bed has not even been disturbed. No one has slept there.

—Impossible. Goffredo has never spent a night away from home...It would be the first time...What new thing is this? Explain yourself.

—Must I tell you everything? On his bed table I found this letter addressed to Your Excellency.

—A letter? Give it here immediately.—His voice trembled. He took the letter in hand and fumbled in his pocket to pull out his eyeglasses.—Where are my glasses? Where are they?—he cried frantically.

Marco started to search through the room, while his master, in the grip of a furious agitation, tried to decipher the writing with his naked eye. His nearsighted orbs started from their spheres and ran up and down the lines without taking in their meaning.

—But where are these cursed glasses, where are they, dammit! There's no more order in this house, no order...everything is going to hell. There's no respect. Everybody is in command here, command if you can and obey if you feel like it. I want my glasses right now! Do you understand, you thick-headed old fool?

—Pardon me, Excellency. Have you searched in all your pockets? For the love of God, try. It pains me to see you like this.

The marchese patted himself, he searched with his trembling hands, and in the small pocket of his waistcoat he found his eyeglasses. He put them on, balancing them unsteadily at the end of his nose, and read, mumbling the syllables that formed themselves with difficulty on his lips and in his mind.

Before he had reached the end of the sheet of paper, don Fabrizio staggered and shrank back, groping with his hands in search of some support, and collapsed with his full weight on the floor. His face blanched, his left hand pressing his heart, his eyes glassy, he gave no signs of life.

Marco flung himself out the door, shouting desperately. The house was in an uproar. Who is it? Who isn't it? A collapse? An attack? A disaster? Family members, servants rushed in from everywhere. Cries of terror and horror. The master is dead? He has had a fit! Jesus mercy! What a commotion!

He is picked up, almost unconscious, heavy, bent in two like an empty sack, and laid down on his bed. He gives no evidence of life. Sprinkles of water, vinegar, salts, massages. Everybody gives advice, everyone bustles about to help. The confusion and the agitation increase. A doctor! Send for a doctor right away!

But how? Why? All at once! He was fine yesterday. He was in excellent humor!

Marco's only response was to pick up the letter from the ground, with a gesture as if to say: The answer is here.

Someone read:

'Dear uncle, I know I am causing you grief. I would have spared you if it were not necessary. Please do not think that my decision depends on the recent *happening,* or that it is caused by resentment or by a grudge. I would not be capable of it. Serious events are brewing for our country and I cannot stay here inactive. My father would be grieved. I feel what his wish would be if he were alive. The dead command more than the living, them one cannot disobey. I have only one duty, to enlist and to follow Garibaldi, who is marching toward Rome. May God help me.

In leaving I thank you for all you have done for me. Indeed, I will never forget your kindness. Yours, Goffredo.'

Donna Ortensia did not break down.

Teodora hid her pallor by burying her face in her cupped hands. When she reopened her eyes, their green pupils were enormously dilated, as if she had emerged from the grip of some indescribable horror that very moment. But since her glazed look was fixed on don Fabrizio, everyone thought, She is overcome by pity for her husband, even if she can't stand him.

Meanwhile the marchese, who at first seemed to have suffered an apoplectic stroke, stirred on his bed and half-opened his bruised eyelids. The bluish pouches under his eyes, more swollen than ever, gave him an appearance of declining and repugnant old age. One would have said that years of his life had suddenly collapsed into the void.

His wan glance wavered listlessly between his mother and his wife, then hid itself again under the withered leaves of his eyelids.

In the meantime the doctor had arrived. He took the marchese's pulse, listened to his heart, administered an injection of camphor, advised complete rest.

—Nothing serious—he declared—only a *lipothemia*, a blackout...The organism is healthy. A bit of rest and everything will be back to normal. I advise avoiding any emotion.

As soon as he had come to, don Fabrizio said quietly and with an effort—as if the words stuck in his teeth—: 'He is dead.'

—Who is dead—asked donna Ortensia.

—Him...it hurts me to pronounce his name. I want Marco. Where is Marco?

The faithful servant, who was standing near the door, drew closer.

—Close the *portone*...in sign of mourning—his master ordered imperiously, gathering all his forces.

—Prepare my black suit for me, for when I go out. You understand? In the meantime I am at home to no one. I don't want to see anyone.

When donna Ortensia left the room of her son, who was improving as she watched, someone heard her repeat to herself:

—Dead...common sense is dead, which was never alive in this house. What will happen when I set out for my last voyage? On my word of honor, in my will I will order that the doors of the palace remain wide open, and all the windows too...and that the bells ring in celebration. If the comic becomes serious, it is right that the serious become comic.

In reality there was nothing comic in don Fabrizio's decision. And if there had existed less incomprehension between mother and son, donna Ortensia would have been able to understand that her son's soul had suffered a wound, a mortal blow, at the departure of his nephew, like a tree from which a branch has been torn off. Men who are closed in themselves, surly and savage, often have the misfortune of being misunderstood. Don Fabrizio, by reason of his brusque manners, had always given the impression that in taking his nephew into his house he had given way to a moral imperative instead of an affectionate impulse, of having suffered his nephew instead of seeking him out, of being unconnected with him except by the thin thread of a family name which must not be left to rot in the swamps of abandonment and poverty. But those who could read to the bottom of Fabrizio's heart would have discovered instead an attachment to the boy, not unmingled with a certain sense of pride, the pride of making him a worthy continuation of his family. From the gravity and the nobility of such unexpressed sentiments one can imagine how harsh was the blow felt by don Fabrizio by the sudden and unforeseen departure of his nephew. He interpreted that flight as a real 'going over to the enemy,' something resembling treason, a proof of insensitivity and ingratitude, and his self-respect was offended and wounded. What a bitter disappointment, what an inglorious crumbling of the sweetest of illusions!

Donna Ortensia (let's not speak of Teodora) was not aware of such an inner state. Had she been able to enter a bit into the soul of her son, she would perhaps have refrained from encouraging the plan that her young grandson had thought up and firmly carried out. On the contrary!

When Goffredo unexpectedly announced to her his decision to enroll under the flag of the Garibaldian legionnaires, she felt a stab in her heart, which was immediately dominated and repressed by a feeling of pride. She had answered simply:

—You must follow the voice of your conscience, my child. If you have decided to leave, then leave. Your father will protect you.

—It will be a short campaign. Rome will be taken. We will soon return victorious. Under Garibaldi we never lose.

—War is war—the old lady commented, with a hint of sadness in her voice, and she turned away to hide her eyes, which were becoming moist.

—You will see, grandmother, that in two months, three at the most, I'll be back here. I'm making an appointment with you in this very room...in your arms.

—That is something different. You must ask permission of my seventy-five years.

—Permission is already given. Indeed, the years will stand still to wait.

—If you don't find me, you shall say, Grandmother has gone *in villeggiatura,* to vacation in the country.

—Why *in villeggiatura*?

—It's what Voltaire said to the friends who were present when his last hour was near: 'I'm going *in villeggiatura.*' Or rather, he said it in the language of Cicero, *Eo rus,* to show Death that he understood Latin. Anyway, the ancients described the kingdoms of the great beyond as an immense, smiling countryside, like a field carpeted with asphodel.

Because the young man was looking at his grandmother a bit dazed, to compose herself and to conceal her pressing emotion she continued:

—Why are you looking at me with such eyes? Has your Latin teacher taught you really nothing? Have you eaten bread without paying for it? I wager that your teacher did not even tell you about the isles of the blessed at the farthest reaches of the world, where the heroes fallen in battle, the demigods of the fourth generation, are strolling in a state close to blessedness: a place which is no longer life and not yet death. Yes, the heroes fallen in battle...(and here the old lady paused to blow her nose, a good excuse for wiping her eyes).

—But let's talk about something else. Instead I want to tell you that your action will have serious consequences in this house. Have you considered that? If you haven't thought of it, I do. Your uncle will never pardon you for leaving his house that has sheltered you, in order to follow his greatest enemy. He will interpret your generous deed as the blackest treason. He is unforgiving in his resentments, he never forgets...even if as a Christian he foregoes personal revenge. In short, my child, you will never be able to return within these walls, to this palace: *never,* I said. Let that sink in (and she touched her forehead to render her words more impresssive). Victorious or defeated, you will never set foot here again.

—And what does it matter? Only one thing is necessary, that we win.

—To you it doesn't matter. But to me? I am a poor old woman, and I had no one but you.

—Perhaps I can stay with you?

—Yes, but not here. But I have considered where you can go...I have thought about it. A grandmother anticipates everything. We'll discuss it when you return.

—You see, you have decided to wait for me!

—Did I say that I wouldn't wait for you?

—You talked about villeggiatura, naughty woman!

—I have changed my mind. If things go wrong when you return, both of us will have a change of air. We will leave this house and go to live together. Far, far away, in a land of dreams. They say that old age is youth, minus the illusions and the dreams. If I add a few dreams to my age, youth is complete. Now go, and God bless you!

The recruitment of the legionnaires proceeded in full daylight, to the serious disappointment of those men of order who were condemning the weakness of the government. Those same ones who blamed the Kingdom of Italy for having imposed mandatory conscription in Sicily were now violently attacking the constituted powers for allowing the formation, to the general scandal, of bands of volunteers to march at the orders of the scoundrel. Having shouted in every tone of voice, 'This is a regime of tyranny,' now they were crying to the four winds, 'This is a cardboard government.' So true is it that the mentality of faction permeates men to the point that they no longer know what they are saying. Now they accuse you doing too little, now of doing too much. They blame you both for what you have done and for what you have left undone. They ascribe to you today as a crime the same misdeeds that they themselves will be stained with tomorrow. They right your wrongs with worse wrongs, calling their own advantage justice and labeling the good of others as injustice. In short, they ignore or pretend to ignore that where politics begins, justice ends. This is what was happening in Palermo, as it happens everywhere, in the turbulent period between 1860 and 1866.

The concentration center for the volunteers was the forest of Ficuzza, a thick and verdant wood lying between Mezzoiuso and Corleone, some thirty kilometers from the capital, which was formerly a royal park and hunting preserve of their Bourbonic majesties. General Garibaldi had set up his headquarters there, where were gathering from every part of Sicily and the mainland the legionnaires to enlist in the expeditionary force for the conquest of Rome. In that July of 1862, anyone who happened to be following the road which runs along the sea from Palermo, gradually enters the plateau of Misilmeri, and rises slowly to the outskirts of Rocca Busambra, would have been surprised by the unusual confluence of people in those parts. In groups, in vehicles, in crowds, one by one, on foot and on horseback, on carts, carriages, and wagons drawn by every species of animal, men of all ages and conditions were marching toward the wood of Ficuzza. Beside the young and the very young—boys still in short pants, like little swallows just fledged from their nest—there struggled along men of middle age, grey of hair although still lively of movement, and really old men, slow of step but nonetheless glad of heart. Aristocratic, bourgeois, and plebeian figures. Red shirts and uniforms of the regular army (deserters who had gone over to Garibaldi, complete with their weapons and kit), peasants' *bonache*, workmen's smocks mixed with gentlemen's frock coats and redingotes; caps and cloth- and shovel-hats, priests' cassocks and friars' habits; women loaded with bundles and suitcases, trailed by snot-nosed urchins romping like little goats. If it were not for the weapons that were waving here and there above the crowd—generally ancient wrecks brandished like rifles, some pistols, and not a few sabres and pikes—that strange and multicolored procession could have been mistaken for one of the popular pilgrimages which every year bring thousands of people to the shrines of Santa Rosalia, the Madonna of Altavilla Milicia, or the Madonna of Tagliavia.

Among the crowds of the irregulars there were sometimes also squadrons of men in military formation. Make way, make way! The National Guard is passing! It's a battalion, commanded by Enrico Albanese, headed by a band, marching toward the General's headquarters.

On the morning of July 25 a little group of three young men is setting out from the Foro Italico of Palermo toward S. Erasmo at a self-confident pace. If their ages were added up they would total little more than a half-century. They are Goffredo and two of his friends, Salvatore Ponte and Giacomino Battaglia. They are dressed in civilian clothes, with their red shirts under their jackets; unarmed, with simple backpacks across their shoulders. They are flying along and whistling with the liveliness of birds migrating toward the spring.

The dawn widens on the sea. One of those splendid and serene dawns without mist and without uncertainties that announce themselves like the prophecy of a perfect world, where freed from mystery every thing seems intelligible, and even the fleshly wrapping of our bodies is as transparent as crystal.

The emerald sea is almost breathless, only at the edge some lacy foam is seething. At the rim of the horizon, the cotton-wool of a new edging is scatttered, down low, in scarlet. It is the breath of the young sun which rises toward the arch of the greenish heaven, where the last star has faded just now. It seems that all the peace of the world has taken refuge in the bay, among the maze of rocks forming random bowls full of sea water here and there. Offshore, sardine trawlers dance softly on white triangles, the watery reflection of their sails.

A cart passes, drawn by a big lively mule. It is driven by a Franciscan friar seated on its edge, the fat nape of his neck bulging over his lowered hood, his plump and rosy cheeks covered by an ill-shaven beard. A member of the joyful rather than the penitent orders of friar, who encourages the animal with frequent slapping of the reins, shouting, 'Aià.'

—It wouldn't be a bad idea if that cart picked us up and carried us for a bit of the way—one of the three youths reflects aloud.

—Ohe! Saint Francis, where are you going?—cries another member of the group, quickly translating his companion's words into action.

—To the convent of Mezzoiuso—answers the big friar.

—Can you take us some of the way?

The friar examined the group, noting with his little eyes—two tiny lines cut into his moon-like face—the bright red of their shirts above their jacket lapels, and said kindly:

—*Acchianate,* climb up. I can give you a lift as far as the turn-off for Marineo, no further. From what I can see, you are headed for Corleone... All of you are for Garibaldi, right?

—Why?—Goffredo asked—are you against?

—God forbid! But in the convent everybody calls him the devil and makes the sign of the Cross. If they knew that I had given you a lift on the cart of Saint Francis they would want *'mpisu,* to hang me. The padre guardiano is a rat and the father provincial is twenty rats [*sorci* = rats: police informers] in one. You should see their tails! But what can they do to me, after all? They can't stop me from saying mass, since I am a lay friar. And if they send me away, who is the loser? The convent. Go find another beggar like brother Rosario, who returns with his knapsack filled with every good gift of God! That's why I let you climb up.

—Then you're on our side?

—Goes without saying. I'm for freedom.

—Then you're against the Bourbons, unlike all the other friars.

—My God, don't talk to me about them. Under the Bourbons my family was taken 'in the eye of the law.' That miserable Maniscalco threw my father and two of my brothers in jail, and if it weren't for Garibaldi they would still be rotting in Favignana, like the lowest criminals. What had they done? It was said that they were hand in hand with the mafia. I would like to see anyone, compelled night and day into the countryside, who could defy the mafia. Did signor Maniscalco spare a gunshot for his spy? Better in prison than under the earth. Prison doesn't consume good people, says the proverb.

—Now they are all free, naturally.

—By the grace of God. But nobody goes to paradise without their saints. And our saint was Garibaldi. When he came, the prisons were opened and all the innocent mama's boys that were shut up came out free. That man has such a great heart! (brother Rosario made a gesture like spreading the bellows of an accordian). You know how much good he did in '60! Everyone who came to him with an injustice to correct, to obtain help, was heard. How many mothers, how many widows, how many poor people have I seen weep with joy as he went past! They kissed his hand like a saint. And where does that blessed man want to go now? They say that he wants to embark for America again to bring back all its riches to Sicily and divide them among the poor.

—No—smiled Goffredo—he's headed much closer. He's going to Rome.

—To Rome? To do what?

—To capture it, of course!

—But the pope is there.

—So?

—I mean, if the pope is there then Garibaldi can't stay there, and if Garibaldi goes there the pope can't stay—the friar objected logically.

—But he'll send the pope packing.

The stout friar looked at the three young men with astonished eyes. He seemed to be saying, You wouldn't be fooling me, would you?

—And you want to leave Rome without a pope?—he objected.

—It's not a question of that. The pontiff will remain the head of the Church, but his State will pass to the Kingdom of Italy.

The friar stopped to think a moment, then he said, with the satisfaction of one who makes a discovery:

—Good. You know what I'd do? I'd make Garibaldi pope. At least he would be a man of character and he wouldn't behave like Pio nono, who turns his coat every other moment. Garibaldi would be a big Christian, a *cristianone,* to put everybody to rights.

The three young men burst out laughing.

In the meantime, having passed the last climb through the efforts of the mule under whose hooves spurted the gravel that had been freshly scattered on the roadway, the cart stopped with a flick of the reins.

—We're at the fork of Marineo—said the friar—you have to go on further. I'm taking my road for Mezzoiuso. I'm sorry to leave you, but it won't be hard for you to find some other cart willing to carry you up there. *Picciotti, u Signuruzzu v'accompagna e si viditi San Giuseppi, chiddu ca commisa russa, dateci un vasatuni pi fra Rusariu!* Boys, Our dear Lord go with you, and if you see Saint Giuseppe, the one with the red shirt, give him a kiss for fra Rosario!

Chapter 9

ON THE stroke of one p.m. of August 30 1862 marchese don Fabrizio appeared at table in his impeccable black frock coat, shining, all dressed up, and restored. Not a lock out of place in his thick iron-grey hair, not an untirmmed hair in the ring-beard which rounded his vast double chin. In his eyes, which had been dark for so many days, there swam a glint of malicious joy, sweetened by a certain hypocritical pity. His hands were clasped on his waistcoat, in a composed gesture, as in a sacristy.

—*Abyssus abyssum invocat,* The abyss calls to the abysss—he said, knotting his napkin behind his neck.—How many griefs would be avoided, if we acted according to the law of God!

—What has happened?—donna Ortensia asked fearfully.

—Nothing more, nothing less that what had to happen. The scoundrel has been beaten, wounded, and arrested by the government troops. A fine ending for the second expedition of the Thousand!

—When? Where?

—Just yesterday. On the road to Rome, naturally—don Fabrizio explained with bitter irony—which is quite long. There are many kilometers from Aspromonte to Rome...

—Where is Aspromonte?

—Almost at the beginning of the Calabrian Apennines, a bit above Reggio Calabria...At the toe of the boot, as the liberal poets say. But this time the toe of the famous boot has kicked the very one who wanted to enlarge it.

—Are there victims?

—Of course there are. The newspapers are talking only about Garibaldi. But in an encounter between troops they're not exactly shooting confetti.

—Poor people—sighed donna Ortensia.

—Poor us—corrected the marchese, without conviction—who will feel the consequences of this ugly episode of fraternal war. And perhaps, why not? poor them too. How many youths led to the slaughter by the gesture of a madman.

—They're all madmen! All crazy! All the same it remains to be seen which side is wrong.

—It seems to me that God has spoken His word.

—It's convenient to attribute to God what are only the works of the devil.

A hum, a confused buzzing, pierced by loud cries, was rising from the street.

—What's going on outside? What is this uproar?—the marchese asked his majordomo, who was coming in to serve the dessert.

—*Un focu granni,* a great riot, signor marchese! According to the coachman, who has just returned, there's the wrath of God. A stream of frenzied people, with flags, is pouring onto the street and is headed toward the Fieravecchia. Workmen, peasants down from the 'Regno' in Naples, gentlemen, and even a few priests, shouting like they're possessed. They have put a red shirt on the statue of 'old Palermo' on the fountain. Jesus, Jesus! There's nothing we can do but watch. They are chasing the *sorci* and have beaten some of them who happened to be passing. They're shouting, 'We want Garibaldi! We want our father!' The police are following the demonstrators, but they don't know which fish to land.

—A fine father!—the marchese commented sardonically.—A model father, who sends his sons to be massacred.

—But the crowd doesn't think of it like that—Marco observed respectfully.

—How do they think about it?

—They say that it shouldn't have reached this point. The government should not have allowed so many mammas' boys to leave, then shoot at them. Everybody knew that the government was in favor of the expedition. If they were against it, why not stop the volunteers while they were still in Sicily? It was so easy to dissolve the bands before they crossed the

Straits. But to let them leave in order to send them to the slaughterhouse, that no. That's what people are saying.

—You speak well, Marco, and anyone, even the shoeshine boy on the street corner would think like that. But what do you want us to do, if we are governed by clowns? The various Rattazzis, who hold the helm of the State, are leading us to ruin.

—*Benedicite!*—said the soapy voice of don Assardi, standing on the threshold of the dining room as if he had sprouted magically out of the air—*Benedicite!* And excuse me for coming in unannounced. But there was no one in the portineria to ring the bell. It's true that I could have rung it myself, but I didn't want to behave like the bagpipers from the mountains at Christmas...

—The gate keeper will have gone along to see the racket at the Fieravecchia. He too will have lost his head, nothing but a coward as he is.

—Curiosity is a sin, but a venial one. Pardon him for it.

—I would have said that you entered through the keyhole, seeing you appear here so unexpectedly—said don Fabrizio, turning toward the comical little man in a cassock.

—It's true that I'm small—the priest laughed—but I never enter through holes. It's rather easy to leave that way, from the many you can count on my robe. It's a real sieve.—And he proudly showed his cassock, where there were indeed more holes than patches.

—All we needed was this bird of evil omen—donna Ortensia murmured softly to Marco, who was changing her plate.

—Marchesa, *Quannu veni iddu, o vozza o chiaia,* When he comes it's either a bump or a sore—answered the majordomo, leaning down to her ear.

It really was so. Every time the plotter or busybody, according to your point of view, the coadjutor of the Madonna of the Catena, appeared at the palace, it was a sign that the weather was changing for the worse. Like a barometer where a little friar either emerges from the tower or puts on his hood, according to the changes in the atmospheric pressure, so the appearance of don Assardi at the palace meant rain, wind, or storm: always a turbulance or a precipitation in the moral atmosphere. Therefore, at the sight of him the servants became alarmed. Some winked an eye, some elbowed their neighbor, some whispered, *O vozza o chiaia.*

—A cup of coffee for our padre—the marchese ordered.

—That's just what I need—croaked the priest.—I have a lump the size of a quince here at the top of my stomach. What times! What times!

On a silver tray Marco brought a deep porcelain cup filled to the brim with coffee. The priest fished two big lumps of sugar out of the sugar bowl, stirred, poured the coffee into the saucer, and started to sip it greedily, whistling though his black teeth. At every sip he licked his lips with his raspy cat-like tongue.

—Life is so bitter that a bit of sweetness puts the soul back into the body.

—What good wind brings you here, don Assardi?

—An ill wind, a west wind, my dear marchese. Above all, it is only by a miracle that I am still alive. Near here, by the Fieravecchia, I was caught up in the stampede (What a mob! What a crowd! *Madonna mia!*) and I got a punch in the stomach that almost sent me to the other world. Someone inspired by the devil, holding one of those awful flags, wanted to pass in front of me, and since I was caught between two fires and could go neither this way or that, he was about to poke me in the stomach with the pole. If I hadn't flung myself to one side I would have been spitted like a sausage. And wave *ciao-ciao* father Assardi! Craziness, madness! I swear to you that the Palermitans have lost their minds.

—The effects of the dog days.

—What dog days?! On August 25 the sun entered the Constellation of the the Virgin, if I am not mistaken, and yet everybody's head is even hotter than before. A volcano, God's truth.

—But what do they really want?

—Do you know what they want? A second Sicilian Vespers, it looks like. They don't undertand that we're already full up. It's useless to shout, 'Hurrah for Garibaldi.' He is lamed, trussed up like a salame, and already in prison pondering his fine vanished megalomaniac dreams. Maybe he'll go to Rome, but only to stand trial.

In the meantime donna Ortensia and donna Teodora had risen, leaving the two men alone to converse in the dining room.

—Now we can talk at our ease. Women...I have great respect for them, especially when they are gentlewomen. But often they do not understand, or what is worse, they do not understand that they don't understand—observed don Fabrizio.

—The disaster of Aspromonte! But let's pull long faces, you and I, as if we were distressed by it. In fact, we should be as pleased as punch. *Felix culpa!* The façade of *their* revolution is crumbling and *ours* is strengthened. It couldn't have gone better for us, *perbacco baccone*. What did Garibaldi want? To grab Rome and the States of the Church and make them a nice present for Victor Emmanuel, as he did with the kingdom of the two Sicilies. That scoundrel is famous for giving to one what he steals from another. Victor Emmanuel gloats and lets him do what he wants. It's nice to enrich yourself with other peoples' property. But suddenly the chastiser wakes up. Napoleon III shouts, Halt! if you take Rome from the pope, I'll jump on you and tear you to bits. Then the great king gets the shakes. Fear gives him courage (the courage of fear is a terrible thing), and he orders Cialdini to stop the march of the Leader. In short, the cat is about to pounce on the rat and make a mouthful of it. But just then arises the dog, who is watching him to attack and sink his fangs into him. So Mister Cat lets the rat go and beats a prudent retreat. You can be sure that as long as a mastiff like Louis Napoleon is on guard nobody will go to Rome. This is certain. But now comes the best part. Victor Emmanuel has had Garibaldi arrested. The Crown has broken with the revolution. The two accomplices are entering into war against each other. And the nation is against the king. Because the Italians can't swallow the wounding and the arrest of Garibaldi. And the Sicilians? The Sicilians are infuriated more than ever, really enraged against the monarchy, which has hurled itself against their idol. You know that Garibaldi's expedition against Rome was incubated, prepared, willed, some say imposed, in Sicily and by Sicily. It seems that Garibaldi himself had not even thought of it until he landed on the island. The result is today's events, which threaten to turn into an uprising. Don't you hear them shouting in the streets, Down with Victor Emmanuel? Believe me, the monarchy is passing a *mauvais quart d'heure*.

—I understand—don Fabrizio remarked doubtfully—but the present upheaval can also play the game of the republicans. And for us one thing alone is important: the restoration of the Bourbons.

—Don't even think of it. The revolt, which is creeping everywhere and which seems about to explode, is helping our cause. We're really the ones who will fish best...in troubled waters.

—In what way?

—I see the thing as clear as a mathematical theorem. The Sicilians do not love the Savoias. They cheered them as long as they were with Garibaldi, that its, with the revolution. But now that the Savoias have set themselves against Garibaldi, the Sicilians will rebel *en masse* against the Savoias, who have offended, betrayed, imprisoned their idol. Is that clear?

—So it seems.

—Well then, we have to focus on this hatred of the Sicilians, never livelier than in this moment, against the Savoy monarchy. What says the philosopher? Give me a place to stand and I will raise up the world for you. We have this place. With this as a fulcrum we will raise up Sicily. Not the world, but Sicily. Our program is much more modest!—And here don Assardi emitted a gurgling rattle of a laugh.

—You see far ahead, father—said don Fabrizio, giving a friendly little tap on the priest's knee.—You have laid out a magnificent strategic plan, without question. But now it's time to descend to the level of tactics. We must act concretely. And *quid est agendum*? What is to be done?

—I'll answer you right away. Listen to me for a moment. Let's look at the local situation: the situation in Palermo, I say, since Palermo must be the center of the movement, as at the time of the Vespers. Aspromonte was a mistake, you agree...

—And in politics a mistake is worse than a crime, according to Fouché—interrupted the marchese.

—Excellent. Now, this mistake, whether by Garibaldi or by Victor Emmanuel, has also transformed the situation here into a camp of Agramante straight out of *Orlando furioso*. *C'sciarra 'nto cammaruni,* There's a quarrel between comrades. It has brought and will bring ever more discord into the enemy's camp. First all the parties of the revolution, so to speak, were united against us, the legitimists. Now each one is attacking the other. The government party, the most dangerous of our enemies because it controls the military, the bureaucracy, and the mafia, is in crisis now, condemned by everybody for having spilled fraternal blood at Aspromonte. The party of action, headed by Crispi and Corrao, friends of Garibaldi, is turning decisively against him. The Mazzinian party is against everybody, because Mazzini, hostile to the monarchy, was also hostile to Garibaldi's Roman adventure that ended with yesterday's tragedy. The separatists are against the government, against Crispi the unitarian and Mazzini the unshakeable antiregionalist...

—The ones in arms against the others, in short. But all of them in arms against us, who are left alone.

-Alone, no. We have with us the clergy, who are almost all for the Bourbons. But the clergy isn't enough. So we must seek new alliances. We cannot remain isolated. In politics, woe to those who are alone. This is the problem.

—So, what do you propose?

—I propose nothing. I'm a poor priest, a servant of God, unworthy, who would like to live quietly and not bother with this sorrowful world.

—But you must have an idea.

—Do you really want to know it, little as it's worth?

—Naturally.

—Here it is. What would you think, for example, if we joined with...the Freemasons?

At this word the marchese started up from his chair like one possessed, falling back with his full weight and staring at the priest with dumbfounded eyes.

—The Freemasons? Never. Are you serious, don Assardi? Come to an agreement with the enemies of the pope, of Christianity, of God?

—I knew that you would be offended—said the priest, more honeyed and calmer than ever—I knew it. I'm not surprised. Indeed, I understand your scorn. But let's think it over. Above all, we are on the field of politics here, not of religion.

—I do not admit that the two things can be separated. Conscience stands above politics.

—Your conscience is a most respectable thing, my dear marchese. But you are too intelligent and cultivated to share certain prejudices, to let youself be led by preconceived and perhaps partisan notions. I am only saying that—in the field of tactics, understood—there is nothing wrong in using our enemies when they can help our cause. Must we hate the Masons? Then let's hate them. But don't let's forget that they are for the revolution just because Mazzini is equally for the revolution. I gather from an unexceptionable source that he is in active correspondence with all the Lodges of the island and especially with the Masons of Palermo. There is only one point of difference between Mazzini and us. He wants the rebellion to break out at the same moment throughout the peninsula in order to create a unified republic, while we want it to occur immediately, for our own purposes, which do not coincide with his. He writes, 'The revolution will be made when the time is right and we will make it together.' We say, 'Sicily will do it alone, as it has always done, without awaiting the word from the mainland.' For us the times are ripe. Aspromonte has speeded up these times. There is no occasion better than this one. All Italy is in an uproar. Let's take advantage of it. There is no time to lose. Strike while the iron is hot. Since the majority of the Sicilian Masons think the same way, let's join with them. In union there is strength... What do you think of it, marchese?—the priest concluded with the satisfaction of a general who has marked out a plan of battle.

—I think that this marriage must not be made—don Fabrizio said firmly.

At this remark, which he did not expect, the priest shrank back in his chair, mortified and surprised.

—Be it as you wish. But remember that this time the part of Manzoni's cowardly don Abbondio is not destined for me. I'm not the one lacking in courage. It's curious, curious indeed, that I should be the brave man and you would play the role of the fearful parish priest.

—There is a virtue which is worth more than courage, dear father: character.

—You are perfectly right. But in politics those who have always triumphed are the men without character. Consider it well, and you will give me your answer...

Chapter 10

'HALFWAY ALONG life's path,' *nel mezzo del cammin,* Teodora had reached the dangerous stage of remorse for virtue. At the age of thirty-six, for the first time she realized that until then she had passed her life among the sleepy mumbling of rosaries, the elegant witticisms of her mother-in-law, and the clumsy and heavy company of a husband absorbed in politics, in a loneliness broken only by occasional visits of some old dragon of the black aristocracy and by the rare little family celebrations, neither amusing nor invigorating, which were dictated by the calendar. Nothing but weariness and boredom. Only haze and shadow. Goffredo's stay in the house had been an interval of light (not for her alone, but for everyone), a breath of youth which had dispersed the unbearable stench of old age that permeated the palace. But since the young man's departure a heavy lethargy had weighed on things and souls. And the soul of Teodora, which had felt the lump of bitterness repressed within her dissolve into a sentiment whose name she herself dared not speak, had fallen back into that state of stiffness that the world called frigidity. She had gone back to being the 'statue of ice' which had become proverbial in the high society of Palermo.

But it is not decreed that even female souls more solid than ice are completely incapable of melting. It is a question of temperature. Even the hardest metals can liquify when they have reached what chemists call the 'melting point.' And such a point arrives even for women who are believed to be the most frigid.

When several months had passed since the disappearance of Goffredo, Teodora was waking to a new life, out of that state of bewilderment and stupor that had dominated her. A new sap was beginning to flow through her veins. A desire for pleasure, a fever of liberation and joy mixed with trembling impatience and nebulous temptations rioted in her inmost being; but her frenzy for livng now flowed outward instead of writhing and exhausting itself within her. The madness of worldly life took possession of her spirit. Where she had written *Clausura et silentium,* Enclosure and silence, for so many years, she now inscribed the Epicurean motto *Carpe diem,* Sieze the day. And accordingly she seized and enjoyed the hours of the day (and the night as well, when she could) in frequenting salons, *conversazioni,* promenades, theaters, balls, and every other pastime which the society of her rank offered her. Was she happy? Perhaps—no, certainly not, and if love is a happiness (which is quite doubtful) one could wager that she did not love, or loved no longer. Love is ascetic, unsociable, fond of solitude. It cloaks itself in shadows and feeds on loneliness, it hides from the crowd and from the world. Society cultivated the *flirt,* coquetry, and every form of sentimental fatuity, in which a woman promises without compromising herself, plays with fire without burning herself, and stands on the brink of temptation taking care not to fall over, while at the same time she condemns delirious loves and overwhelming passions. Society, to whom the grace of woman is as necessary as the seriousness of man, wants the woman to belong to everyone, like a work of art, and not to become the exclusive property of one person. Woman is, by definition, a wordly being, as man ia a political animal. With a division of labor which has something marvelous about it, they co-operate for the common good.

Naturally, in throwing herself into the toils of the living joyfully, Teodora was not thinking at all of performing a social function. She was obeying her instincts. She felt a need to *exist.* Until now, had she ever existed for anyone? Not for her husband, not for her mother-in-law, not even for Goffredo himself, who had given her for a moment the illusion that she was a woman. Since she had existed for no one, now she wanted to exist for everyone, to transform her solitude, the negation of her being, into a multi-souled cohabitation, into a plural and nameless existence, such as worldliness. She had belonged to no one and now she belonged to everyone. And if among so many there was one who would be happy to dedicate himself to her...No. She did not wish, she did not even dare to think of it. After the departure of Goffredo she felt that there would no longer be a place for only one single person in her heart.

Night. The darkness was crawling along palazzo Geraci like a thief hunted by the cones of light that projected from its windows.

The splendid eighteenth-centuy building, commissioned by the Ventimiglia family from the architect Venanzio Marvuglia and finished by the imaginative architect Ignazio Marabitti, was open that evening for a celebration in honor of the English naval squadron anchored in the bay.

In the Cassaro, amid the pawing of the splendid pairs of horses, the blasoned coaches passed slowly and paused before the entrance to the palace, which was guarded by a gigantic doorman, proud of his top-hat with its cockade and his enormous mace with its silver handle, which he leaned on with the dignity of an Ercole Farnese. There descended fron the carriages women in cloaks, sparkling with silks, velvets, feathers, and jewels, gentlemen in tailcoats and top hats, Italian and British officers in gaudy uniforms. The broad stairway, flanked by plants and covered with soft carpets, was thronged with elegance, with conversations, with whispers, among harmonies of perfumes which caressed the sense of smell. Footmen in livery with powdered wigs stood rigidly at every landing, like manikins with porcelain heads.

The vestibule of the palace was thronged by the continual arrival of guests who crowded together in front of the cloak room. The facing mirrors reflected between them the momentary images of the ladies removing their varicolored outer garments. Rainbows of rubies and diamonds, of emeralds and sapphires, exploded on their bare shoulders and arms, on their dark or golden hair, on their snowy bosoms. At the threshold of the drawing room the voice of the majordomo gave out the names most famous for nobility, for wealth, for high rank in the army, in politics, in the republic of arts and letters.

Teodora made her entrance alone, dropped her mantle of blue velvet into the hands of a footman; after a few steps she halted under the chandelier—a monstrous crystal dahlia with fire-colored petals—to gaze casually at her image, which the mirror returned in its entirety. A simple amethyst-colored crinoline, of Chambéry gauze in several rows of ruffles, light and airy as a cloud, harmonious as a distant bell. A rose of pale flesh color in her hair, which was parted by a thin line into a double raven's wing, cascading in graceful curls along her temples and reknotted at the nape of her neck, leaving her finely-modeled earlobes free. No jewels except an artistic clip of antique gold at the top of her décolltage. By comparison with many other necklines hers was not a bold one (one must sacrifice a bit of flesh to the conventional *pruderie* of the black aristocracy), but neither was it so modest as to conceal a tempting line of shadow between the globes of her breasts.

On that shadowy line ran the aroused glance of the magistrate Camarda, who stood frozen in the doorway like a faun ambushing a dryad. As the lady passed, the black tailcoat of the magistrate split in two as he bowed, making his coattails ripple. His lips rested on her lovely ringless hand.

—For such a stupendous creature I would be capable of committing... an injustice—murmured the public prosecutor, dropping the words into the funnel-shaped ear of the marchese d'Aci.

—It wouldn't be either the first or the last one you had committed—the marchese answered.

—The first for a just cause—intervened in defense of the magistrate the little duke of Villaverde, twisting all his facial muscles to hold in place an enormous monocle which threated to pop out of its orbit.

—Here is the star Sirius—poetized baron Mazza, affectedly kissing the finger-tips of Teodora, who rewarded him with a smile full of charm.

—Forget Sirius! This is the midnight sun, as I have seen it in the northern regions—admiral Turchi redoubled his admiring remarks, jokingly pointing his rolled-up hands like a binocular at the stunning sight.

Bit by bit as Teodora advanced into the room between two dense rows of guests, opinions and comments rained down like flowers and shot like arrows around her.

—Do you like her?—asked donna Oretta Strongoli, proud of her heart-shaped decolletage which was flirting with her stomach, to her neighbor, who was speechlessly contemplating the majesty of the new arrival.

—Why not? It's true that I don't see much, but I'm not blind yet.

—I agree that she can be pleasing. But allow me to say that she does not have 'class.' Those hands and those feet, please...

—And that swanlike neck?...—agreed signorina Anonymous in a sea-weed green *toilette* trailing behind her, laughing with all her little teeth, tiny white seeds in the scarlet fruit of her mouth.—You who are an artist, what do you say of that?

The person questioned—a sculptor, the student of Valerio Villareale, and therefore of Canovan tastes—answered, tossing back his flaming red hair.

—The shoulders are beautiful, especially the place where the arms are attached, where two delicious little dimples are smiling. If I could sculpt them...I would make a second Paolina Borghese.

—You only have to ask—said donna Oretta, maliciously—the model will make you free of her beauties...and not just of her shoulders.

The talkative group suddenly broke up. There was an unexpected rush of everyone, men and women, toward the gallery, which was boarded by the officers of the Britannic navy led by admiral MacDonald. Commodores, commanders, cadets, in gaudy uniforms, shining with gold and multi-colored decorations, dropped from their great heights honeyed smiles and superior glances on the ladies, who collected them with humble servility, competing for the honor of a foreign signature on their dance cards.

That outburst of Anglophile infatuation left Teodora alone and disappointed. In her first passage of arms with the life of society, not sufficiently bold to push herself forward nor humble enough to remain in the background, she felt neglected, forgotten. A veil of sadness, embittered by a passing annoyance, descended on her green eyes. Having lived for years and years in the cloistered tedium of an ancient palace, was she not perhaps a stranger to this world? She raked a dark glance over that sort of electrifying witches' sabbath of splendid garments, elegant uniforms, rosy and excited faces, smiling and longing little mouths. Over such splendor of jewelled flesh drunken with exhibitionism and sensual joy, on all that fairground seething with eroticism and lightheadedness.

—It's suffocating in here—she said to the gentleman standing next to her—accompany me, please, to get a bit of air.

The gentleman led her to the central balcony, which opened on the Cassaro. The air was soft in spite of the winter night. There was resting lazily on the Conca d'Oro one of those mild winters which already bring a message of spring along with the first violets. The street below was deserted. A row of carriages stretched like a black snake, disappearing at its opposite ends between the Quattro Canti and piazza Vittoria. The silence was punctuated by the chatting of the coachmen and grooms and broken from time to time by the rasp of the horses' hooves on the pavement and some sudden neigh.

Lined up along the balcony, leaning on the railing, were several officers, who bowed at the arrival of the couple and moved off into in a corner.

The heavens opened on high like a monstrous peacock's tail starred by many golden eyes. Above the houses, the roofs, the chimney-pots, which the calm brightness of the stars underlined with shadows, stood out the dome of the Santissimo Salvatore with its graceful flight of arches, bathed in an unearthly light.

The gentleman made the introductions.

—Allow me, marchesa. Captain Assanti, liuetenant Diatto, lieutanant Spada...

Teodora held out her ungloved hand.

—Are we disturbing you?—she asked.

—Of course not! We were looking at Palermo by night. Conversation multiplies the joys of art.

—Do you know Palermo?

—We two, yes—assented the captain, indicating lieutenant Diatto—we have been here for almost a year. Spada has been in Palermo for several weeks.

—Where are you from?

—From Genoa—answered the handsome lieutenant of the Guides, standing rigidly at attention and displaying an irreproachable double-breasted uniform jacket with silver buttons, blue cuffs, and a blue collar blazoned with white flames.

—Genoese?

—No, from Asti. My regiment is stationed in Genoa. I am detailed here as the general's orderly.

Leaning on the railing, the young man was silhouetted against the sky with his great height, while his face disappeared into the shadows.

—What is that church opposite, on the right?—he asked, turning toward the street, just to keep the conversation going.

—The church of the Salvatore—lectured Teodora's companion, happy to show off his historical knowledge—fine architecture by fra Paolo Amato, with agreeable frescoes by Vito D'Anna and Antonio Mauro. The present seventeenth-century building rises on the site of the ancient church founded by Robert Guiscard in 1073. According to a tradition mentioned by Dante, Costanza, the sister of king Ruggero, had been shut up in the convent next to the church, from which she was taken by force to be married to Henry VI of Hohenstaufen, who sleeps in one of the porphry mausoleums in the cathedral.

—It's a pretty story, but not for a party—observed Teodora, stopping her loquacious friend, who, having got started, would never have stopped talking—Happiness is always tied to the present moment, it isn't burdened by the past.

—However—observed lieutenant Spada—there is one who maintains that pleasure is always past or future, never present. Giacomo Leopardi.

—Future, perhaps. Past, no.

—Doesn't it seem to you that the past, in memory, is as if it were present? With this advantage: that the future is uncertain, the present inconstant, while the past is not subject to change. It is what it is. Indeed, in memory the past often appears to us even more beautiful than what it had really been.

—Are you by chance a pessimist?

—Not at all, marchesa. I love life. And you?

—Do I love life? In truth, I would prefer that life loved me—said Teodora enigmatically.

—It's clear that if we don't love life, it doesn't love us. Our whole existence is fundamentally a problem of the will.

—Do you think so? Do you assume that it is enough to will in order to exist? And what if life deceives us, betrays us?

—Then we create a life with our own imagination.

—A poet's luxury. We are not all poets.

—Each one of us can be. Everything consists in knowing how to construct one's life poetically, said the lieutenent, fluttering his eyelids behind the flame of the match with which he had lighted his cigarette.

—Are you a poet?

—I have been. Who hasn't written verses at age twenty? After that my military career caught me up completely. The active life kills the contemplative life.

—It's a sign that you love the active life more.

—I wouldn't say so. I love difficult things, and art is the most difficult thing in life. It is more difficult to describe a fine action than to perform one. Not having the possibility of describing and writing, I content myself with reading what others write. I read a lot.

—What do you read?

—A bit of everything. I like novels.

—Whose, for example.

—Any author who knows how to write them.

—The French are the best.

—There are also beautiful novels among our own writers. We will soon be reading one that will make a great stir.

—The author?

—Ippolito Nievo.

—What did you say?

—Nievo. One of the Thousand, you will have heard him spoken of. The Garibaldian captain who was drowned in the Tyrhennian with the *Ercole* while he was returning to Genoa from Sicily. Very young, barely thirty.

—What is it called?

—*Confessions of an Italian.* It will come out soon, posthumously. The author read me a few pages years ago, while we were both students in Padua. What talent! What imagination! What a loss for our literature! A sorrow to die so young!—sighed Spada, extinguishing an umpteenth match along with the sentence.

—The death of a poet is sad.

—The poet never dies. It is we who are dying, a little bit every day. In the meantime, if you like literature, I will allow myself to lend you some books.

—Thank you. I don't read much, but a bit, yes. It's a way of killing time.

—You deceive yourself, marchesa. Time is never killed. Occasionlly it is wounded, but it remains more alive than before. So it's better to make a treaty with time, and to spend it in the best way possible. Will you do me the honor of a dance?

—I'm really sorry. I'm not dancing, I have a migraine.

—What a pity! I'm sorry for you since you are suffering. Fortunately, the migraine is a...fickle illness.

—What do you mean?

—It passes. It passes, by dancing.

—Bravo! But if the migraine is fickle, I don't want to be like the migraine.

—Now it is I who ask you: What do you mean?

They had remained alone on the balcony, since all the others had left to take part in the festivities, which were now at their height.

—You understand—said Teodora softly—until a short time ago I refused the many gentlemen who had come to engage me: 'I have a horrible headache.' What will they say if they see me dancing?

—They will say that you are a woman without character.

—That seems little to you?

—And you will answer that only ugly men are asked if they possess a character, not beautiful and elegant women.

A moment later Teodora–who had gently let her inviter take her by the arm—made her entrance into the gallery, where the dance was in full swing.

The party was celebrating with the frenzy characterisic of the small hours of the morning. The rustling of silk, the scrape of shoes; wafts of perfume, heavy scents of decaying flowers, of perspiring armpits; splendors of naked flesh, fireworks of eyes, of jewels, which lit up sensual and bloated faces. The Strauss waltz, 'Wo di Zitronen blühn,' floated through an air loaded with desire like a lazy stream, from which the naked arms of the female dancers emerged from time to time like sinuous swan-necks.

Holding tight to her officer, absorbed into the mazes of the dance, Teodora passed with a smile of wandering happiness on the edges of her half-open lips, arousing words of admiration and glances of jealousy.

On the last beat, while the couples made their way bit by bit to the *queue* to start the cycle again, she said with agitation:

—I would like to rest.

—Are you tired?

—Not tired. My head is splitting. A feeling of confusion...

She sat down, more pale then ever, waving her great feather fan to give herself some air.

—Faithless one!—baron del Monte reproached her in a fatherly tone, slicing the air with his open palm, miming a threat. — It's really true that 'la donna è mobile,' 'woman is fickle.' You have a migraine only for dancing with the undersigned. On the other hand...! Yes, the migraine—hemi-crainia—is the illness of the divided brain. One half was against the dance, the other in favor. This explains everything.

—It could be—she agreed, in the throes of a pleasant exhaustion.

—I allow myself to remind you that a woman, even though she has never saved any one, will always do well to save appearanes.

—If it is like that, I grant you the next dance.

And she allowed herself to be led into the rhythm of a mazurka.

Now Teodora is galvanized. She seems to have drunk a stimulating potion. She talks, laughs, jokes, frolics. One would say that the 'melancholy beauty' had lightly let the cloak of sadness slip from her sculptured shoulders, from her magnolia bosom, to throw herself into the enchanting whirl of the party free of any restraint. She passes happy and light like a lilac cloud through the gilded circles of the dance. She no longer tires of dancing, of generously bestowing smiles in order to express the joy bubbling in every move of her body, in every vibration of her soul. It is no longer Teodora, they say, she is no longer recognizable. And if the ancient and forgiving air of the Saturnalia, more concerned with its own enjoyment than with the failings of others, did not weigh on the vast hall, every mouth would be spouting the poison of envy and the acid of slander against her.

—I'm becoming aware—lieutenant Spads says to her, approaching the beautiful marchesa who has just finished the last turn of waltzes—that melancholy is just barely creeping on your skin. You shake it off like a light veil of powder.

—What do you know about it!—she answers, visibly annoyed.

—I saw you passing happily from one dancer to another.

—Sometimes appearances are deceiving.

—We can fool others, not ourselves.

—Ourselves too. What do we know of what is within us? We are ignorant of it, my friend. Does the oyster know that it contains a pearl? What is a jewel for others is a sickness for her. And yet she does not know it.

—Now I understand why you do not wear even the shimmer of a pearl. You are afraid of catching her disease.

—True. I prefer not to become ill. You will agree that I am a wise woman.

—The greatest wisdom would be that of going wild in a final *galop*. I hope you will have the kindness of allowing it to me.

—No—she smiled with all the energy of her strong-willed mouth.—Everything has its event, its cycle. And for me the cycle of dances is concluded...

—Is another cycle opening? and of what sort?

—I could be annoyed by your insistence. I tell you that I like living day by day, indeed...by hours...by minutes. And in this minute I am deciding to leave. Naturally, I will slip away without taking farewell of anyone.

—To any other woman who was not you—joked the lieutenant—I would say that this is behaving deceitfully.

Seated on a low *pouf*, she was indeed shining like a lovely perfidious flower, an enormous calyx of lilac silk reversed on the fleshy stem of her body. The green of her eyes, enlarged and pale as in an hallucination, held something enigmatic and elusive.

—Will you accuse me of deceit—she said—if I ask you to accompany me to the cloakroom?

—You want to leave? So soon?

—'Soon' and 'late' have no meaning for happiness. Give me your arm.

At the cloakroom the officer helped the marchesa put on her *sortie* and kissed her fingertips, which she offered uncovered before pulling on her second glove.

—So, will I have the pleasure of seeing you again?—asked Spada.

—Perhaps yes, perhaps no—she smiled ambiguously. —What do we know of tomorrow?

And she disappeared among a forest of flowering plants on the landing of the stairway, swallowed up by the watery surface of the great mirror.

The afternoon of the following day her majordomo presented to the marchesa Teodora on a silver tray a calling card with the corner turned down in sign of a personal visit.

She read absent-mindedly:

Nob. SERGIO SPADA
Lieutenant of the 19° Guides

With a little click she dropped the card into a tawny alabaster tazza, an antique funerary urn intended to inhume all the calling cards, the invitations, the wedding announcements, the social engagements that arrived at the palace.

After it had fallen, she rummaged in the heap, picked up the card, and read it again.

Was she feeling that it *must not* end up among the dead things?

A flash of rebellion, and the card, fiddled about by her nervous fingers, fell to bury itself again in the urn.

—After all,—she murmured, angry with herself—what can there be in common between me and this little lieutenant whom I met yesterday evening at some sort of ball?

Chapter 11

A TRYPTICH of naked shoulders. A sight reserved for those entering box number 11 of the Teatro Santa Cecilia. Anonymous shoulders (since the nude avoids the married state), but not all of them. Anyone could recognize the duchess of Montescuro by the two large moles nestled under her left shoulder blade, resembling the two of spades. The owners ot the two other spines sculpted in young flesh and furrowed by soft shadows are two ladies who turn like sunflowers toward the stage lights.

The Teatro Santa Cecilia—today degraded to a common storehouse of scrap iron—was the second theater of Palermo between the end of the eighteenth century and the first half of the nineteenth, and it remained such at the time of this story. It was later dethroned by the theater of the Travaglini or the Caroline Theater, as it came to be called with the more imposingly brilliant name of royalty. Erected in 1693 by the initiative of the 'Union of Musicians,' or the corporation of 'Virtuosi of song' (since at that time corporate life was flourishing on the island) on the spot where the church of Santa Cecilia had once risen, in the period of its highest splendor the theater saw the greatest artists of Europe pass under its proscenium arch, and on more than one of them it bestowed the kiss of glory and the garland of immortality.

Whoever pauses today to look at the old building,—faded, cracked, leprous, despite the symbols of the Muses of song which still survive on the top of its pediment that is humiliated by a swarm of ignoble houses on every side and a piazza which has now become a plebeian market— is drawn to reflect sadly on the transitory nature of human things: *Sic transit gloria mundi.*

They are performing *Lucia di Lammermoor*. The air is charged with electricity. Currents of tension are passing between the stage and the house on a thousand invisible wires, and if a spark chances to explode there is trouble Why such concentration of electric fluid? For political motives? For artistic motives? Far from it. The spectators in the theater are not divided for reasons connected with public affairs, although the political climate is overheated, nor are they championing the music of Donizetti against that of Bellini. They are polarized, with the greatest passion, around the two prima donnas: Barbara Marchisio, who is singing *Lucia*, and Erminia Frezzolini, who is singing *La sonnambula*. The republic of opera patrons—where there is no distinction between connoisseurs and laity, between men and women, between nobles and commoners—is divided into two factions: the *marchesini* and the *frezziolinisti*. Every evening they argue, they gesticulate, they fight, whether the stage is visible or the curtain is down, in the boxes and in the orchestra seats, in the corridors and in the foyer. The verbal battles, the squabbles, the brawls are prolonged outside, in salons, in cafés, in clubs, with exaggerations and excesses that end in angry words and sometimes deeds, not to mention legal and social consequences.

The stage lights awake from their sleep, yawning at the house lamps.

The *professori* of the orchestra enter one by one or in little groups, as if conjured up, sidling cautiously between the music stands and the instruments. The prompter's head is glimpsed in his box.

The violins moan, the violas throb, the contrabasses and the bassoons snore, the oboes and clarinets gargle, the trombones shout, while the timpani thump from time to time as if to put a bit of order into that infernal din.

Nonetheless, the conversation between the floor and the boxes and the boxes and the gallery is a hundred times more discordant:

—What do you think of the Marchisio?

—She's a nighingale.

—She's like a cat in heat.

—It would take ten Marchisios to make one Frezzolini.

—As a voice it's passable. But as an actress she's a disaster. She moves like a servant girl. Doesn't know where to put her hands.

—But you don't sing with your hands. You sing with your throat. And Marchisio's is a voice of gold.

—Let's see how she does in the mad scene.

—Bring out Barbara!—they call from the peanut gallery.

—Hooray for Erminia-a-a...—other shouts answer.

In box number eleven as well the disagreements and polemics are seething among the women and some gentlemen who have come in to greet them. But one of the three women seems abstracted, detached, almost absent among such boiling passions. When she is questioned, she deals with it by some friendly smile, interspersed with monosyllables. Meanwhile, with her opera glasses she is seeking, searching the hall, among the seats, the boxes, the officers' *barcaccia.*

Edgardo and Lucia have finished the duet 'Verranno a te sull'aure.' A scattering of applause disputed by shushes and a few whistles; even more enthusiastic acclamations from one faction, more angry and impolite protests from the other. The whole theater is in an uproar. But the faction of the 'marchesini' finally prevails, and the commotion fades and dies.

—So, what is your opinion—the duchess of Montescuro asks her friend, who has laid her opera glass down on the red velvet ledge of the box and sits contemplating the hall, which is now dominated by the house lights.—You can emerge from your silence now.

—My opinion about what?

—About the prima donna, of course!

—She's pretty.

—That isn't what we want to know. Every prima donna is pretty onstage: well dressed, carefully made up, shining with jewels, even if they're false. But the voice! your opinion about her voice is important because you understand music. The Marchisio or the Frezzolini?

—The Frezzolini?

—Yes, the one who sang *La somnambula*.

—I didn't hear *La somnambula*. How can you want me to give an opinion?

—For me the Marchisio is a hundred times better—the marchesa di Montescuro decrees.

—I'm for the Frezzolini—the solemn judgment of the second of the friends.

—The Three Graces are not in agreement—said a warm male voice behind the gentle spectators.

—You, lieutenant!—exclaimed the duchess, turning quickly.

—*Pardon*—said Spada, in a complimentary tone—if Paris intrudes on your discussion. It is understood that I will not decide who is the most beautiful among you three graceful contenders, if only because I have no golden apple available.

—You don't even have the habit of asking permission.

—Please, I did ask permission. But the three lovely ladies were so taken up by their discussion that...

—I wager instead that you entered on the sly to spy on...our shoulders. But you forget that my shoulders have eyes, two eyes with good sight. Everybody in Palermo knows the two birthmarks of the duchess of Montescuro. It's obvious that you're not from here.

—I beg pardon for my ignorance.

—And I grant it. But bring yourself up to date. Look at me well—and the lady turned her shoulders to the light—and do not forget your astronomy. The constellation of the Twins is my identity card. Have you seen it? And now enough. Don't imagine that I want to show you any other signs of the Zodiac. Sit down instead and we'll talk about politics. At this moment politics is more interesting than art.

—I think that something is in the air... Something is preparing. People are on the alert, we're arming ourselves... There is talk of troops massing at the approaches of the Trentino...contingents of troops are being transported up there from lower and central Italy, officers are being consulted as to whether they wish to be combined with the border corps. I too have received the invitation...

—And what have you answered?—asked Teodora, in the grip of obvious anxiety.

—Naturally I accepted...but the decision depends on the consent of my general.

—You will leave, then?—Teodora pursued, visibly pale.

—What do you want? We are soldiers. War is our profession.

—A horrible thing, war. It should be abolished. A barbarism!—Teodora burst out.

—Naïveté!—exclaimed the duchess, with the scorn proper to persons who have a long experience of life.—To abolish war you would first have to abolish class struggles, the clash between social classes, the conflicts between friends and relatives and even spouses. Where there are people, there will always be conflicts and wars.

—And is this war imminent?—Teodora insisted.

—In life nothing is near and nothing is far—said Spada, with serene philosophy.—It is not in our power to measure the distances between ourselves and events. We summon them and they distance themselves, we discourage them and they rush toward us. We are conceited masters who are always mastered. We barely command the fleeting present moment. A minute earlier or a minute later and we become the playthings of fate.

—I propose to command the present moment—said the duchess of Montescuro—to get a breath of fresh air outside. It's stifling in here.

They went out (the troop had been increased in the meantime by other gentlemen) into the corridors, which were lighted by infrequent oil lamps and thick with a crowd animated by conversations, shrieks of laughter, and voices.

The crowd has the same effect as the desert, so true is it that extremes meet. In a great number of people, man feels alone, set apart by himself, the exclusive companion of his soul. Therefore the solitary man—the man devoid of social conversation, the enemy of the salons, of the clubs, of lectures—loves to lose himself from time to time in great crowds where it is easy to preserve his incognito. The proverb 'poca brigata, vita beata,' 'small crowd, happy life,' is the motto of the sociable man. The unsociable man is for 'no crowd.' His hermitage is either the silent monastic cell or the great anonymous mass. Everyone knows that lovers are equally at their ease in the cave or in the hurly-burley of the crowd.

Teodora and the lieutenant found themselves side by side, as if led by an obscure instinct.

HE:—You are delightful this evening.

SHE:—That's what they say when a lady is tastefully dressed.

HE:—I don't have the habit of talking about clothes. And anyway, if it were for that, I would have said 'elegant' and not 'delightful.'

SHE:—Is there a difference?

HE:—The *admiring* adjective 'delightful' covers the whole person.

SHE:—What does that mean?

HE:—That an irresistible fascination breathes from your whole being.

SHE:—And yet you have resisted for so long the temptation to see me.

HE:—It isn't my usual habit. In the matter of temptations, I know that the best way of resisting them is to give way immediately. But permit me to say that this time the merit of resistence belongs to you.

SHE:—I don't understand you.

HE:—I have encountered you several times and you have returned a perfunctory greeting. I sent you a book and you didn't even thank me. I wanted to send you some flowers...

—You were right not to send flowers. They have a secret language.

—And books are silent?

—They tell the stories of other people. Flowers are part of ourselves.

—Precisely for that reason I wanted to send them to you.

—You forget that I have a husband, a house, my duties...

—I forget nothing. Nor would I want you to forget me.

—Do you doubt it? Did you not *feel* this evening that I was looking for you, I was seeking you throughout the theater, without finding you?

—And were you sorry not to find me?

—Don't ask me anything more. It's up to you to understand.

Spada looked into her eyes, which were immensely large and of a green shining like a precious stone. In truth, not only were her eyes speaking, but her whole body.

—This is the first time that you are sincere.

—Why? Have I been insincere until now?—she wondered innocently.

—One is insincere when one conceals what one has in one's heart.

—What do you know of what I have in my heart?—she said with a hint of pride.—Often we ourselves don't know. And are unhappy.

—Therefore I am happier than you are, because I know well what I have in my heart.

—What do you know?—asked Teodora fearfully.

—That I love you.

Her long eyelashes trembled, while her green pupils rose to him in an offering of happiness.

—What are you doing here in a trance?, shrieked the duchess.—Don't you hear the bell for the beginning of the second act? And you, lieutenant, stay with us. The judgment of Paris is only suspended, not postponed.

All the circles of the Palermitan aristocracy were talking of nothing except the *béguin* (the French language allows a greater indulgence to the sins of love) between the marchesa Teodora, the 'statue of ice,' and the fiery lieutenant of the 19° Guides. Surprise, curiosity, the appetite for scandal, political interest, gratuitous malice or the pleasure of evil for its own sake, and above all jealousy—all these were working to spread news of the event like an oil stain on a sheet of blotting paper.

Once it is established that public modesty is nothing but socialized jealousy, we can imagine what senses of horror were aroused in social circles in the name of offended chastity about the 'relationship' of Teodora, who was envied for her beauty, her wealth, her prominent position in society. It seemed that a trumpet, blown by that invisible personage, public opinion, repeated everywhere with unceasing echoes the refrain: Teodora is a sinner, Teodora is a dishonest woman, Teodora is a Messalina...

Let it be said in honor of truth, that nonetheless there were some who sympathized with her. They did not defend her openly, but they did try to undertand her. And *tout comprendre c'est tout pardonner.* If not everything can be pardoned to an adulteress, at least something of her sin can be forgiven. Jesus gave the first example of it.

Above all, mitigating circumstancces are allowed to a woman tied to a much older hunband, to a husband who neglects her. Don Fabrizio had only one spouse: politics, to whom he dedicated his whole being, forgetting that he had near him a creature of flesh and blood, exposed to the weakness of her sex. Even if she does not hear the cries of lust, a beautiful woman who has already crossed the threshold of her thirty-fifth year is subject to the anxieties, the upsets, the inevitable impatience of summer declining into autumn. Nor is she so armored against the temptations of the noonday devil as to be able to say to pleasure, Let this cup pass from me. And the more she is ensnared in the cycle of endless desires, the more difficult her self-defence becomes. The life of a woman condemned by her beauty to carve constantly a path for herself through the forest of impure desires is difficult. It is easy to guard oneself from unexpected falls, but how to resist gradual poisoning?

So thought the less nasty-minded critics of Teodora's behavior. They did not hesitate to blame a good part of her departure from the straight and narrow path on her husband, who had loosed the reins on her lovely neck without considering her uncontrolled race on the dangerous paths of high society. Strange: the fearsome and irreconcilable enemy of liberalism practiced a proverbial liberality toward his wife, letting her gallop happily toward destruction.

By the mercy of God, Teodora had not yet lost everything. But she had certainly lost her head, her powers of reasoning. If she had been a bit more reasonable, never ever would she have been surprised with the young officer in frequent meetings in the main throughfares of the city, and worse, in hidden back streets. She would not have appeared in all the social gatherings where she was sure to find herself with him; she would never have formed with him the 'usual couple' at dances; she would have been careful to keep him from coming to the palace on days when she was not receiving...Now she was passing from one folly to another, she allowed herself to be carried thoughtlessly on the back of recklessness, as if the world no longer existed for her. And the damage, more than in her behavior, was in her mind.

It is jealousy—she said to herself—that renders forked and slanderous the tongues of my lady friends who preach sermons to me. It is the envy of the poor against the rich, of those condemned to meanness against the joyful, those who arm themselves with false moralism against a creature who does no harm to anyone. After all, what does it matter to me? I rejoice in being envied. When I was the honest wife, irreproachable, no one cared about me, not even to commiserate with me. I was an insignificant little goose without character and without warmth. Now that I have become aware of my freedom and have awakened to a sense of my beauty, every woman who would like to be in my place is gnawing herself with rage and spitting poison. Is there someone who is longing to do what I do? Let her imitate me. Let her surpass me. The world is wide. There is room for everyone. What am I doing? I am enjoying my freedom. And if I make a bad use of it, I have to render an account to no one but my husband. An account of what? Of my feelings, if anything, since my body is without stain. I may have committed sins, but sins of the imagination, against which religion itself is indulgent. My life is lived in broad daylight. I challenge anyone to convict me of adultery. If I had sins to conceal I would hide in the shadows. Everyone can examine my acquaintances, my friendships, my affections. Is it forbidden to have affections, when they are innocent?

To defend Teodora some of her friends, real and not jealous (we do not intend by this to invalidate the principle that a friendshp between two women is a conspiracy against a third) grasped this fundamental argument: as long as a woman acts out in the open, do not mistrust her virtue. A woman who has a lover is never a great socialite. And who is more social than Teodora?

The Kramer equestrian circus in piazza Castello (neither the castle nor the piazza exists today) was presenting that evening a special performance for the curious public.

Eye-catching banners attached to the bleachers shouted in red and black: 'An unprecedented *high life* show—great charity spectacle for the flood victims—with the kind participation of the Palermitan aristocracy—and the generous assistance of the army. An absolutely unique program.—The entire company is offering their services without remuneration.'

Some days previously the city had been devastated by a terrifying flood: destruction, collapses, ruins, victims, misery, mourning. The charity of the common people had reached out its hand to the unfortunate disinterestedly. The charity of the middle and upper classes, always ready to dance on the misfortunes of others, had undertaken to organize diversions and entertainments to convert their thirst for enjoyment into money. Two philsophies—that of the poor and that of the rich—were mobilised for the same purpose.

The circus: a gigantic funnel of waxed cloth which flared out over the arena from on high. Spider-webs of ropes, light caves, tight and swinging wires which controlled rings, bars, trapeezes, glass globes: thick drops of light.

A blast of music. Only brass. Horns, keyed horns, flugelhorns, trombones, bombards, cornets, with cymbal crashes and thumps of bass drums. Crowds of children dressed in their best, shouts of candy- and salted seed-sellers, the hum of the impatient crowd, a shower of many-colored leaflets like lazy butterflies.

Quiet! The show is starting. It is the great *charivari,* the group parade announced in the program. A fabulous fantasmagoria of doublets, overcoats, shirts, tailcoats of the most bizarre cuts; of shouts, of barking, of jeers, of jokes, of capers, of death-defying leaps. The carnival of the grotesque, the misshapen, the deformed. The audience laughs. Perhaps each of them discovers a bit of himself in those beings, in those disjointed gestures. We are all in some manner clowns of the soul and buffoons of our feelings. Behold the contortionist and the tightrope walker: the portrait of the politician. The busybody dwarf wasting his breath by throwing a monkey wrench into everyone's works: a parody of the man of action. The nonsense and the imbecilities of the dandies: a parable of the everyone's idiocy. The animal trainers: what a waste of effort! Why don't they employ it to tame the most savage of all beasts, man?

A shining quadriga bursts into the arena. Four horses the color of of Parian marble that seem fallen from the crown of a triumphal arch, obeying the whip of their helmeted charioteer. They caracole, they dance, they bow to the public, they kneel, they pretend to fall dead at a pistol shot. They are unaware of their beauty, they are patient and sorrowful. What does applause mean to them? Nothing is sadder than an animal forced to imitate the absurd customs and shabby vices of the so-called king of living beings.

Ten minutes' intermission. A donkey circles around the track ridden by a monkey waving a placard with written on it, 'Ten minutes' pause.'

The tension builds for the last number of the program in which the cream of the Palermitan aristocracy, both men and women, will participate.

A flourish of horns. The beaters in black velvet uniforms come first, armed with drums. A pack of dogs follows: Irish wolfhounds with a rough grey coat, curved tails, nervous hindquarters; Persian hounds with silky coats, fluffy tails, human eyes, their muzzles sharp as nails; Arab salukis, red, slender, savage, ribcages naked under their thin skin, with their look of cruel predators.

Behind the Master of the Hounds caracole four horsewomen in red coats: moving scarlet patches on the tawny, merlin, chestnut, black coats of their fiery horses. Teodora, paler than ever, with an air of command mounts her sorrel sprinter, impatient of the bit, in perfect form. Numerous gentlemen riders, all in hunting pink, the fine flower of the Palermo racing-club, close the hunting meet.

—Hallalì, Hallalì, the cry of the kill.

The carousel of fox hunting now turns into an obstacle race. The grooms are holding a plank that divides the arena into two sections.

Male and female riders take a runup and jump the bar, landing on the far side.

It is Teodora's turn. She makes a little sign to the grooms, who raise the bar higher above their shoulders. The beam, forming a single unit with the men, seems a monstrous animal with many feet. The horse takes off, gallops, but near the jump he balks, curvettes, and falls back on his hooves as if fearing the height of the beam. With a violent wrench of the bit, his rider turns him back to the starting point and gives him a shout, digging her spurs into his side. The animal takes off like an arrow. Before the barrier he hesitates for a second, gathers himself, and with a magnificent leap launches himself into space. His bold rider seems to hang suspended in the air as on the back of a winged Pegasus. Then she lands like a feather and returns to the track with the trumphant smile of a Valkyrie.

Delirious applause from the crowd.

Last, lieutenant Spada comes onstage. Acrobatics on horseback. In the costume of a jockey—a doublet of red and yellow stripes, the heraldic colors of Palermo, and a peaked cap of the same colors—he rides bareback astride a dappled roan horse and performs miracles of skill and daring.

He leaps onto the back of the running horse from the center of the ring as if he were climbing a sidewalk. He mounts, turns, from a sitting position he springs upright onto the spine of the animal, he capers, he somersaults, landing facing the tail of the running horse....

The adagio. It is the most dangerous of the excercises. The music falls silent. The public holds its breath. The inspired jockey will leap through a ring of paper, will smash it in one bound, and will land back on the galloping horse without losing the beat.

A moment. The horse shoots off. The jockey is standing on his horse, smiling. The paper disk is shining like the full moon. Into the air. Hop là!

A tear in the paper and a thump. Bravo! *No!* The leap was too short and the rider has fallen sideways, striking the border rail of the arena. Cries of horror from the public. A rush of clowns, grooms, horsemen. The body of the fallen man is carried off the track. Dead? Wounded? Has he fractured his skull? Has he broken a leg? There is blood on the sand. Cries, shrieks, shouts, stampedes.

The director of the circus appears, in tailcoat with his whip still in hand. He advances to the center of the arena, he asks to speak.

—An unfortunate accident—he says—but nothing serious. Ten minutes' intermission. The show continues. Everyone please return to your seats.

Chapter 12

THAT EVENING, to put a damper on the hornets' nest of comments, malicious talk, and gossip that was buzzing around the city in a disturbing crescendo, Teodora had gone to the theater. She urgently needed to show that the misfortune that had happened to lieutenant Spada in the Kramer Circus was, yes, an unpleasant occurrence but without any relation to what had followed it.

Everyone was saying that at the sight of the unfortunate jockey, dragged out of the arena like a dead body, a noblewoman who had taken part in the fox-hunting carousel had given way to an attack of despair and had fainted. To be precise, the noblewoman was the marchesa Teodora. So? Is there something strange if a woman cries out in anguish and faints at the sight of a disaster? So much the more if the woman were exhausted, *surmenagée*, over-excited by 'exhibiting' herself for the first time in a public spectacle, albeit a charity one, and the accident had happened to a friend. Is it forbidden for a fragile creature, made of flesh, to be moved by another's mishap? Is it a crime to feel the misfortune of one's neighbor? Who had not shared the bad luck that had struck the young and generous officer? He enjoyed the sympathies of all the good society of Palermo, and the hospital where he had been taken and the Military Division had been deluged by lady admirers with bouquets of flowers and calling cards bearing good wishes. Fortunately, the fall had had no other consequence than a slight cerebral disturbance, from which the young man was already on the way to recovering. Nothing else. Therefore there was no reason to dramatise. And in order to marginalize the malicious comments that embroidered fantasies of love, of affairs, of immorality, around an unimportant event of everyday life, it was necessary to react with a disciplined attitude of serenity and indifference.

This was Teodora's program, immediately conceived and immediately carried out. And there was nothing to criticise about its wisdom. It was necessary at whatever cost to deflate, to minimise the event at the circus. To dilute its intensity, like soaking a stain in water before removing it.

Now that her friend was safe, it was necessary to save her own reputation as a sinless and irreproachable woman in the eyes of her husband and the world.

Therefore on the very evening of the 'terrible event' she had steeled herslf, she had assumed a mask of impassivity, she had called her hairdresser, busied herself with her toilette, and decided to go to the theater as usual, to ease, she said, her unbearable migraine.

Alone with herself—despite the presence of one of her most faithful women friends—in the shadow of her box, completely unmindful of the performance, she lowers her eyes and mulls over the events of the unforgettable afternoon in the depths of her heart. Disconnected, fragmentary memories. What an effort to put them in order, to link them to each other in their sequence of cause and effect, of 'before' and 'after'! Her memories moved, they stirred themselves, they shouted with the mad tumult of the *charivari* at the beginning of the performance. Horses, wild beasts, clowns, acrobatics, comic antics, wild music, red splotches of tailcoats and a many-colored palette of greatcoats, top hats and felt hats...laughter, whistles, tears, shouts, races, precipices, dizziness, dizziness...And love? Is it possible that the most sublime thing in life should be at the mercy of the most commonplace and insignificant events? Is it indeed true that it is the great loves that die at the impact of little setbacks? Would her own affection also perish so inglorious a death? Certainly it was on the edge of a precipice. And yet it was necesary to revive it at any cost. She rebelled from the idea that her passion could have an end. It could not, it must not. She would prefer to die herself. But what so irreparable had therefore happened that afternoon, to put her love at risk?

The last clear memory that came to her to pin down among the many that ebbed and flowed, dark and unfocused, was her jump at the gate. While she hung high over the fence, like a goddess on a cloud, she had met *his* eyes. He was dressed as a jockey in red and yellow, anonymous, mingling with the other performers near the entrance of the circus. They had smiled at each other. Then the deafening burst of applause, the shouts, the congratulations for her triumph, the calls for a bow, the unforgettable clasp of *his* hand with a murmured 'divina' that still whispered in her ear like a caress.

Happy and overexcited, she had not wanted to be present at *his* 'number.' She did not have the heart to watch *his* acrobatic exercises, which she knew were dangerous. Not that she had evil premonitions, but her nerves were horribly taut and she felt an intense desire to weep. And in order to calm or conceal her agitation she had preferred to remain during his exercise in the green room of the circus to chat with the men and women of the troupe. No, it was not a test of love. But she could not bear it, and he would pardon her. Suddenly, an unexpected pause in the music, a cry of astonishment and horror, everyone rushing into the arena, an unconscious body dragged out by the grooms and clowns...*him.* Here a gap in her mind. No memory. Impenetrable night. When she had re-opened her eyes, there were only a few actors around her, dosing her with smelling salts. *He* had been taken to the hospital. How her heart still pained her! Two wounds, one to her love, the other to her self-respect. And she did not know which was the more cruel. A disaster for her heart as a lover and for her reputation as a respectable woman. Would she not perhaps have been better off dead? What good fortune was it, if her momentary swoon had turned into the annihilation of her existence?

Between one act and the next a crowd of friends and acquaintances rushes into her box to congratulate her, to inquire about her health, to recall her bravura as a horsewoman, to sympathise with poor lieutanant Spada, to suck affections, impressions, secrets, from her eyes and from her heart.

—How tiresome! How disgusting the life of society is!—Teodora says.

Anyway, her self-control could not be more perfect. She thanks, smiles, laughs, chatters, deftly managing the conversation with unexpected transitions and ingenious complications.

—My friends—she answers to someone attempting to torture her by recalling the past day—don't wish to stop time. You will not succeed. It is a wayfarer too much in a hurry. Life resembles a play composed of several acts. When the curtain falls on the second act, we have the right to forget the first. And tomorrow—since midnight has already struck—we don't even remember the play.

When her carriage, on its return from the theater, had arrived under the palace, Teodora noted (unusually) that her husband's bedroom, which faced on via Alloro, was still lighted. Strange. It was already one o'clock. And usually he never went to bed after eleven.

She looked up again as she dismounted the carriage-step, and the light irritated her. She felt horribly tired. Not so much from the emotions of the day as from the continuing effort to overcome them. She had lived hours of maddening tension. The idea of going to the theater had been excellent: above all, to free her from the presence of her husband and mother-in-law at dinner. She gave orders that she be served coffee at table. But she had not drunk it because it would have flayed her already shaken nerves inhumanely. With the excuse of dressing she had risen hurriedly and left.

In the theater it seemed to her that she had acted out the play rather than just listening to it. And what sort of play had it been her luck to hear! Just the thing to console an agitated soul: *La morte civile* of Giacometti, a *mélange* of prison, divorce, and suicide. Athough she had planned to withdraw into the shadows, all the glances, all the opera glasses, hungry for scandals and gossip, were directed toward her box, to peer into her, to question her, to disrobe her. Finally, the visits between the acts as well. And God knows with what laceration of all her womanly feelings and dignity she had accepted their remarks, composing an impassive mask on her face. Now she was returning home with a desperate need for a bit of rest, a bit of oblivion, at last. To be able finally to throw herself on her bed, to think, to weep, to suffer without being seen, without being obliged to pretend and playact. To be able to close her eyes in order to forget, to sleep, to die! Instead, here is that light calling her back to reality. So the tragedy was not yet finished?

Her husband was there. *He existed.* For how long had she deceived herself that he did not exist, for how long had she behaved as if he had never existed. He had allowed her the greatest liberty, which she had used and indeed abused. They lived together under the same roof, but their worlds had lost any point of contact. There was no longer anything in common between them, nothing except their name. Now that yellow light seemed to re-establish all at once the contact which ought to have been considered definitively abolished. No, it was not possible. She would not allow it. And to avoid it she would break that evening the only link, more of propriety than of affection, by which she was bound to her husband. When she came back late from the theater or other evening gatherings, she had the habit of tapping lightly on don Fabrizio's door and announcing her return with a low 'good night.' This evening no. She would go right off to her own room on tiptoe, silent, so as not to be heard...Except that to her great surprise, on reaching her room she discovered her husband waiting for her at the door.

—Good evening—she said, with a shudder of her whole body, while her hands instrictively clutched the collar of her evening wrap to cover her low neckline.

—Good evening, my dear. I would like to allow myself...

—Aren't you well? Why haven't you already gone to bed?

—I am fine. But I would like to allow myself to speak to you. I have something to tell you.

—At this hour? I am so tired. Would it not be better to put off this ... conversation until tomorrow?

—Now—answered don Fabrizio in an exceptionally peremptory tone.

—Where?

—Either your room or mine. It makes no difference.

—I prefer yours. Since I am still dressed—answered Teodora, to whom it was distasteful, almost from a sense of modesty, to admit the marchese into her private quarters in his authority as husband. And she followed him hurriedly.

After her first astonishment, she recovered her sense of dignity.

—Is it something long or short?—she asked, with the expression of an offended goddess.

—It depends on you. Sit down, I beg you—and he held out a chair for his wife.

Don Fabrizio struggled to find speech. There could be read in his contorted face the effort to dominate his resentment and his contempt. Authoritarian, imperious with everyone, by temperament and by the style of his class, but whenever he was in the presence of his wife he always reverted to being the great lord, for whom respect for women is a law of the chivalrous gentleman.

Suffering, in that moment he was afraid to inquire into the nature of his suffering.

Resentment? hatred? offended dignity? desire for revenge? No. Jealousy? Even less. If these emotions had struggled for a moment up from the abysmal depths of his soul into the light of its threshold, from his shadowy subconscious into the clarity of his conscience, he would have rejected them proudly.

Certain of his own infallibility as he had always been, he could not admit that he had been mistaken in his choice of a life companion, although she was younger than he. To those who before his marriage had warned him to beware of missteps, he had replied haughtily, 'I need no advice. I have consulted with God, and that suffices. He cannot have deceived me.'

On the other hand, jealousy appeared to him to be a feeling damaging to married dignity—a form of moral suicide—and to the duty of charity, an essentially anti-Christian feeling. The jealous man lowers himself by admitting even the possibility that another is preferred to him. He believes that he is offended and instead he gives offense, since no one can be offended except by himself. At the same time he lacks charity toward his lady and promotes her depravity. With his suspicion he solidifies in her heart an as yet undefined feeling, which lives in a nebulous state. By the coldness of his heart—since jealousy is an egotistical feeling—the jealous man ends by hardening his own heart to sin and vice. All of which, it must be admitted, is not Christian. The religion of Christ cannot wish the condemnation of a woman out of anger, *ab irato,* of his own woman, but only her amendment through pardon.

And finally, what proofs had he had until now of his wife's fall in the sight of God and man? Nothing more than whispers, murmured remarks, slanders. Nothing except a vague and inprecise 'they say,' except for the vile accusations hurled by those extremely vulgar anonymous letters which he systematically consigned to the wastebasket. The equally anonymous gossip that had reached his ears had suffered the same fate...until the scandal of the Kramer Circus had exploded like a pistol shot the day before. Now the situation was compromised beyond saving. You had to be blind and deaf to ignore it. Far from repeating with the Gospel, *Oportet ut eveniant scandala*—It is necessary that scandals come—Don Fabrizio would have wanted certain facts never to become food for the unhealthy curiosity of the public. But when had the scandal occurred?

The fall and the wounding of lieutenant Spada, the scene of the despair of the horsewoman—identified by her full name—and her collapse, with all the embellishment of spiteful remarks that sprouted up around the event like a poisonous mould, made the rounds of the city, it mounted up, swelled, foamed in an impressive manner. Therefore it was necessary to intervene. One could put up with sin, but scandal had to be smothered to avoid worse evils. When to intervene, if not immediately? The dilemma was choking him: now, or never.

So he had decided to confront his wife face to face for the first time.

—I will remain standing—she said, refusing the chair. —That's how a prisoner stands awaiting his sentence.

—No sentence—he said politely and sweetly.—I am not here to condemn. One human being is not allowed to judge another human being.

—And so?

—It is only an advice, a request.

—If it is only for that, I don't see why this...torture can't be put off until tomorrow. I am so tired.

—Today or tomorrow is the same. Unfortunately, the fact itself cannot be undone. At least believe that I would like to do without it.

—It would be the best thing—said she, evasively, almost distantly.

—I cannot. At the point that things have reached, it is a duty of conscience. Do you have a conscience?

—Who does not?

—Then question your conscience, in the sight of God. What does it tell you?

—Nothing.

—Nothing?—marvelled the marchese.—And what happened yesterday?

—Well, what happened?

—You are asking me?

—Are you referring to what happened at the Circus? Nothing but a painful accident, painful for everyone, I suppose.

—Not in the same way... for everyone.

—Not everyone has the same sensitivity. Each one reacts in his own way.

—But your reaction, as you call it, goes beyond the ordinary. You must admit that it was very strange.

—Because I fainted? I don't believe that one should be put on trial for a sudden collapse. One has the right to suffer, to lose consciousness and... even to die.

—It is not a question of rights, my dear, but of duties. One has duties to God and duties to men. Finally...it is not your fainting that matters.

—So, for you suffering does not count. Pain and sorrow do not count.

—What matters—continued don Fabrizio coldly—is not the fact, but what lies behind it, what had caused it. It is necessary to establish where chance ends and sin begins.

—Are you perhaps my confessor? I was not aware that I had two confessors.

—God forbid!—esclaimed don Fabrizio bitterly. —It is not up to me to judge sinners, only to God. I judge outward behavior, as does the world.

—You said 'the world'!—she laughed sarcastically. —I scorn the world, since my conscience is at peace.

—There are duties toward people as well as duties toward God. So much the more if those people constitute our family.

—Do I have a family? Do we have children?

—What difference does that make? Does marriage cease to be a sacrament only because it is not blessed with children? Who says that a childless spouse can trample with impunity on a union made in the sight of God? If anything, the absence of children increases the responsibilities which we have toward a creature entrusted to our affections. If God has willed that no children be born of our union...

—Certainly the blame is not mine.

—That does not alter the fact—continued the marchese, without reacting to her provocation—that a wife must conform herself as prescribed by the duties of her married status and her social rank. You, instead, have failed in your respect toward yourself, you have brought ridicule on this family whose name you bear, you have thrown a shadow on me...in one of the most delicate moments of my life, when I am engaged in a relentless politcal struggle.

—I've got you where I wanted you—Teodora exploded, mocking and victorious, like a wrestler who discovers the weak point of his opponent and pins him to the mat in a flash—now I undertand. It is a question of your good name, your personal prestige as the head of a party, as a demagogue. A 'political' jealousy in short. My happiness, my respectability, my honor are nothing finally but the stakes in a game of vulgar ambitions.

—Let's not change the cards on the table—argued don Fabrizio, not without hesitating like the wrestler who is about to be overcome by a stronger enemy—let's not wander from the point. Answer me: is it true or is it not true that the whole world is talking about a 'relationship' between you and lieutanant Spada?

—Relationship!—exclaimned Teodora scornfully—Nothing but a good friendship.

—Friendship! I do not believe in friendships between a man and a woman. Between two persons of opposite sexes, what is called friendship is either nothing or it is love. When a married woman is seen with a man who is not her husband, here, there, and everywhere, when she encounters him in drawing rooms, in clubs, in the streets, and even in the public gardens, when they exchange secret notes, when she makes operatic scenes because *he* has fallen from his horse...honest people have every right to suspect that the two are lovers.

—I rejoice with the marchese Cortada, *Chevalier sans peur et sans reproche,* Fearless and blameless knight! A cleverly organized spy system, with investigations, interrogations, shadowers...Perfect Bourbon style. The tactics of a Salvatore Maniscalco. Your painted ancestors can glory in such a descendant.

—I have never stooped to such low conduct—the marchese protested indignantly—no matter how much I recognize that a husband may have the right to it. I swear to you that I have never used such means. But if the law gives me rights, you may be sure that I intend to avail myself of them.

—What rights, for example?

—The right to demand that you not destroy yourself, that you no longer see that man either here or elsewhere.

—You are perfectly correct. The house is yours, it is your kingdom. The street belongs to everyone and is mine too, you will agree. Unless you wish to put me under lock and key...

—I do not want slavery, but neither do I want anarchy. Every freedom of yours will be supervised from now on. I did not want to reach this point, but your behavior forces me to it.

—Freedom of what? to move? to go out? to breathe? to think? You can imprison the body, not the soul. I defend my soul. It is mine. I am free to give it to whom I wish.

—To whom? Tell me, then.

—To the one I love. To the one who loves me. You wanted to know my truth. Here it is. And now make of me what you wish. Up until now who has loved me? Who has even been aware that I had a soul, a heart. *You*? No one, no one.

And she burst into heavy weeping, the heartfelt lament of a creature who has never once seen the face of happiness.

Chapter 13

AN UNKNOWN man, who announced himself with a great tug at the entrance bell, asked to speak to the marchesa *grande*. To her in person? Yes, face to face. Marco scanned the man from head to foot, surprised that the concierge had let him pass. You never know. When times are murky, certain types whom it is well to keep an eye on are in circulation. He was a moth-eaten little man, with a brick-colored face and the mask of Cyclops—by reason of one missing eye—badly dressed, with a crumpled hat in his hands and dreadful shoes resembling open-mouthed crocodiles. From the man's expression, halfway between the beggar and the criminal, the majordomo would without doubt have shown him the door if the man had not insisted that he was the bearer of a personal message from signorino Goffredo.

When he was admitted to the presence of donna Ortensia, the unknown rummaged around in the messy inside pocket of his *bonaca* and pulled out a large sheet folded in two and tied with a string, which smelt of tobacco and grease. When asked who he was and whence he came, he winked his one eye and gurgled with a distant voice, like a ventriloquist.

—From the *collegio.* Where we were there together, companions in misfortune.

—What do you mean?—asked the old lady, who was dying of impatience.

—From jail... Your Excellency understands me.

—From jail?—trembled donna Ortensia.

—*Non si scantassi,* Don't be shocked. Jail doesn't consume good people. I'm coming out after seven years, and by the grace of God and the Most

Holy *Bedda matri* I'm better than before. Death is the only thing there is no remedy for. What do they have to do with signorino Goffredo, who is as innocent as water? Whoever was with Garibaldi is a man of honor. He deserves great repect. One should only be ashamed of having been thieves. But honor is honor.

—And you?

—I understand what the signora marchesa means. What was my crime? *Singalai* a '*mala carne*,' I offed a bastard who was bothering my fiancée. So that when she looks in the mirror she remembers the undersigned. *Cose da piciotti,* kid stuff.

—And now?

—I'm going back to my home town and I hope to work. With the help of God and my friends. I'm going to Montelepre. If Your Excellency has any orders...I'm Turi Pitarresi, called *u pappagaddu,* the parrot. *Baciamo le mani.*

The man stretched out from his shabby sleeve a large hand (on whose wrist was tattooed in blue a heart pierced by an arrow) to grasp the marchesa's gift and hurried out the door, pleased as punch.

Donna Ortensia, after the first shock to her heart, had recovered herself. Goffredo was safe and healthy, even if in prison. In the end, there was a grain of sense in the the jailbird's remarks. Freedom is a great good, but life is an even more precious one. And if Goffredo was alive, then for her also life became worth living. To live until she could embrace her nephew again! This was her dream, nor did she desire anything more. When God had given her the blessing of placing her lips on the blond hair of the young man who was her pride, blood of her blood, she could call herself happy. What other happiness could she ask of the world?

She withdrew into her bedroom. Clutching the paper package as if it were a treasure, she sank into her armchair, she slowly unwrapped the covering (it was a little bundle of papers of various sizes spotted with dirty water) as if to prolong her pleasure, and read the letter, which served as a covering sheet to several pages of a diary.

"*My dearest grandmother,*

I am writing you, as you see, from jail. It would be something to lament if what my 'friends' here say were not true: everyone of us has his share of the jail and of the hospital. Take heart then, and smile as I do, in the hope that my words can reach you soon. I do not hide from you, however, that I would prefer to be in hospital, wounded like Garibaldi, rather than rotting in a prison, associated with common criminals. We members of the legion ought to be classified and treated as prisoners of war. But the government, in order to humiliate us, to give us, as they say, a lesson, has thrown us in here along with thieves, robbers, and common murderers: in short, among the damned. Believe me, nothing is more degrading than fighting bedbugs and lice in the unhealthy darkness of a prison cell, instead of exchanging gunshots with the papal troops and their worthy supporters the French. Unfortunately, the bedbugs, the lice, and the worms are not only present here inside. They are marching over the body of the Fatherland and are leaving their slimy traces. The Italians are despicable. They look happy when they are struck, they wag their tails between the legs of the foreigners, and when they arre kicked again they answer, Thank you. Believe me, grandmother, we ourselves are our own worst enemies. Aspromonte may have been a mistake, but it remains in history as a proud and generous gesture amid the general cowardice. They call us rebels, ambitious men. The newspapers, the false politicians, the judges, the jailors, spit in our faces. They use against us, volunteers for an ideal, rigors without name, they treat us as criminals, they scream in our faces that all Italy is against us. History will say that the real Italy was on our side on the unhappy day of 29 August 1862. The truth about this episode will be known better from the living voices of those who took part than from the lies of the treasonous newspapers, and you will have an idea of it from these notes that I am sending you. Brief notes written between one march and the next, in the halts at the bivouacs, under a tent or even *à la belle étoile*, and finished in jail. After you have read them, I want you to keep them with the sacred relics of my father. Those who come after us must know how Aspromonte could have been a new Calatafimi—a sad victory of Italians against other Italians, but a victory nonetheless—if Garibaldi, in his great humanity, had not forbidden us to use arms.

Now we are all lumped together like common criminals. You shall know this shameful story as well. Since Aspromonte is in Calabria, we must be tried in the Court of Assizes of Catanzaro. Unless—unheard of, say the lawyers—the Court of Cassation of Naples raises the precondition of legitimate suspicion and turns to the Cassation of Turin to appoint another judge. Southern Italy is suspected of Garibaldinism (don't forget that the expedition of Aspromonte was organized in Sicily) and they are re-assigning us to the north so that we do not escape our well-merited (!) punishment. Crispi has protested against this obvious illegality and is busy putting together a defence team to demand the observance of the law. What will happen? Whatever happens, I await without fear. You too must take courage and wait in faith. Justice will finally triumph. And may it be God's will that the Italians, laying down their hatreds, will remember for once that they are brothers. I send you the present letter by a jail comrade who is returning today to Sicily having served his criminal sentence. Big kisses and a thousand tender thoughts from your

GOFFREDO."

Goffredo's diary sleeps in his grandmother's coffer, a Moorish chest with an arched cover shaped like a horseshoe, made of sandal wood encrusted with mother of pearl and decorated with figures of animals in complicated arabesques and verses from the Qu'ran.

The diary's rest is not tranquil. Every evening before going to bed the old woman takes out the creased manuscript and reads a few pages of it, marking with notes and signs the sentences that especially hold her attention. While reading it, she seems to be talking with her nephew, of whom there arrives only rare and laconic news. The prisoners are kept rigorously segregated and their mail is minutely scrutinised by the censorship. It is a great favor if the censors pass a letter which has some sketchy news about health and some banal messages. Unfortunately, all the newspapers are against the expedition, and they agree in calling for severe measures against Garibaldi and his followers. They are all 'disturbers' of the public peace and must be exiled for life. So it is, and perhaps so it must be, Ortensia thinks. For the mediocrities, every generous person is a 'disturber,' an infected branch that must be cut off from the great tree of society.

She has read the faded pages of the diary several times, and now she pauses on the observations of the last days of the drama.

28 August.

Here we are on the Aspromonte massif. We have the royal troops at our heels. We must scale the Calabrian Apennines as soon as possible and reach the heights by the most impassable routes, in order to put ourselves in condition to face an attack. We can no longer count on the coastal roads: they are swarming with enemy troops (what sorrow to call the sons of the same earth our enemies!).

A terribly tiring march, especially for those unaccustomed to Alpine climbing.

Aspromonte: rocky, dull grey, ferrous mountain: harsh with ravines and cliffs, slashed by crevices and ditches: bald and barren, without a blade of grass, without a drop of water. We can no longer feel our legs, our joints are stiff, and our empty stomachs stick to our backbones. Again today a handful of raw potatoes for rations. We lack wood for cooking, and anyway there is a strict order not to light fires so as not to reveal our presence to the troops that are hunting us and spying on our every move. The few shepherds who are wandering on the heights with their sheep, dressed in rags and shod with rope, gaze at us with eyes between fascinated and distrustful. They find every excuse to refuse us not just a lamb but even a basket of ricotta. They seem to consider the Garibaldini as robbers. What a difference from the enthusiasm with which we were welcomed in Sicily, from the nobleman down to the last peasant!

We walk, or rather we climb like goats, breathless and footsore. No path, no lane, no mule-tracks: rocks, rocks...

29 August

Reveille before dawn. We have spent the night without shelter, on the bare earth. From yesterday evening, when we reached this plateau, we haven't eaten enything but a few biscuits. We are awaiting the return of the scouts who went in search of food. Since it is forbidden to light fires, we warm ourselves by stretching, rubbing our arms and legs by turns. The night is cold on these camel humps. The dawn is full of shivers. The sky is low, and thick clouds are crushing themselves against the peaks of the mountain ranges. The whole camp is in a turmoil. There is one password: It is the odor of gunpowder.

A modest distribution of food and cartridges is made. The captains pass us in review. We are not more than fifteen hundred. The rest of the column is disbanded or was lost during the ascent. They arrive in groups or drift in, some in a pitiful state, to join the main body. A new order of march. We must reach the ridge of the mountain. Once across its saddle, whose name I do not remember, we must launch ourselves out toward the coast and aim for Catanzaro, following the eastern watershed of the Sile river.

—This is the *Anabasis* of Xenophon—comments a volunteer, a professor of Greek—it's the retreat of the Ten Thousand.

But everybody knows that it is a provisional withdrawl arranged by the General, to avoid an encounter with the royal troops at any cost. He has an horror of fratricidal combat.

Unexpeectedly the 'Halt' sounds. Whatever it is or is not, it seems that the royal troops, following our tracks, have succeeded by an unknown shortcut in gaining positions which threaten us directly in front and on our flank.

We are in the shelter of a thick pine forest, which lends itself excellently to defense. Here every tree trunk can become a fortalice, every boulder a trench. Battle order. My battalion, under the command of Corrao, forms the right wing. Menotti and Bedeschini hold the center; two companies are disposed on the left under the command of a major to oppose any attempt to outflank our positions. The fog which is rising from the valley appears created precisely to hide the movements of our enemies. Anxiety grips us by the throat. Are they advancing? What do you see? Is it a false alarm?

Bit by bit the fog dissolves, the mist thins. On the most distant hills the shadows of the clouds are racing, chased before the rapidly rising sun. There, there! Look way down there. At the feet of the opposite heights—not more than three miles, as the crow flies, from our position—you can see a movement of troops, which are drawing up in two columns. The vapors, which thin and then thicken again by turns, do not allow any more to be seen. But not a half hour has passed when our reconnaissance battalions bring news of the royal forces advancing in our direction in a fan-shaped formation.

The dance has started. The fatigue, the hunger, the adventures of the terrible march are forgotten. Only a single will rules: To fight.

Crisp orders from the leaders. We load the rifles. Synchronized clicks of the rods pushing the cartridges into the barrels, snap of hammers being cocked, metallic jingle of bayonets, thuds of bodies that kneel or stretch out on the ground in firing position.

The first enemy battalions advance at quick march through the underlying terrain. We recognize the Bersaglieri from the waving of the cock feathers on their hats.

Voices of volunteers.

—See that officer, showing off waving his saber? As soon as he's in range, I'll lay him out on the ground for you. The first ones to arrive will drop like hares. Aim well, so that no bullet misses its mark.

Voices inside me.

—What wrong have they done to you, these poor people whom you are about to shoot with your rifle like wild beasts? They are men like you, in the prime of life, who have a mother, a wife, maybe children fearful for them. They are your brothers who speak your own language, they have grown out of your same earth…An inflexible law impels them against us unknowing sowers of death: a law forces us to use arms against them. We will kill each other, perhaps without hatred, but we will kill each other. What a horrible thing war is!

—Silence!—what is the lieutenant, who is hurrying across our front line, saying?

—Dammit, let us hear him. Look, he is talking and waving his hands!

—He says: By order of the General, no one is to fire.

—Exactly. Do not shoot. In desperate situations use your bayonets.

—This is new. Are we soldiers or extras at the opera?

—So we are to let ourselves be slaughtered like beasts for the knackers?

—An order is not to be questioned.

—And I am questioning it. At the first shot I will answer 'per le rime,' in kind.

—I see you are a poet.

—Gentlemen, naturally it is forbidden to fire with bullets. But not with buttons. I'm ripping the buttons off my tunic and loading my rifle with them.

—Get down, for God's sake. This is serious business.

A hail of bullets whistles over our heads. The projectiles hiss and bury themselves in the tree trunks with dry thuds, or they knock a hail of leaves from the branches. A legionnaire folds up on himself and collapses on the ground, calling for help.

Ever more numerous, the Bersaglieri advance in waves. They run, they stop, they fire on foot or kneeling, they rise and continue to advance. We are about to be surrounded.

The men swear, they blaspheme, no one can restrain them any longer. A hearty discharge goes off from my platoon, as if the guns were firing by themselves. We are wrapped in a fog of black smoke.

The couriers run about out of breath. Officers plummet down among our ranks shouting, pushing down our gun barrels, which are about to be reloaded. Shouts, protests, curses. A trumpet signals: Cease fire.

Immediately a freezing silence. The rumor spreads: the General is wounded, the General is dying.

Where? How? It's not true. Yes, it is true. What is happening? Retreat? Surrender? No, a thousand times no. Better to die on the spot. Load your bayonets! Some ask questions, some shake like animals, some run with the others toward a rise of ground crowded with officers. I run too. Anyway, we are already trapped. The Bersaglieri surround us on every side. Among the officers I recognize Enrico Cairoli, Giocanni Civinin, Tullio Malato, Ruggiero Maurigi. Yes, the wounded General is lying under that tree. He is attended by Dr. Albanese, with the surgeons Ripari and Bauli.

While I am about to reach the group under the pine tree I am grabbed by two strong hands and sent toward a clearing where the prisoners are being collected. I too am a prisoner of war: nothing but a number, kept under guard, waiting to be transferred elsewhere. Isolated as I am, I know nothing more of our General. Incomplete and contradictory reports are gathered from the prisoners, rounded up bit by bit, who reach our holding pen. They report that colonel Pallavicini, summoned by the wounded Garibaldi himself, has already presented himself hat in hand and has expressed his regret, saying, "I have fulfilled a painful duty." Garibaldi only requested to be embarked on a British ship for England.

At sunset the rumor spreads through the camp. They are moving the General.

From a distance (since the sentinels do not allow us to leave the enclosure) we glimpse a sad procession emerging from the pine grove. Amid the forest of royal bayonets that flank it we see a stretcher made of tree branches carried on the shoulders of eight Garibaldian officers.

It is all that remains of our expedition.

The legionnaires remove their hats, someone weeps. I too swallow my tears.'

That evening after her customary conversation with the absent one, after closing the manuscript in its box donna Ortensia was preparing to go to bed. Before laying herself down to sleep she was accustomed to check her bedchamber to assure herself that nothing was out of place. She wound the clocks, put the scattered books back in the bookcase, straightened the misplaced table ornaments, replaced her worktable in its corner. 'If death arrives suddenly, like a thief in the night—she said—one must give him the sense of perfect order and not create obstacles, so he can work in silence...It's the best way, not to be aware of it. To die without being aware of death is the greatest gift that the gods can bestow on us.'

Now, in front of her mirror, she is about to change her black cap for her white nightcap.

An unexpectedly vigorous knock on the door.

It's Marco. The majordomo is so distraught that if his eyes were not shining with joy one would think him the bearer of bad news.

—Marchesa—he says, choking on his words,—something great, incredible...

—Speak up, I say, don't make me feel ill.

—He's there, it's signorino Goffredo who...

His sentence is not yet finished when there bursts into the room a badly-dressed young man, with a worn-out and tattered jacket and a thick untended beard like a Capuchin novice.

The old lady can hardly recognize him, but she doesn't have time to look at him before she disappears into the arms of her nephew.

—My child!

—Are you happy, grandma?

—Did you expect me?

—Never and never. If an angel had come to tell me I would have sent him to the devil.

—And yet I'm here, in flesh and blood.

—Tell me, my child, how did you do it? Are you free?

—Hush, grandma! If you only knew. I am (and he put his mouth up to her ear) a fugitive.

—A fugitive from jail?

—And from where else? You know I wasn't in a monastery.

—Mercy! And how did you do it?

—A professional secret. We'll talk about it later. After many months the life of a prisoner becomes a profession, whose secrets one learns.

—You have been very bold.

—I once saw written in one of your books: *De l'audace, encore de l'audace, toujours de l'audace.*

—It's an old phrase of Marat's. But you are not a Marat, my boy.

—Who am I, then?

—To look at you, you could be mistaken for the Prodigal Son. My God, what a state you're in!

—Was the prodigal son this happy when he returned to his home?

—Happy, yes. Except that you, unfortunately, are not returning to *your* home—the old lady sighed, stressing the 'your'—Don't expect them to give you purple garments, to put a ring on your finger, and kill the fatted calf for you to make merry. Here you are in the house of my son the marchese, who regards you like a thorn in his eye.

—I know it well.

—And you will also know that not only in this palace, but in town, in Italy...no good wind is blowing for you legionnaires. Whoever has fought for the honor of his country is now a reprobate, a criminal. Valiant men have always worried the despicable. And unfortunately the despicable are in the majority. I didn't believe there were so many of them. It's enough to read the newspapers...

—I haven't read a page for months.

—Well, I will tell you that not only the government, but a great part of the public opinion...up there, on the continent, is enraged against Garibaldi and his followers. I am not surprised. The Italians are fickle, like the French, and worse. They pass from enthusiasm straight to hatred. Today they set an idol upon an altar, tomorrow they smash it and drag it into the mud. Garibaldi, the hero of the two worlds, the liberator of his country from tyranny, has become a scoundrel and a fraud. Some want his death, some want him imprisoned for life as a criminal. Yes, whoever dares, whoever has a sense of the honor and the dignity of a people, whoever does not let the foreigner spit in his face, today is a criminal. The 'men of valor' are all on the other side. And along with Garibaldi, all those who had faith in him are guilty, because his original idea of marching on Rome began in Sicily, because the cursed expedition was organized here amid the enthusiasm of the people. In short, Sicily is responsible for Aspromonte. As if Piedmontese, Romans, Ligurians, Venetans, Emilians, and such generous youth from every part of Italy were not marching in your ranks! But our little Savoyard Napoleon hurls his thunders like an angry Jove and must be appeased. We must turn the right cheek after being slapped on the left one. To satisfy the mob a state of siege has been proclaimed, thousands of citizens have been thrown in jail, extraordinary tribunals have been set up. Beaters are combing the towns and the countryside, they are searching the houses of peaceful citizens, they reward informers...and heaven help you if they find a red shirt, if they catch you singing or even whistling the anthem of Garibaldi!

While his grandmother pictured the situation in her caustic and imaginative style, Goffredo stood and listened to her with his great eyes calm, stroking his beard. He was neither surprised nor dismayed. It seemed as if all those sorrows and those nasty tricks did not concern him.

—Courage, grandmother—he smiled when she had finished—the Idea cannot die.

—As much courage as you wish, my boy. But you won't, you mustn't stay here. Do you understand? Courage, yes, but not foolishness. And until this storm blows over you will stay quietly in the country with your uncle Federico.

Tomorrow at dawn the cart will be ready and you will set out. Do we understand each other?

PART II

Chapter 1

By a public testament of 1 November 1810 marchese Alfonso Cortada named his firstborn son don Fabrizio as heir of his entire fortune according to the feudal laws of primogeniture, intended to maintain the 'generous pride of noble lineage.'

As universal heir, Fabrizio's share was the fortune and the titles of nobility. His other brothers had to content themselves with the bare legal minimum of inheritance and the modest title of 'cavaliere,' according to Sicilian noble custom.

The portion that devolved upon the second son consisted of the former fief *Tre Pernici*, Three Partridges. Don Federico had never bothered with his property, following the custom of the Sicilian aristocracy, who for nearly a half century had divorced themselves from their fields to embrace the ease and splendors of the cities. It was a condescension if Federico absent-mindedly received once a year the *gabelloti* to whom his *latifondi* were parcelled out, for their accounting in the presence of his administrator.

Here we insert a parenthesis necessary for anyone who is not familiar with the rural economy of Sicily. This rests on the distinctive word-pair, *latifondo* and *gabelloto*: two institutions, one tied to the South, the other to the sunset of the feudal regime.

We do not wish to recount here the history of the latifondo (which is not to be confused with fallow land, since among the latifondi of Europe none is more cultivated than that of Sicily). We will only say that, as the result of royal donations, individual acquisitions, exchanges, usurpations and so forth, and by escaping the compulsory breaking up to which the latifondo was subjected among the teeming small fiefs in the area of Naples, it ended by being almost totally concentrated in the hands of the baronial class, except for church property. It is calculated that up to the middle of the eighteenth century two thirds of the land of the island was enfeoffed to the nobility. It was not by chance that the viceroy Caracciolo reported to his sovereign that barely seventy-five families could consider themselves owners of the greatest part of the landed property of the Regno. Was it a good thing? was it an evil? There is no doubt that the original concentration of landed property in a few hands is one of the outstanding causes of the decline in the Sicilian economy. But we would be less than just to our duty of historical impartiality if we were to deny all merit to the original feudal regime.

With the resurgence of new spirits in the mid-fifteenth century the conflicts of the dark and disorderly medieval society had been pacified, anarchy had been reduced to order, the shock of hammering passions tamed, customs made polite once again, and the general clash of arms muted. The barons lay down their warlike finery and weapons and retired to their castles, which were rendered festive by celebrations and knightly courtesy, to attend to the arts of peace in a more humane manner. Bursting with initiatives, they drained swamps, dammed streams, channeled springs of fresh water, opened roads and trails through forests and up harsh and rocky slopes. They granted civic privileges, they promoted useful cultures, they encouraged the peasants to move to the latifondo in houses which, grouped together, formed the first inhabited centers. It was a competition of good works, an outburst of rural enthusiasm, that signalled a new pact between man and the earth. Never had the Regno of Naples, which for two centuries had been the theater of bloody turbulence, breathed a climate of greater well-being than when the barons, reconciled with the soil, realized that all their power and glory proceeded only from there.

This happy season lasted until the second half of the eighteenth century. At that moment there occurred an unusual phenomenon: the exodus of the nobility from the countryside to the city, their separation from the ancient mother who had nourished the feudal regime with her vital fluids. Bored by their long solitude, tired of contending with rough and ignorant peasants, tempted by the leisure of the city mingled with sin and vice, puffed up by the splendor of their ancestry, the nobility swarmed from their manors toward the capital, which promised them savory enjoyments, committing their goods, and with them their power, to the *gabelloti*.

Anyone who does not know the figure of the *gabelloto* in its proper frame cannot form even an approximate idea of the Sicilian economy.

From the legal point of view the gabelloto is nothing more than a renter: one who obtains for a rent, or *gabella*, another's property by paying an annual fee. In reality it is a social institution with political overtones, the symbol of a form of twilight economy tied to the ruin of the nobility, the elevation of a new class destined to become the masters of the entire rural life. The gabelloto was often the chamberlain of a noble property, a small landholder, or even a jumped-up peasant. Before becoming a gabelloto, he had assembled a small fortune by serving as a middleman in the sale of sheep or grain, or he had scrimped like a miser and enriched himself by dint of sponging and deceit, of arrogance and villanies, in collusion with the worst criminality, until he succeeded in leasing a bit of land where he became little by little the *alter ego* of the owner. Not possessing notable capital, he has no other program than to milk his property to an unrealistic extent. He knows no other form of agriculture than constant expansion. By incessantly alternating the planting of cereals with pasturage, he impoverishes the soil with ill-judged replantings, he neglects every effort of land drainage, he deforests wooded areas without pity, he breaks down stream banks, with his continuous encroachment on the government trails he ruins the road system instead of improving it.

Often, impelled by excessive greed, tired of overseeing directly the cultivation of the estate, he sublets it for heavy and usurious rents to farmers burdened with loans, forced labor, and the *angaries* and *perangraries* formerly levied by the barons on their fiefs. The settler binds himself to sow, harvest, and thresh at his own expense; to pay for the use of the millstone, the mill, the slaughterhouse, and even the owner's oven, which he is obliged to employ. He is bound to pay the so-called 'carnaggi,' payments in kind (wheat, fruit, wine, oil, forage, lambs, chickens) and sometimes to serve without pay for a certain number of working days, the *corvée*. If he becomes a defaulter or insolvent he can be subjeted to the coercive methods formerly employed by the so-called *mano feudale* against recalcitrant vassals. The least that can happen to him is to see his foodstuffs impounded and carried away, the door of his house sealed or broken, or even to be thrown, with the connivance of a corruptible judge, into a *dammusu,* a prison. Many farmers, tired of so many vexations which make them regret the darkest days of feudalism, renounce the agrarian contract and prefer to work as simple farm hands or *jurnatari,* day laborers, lowering themselves to the status of peasants. The peasants, in their turn, being constrained to sell their labor for a pitiful wage, lead a more than wretched life, inhuman and indeed bestial. They are ill-nourished, worse clothed, housed in filthy hovels, when poverty and unemployment do not drive them into the cities to stretch out their hands as beggars.

Such was the state of the Sicilian countryside which lasted from the mid-seventeenth century until the period of this story, despite the laws passed in 1812 abolishing feudalism. Which state can be summed up thus: On one side the baron living in the capital, a kind of unknown god, whom the peasant respects and barely knows, a sovereign who reigns and does not rule, satisfied to receive from afar the not abundant income from his estates and reluctant to divide and break them up, respecting the old proverb 'chi vende scende,' 'the seller loses caste.' On the other side the gabelloto, the exponent of an agrarian middle class, which having enriched itself unscrupulously at the expense of the owners, having become ambitious and arrogant, acquires lands and palaces, dreams of a lavish life, goes chasing after titles of nobility, and dreams of marriages—not always illusory—with the impoverished nobility.

As a good aristocrat, until the age of thirty five Federico knew nothing of his possessions except what the 'mastro razionale,' his bursar, reported to him in an annual account of profits and losses. Since after his earliest years Federico had not set foot again on his property, he might not even have been able to describe its boundaries. Only 'nel mezzo del cammin,' 'half along life's way' had he become aware that he was a landed proprietor, and that there exists a problem with property that opposes economic interests to the demands of justice. He had made this problem the essential purpose of his life, but his evolution had been slow and tiring.

His external history, let's call it that, was that of a failed priest. Only two roads were open to the younger sons of ancient Sicilian families, both tied to feudal law: the profession of arms or the Church. Federico certainly was not cut out for the military. The division between the active and the contemplative life is not an invention of theologians and philosophers, it is rooted in reality. There are men born to act, others are cut out in physique and discipline for meditation and prayer. It is useless to debate here whether it is better to act or to think, whether the part of Martha or that of Mary merits greater praise. In life, none of us can choose our role as in the theater, and play it according to our own talents. If Federico had chosen the way of religion, so it must be.

As a boy he had frequented the Oratorio of San Filipppo Neri, which was attached to the church of the Olivella, and he had become known for his rare piety accompanied by an exemplary mildness. He divided his days between the Oratorio and the villa Filippina, where the boys were trained to serve the Lord with gladness according to the educational system of the Florentine saint of joyful faith and devout cheerfulness.

At age fifteen Federico had entered the novitiate of the Oratorians, to the great satisfaction of his father, with patience not unmixed with scepticism of his mother, donna Ortensia, who was moved by her invincible *esprit fort* to anything but benevolent feelings toward the religious life. But the custom of the times and her spirit of tolerance did not allow her to obstruct her son's vocation. Going areound the family portrait gallery, she thought, After all, who knows if our collection will not be enriched one day by the image of another Malebranche or Massillon, some great priest who will do honor to the house of the Cortada, which is now falling into decline.

The Fathers were enthusiastic about their novice. He lacked nothing: sweetness of character, submissiveness, intelligence, religious feeling. He would have approached perfection if only he had been less imaginative. Imagination is certainly no sin, but it somewhat resembles a rust which imperceptibly erodes piety. Imagination is a sweet somnolence of the soul effused in contemplation, a resigned abandonment to the mystery which surrounds us, whose key remains locked in the hands of God. Imagination generates curiosity, curiosity ferments in disquiet, disquiet often corrupts faith if it is not the right disquiet which reposes in God, of which St. Augustine speaks: *Inquietum est cor meum donec requiescat in te,* My heart is restless until it rests in Thee. But the disquiet that is never eased, which feeds on its own torment, which beats like an insect against the opaque glass of the inscrutable in its frenzy to escape, can kill the Christian soul. The emotional excess of contemplation is as dangerous as the intoxication of action. For that reason San Filippo Neri—expert in the damage done to the Faith by the excessive rationalizing of the Reformation—advises controlling the excesses of the imagination and the diabolical train of its particular temptations by means of physical exercise and games which create a healthy well-being. Even a few Oratorians had allowed themselves to be drawn into the turbulent maelstrom of Jansenism, that dark disguise of the Protestant idea, by the disorder of their contemplative imagination.

A treasure, that Federico, but one to keep an eye on. He does nothing but dream of plans to reform mankind, society, the State, even the Church and the religious life. A little head that finds errors to reform everywhere, wrong ideas to straighten out, injustices to redress, intolerant of tradition and history: a brain too fertile in ideas and too thirsty for novelties for his young age. Of course, everything is to the greater glory of God. But...

The good fathers of the Oratorio were not deceived. And they were not greatly surprised when the novice Federico, on the death of his father, left the Congregation and returned to the world. It was easy to foresee that his mysticism, misled by worldy daydreams, would turn aside into another path sooner or later. Mysticism is a Proteus that clothes itself in the most various forms. It inhabits the stratosphere of the spirit, but is equally germinated from the worship of material things, the same way that coarse fumes are generated from heaps of manure. Alongside the mystics of the soul there are the mystics of the muscles, of the stomach, and of even less literary body parts. Federico's mysticism had not evaporated, it had only changed direction. He no longer had heavenly blessdness as his goal, but rather the earthly happiness of mankind. Tired of aiming at spiritual salvation, Federico now desired nothing but the material well-being of the human family, and he decreed that such well-being demanded an equal share for everyone. All men, equal in the face of nature, have an equal right to the goods of the earth. If these are distributed unequally it is a sign that we are living in an unjust society which must be led back under the emblems of justice, even by force.

This metamorphosis astonished everyone except donna Ortensia.

—Even this son who seemed so different from me—she noted, not without a bit of satisfaction—has at bottom something of his mother, *l'esprit frondeur,* the spirit of rebellion...

And turning the page with a friendly uninterest on the names of Massilon and Melebranche, servants of God, she was pleased to remember that the Oratorio had also always been a nest of rebellion. From there had come, in the seventeenth century, the first of the libertines and free thinkers, Richard Simon, and a century later the most unscrupulous of political chameleons, Joseph Fouché.

Which does not alter the fact that other times she regarded her second son with a feeling of compassion and sighed, bowing her old head:

—You've picked a fine cat to skin, my boy! Don't you know that all the benefactors of humanity, from Christ on down, have ended badly?

In the meantime, aroused from his sleepy meditation on books of theology and asceticsm, Federico threw hmself into reading the great social reformers. The names of the celebrated Oratorians whom he had endeavored to imitate—Cardinal Baronio, the blessed Sebastian Valfré, Melebranche, Masillon, father Cesari—vanished bit by bit from his memory, replaced by Rousseau, Saint-Simon, Fourier, Proudhon, Owen, Carlyle. His reading of Rousseau's *Discours sur l'origine et les fondements de l'inégalité parmi les hommes* (*Discourse on the origin of inequality,* the first book that he happened to find in his grandmother's library) raised a storm in his sprit. The famous prophecy of the man of Geneva, 'When the people have nothing more to eat, they will eat the rich,' rang in his soul like a summons to battle. He must use this as a lever to transform the world: this was now his task. Quite different from mumbling psalms and ejaculatory prayers in the gloom of choirs and in his lonely monastic cell. He read. He read, and he grieved that the Italians, with the exception of Campanella, had lagged so far behind the foreigners in preaching the crusade for the conquest of a realm of justice open to all.

When he recognized a socialist *avant la lettre* in the great Sicilan poet Giovanni Meli, who had died in 1815, it seemd to him that he had made an important discovery which ransomed the Italian people from their inferiority in this field. With great gusto Federico recited from memory the verses of that famous Theocritus of Palermo, a proud rebuke to the dictators of the earth and the exploiters of the poor:

Vui autri picuara e viddaneddi/ chi stati notti e iornu sutta un vausu/ o zappannu o guardannu picureddi/ cu l'anca nuda e cu lu pedi scausu/ siti la basi di città e casteddi,/ siti lu tuttu, ma unn'aviti lausu:/ l'ingrata società scorcia e maltratta / ddu pettu, chi la nutir e sinni addatta.

You shepherds and peasants, /who stay night and day under a rocky spur,/ either hoeing or looking after sheep,/ with bare heads and barefoot,/ you are the foundations of towns and castles, /you are the all and have no leisure, /the ungrateful society hurts and maltreats /the same bosom that nourishes it and the breast that feeds it.

Just so. O poor workers (the term 'proletarians' had not yet been coined), you form the columns of society, the primal source of riches and production, but you are condemned, like Lazarus once a beggar, to gather up the crumbs fallen from the tables of the rich gluttons.

—Careful, careful! not all that glitters is gold—observed donna Ortensia, throwing a dash of cold water on her son's *emballement.*— I knew Meli better than you do, my boy. Our abbé exalted the humble and meek and cozied up to the powerful. He condoled with the oppressed while he praised the Bourbon court, the very symbol of oppression, to the stars. He was progressive in theory and a conservative in practice. I don't know if he would be better defined as a reactionary hiding a Jacobin or a Jacobin decked out as a reactionary. I will tell you that in publishing the complete edition of his poetry through the generosity of don Leopoldo di Borbone, prince of Salerno, in the preface to his poem *Don Chisiotte* Meli was quick to point out that he was not attacking the State but only satirising certain political and economic reformers who, having no finger in that pie or no dog in that fight, want to remake the world according to their crazy ideas. The reason is that at time he was angling for the reversion of the abbey of San Pancrazio, one of the richest on the island. In short, as a man and as a politician, to Meli I prefer don Francesco Paolo di Blasi, who for love of his revolutionary ideas lost his head on the gallows.

Federico let her talk. Her totally romantic revolutionarism, supported by the stale ideas of liberty, equality, and fraternity, seemed *vieux jeu,* to quote a phrase dear to his mother. 1789 had been a typically bourgeois revolution, an uprising of the middle class against the nobility for the abolition of feudal privileges, for the recognition of the equality of everyone before the law, for the affirmation of the liberty of man as a person. But the people, the masses, what part had they had in all that, except during the brief Reign of Terror? What advantage had the multitude of the workers gained from the middle-class revolution? What difference did it make to those who are denied the right to live, to be declared free and equal in the sight of the law? Marat had said, 'The voice of Liberty says nothing to the heart of the poor man, who is dying of hunger.' The poor man wants to eat, and liberty and equality don't fill his belly. What difference does it make that the law is equal for all on paper if in practice it condones injustice?

What good had the Constituion of 1812 done, when the masses were left to faint with hunger? Yes, the nobles had renounced their feudal rights. But it was nothing but a theatrical gesture. In fact, the land had remained in the hands of the great proprietors, the latifondo was intact, the condition of the workers had not been raised at all.

Instead, their poverty and their degradation were increasing visibly. Only in the north of Europe did the successors of the Florentine revolt of the Ciompi, the disinherited, the oppressed, begin to make their voice heard in uprisings. There was talk of arson in the factories of Ulster, of dyers' disturbances in Germany in 1840, in 1831 uprisings of the weavers of Lyon, where the crowd had marched raising the banner, 'Live working or die fighting.'

Why not keep *au courant* with these examples of more evolved countries, why not study at close hand these still uncoordinated movements which were harbingers of wider and deeper social upheavals?

So Federico matured and executed his plan to leave the narrow domestic circle of the kingdom of Sicily and to undertake a voyage beyond the boundaries, not only of the island, but of Italy itself. He would have liked to go to France. He decided instead for Austria, because the relations between the Italian Bourbons and the court of Vienna promised to facilitate his undertaking. Thus, on the eve of 1848, our thirty-year-old visionary, laden with letters of recommendation to various influential personages in the Habsburg capital, climbed into a stagecoach headed toward the Brenner pass.

Vienna. The hedonistic metropolis, with its outermost houses kneeling beside the mirror of the blue Danube and its flowery gardens rising on the verdant Alpine foothills, was certainly the most welcoming land in the world. Crowned with the glories of well-merited political power; a symbol of peace for having hosted the Congress of Vienna, which boasted of giving Europe its definitive politcal order: cosmopolitan, multilingual, fanatical for culture, the friend of art; full of stunning women, foaming beer, exquisite delicacies, in those days it still merited the name 'the Capua of the spirit,' the proverbial capital of luxury.

Like a jewel set in a precious ring, its *Ringstraße,* Vienna shone with a calm and restful light, whose liveliest rays were softened and whose most strident colors were sweetened into a wonderful *impasto* without clashes and without disharmonies. More than a musical city, it could be called a living symphony of stones, of manners, of souls, as if it had been constructed by its wonderful architects of sound—Gluck, Haydn, Mozart, Schubert, Johann Strauss—new incarnations of divine Orpheus. Ethnic, racial, linguistic, religious contrasts were reconciled there, the nobility mixed with the people in the dances at the *Prater* and in the festive flower parades, the emperor went for walks in the streets answering the greetings of the passers-by, he followed the procession of *Corpus Domini* on foot, flanked by the common people. In short, the goddess *Gemütlichkeit* ruled everywhere, with her humane entourage of Understanding, Solidarity, Tolerance, and Forbearance, which are the bases of happy living. And no other philosophy was admitted except that of 'live and let live,' which is without question the height of all wisdom.

When Federico set foot in the fascinating Danubian capital he had the sensation of entering a warm bath of serenity. He came from a Sicily bristling with discord and conflicts, agitated by political movements and revolts between the intransigent authoritarianism of the governments and the bad faith of the subjects. A land smiled on by a beautiful nature on which the black wires of prejudice, distrust, jealousies, and fears, joined in a thick tangle, were tightening in order to strangle her. He understood what an incomparable divine gift is freedom. He felt alone and liberated from himself, he relaxed his cramped limbs, he breathed lungfuls of air, he felt a sense of indescribable lightness whose like he had never known. He walked, he made excursions, he attended some lectures at the university, he danced, he courted blond and sighing girls who led him through unexplored mazes of love: love, light and transitory like a Strauss waltz, without the unknowns of drama and the poisonous darkness of jealousy. Oh Vienna, sweet Vienna!

And yet—certain nuances elude the foreigner—the beautiful city that lay stretched out like a nymph on the banks of the river, the foolish and lazy city, tempting and dreamy, drugged by the madness of pleasure, was already betraying something new in its expression. Did not the signs of an unaccustomed disquiet breathe from her festive appearance?

To the eye, nothing was changed. At the *Prater* the *Burgmusik* played and the citizenry danced; plays were performed at the *Burgtheater* and the *Hoftheater*; incredible elegances paraded in the *Ringstraße*. In the drawing rooms Franz Liszt, shaking his locks, tamed the keyboard with his fantastic virtuosity, while Johann Strauss, his violin under his chin, led the world by the string of his waltzes. The demigod Metternich, that old unrepentant libertine, methodically betrayed his third wife, the irresistible Melania, with other supplementary wives. All as before. Except that something like an exciting pollen, spread by poisonous flowers, which pierced the sense of smell and whipped tense nerves, was sparkling in the air. In the arcades of the University, in the *Studentenherbergen*, in the clubs, in the beer-halls, in the cafés, mysterious spirals of smoke, not emitted from pipes and beakers of over-heated punch, gathered and dispersed. They were the fumes of red-hot minds, who were discussing social and governmental problems (a thing never seen in a country where politics was a jealous monopoly of the *Hofberg*), projects for reforms, for new orientations of the history and geography of Europe.

One evening in January Federico found himself by the *Kremer-Café*, one of the most animated meeting places of the *Kärtner Ring*. Outside it was snowing. Suddenly an arm was inserted into his. From the nest of a hood two great eyes looked up at him, while from a little rouged hare-like mouth came the words:

—*Kann ich dich erwärmen? Ich bin ein guter Ofen. Ein Fleischofen!* Can I warm you up? I'm a good oven. A flesh oven!

It was one of the many girls who patrolled the sidewalks of the lazy metropolis in the evening, sellers of pleasure.

Federico, embarassed by the unexpected and unwanted encounter, tried to escape, stammering:

—It's too late...*Es ist zu spät.*

—*Nie zu spät mit der Freude, mein junger Sperling!* Never too late for pleasure, my young sparrow—whispered the flighty streetwalker.

To deliver himself from temptation, Federico said that he had an appointment with friends at the *Café Kremer,* which they had reached in the meantime; and he entered, pushing the revolving door and detaching himself by force from his suppliant.

The hall was crowded and joyous with shouts, songs, the tinkling of metal and crystal, of smoke, and above all with giddiness, like all Viennese cafés. Without its like in the whole world, a café in the Danubian capital is more than a place of amusement, a social institution. It is an extension of the home, of the university, of parliament, of the stock exchange, of the chamber of commerce, of the arts: a place where business is transacted, where disputes of honor are resolved, political events are discussed, love is made; where people read, argue about philosophy, invent theatrical works and poetry.

The most varied types of humanity were jammed around the tables loaded with endless *Krüge* of beer, cups of coffee, every sort of *Küchen.* Alongside the aristocratic Viennese there stood out the jovial and noisy Bavarian, the cold and silent Berliner, the plump and practical denizen of Westphalia, the Jew with his hooked nose and dark hair over his olive skin. There were students with faces gashed by duelling scars, bearded artists in velvet jackets, lawyers and noblemen starred with decorations, officers in immaculate uniforms, female Russian students with short hair and mannish garments.

From a cluster of students of the most fanciful goliardic Bohemianism there suddenly arose the verse, declaimed with a great profusion of gestures:

Drauf sing der Tanz in Welschland los,/die Scyllen und Charybden/Vesuv un Aestna brachen los/Ausbruch auf Ausbruch, Stoß auf Stoß.

At the names of Scyllla and Charybdis, Vesuvius and Etna, pronounced by German mouths, Federico felt warmed as by an electric shock. Since he was not too expert in the Teutonic tongue, he rose from his table and asked a Jewish student, known as a polyglot, the meaning of the verse.

—In Italy they're dancing—he answered.

—There's fire—another added—volcanoes go fff...—and he sketched an explosive eruption with his throat.

—Don't you know?—said a third, better informed—the revolution has broken out in Palermo.

—How? When?—Federico answered, stunned.

—January twelfth. The Bourbons are packing up. Down with the tyrants! Pfui!

—Hooray for freedom—they all shouted in unison.

Ridiculous cries, manifestations unbelievable in Vienna, the symbolic advance-trench of reaction and the stronghold of the restoration. Can the revolution be about to arrive even here, where everything is unchanged and everything seems unchangeable? Metternich must be asleep or fallen into a lethargy if the republic of mice, defying the great terrifying cat set to guard the Habsburg monarchy, gives way to a burst of temper.

But no. Clement Wenceslaus von Metternich, the 'Grand Inquisitor,' as Lord Canning called him, the man who from 1789 has opposed the revolution and exorcises its ghost, the man who made anti-Jacobinism has masterpiece, is alive and in perfect form. His seventy-six years notwithstanding, he stands as straight as a grenadier, he dresses like Beau Brummel, he courts women, he is lavish with his smile of a great *charmeur,* he dances with perfect elegance, and he is an unbeatable chess player. They say that the webs of thick wrinkles around his temples, his overly rosy cheeks of a porcelain firmness, and his senile glance all betray his decline. You deceive yourselves—he thinks—it is the world that is declining, with its humanitarian bugaboos and its revolutionary follies. But the old chancellor will keep it on its feet. Is he not the famous dancer who for a half century has led all the quadrilles of the European powers, is he not the formidable chess player who has checkmated the most famous politicians of many nations? Let the times change, it will not be said that Metternich has turned his coat.

Certainly, the times are fickle if the Indiscussible begins to be discussed, if the Irresisible walks through the city no longer revered and bowed to, but made the target of scornful gestures, if in the morning the walls of buildings awake inscribed with insulting messages, 'Down with Metternich! Away with the senile old man! We want the Constitution.' We must be optimistic. If some disorder breaks out, it will only be a little comic revolution in kid gloves, *en gants glacés, gemütlich,* that is, domesticated and polite. The good Viennese are not the stuff that sansculottes are made of. Please! It is true that in the torbid days of February the French overthrew the monarchy and proclaimed the republic. But Vienna is not Paris, nor is Metternich Louis Philippe.

The morning of 13 March 1848. Unusual liveliness. People everywhere. The windows, jammed and crawling with people, look like eyes constantly blinking their lids. The houses, swarming up to the attics and on the dormers with human figures, seem to be alive. A procession of men and women of every rank and condition—a black ribbon, an endless ribbon, a swollen and enormous worm—is headed toward the *Rathausplatz,* where the Diet is debating. Princess Melania, with her mouth enclosed between two sardonic commas, looks on and exclaims, 'We'll see how the Viennese make their little revolution. For these people, all you need is a wagon full of sausages and everything would end in a sentimental *embrassons nous.*' Metternich paces the room with measured steps. Slender, slight in his impeccable bottle-green redingote, his neck oveflowing between the points of his wide collar, his throat moving up and down like an ill-swallowed apple, he torments the carpet with the point of his gold-handled cane. 'It's unbelievable—he says to himself—it's just a passing storm.' Shouts, noise, shots, cavalry charges, barricades, dead, wounded...It is History happening.

A fooотman arrives from the Hofburg out of breath. His Excellency is urgently entreated by the Archdukes. His letter of resignation is all ready. All he has to do is sign it. The old man signs with elegance. A carriage is ready to carry him to safety beyond the borders. There is no time to lose.

—So, are we all dead?—Melania asks him, reproaching his weakness with a severe glance.

—Yes, my dear, we are dead. Who can prevent a monarchy from committing suicide?

And the dictator of Europe flees with a few ducats borrowed from the banker Rothschild in his pocket.

Federico was present at the revolution as a spectator without overwhelming enthusiasm. One might say that his sensitivity was more social than political. Yes, the upheavals in Europe followed each other with impressive continuity, like heaps of powder, united by a single fuse, which take fire and explode one by one. France, Italy, Austria, Germany make their constitutional revolution. Instead of an autocratic power or a paternalistic regime the nations will have their representative assemblies which dictate the law in accordance with a written charter sworn by their respective sovereigns. In the meantime the masses will continue to rot in the same state of subjection and poverty. What difference does it make to be governed by an absolute prince or by a constitutional monarch when your stomach is empty and new injustices are added to the old ones? Political revolutions are short-lived, they resolve into alternating fluctuations of powers and their abuses. Only social revolutions, which represent real conquests for the masses, leave an indelible trace on history.

Events proved that Federico was right. A year had not yet passed when the revolution had been crushed everywhere, and reaction had triumphed once again.

The situation was now such as to render problematic both his return to Italy and his further sojourn in Austria. The entire Italian peninsula was on fire, subjugated but not tamed by reconstituted tyranny. Sicily, conquered by the prince of Satriano, groaned under a reign of terror. In Austria, at war with Piedmont, every Italian was considered undesirable or was subjected to a regimen of inquisition and suspicion. For this reason Federico moved to Germany. Here life was less pleasant and society less approachable than in Vienna. It did not breathe that air of carefreeness, that climate of sympathy, of mutual understanding and forebearance, which make everyone feel a citizen of the country whose guest he is. Everywhere coldness without spontaneity, a perfect exterior order without the warmth of intimacy, an atmosphere of the boarding-school and the barracks which choked off the breath. Above all, as a good Sicilian Federico mourned the perfumed and strengthening coffee of his country by comparison with what was served in every *Cafe-haus* and *Konditorei.* As often as he gulped down a cup of that swill which with Germanic honesty was called *Bohnekafé,* bean coffee, he grimaced as if grieving for a lost happiness. It was therefore necessary for him to restore himself with other aromas of the spirit.

It seemed indeed to Federico that he was getting drunk at the fumes of a new drug when in Düsseldorf he happened on a little book printed clandestinely, without indication of publisher or place, the *Communist manifesto* of Marx and Engels. It was like a flaming rocket in a sky covered by a curtain of fog. The pages were written in a style at once spare and yet angry, dictated by a mind without prejudice and a will without scruples. They disentangled the complexities of his ideas, they resolved an infinity of his doubts, they instilled a sense of illumination and clarity.

The book became his Gospel. He devoured it, he meditated on it, he commented on it, he learned its most meaningful passages by heart. There were sentences that ending by obsessing him. Reading, studying, walking, resting, the famous phrases whistled in his ear like the buzz of a wasp: 'Workers of the world, unite,' 'The whole history of humanity is the history of class warfare,' 'The exploiters will be exploited,' 'The middle class is producing its own undertakers and digging its own grave.'

He thought of his own Sicily. The *Manifesto* had been written for the workers of large-scale industries, such as the mass of northern laborers, among whom Karl Marx had lived. In Sicily the conditions were quite different: no large industries, not even one. On one side the aristocracy of the latifondisti, who accumulated the surplus value of endless extensions of lands made fertile by the hands of others. On the other side a poor, skeletal, ragged horde of day workers obliged to sell their labor for starveling wages, subjected to all the oppression and humiliations inseparable from a feudal regime. Class hatred could exist in Sicily, but not class warfare. Warfare implies a clear knowledge of reciprocal duties and rights, a collective understanding, a solid organization that knows how to use the weapon of strikes: in short, a certain spiritual maturity. And how was all this possible where the mass of the peasants lived in a state of total ignorance, of degradation, of terrifying subjection, still crouching in underground caves? What effort would it take to awaken in this immense mass of sub-humans the knowledge of human rights and a class consciousness?

The problem was immense. It did not seem completely insoluble, but only if one could work for years with patience and tenacity in the spirit of Marxism. Rather, in the Spirit (with a capital S) of Karl Marx, since he was not a man. He was rather the incarnation of the Holy Spirit, the Messiah, the Apostle of the new light. All the believers in a renewal of suffering humanity turned to him, all the neophytes of the new social religion, the prophets of the newest covenant among men yearned for him. Everyone was fortunate to be able to hear him, to approach, or at least to touch the hem of his garment, when, eluding the vetoes of the authorities who were hunting him across Europe, he slipped into a city to propagandize his word.

Fate smiled on Federico, allowing him to see the man of the day at a *Versammlung* held at a beer-hall in the suburbs.

The Lion of Trier spoke in a forest of red flags. A flowing mane of jet black hair mingling at the temples with a great ruffled beard, a bulging brow pierced by two melancholy eyes like those of an Old Testament prophet. Altogether, an expression like a poodle without the goodness of a dog, indeed embittered by a shade of resentment and pessimism. It seems that he is confronted only by evil, which poisons and perverts the world to its roots: an evil without a ray of good, which must be exterminated at any cost, like a poisonous plant, with plow and harrow. From the energy of his every gesture there breathes a will power without love, a cold and peaceless resolve. He is not a demagogue, as Federico expected. He does not overwhelm with the blaring impetus of his phrases, he leads and persuades. A slow and calm reasoning, a sophisticated and logically irrestible argumentation. His thoughts march like an army, like an armored battalion which takes enemy positions now by frontal assault, now by surrounding them: but when it reaches its target gives no quarter. It is the tactic of total war.

—What a difference from Bakùnin!—Federico says to himself as he listens.

Bakùnin—whom he had heard on another occasion—seems a refugee bear from the steppes. A magnificent example of the Slavic race: broad head, eyes of a lacustrine bright blue, luxuriant hair and beard the red of dead leaves; gigantic and superb, staturesque and scornful. When he grows heated in declamation (and he never loses his declamatory manner) he becomes immense, so as to touch the ceiling with his head, it seems, and the opposite walls of the hall with his open arms. In his perorations he imitates the Pantocrator God depicted in Byzantine apses, who like lightning and cyclone threatens revenge and punishments in the name of Justice and Wrath. 'We have no other fatherland—Federico remembers him saying—but the universal revolution. The enfranchisement of the masses demands that all institutions, political, religous, civil, and social be destroyed! We must tear up the State, the Church, the tribunals, the banks, the administration, and the army. The total revolution can only fulfill itself with a massacre. It will surpass in horror everything that history has known until now, everything that the West can imagine!'

—The Slavs love catastrophes, thought Federico, who owing to his mild character detested violence and bloodshed. But then he reflected that Marx, German by birth and Jewish by race (although a Christian convert), also preached hate and destruction. And he was really appalled when during the troubled days of the Dresden revolution he saw Richard Wagner, then Kappellmeister to the Royal Court of Saxony, mingling with the shirtless rabble and taking part in the popular uprising—Wagner, the Olympian musician. He wrote in a pamphlet, 'I will destroy our social state from top to bottom, because it is born from sin. Its flower is poverty and its fruit is crime. I will destroy any dominion whatever, I will break the power of the governing class, of the law, and of property, I will annul the order of things which divides men into the powerful and the weak, the rich and the poor, the privileged and the disinherited. Arise, ye miserable and oppressed! One thing alone will last for eternity: the ninth symphony of Beethoven.'

But when everything is destroyed and only the desert remains—commented the moderate middle class, mocking the fiery maestro—who will listen to the symphonies of Beethoven? To the sound of his lute Orpheus calmed the beasts and brought to life the stones, which hastened, moving by themselves, to raise cities. Herr Wagner employs music to overturn and devastate the world.

The revolution of the forty-eight completed its parabola. It arched across the European scene, its gleams going out one by one, like a night watch. When the earthquake had ended, everywhere the ancient orders had returned, the conservative regimes were restored. The political revolution had failed, as it had to. No political revoltuion is possible unless it is preceded by a social upheaval. Tired of inflammatory speeches, of fights, of gunshots, of barricades, Federico mulled this over. The Bourbons again ruled in Sicily, the barons were again the bosses. Police and feudalism tyrannised over two million inhabitants, the majority of whom were exploited by a minority of those privileged by wealth and power. Therefore it was necessary to go down there, to his island, to set to work on the liberation of the masses, to resolve the problem of the land, the keystone of every social ordering. There was no time to lose. Justice that arrived too late would sooner or later fulfill the prophecy of Bakùnin: 'The instincts of the workers of the land will be unchained as soon as it is said to them: the land is yours. Take possession of it.'

That was how Federico re-entered Italy. There he met with friends who informed him about the political movements writhing and the ideas bubbling in the peninsula. Concerning ideas, they gave him to read several writings of Carlo Pisacane, a well-known deserter from the Bourbon army, a volunteer in the campaign of the '48, formerly commander in chief for the defence of the Roman Republic, and presently an exile in the States of Sardinia. The clearly socialist position which the author assumed in his writings (it was the first time during the Risorgimento that the social problem was met with such a lack of prejudice) encouraged Federico to make his acquaintance.

He found Pisacane in Albaro, above Genoa, boarding with a modest family of artisans. With overflowing southern effusiveness Pisacane treated him as an old friend. Two restless little eyes smiled, crouched under a forehead pale and vast like a church dome on which the sun beat down, while his aristocratic hands tormented the mustaches pouring over the tawny beard of a Nazarene. He spoke with an abundant and liquid Neapolitan accent, with a great profusion of *d's* in place of *t's* and a mutilation of final vowels. He concluded his long rhetorical periods by inserting, 'curragge! avande!,' and the smoke of the cigarette which he clenched between his lips settled on the flourishes of his torturous and convoluted arguments. He criticised Garibaldi (who had shown himself more guerilla than general in the defence of the Roman Republic), he criticised Mazzini (who did not understand an iota of socialism), he criticised Christ, whom he stripped of the title of God as one dismisses a gossiping and lazy servant. He declared himself an atheist, he spat on tyranny, he burned incense to the republic, he thundered against capitalism, he repeated with variations Prudhon's dictum that 'property is theft,' he threatened to unloose against the reprobates the lightning of the revolution, predicting that it would break out in the south. 'From the South—he kept repeating, drilling the air with his index finger at a level with his rolling eyes—will come the salvation of Italy...But we must strike while the iron is hot...Have no scruples about violence.'

Federico left the encounter disillusioned. The atheistic socialism of the Neapolitan disgusted him and the preaching of violence wounded his sensibility as a Christian, which had survived the dissolution of his religious vocation. To reform the economic system, yes, to float society off the shoals of injustice on which it had run aground, certainly; but without arousing hatred, without unloosing war between brothers. To hold out the hand of pity to the poor, to the destitute, but without inciting them to revolution and urging them to bloody expropriation. To bring the kingdom of God on earth voluntarily, without waiting for the outcasts to seize it with violence.

In Sicily.

Donna Otensia's lips were edged in a double smile when Federico, after so many years of absence and the exchange of repeated embraces, sat down before her to entertain her with his journey. She smiled with happy satisfaction on hearing that her son, at the conclusion of his experiences, would retire to the country, to occupy himself exclusively with agriculture. She remembered that even Voltaire's Candide, finding peace after touring the globe and passing through so many adventures, was finally reduced to *cultiver son jardin*. She curled her mouth in a little *moue*, between doubt and amusement, on hearing her son's proposals to attempt a collectivist experiment on his property to insure bread and peace for his peasants.

Don Fabrizio, who was present at the conversation, showed that he did not take the discussion seriously by simply pointing out with amusement that the first socialist had been Ferdinando IV of Naples and I of the Two Sicilies. In 1789—the same year as the French Revolution—he had founded at San Leucio a colony where the right of heredity was abolished, property was held in common, the age for marriages was fixed, labor was obligatory for everyone ...Was Federico now looking for anything better?... The historian Pietro Colletta had defined it as one of the seven wonders of the world.

Chapter 2

'ASTREA' OR 'Happy Island?'

The two words—two hallucinations—battled each other in Federico's mind from the moment that the plan of creating a collectivist colony on his estate had solidified there.

'Astrea,' a rich classicizing title, was all a hum of stars in a springtime Hellenic sky. 'Astrea' or *Virgin of the stars,* the ancients called the daughter of Jove and Themis, the immaculate goddess of Justice. Like a tunic modelled on a well-made body, that name fitted his project to achieve an institution intended to give each his own (or better, to each according to his need) in harmony with the Aristotelian definition of what is just.

'Happy Island,' was more tempting. And temptation has such power over the human heart that the Our Father is a prayer made on purpose to avoid it. Happiness attempts justice, sometimes it repels it. And Justice is regarded with a certain suspicion by the Sicilian populace and peasant. To them it smells of soldiers, of judges, of policemen and executioners: a whole parade of personages who do not exactly arouse their trust. What is the mafia, if not distrust of the 'law' of the government and the aim of doing oneself justice with one's own hands? You *assume* (Federico said to himself, ornamenting his mental discourse with a verb much in use in his seminary) you assume that the word 'island' exercises a natural fascination on the Sicilian, proud of his insularity.

All the same the more difficult name ended by prevailing. It had the advantages of obscurity and mystery, and the people only feel respect for the things they don't understand. In addition, it did not bind Federico to an over-confident promise. To promise, what a responsibility! It is true that he mulled over in his mind a sparkling and energetic thought of Goethe that he had learned in Germany: *Was das Leben mir versprech, werde ich ihn halten,* The promise that life has made me I will keep. But sometimes instead one must expect the unexpected from life. And the public laughs at good intentions when they fail of success. What would become of him, facile promiser of happiness, if the experiment on which he was about to wager everything failed? Better therefore to put the accent on justice rather than happiness. So the name *Astrea* appeared on the documents that constituted the baptismal certificate of the new republic, as he liked to call it. And the magic word was printed in registers and engraved on stamps and dies, as well as on the commemorative medal which on the day of the dedication would be buried in the estate under a two-faced herm. On its *recto* the bronze medal bore a yoke of oxen with a plow digging a furrow in the earth, on the *verso* a three-legged Trinacria, with underneath the Biblical motto, *Iustitia et pax osculatæ sunt,* Justice and peace have kissed each other.

The estate *Tre Pernici*—nearly five hundred acres in extension—was, like all the latifondo which occupies about the half of the island, a vast terrain planted in cereals and grain, with some areas of grazing and fallow. Greening in spring, yellow, squalid, and scorched by the sun after the harvest. A characteristic landscape of loneliness and sorrow. The traveller who ventures any distance from the inhabited centers—those smiling oases of gardens and fruit orchards beyond the cloister of dull grey houses climbing up their slopes—when he has bidden farewell to the last olive trees, loses himself in the immensity of the depopulated and deserted land, absolutely devoid of any rural life. Not that it is a matter of uncultivated terrain, as is generally believed. Indeed you could say that in all the limitless extension, sweet with easy hills and suddenly torn by crevices and deep valleys, tamed by plains and made savage here and there by shapeless erratic boulders, there was not a yard of earth that the effort of man had not sought to make fertile. From the highest hilltops to the deepest channels carved by the loosened flood waters in winter, from the open plateaux to the most impervious ravines, the lazy and reluctant earth appears tilled, worked, constrained to generate without rest. But man, having violated the earth by forcing it to give birth in sorrow, draws back from it almost frightened. Only his work remains there as the trace of a mysterious and invisible hand.

Except for the season of sowing and harvest, the countryside remains wrapped in solitude. In autumn some plows are seen—the antediluvian nail plow—drawn by a mule or a gaunt cow, and some peasants intent on hoeing the grain and the fava beans. In summer the angry sun comes into play, deforming the countryside according to the time of day with the shadow of a poor donkey who scatters under his heavy tread clouds of chaff freed from the grain. Only during the primeval threshing does life pulse on the threshing floor. After that the countryside falls into a lethargy. For months and months from the bottom of the valley to the hill tops not a human figure appears. Look all around, and your glance does not encounter a living soul. You can shout at the top of your lungs without an echo answering you. No laughter of children, no chatting of housewives, squeaking of carts, stamping of horses, lowing of herds, howling of dogs. Instead of houses, miles away a straw hut resembling an African *tukal* surfaces from a crevasse in the earth; some thin cows wandering in the *campia*.

The owner never lives here. He only makes an occasional appearance from time to time, arrogant with feudal authoritarianism and a predator of rustic female virtue. The peasant lives here only during the work in the fields. The rest of the time he prefers, even at the cost of traveling tens of kilometers on foot between going and returning, to live crouched in his hovel, 'in town,' in a primitive togetherness of men and beasts. Owing to a misunderstood point of honor, women scorn the work of the countryside. Only after the harvest will you encounter in the yellow stubble some wretched gleaners, their bodies worn out by frequent pregnancies, consumed by malaria, in the process of gathering the crumbs from under a table to which they were not invited.

Between the distrust of the owner and the resentment of the gabelloto, who, as a typical exponent of the rural mafia, is often the exploiter of the same proprieter, the peasant does not love the land. And his lack of love often ferments into hate. How can you grow fond of that which does not belong to you, which does not give back to you in proportion to your work, which denies you the necessary well-being? The earth was not created by God only to gather the peasant's bones, but to give herself to him in a dedication of joy. Tormented by her betrayal, the peasant betrays her in his turn.

With his head buzzing with ideas, Federico set out for his estate. It had been years since he had set foot there. He was bitten by a mixture of nostalgia and curiosity. What new things would he find there? Perhaps nothing. Rural life is resistant to changes: it runs on timelessly, its minutes have the duration of centuries. It seems rocked by a lullaby alternating between 'always' and 'never' with a rhythm of eternity.

When he had climbed down from the coach which had brought him in five hours from Palermo to the town of Adrianica in the company of the factor, his estate manager, at the edge of town Federico found his mount, a two-year-old merlin-colored mare all leaps and liveliness, with a short head and nervous hocks, her halter held by his steward Paolo Mancino. Since Federico teneded toward corpulence, he mounted with some effort. The animal bent willingly to his unaccustomed weight, turning her neck back as if the photograph the figure of her new master in her lively eyes. A word and a nudge of the knees were enough to start her off.

The group set out. Federico and the factor at the head, two field guards at the tail—grim types, whom no one would want to meet along a road at night—with their rifles balanced on their saddles. They took the path up the slope toward the latifondo at a good pace. The ancient *trazzera*, reduced to a miserable little trail by the continued encroachments of the local land owners, snaked and stretched across the undulating plains, from hill to hill, from ravine to ravine, in soft waves. Sometimes it was split by a little bridge which covered a thin stream—a muddy strip—to continue on the other side. Between the end of summer and the beginning of autumn, the earth was drowsing in a sweet rest. Caressed by the dry breeze, the immense untilled terrain extended as far as the eye could see: pale, cracked, devoid of green, bereft of houses, deserted of human life. An endless yellowish steppe, where a horse bent his gaunt neck to graze on a bunch of wild thistles like a ghost wandering through those places from time immemorial. On high, the blue arch of the heavens; beneath, the violet bastions of the mountains in their granite immobility.

After two hours' travel the party was in sight of the settlement. The howling of dogs shattered the crystal air. Tiny outlines of people dotted the whiteness of the buildings.

Even before the party had entered the vast courtyard the stableboys took over the horses to cleanse them from their sweat and feed them, after the animals had quenched their thirst at the watering trough.

Cheerful and fresh despite the long trip, Federico looked around with joy at the places perfumed by the most pleasant memories of his infancy. He felt young, as if a sudden vigor were flowing through his entire body.

Paolo the steward—whom he had left almost as a young boy and now saw again as a man with a blue chin from his recently shaved beard—took off his cap, bowing to the padrone with the obligatory greeting, 'Voscenza benedica.' A big clumsy snotty baby of about four years old romped around between his legs, all eyes like a nesting canary.

—Is that your son?

—Yes, Eccellenza—the steward answered with pride—he's one of the three.

—You've been quick to set up a family. How long have you been married?

—We begin our fifth year at Saint Martin's Day, if I'm not mistaken. When Your Excellency left me I was 'schietto,' unattached.

—Is that your wife?

—Come here, Orsola. Kiss the master's hand—said Paolo, turning to his companion who was hesitating to come forward.

She was a girl between twenty and twenty-five who was striking even at first sight. Tall, flourishing, well formed, her hips springy, beneath a bosom that was firm and unyielding despite her repeated pregnancies. It was a pleasure to see her move in the abundant folds of her best dress. The light took the black of her crisp hair and shone on her strong white teeth, over which an aggressive smile played. From her body—especially from her inviting glance and the movement of her hips—there exuded the odor of restless flesh nourished by the abundance of pleasure. Perhaps for this reason, whether it were truth or slander, the rumor spread insidiously about her provocative figure that she was an insatiable man-trap.

And this is my mother-in-law—continued Paolo, pointing to a woman of medium height, solid and robust, her upper lip adorned with little brown hairs which gave her an air of manly boldness.

Federico entered the house of the master followed by the steward's family.

Everything was in order. A sense of freshness, a perfume of cleanliness arose from the terracotta tiles, breathed from the recently white-washed walls, from the furniture polished to a glow.

On the large oval table a jar of Sicilian majolica overflowed with wild flowers, smelling of thyme and spearmint.

Because the wind filled the curtains and made them flutter, Orsola closed the window shutters, making sure that the spindle was inserted in the hook, and at the bottom, in the clamp. In the effort her loins contracted between her sickle-shaped hips, and her muscles stood out on her strong and well-planted legs, like the legs of a young mare scrambling up a steep slope.

She asked permission to set the table. She unfolded and stretched out on the table a laundered cloth which smelt of lavender, distributed the plates, then a round-bellied bottle of old wine with ruby-red glints, a brown and fragrant loaf of bread.

The shaggy head of shepherd dog pushed open the door. The animal looked around suspciously and started to bark.

—Come in—Paolo ordered.—Don't you know your master?

—How can you expect him to know me?—objected Federico.—It's so many years since I turned up in these parts. For this animal I'm a stranger.

—*Voscenza* is always the master—flattered the man.—Even the animals must respect you.

It seemed as if he had not spoken idly, because the dog, after looking around, came closer and began to stretch out at the master's legs, looking up at him with his submissive yellow eyes.

Federico sat at table with the steward and ate with a good appetite, served by Orsola, who had surpassed herself, so that in the countryside the master should not regret the pleasures of his city palace.

When they finished night was falling.

In the smoke that rose in spirals from their pipes, the two spoke of the farm. The conversation fell on the mare which had brought Federico from town to the estate, and since he praised her docility and her stamina, the factor proposed a visit to the stables.

The swinging lantern cast a fan of light. Enormous shadows of three horses and as many mules were projected on the walls. The eyes of the animals, who had recognized familiar voices, turned around, lighting up with violet flashes. From their moist nostrils thick vapors smoked, a sign that the air was cooling with the fall of the night. A few terrified hens rushed out of the mangers clucking wildly and fled blindly. When the light of the lantern was lowered to illuminate the bedded straw, a rectangle of sky trembling with stars appeared framed in the opening of the high window.

The promise of a serene autumn was descending on the earth.

The next day—Sunday—the gabelloti, the field guards, and a group of some hundred peasants who had come from town were congregated in the courtyard of the farmstead. It was a gray November morning, on which thick and swollen clouds weighed down like the heavy leather curtain in front of a church door. It was not raining, but 'the water was in the earth,' as the farmers express it in their jargon when rain is imminent. In the folds of the valley the outlines of the mounds unwound lazily from a thick ground fog that streamed low and covered everything like a leaden carpet. As soon as the gusts of wind had calmed and the flight of the clouds had ceased, a few big drops fell tapping on heads and clothes.

Someone from a group exclaimed:

—We need a bit of water, God's truth. It's November and the earth is dry as fish bait.

—If it goes on like this, when will we sow the seeds?

—How can you expect *u Signuruzzu,* the dear Lord, to take care of us? There are too many sins in the world. Too many injustices!

—Do you believe that there were fewer sins when the seasons gave rain and good weather 'as is right'? The world has always jogged along in the same way.

—Be quiet—a gabelloto interrupted sardonically—now our master will set the world straight.

—If you've got money you've got everything. The rich have always made rain and fair weather.

—What do you expect? It's been like this since the world was created. *'A furca è pi lu poviru,* The gallows is only for the poor man.

Federico the *padron* appeared on the steps of his house.

Everyone gathered closely around in a semicircle as soon as he indicated that he wished to speak.

—I have had you come—he said—to give you good news. The gabelle are expiring this year, and I do not intend to renew them.

(—This is the good news?—softly complained the gabelloti, who had suddenly turned yellow with bile. What does this kind of talk seem to you, brother?)

—It's not that I am displeased with you. Each of you has done his duty as well as he could. But I want to inaugurate a new epoch for everyone. A period of real well-being will begin for you peasants, and for your families. Within the year each one of you will have his own land...

(At these words the attention of the the hearers became acute. Some took a step forward, some put their hands to their ears, rolled like a shell so as to hear better.)

"...No more masters, no more gabelloti, peasants, and field hands. The earth is God's and belongs to everyone. In His sight there are no rich and poor. Every man has the right to work and to live from his work. I mean that the fruit of his labor belongs completely to him...Today it is completely the opposite: the land is in the possession of a few and these exploit the sweat of the poor (great applause)...This state of things must cease, and I will be the first to give the example...The land will be divided among the peasants... (new burst of applause). Two problems present themselves. One is a problem of justice. It is unjust, I mean, that a human being should labor like a beast, like a slave, to enrich his masters. The other is a problem of general prosperity, because under the present system the earth does not not render as much as it should, a part of its riches remains hidden in its bowels. The peasant who is paid by the day, moving from one place to another at the mercy of the padrone who pays him (and always pays him just enough to keep him from dying of hunger), the peasant who unwillingly works a land that is not his, gives it the least possible effort of his labor....To increase the yield of his effort he must be made to love the earth, to make him feel it is a provident mother and not an enemy. To make him love the earth he needs to be involved in its product, so that this product goes to him as a salary (cries of agreement from all the bystanders)...

My estate will be divided into one hundred plots of land, and each peasant will get one plot, where he can settle with his family, with his animals, where everyone will have a decent house and enjoy the comforts of life... The assignment of plots will be decided by drawing lots...An assignment will last for ten years, but it will become permanent when the experiment can be called a success, as I hope. It cannot fail of success, since God is with us.

A voice broke in (it came from the group of gabelloti):

—But the roads, but the water! and the houses?

Federico explained that the roads would be built when the land belonged not to a single person but to everyone, because good roads represent a collective interest. The roads between holdings would be constructed at the expense of the landowners directly involved. The expenses of the roads in common would fall on the entire collective organised as a consortium. Dwellings would be provided by means of bank loans with mortgages on the building to be constructed. There remained the problem of water, and that was a more serious one. It is not true that water is lacking in Sicily. The wells that one sees more or less everywhere demonstrate the existence of springs. Let acqueducts be built and the patrimony of water will be sufficient for the needs of everyone, even if it is not rich. Here too a consortium of neighboring landowners would solve the problem. In union there is strength, and Federico was certain that union would not be lacking when everyone was convinced that the interest of the individual was in harmony with the interest of all. It was a question of raising that collective conscience, that spirit of solidarity that until now unfortunately had not existed. And if that spirit is with us, who can be against us?

At the end of his speech he was lifted on the shoulders of the peasants and carried in triumph, to ecstatic cheers.

Only the gabelloti stood off to one side, frowning and sullen, conferring together, shouting and arguing among themselves. The kindest judgment to be read in their dismayed eyes could be translated by the words, 'This man has lost his mind.'

The inauguration of the settlement was a great event. Federico intended it to have both a religious and a civil significance. For this reason he invited to the ceremony, in addition to the clergy, the mayor of the comune and the leading members of his administration. But since the admnistration was in the hands of the mafia, none of the civil authorities was present. The upper hierarchies of the criminal association disapproved that Federico had broken his contracts with the gabelloti, who were affiliates or clients of the *onorata società*. This disrespect was defined in slang as a 'slash in the face.' The stars of the *cosca* of the comune and the province and their asteroids had therefore decided not to take part in the dedication. How could it be tolerated that the padrone had thrown so many fine people out into the street in order to distribute the land to the 'hungry beggars'?

A bigger imbroglio arose about the religious ceremony. The town had two churches, a Latin one and a Greek one, hence a dualism that was often pushed to a rather grotesque point of irritation. The Greek-Albanians, settled in Sicily since the fifteenth century, maintained that they were the founders of the colony and therfore of the town, and boasted the priority of their rite, the authentic one of St. John Chrysostom. The Latins defended with drawn sword their opinion that the town was of Roman origin and that the Albanians were nothing but guests resembling the cuckoo, which lays its eggs in the nests of other birds. From this came an infinity of misunderstandings, disagreements, and squabbles, in the religious, political, and even familial fields. Real fights broke out at Easter, for example, which according to the two liturgies fell on different days. Jesus rose on Saturday, according to the Latins, on Sunday, swore the Greek rite: whence the two churches—side by side on the only piazza—rang their bells at the same time, the one in celebration, the other in mourning. The conflict between the glory and the mourning was so strident that it often erupted in acts of mutual intolerance and hostility, when their souls were swept away by mystical fervor. More than once the two processions, the one to the glory of the Risen Christ, the other following the Deposition of Christ and the Virgin of Sorrows, ran into each other, exchanged insults, and came to blows, and not infrequently some corpses emerged from the conflict. Unfortunately, humankind loses no opportunity to rejoice in blood. Even the symbnol of pardon can become a pretext for hate.

Becaue of such antagonism it was not easy for Federico to organise the religious ceremony. In order to resolve the question he was conciliatory, he invited both one and the other clergy. The remedy was worse than the problem. The Latin priests, imitating Pontius Pilate in washing their hands, said, Haven't you turned to the Greeks? They are sufficient. We are *de trop*. The Greek priests said Byzantinely, The benediction is an indivisible action: *mezzadria*, sharecropping, dear sir, is a Latin institution. The Greek church does not share her prerogatives with anyone. After so many quibbles and much beating aroud the bush, Federico opted for Latinity. And naturally he made enemies of the legitimate successors of St. John Chrysostom who, God be praised, did not easily give up their hatreds.

That May morning the roads, the lanes, the mule-tracks betwen the estate and the little neighboring towns, made a fine sight, swarming with people on holiday. Peasants in their Sunday best, women attired in gaudy colors, babies all dressed up. They climbed up the hills in groups, in little bunches, or a few at a time: the poorest on foot, those who had a bit of land in the sun mounted on mules and donkeys of the most varied sizes. Only the richest *burgisi* did not mingle with the crowd. Mounted on mettlesome horses with a display of harnesses and tack, they wheeled left and right in groups, then suddenly split up and raising their guns in the air fired off salvoes as in Arabian fantasies. The peasants, at the passing of that violence, which disappeared and reappeared amid clouds of dust, just managed to escape onto the grassy roadsides, darting sideways menacing glances full of anger and spite.

In the center of the estate a wooden altar arose on a hillock. Around it fluttered a forest of flags, of pennants, and banners belonging to civil societies and religious confraternities. Beside the tricolor there appeared undisturbed a flag with the Bourbon lilies (the tenacity of the conservative tradition!), a cohabitation which had nothing unnatural about it in a town where the mafia, in view of its multifarious interests, extended its protection to all parties.

Lined up on the right a band, whose musicians showed off dark blue tailcoats with crimson linings, with swords at side and cocked hats on head, was blowing its lungs out on newly polished instruments with blasts savage enough to terrify even the birds. The lively and excited crowd of children were amusing themselves by turning somersaults and cartwheels on the grass.

A moment of silence. There echoed only the pecking of hoes cutting through the dry ground to dig the hole for a terracotta cylinder containing the commemorative medal and some recently struck coins. During the psalmody of the clergy a yellow hand, its purple veins entwined like a nest of worms, shook a holy water sprinkler. The notes of the *Te Deum* arose. The band attacked the first notes of a sacred hymn. A red banner was raised on a flagpole (what does this red mean? many people asked themselves).

Then the merrymaking began. Rural dances struck up, poetic *rispettti* and *stornelli* flew from one chorus to the other. Wine poured without stint from a barrel, ran into glasses, into the wine jars which were passed from mouth to mouth, drenching clothes and the ground. Some men, already drunk, were staggering back and forth. The noisiest rejoicing erupted in laughs and shouts as if greeting the arrival of universal happiness.

Months passed. Federico was pleased with 'his' Astraea. Why that posessive? Didn't the colony belong to the collective? Certainly. No doubt about it crossed the mind of its founder. But so it is. He did not hesitate to call the colony 'his' even though he was convineced of the opposite. Man loses more easily the instinct of life than that of ownership.

Anyway, everything was going well. It couldn't go better, even if the proverb remains true that 'not all that glitters is gold.' In this world there is no perfection without its counterbalance. Even the sun is afflicted by a few spots. And you would have to be blind not to discover the first flaws in the fine edifice raised by the daring of don Federico. What good and noble work does not run up against misunderstanding, distrust, and criticism?

It began with the feudal landlords. For them a socialist experiment attempted by one of their own class was a thorn in the flesh, an insane undertaking, a real stumbling block. While not unknown in Italy, collectivist ideologies were confused, were not understood. The echo which came from abroad was barely absorbed by a few scholars. Socialist ideologies found neither propagandists nor apostles. Filippo Buonarotti had lived in France. Carlo Pisacane was better known for his political ideas than for his social beliefs. Cattaneo was a lonely theorist. Gioberti flirted only skin deep with the social-Christian philanthropy of Lamennais. Mazzini, the tribune of the people, was too vigorous a personality to embrace the socialist doctrine whose enemy he had declared himself. There was a lot of talk about the collectively-based colony instituted by Ferdinando I at S. Leucio, but no importance was attributed to it other than as a royal trinket. *Le roy s'amuse,* the great ones of the earth said with an indulgent air, faithful for life to the house of Bourbon. Federico, in their opinion, was also amusing himself. All the same they did not conceal their opinion that it was a dangerous game, a game that inflamed the minds of the peasants and could spread a harmful contagion. Utopias have their poison. And naïf Federico—without doubt a noble who had lost caste—was playing the role of the poisoner without realizing it. It would be a good idea for the authorities to keep an eye on him. But where *was* authority any longer in these revolutionary times?

In the meantime the mafia were masticating the real poison. They could not pardon *padrone* Federico for having thrown the gabelloti out on the street, all of them emissaries and protégés of the dark society, and for having fired supervisors, guardians, field guards, and other parasites of the latifondo in order to divide the land up among a handful of slackers who were now bloated with pride. What to do? For the moment, nothing but wait. *Pazienza, pazienza*! said the great hierarchs, the high-ranking mafiosi, to their subordinates, who were complaining about the wrongs they had suffered. The day will come even for those plucked cockerels, 'The wife of the thief doesn't laugh for ever.' And what were they if not thieves, those deadbeats tarted and puffed up through the fault of a madman?

But there was worse. As if the rest were not enough, there was a rot working within the colony itself. The falanstery (the founder indicated his community with this name borrowed from the utopian socialist Charles Fourier) had not yet began to function according to the plan meticulously prepared in all its details when it was already showing signs of impatience and unrest.

The Sicilian peasant is perhaps the one of any latitude and longitude who is most individualist by mental makeup. He only sees 'his' person, 'his' honor, 'his' family, 'his' property. The social sense which he should have in common with every man, who is without doubt a herd-loving animal, is short-ranged. It never moves beyond the limits of 'his-ness,' or, in simple language, egoism. Talk to him about solidarity, association, collaboration as much as you want. He will simply repeat to you the old proverb, 'La pentola in comune non bolle mai,' 'The common pot never boils.' It would be easier to pull out ten of his teeth all at once than to extract this conviction from his mind.

The first symptoms of discontent broke out with the distribution. The parcels of land were assigned by drawing lots. And since all land is not the same, one got a plot on a hill and another a plot in a valley, one got a place more in the shade and another one more in the sun; this one got an allotment bathed or crossed by a stream, that one got a tract of land swarming with rocks like unburied bones. Whom to blame if not chance? Except that the countryman, accustomed to struggling with vipers, sees snakes writhing everywhere. He always bears in his heart a tangle of suspicions to which he is trying give a form. A lot of notaries took part in the drawing, yessir: but it isn't the first time that notaries have messed up things. And who says that the padrone had not managed to favor someone with the complicity of the solemn-faced actuary? Nobody is born the son of the black hen by accident.

And then, eh, that clause of the ten years' trial, that was a real trap, for sure! What are you, finally? Nothing but a puppet owner. When the ten years expires the padrone will take back the land watered by your sweat, and that's that. You've made soup for the cats. You won't even keep your working tools, which you have to give back to the community as sole owner. Nothing for you, everything for the community.

The thing which finally most unhinged the colonists, or rather the *falansteristi,* was the obligatory consignment of the harvest to the collective granary. Some justice! The charter of Astrea stated clearly: 'The product of the each single farm will be bestowed on the granary and divided by the irrevocable decision of the Elders for each hearth, according to their respective needs: to equal needs the division will take place in equal parts.' It boils down to, you spit blood to work, you kill yourself increasing the production of your farm, and you have to divide your benefits with the layabouts who suck your blood like leeches. To each according to his needs, it's true. But the needs get measured by the rod of their lordships the Elders, who tip the scales in the direction of their friends and their friends' friends. *Cu sparti, avi a' megghiu parti,* The one who makes the division gets the best share And what for the workers, for us? Not for ourselves, because we're cheated of the product of our own personal labor which goes to benefit the slackers and the spendthrifts. Not for our children, to whom we do not have the right to leave the land, which does not belong to us.

The effect of so much bad temper, of such distrust and recriminations, was that in the second year of Astrea several *falansteristi* took to hiding part of their production in order to sell it at more profitable prices instead of turning it over to the granary, and the quantity of grain and fava beans to distribute to the community diminished notably. Hence loud protests from the other peasants who had had the credulity to hand over their harvest to the common stockpile. Intervention of the Elders, who threatened to take drastic measures against the defaulters: in the general division they would get a smaller share. Even more furious protests and rebellions. The victims decided to down tools and not to take part in the sowing for the following year. To hell with the community! The devil with 'the land for everybody'! The discontent increased out of all proportion and boded nothing good.

Chapter 3

THE THIRD year of the colony's life closed deep in debt, both material and moral. Materially: when the accounts were added up, the fief *Tre Pernici* had never produced so little as in the years of its collective experiment. Even nature had been hostile. First a rainy season, which had rotted the seed in the furrows, then a heat wave that had burned the grains in those sheaves which had been spared. As if the fog and wheat rust had not been enough, a plague of grasshoppers had been loosed on the fields. A real scourge of God. Poor God, always blamed when men cannot bear the weight of their faults and errors and believe that they can lighten them by unloading them onto the shoulders of a Being more powerful than they!

In reality the consecutive bad harvests were explained not only by the whims of a sulking and angry nature. The evil was deeper. Among the colonists the enthusiasm of the first days wilted more day by day, flagged, went out; and with it declined the spirit of initiative and sacrifice which is the driving force of every success. Some distrusted the institution, some trusted it too much. Some slept on the pillow of a gilded optimism, some fell into the arms of a dark pessimism. Some recited 'mea culpa,' but there were more who accused others and bitteerly attacked the padrone. Some thought of reforming the founding statute, others meditated revolutionary uprisings. In the meantime the economy of the undertaking was unraveling. The common patrimony was shrinking before their eyes, and Federico was obliged to fill the cracks that were opening up in the company by turning to the banks for loans, thus endangering the remainder of his resources by means of mortgage guarantees.

More serious were the debts of a moral order. Dissent, frivolity, competition, jealousies undermined the harmony of the colony. Ill-concealed envies and hatreds, repressed but ready to break out, were sharpened like poisoned arrows against the council of the Elders and against Federico who, although seemingly on the sidelines, was always the presiding deity of the institution.

It is a frequent fact that every discontent and vague resentment tends to coalesce around a specific object: widely diffused hatred seeks an immediate target. So the rancors, the recriminations and the suspicions of the falanstery were quickly concentrated around the family of the steward Paolo, nicknamed the *turdu,* the thrush.

That he had a frisky and sexy wife—one of those women predestined by nature to live in the orbit of male desires—was notorious. That she was *sciddiata,* that she had 'slid' into many infractions of the sixth commandment, was trumpeted in whispers or out loud by everyone. But that with the complicity of this woman the Verderame family had won the heart of the padrone, creating for them a situation of privilege, was a new and spiteful accusation, one now making the rounds of the colony and assuming the proportions of a scandal.

Goodwife Orsola—the *strània,* the foreigner, as they called her, because Paolo had brought her in from abroad, from Ragusa to be exact, where he had done his military service—had become a primary figure, the center of the general gossip and backbiting from the time that padrone Federico had moved to the estate. She hung about the master's house at all hours under the pretext of seeing to the service of the household, she did not allow anyone to approach the padrone except through her. The privileges that she enjoyed with the padrone flowed back in favor of her complacent, *pacinziusu* husband, who had in fact become the master's factotum and gave himself such airs, like God almighty, that it was disgusting to see him. And all of this for what? For that woman, the Ragusan, with her freckles, her yellow eyes, her long face like a wild goat, a real animal in heat.

Yes, goodwife Orsola, if not of the goat, has something of the gazelle, with her oblong face in which are set two almond eyes lightly inclined toward her sharp nose, with her mouth of a shameless red half-open on the ivory of her teeth. And her thin nervous legs, contrasting with the soft counterpoise of her pelvis, seem made for racing toward naughty adventures.

When she passes swaying her hips, wrapped in her brand new shawl that changes all the colors of the rainbow, with a provocative air of 'I don't give a damn,' the women appear at the doors and form a group, commenting:

—Goodness, what *sfrazzo,* what showing off! Have you seen the shawl? She didn't have that last week.

—Yes, but last week the padrone had not yet gone down to Palermo.

—And what earrings!

—She says she bought them with her own savings.

—Just you try to save. It's a *festa* if you can even manage to put the kettle on.

—Don't forget that she ...works—emphasised *zia* Lisa with viperous irony.

—The art of flirting is a fine thing—added another.—It's enough to open your...arms to earn what we don't scrape together in a year.

—*Bocca d'inferno*!—protested *zia* Saveria, a churchgoer, scandalized by the obscene reference, mobilizing all the muscles of her old face furrowed with wrinkles.—You'd feel like doing the same! So be quiet.

—I kiss the earth, thanks be to God. My husband can walk with his head high—said the woman who had been scolded, kissing her fingers aftrer touching the earth.

—My God, what arrogance! See how she walks up straight with her bosom stuck out. It looks like she's swallowed a broom handle.

—Let her go. It's her moment. But...the wife of the thief doesn't laugh forever—concluded the midwife of the community, beating the air with a threatening gesture, looking like a dishevelled sibyl.

As long as it was a question of gossip, little harm. The trouble was that the noose of ill-will and resentment tightened more around the family of the *turdu* every day, while on their side they did nothing to loosen it. On the contrary! The burst of dislike that the two spouses aroused in the hearts of everyone was exascerbated by their arrogant and indeed provocative behavior. The world seemed to be made for them. And with what malicious pleasure did husband and wife flaunt their well-being in everyone's face and make their condition as 'favorites' felt! What an insult to the poverty of the others! When the *turdu*, dressed in an impeccable corduroy suit and shod in honey-colored leather boots with a great display of knightly spurs, entered the fattoria, riding the best horse in the stable, he seemed to be the padrone in person. And when on Sunday Orsola flaunted silk dresses, tortoise shell combs, and twenty-four-carat gold pendants, with her libertine and insolent haughtiness there was no difference between her and a queen. The goodwives elbowed one another in sign of recognition and exclaimed in low tones, 'Go it, somebody is paying!,' and the men went *mmch*—the sound of the sheep—at the risk of being overheard by the man whom everyone now called a cuckold or *beccarone*.

If their resentment had stoppped there, nothing irreparable. But one morning an unpleasant incident occurred. The few lemon trees painfully cultivated on the *turdu*'s allotment awakened stripped of their bark. Wide white slashes stood out on their thin brown trunks. On a sturdy pedestal, a bit below the incision, laughed a sinister skull worked with the point of a knife. A death threat, in criminal slang. The peeling of the trees, according to this, represents both an insult and one of the most active forms of intimidation.

The deed aroused serious alarm in the family of the victim. With the lemon trees, destined to certain death, the peace of the household was also lost. Since the disaster had occurred, it was necessary to consider the remedy. There were two possibilities: to go to the police (which in such matters never flushes the spider out of the hole), or to turn to the mafia, which when it wants to doesn't joke around and doesn't make mistakes. Paolo hesitated for several days at the crossroads. There was no question of denouncing the deed to the town's policeman. Paolo would be called a *cascettone*, a squealer, and would meet with the contempt of the 'men of honor.' In the countryside, to fall into their disfavor is worse than anything one can suffer from a crime. As for bringing the matter before the tribunal of the mafia, there was a serious difficulty, that its upper hierarchies were terribly irritable.

Therefore, on that side, nothing to be done. The only thing left to Paolo was to take justice into his own hands. And if he had the guts (oh, if only he were able!), he would have eaten the hearts of those 'mascherati' (it is difficult for a Sicilian peasant to find a more insulting expression than 'masked ones'), burying their filthy bodies under the trees that they had ruined. But how to go about identifying them? To know, that was the problem. And at the time he did not see how to solve it.

On her side, Orsola didn't hesitate. Without bothering with the police or the mafia, she decided to do something different to draw the snake out of its nest. One morning she put on her shawl, tamed her unruly black hair with a fine kerchief of red silk tied under her chin, and went off—so she said—to do some shopping in Palermo. In reality she stopped half way, at Villafrati, where there lived a *magara,* old auntie Tofola who was expert in all the arts of witchcraft. No one would know better than she how to put Orsola on the track of the criminals who had dared such an insult against her family.

Maintaining the strictest incognito, Orsola entered the maze of the dirtiest streets, slipped into the fortune teller's hovel, put two *tarî* into the old woman's gnarled hands, laid out the mystery to her, and fearfully awaited the oracle, which would come out of a smoking pot where there boiled tails of newt, eyes of toad, fragments of bones of the dead, and other deviltries. On the drooling toothless mouth of the witch, who had fallen into a trance, there formed syllables, mumbled words, and finally obscure sentences. There was not a name, but there was more than enough to identify the authors of the crime.

As if a light had flashed on in her head, Orsola bit a finger, bursting out with the oath, 'You're right! But they'll all pay it to me in one go, the murderers.' Her eyes were boiling with blood.

She returned to the settlement, more silent than a fish, like a real 'femina di panza,' a woman who can keep a secret, as if nothing had happened.

But the matter did not end there. After a few days, more or less, there began to circulate a rumor among the women that she had gone to the witch to make the *fattura,* a spell against some poor man. If they had at least known the name of the unfortunate person who was her target, they could have resorted to the necessary exorcisms to turn aside the evil fate! Even the most secret spells have their counter-spell, the *fattura* can be neutralized by an energetic counter-*fattura*. But you can't work in a void, you can't act in these witches' businesses by groping in the dark. You must first know where to put your hands, you must know name and family of the person against whom evil spirits have been unloosed. And all that was unknown. This state of uncertainty held the settlement under a heavy leaden mantle—more than just a threat, a real nightmare.

—This isn't going to end well—the goodwives chatted mysteriously when they got together in the evening—here, you'll see, one day or another it will finish with the *botto,* the explosion. The evil spirits, once they are disturbed, do not have peace and do not give it. Cursed is the one who has unloosed them. It was as peaceful as a convent and now...

—And now? tell, tell—pressed the most curious of the women, in a devilish chatter.

—What can I say—sighed another, who seemed the most informed and shrewd.—Certain things it's better for such as know them to keep bottled up.

—But finally?

—Finally...don't play the innocent. Don't you know that here...one hears. Certain things are happening...Father, Son, and Holy Ghost.—And they all made the sign of the Cross.

Rumors of strange and alarming events were already spreading.

There was someone who had seen one evening a *buffa,* a toad, start off with little hops toward the door of *zia* Lena. The awful little animal suddenly ran into two crossed stems of straw, shot fire from its swollen eyes, and disappeared. The next day the old woman was found on the ground with a lot of foam on her mouth...But alive. She had been saved through the merit of that cross.

And this other story, stay and listen. How do you explain that the little son of the Straticò family, a *nutrico,* a suckling of three months, put to sleep at evening in his cradle woke up the next day in the cow's manger? She was looking at him and did not dare to touch him. She seemed petrified by fear. Who knows what she had seen during the night, the poor animal! Some 'woman from outside' had certainly transported the baby there.

And this is still nothing. The 'women from outside' had done worse. They had actually *changed* the baby girl of the Lenzitti family. A flower of a child, beside whom the most beautiful rose turned pale. Well, from one day to the next the child was no longer recognizable. She was seized by convulsions, her legs shrivelled like rags, she became a tiny deformed and disfigured creature who whined like a dog. Her own mother no longer recognized her. She even had a mop of red hair that was not her own. She had been exchanged, you understand? Exchanged for a little monster. Without doubt the work of witches; instigated by whom, if not by the usual 'infamoni'?

Nor was that all. The evil spirits continued to work. And the most terrifying fact was that one day the devil was born in the village, the devil in flesh and blood. The cow of Pasquale Catena labored and brought forth a horrifying creature, a real monster with seven heads and ten horns, goats' hooves, and a tail like a serpent. The monster stretched out on the straw litter looked around with basilisk-like eyes and breathed smoke from its nostrils, a horror to see. And such was the horror that the people who came running—a real parade—threw themselves on this deformed creature and finished it off with blows of stones and sticks. The news spread immediately through the nearby towns. More than one priest, on hearing the description of the monster, declared that it was the Beast of the Apolcalypse. Precisely: the seven heads and the ten horns, aside from everything else, were enough to recognize it. Perhaps terrible things were preparing for the settlement, a real scourge of God. Let the inhabitants of the accursed place consider doing penance and begging forgiveness for their sins.

While the more frightened and pious spoke of reconsecrating the village and of rites of expiation, the bolder ones, as often happens, instead of resigning themselves to the will of God and imploring forgivenenss for their own guilt, began a prosecution against the responsibilities of men. This time it seemed that they were on the track of serious indications against someone. Was or was it not true that on the day before the Catena's cow went into labor, goodwife Orsola had been seen circling about near the stall making mysterious signs? And if that circumstance corresponded to the truth (more than one perosn affirmed it, ready to wager the 'sight of their eyes'), could it be doubted that the woman possessed by Satan, with the co-operation of who knows what witch, had performed the spell? The reasoning fit perfectly and glided right into the minds of an excited population like a sword into its sheath. Now that they knew the source of the rot, the cause of so many misfortunes was clear. 'The abomination comes from there'—the boldest ones affirmed without restraint, pointing their fingers at the house of the *turdu*. It's them, that *mascherato* and his wife, who have to 'dig the earth from the ditch.' 'Either let them confess their crimes, or we'll make them sing to the sound of the whip.'

The comments and the subdued grumbles burst out in the whole settlement into public accusations. Unruly clusters and knots of people were formed. Threatening hands were raised. Old hatreds rekindled by superstition and fear were ready to explode. Some restraint and some words of prudence were not lacking on the part of the most sensible. But, as always happens in popular uprisings, the opinion of the most extreme and of the violent ended by prevailing, breaking through the weak barriers of rationality. And in the unchanneled river of the passions the bad and the less good (if not the best) get swept away, finally, to make common cause with the masses.

—You know that I say?—exclaimed one of the big shots, reckless and respected for having done time in jail.—Do you know the proverb, 'If you don't break it you can't fix it'?

—So?—asked several of the most aroused, who crowded around him.

—It's time to finish it off. A good lesson to the wicked, and the peace of the angels will return here. But one of those lessons that they don't forget—and he drilled his scarred cheek with his joined thumb and index finger.

—Inspired words!—shouted the others all together. *Ci vonnu l'agghi pi' vicini,* You need garlic to keep the neighbors away.

—When?

—As soon as possible. Even tomorrow.

—And why not right now? Let's break it, since it has to be broken.

An involuntary understanding ran like an electric current over the faces of all. The group, which had increased into a crowd, wavered, recomposed, formed a line, as if it obeyed the order of an invisible commander, and marched as one man toward the house of the *turdi*.

At the head were the women (who are always the first and the most venturesome in popular uprisings), howling and gesturing like possessed Mænads, mixed with a bunch of kids armed with stones and clubs. They were followed by many men, mostly unarmed, others furnished with scythes, bill hooks, hoes, and pitchforks.

When they arrived in front of the house there arouse deafening shouts, piercing shrieks. Door and windows were closed. The squat building, canary yellow with a hunchbacked roof painted red, seemed uninhabited.

—Out with the witch. We want the *magara.*

The silence provoked the rioters. Their cries became more threatening and furious.

—Open, you murderers, or we'll break the door down.

The first stones flew, shattering the glass of the window.

The barrel of a rifle emerged through the crossbars of the iron grating and fired off a blast with a red flash. It was a shot into the air to intimidate the besiegers. At first they fell back, then they closed up around the house with renewed fury, trying to break down the door.

—He's shooting to kill, the murderer! Come out or we'll burn you like a rat in its hole—cried the crowd of peasants like beasts.

—Come out, *cornuto*!

—We want the witch, we want her!

Suddenly a messenger, a shirtless boy, arrived with the news that the woman was not there. She had taken refuge with the padrone. They had to flush her out there.

The news disoriented the crowd. There was a moment of uncertainty. The pressure around the house of the steward loosened. After a short consultation, part of the people remained to guard the building, while the majority moved in a crowd toward the house of the padrone.

Here the tumult flamed up again more furious than before.

Federico came to the door, on those same steps where he had so often been hailed as a benefactor and father of the poor, and dominating the uproar with his voice and gestures he asked to speak.

Assisting himself more by movements than by voice, he tried to tell them to remain calm, that they would have every satisfaction, that if someone had done wrong he would be punished. But their shouts overpowered his words.

—We want the witch! Bring out the mangy sheep!

—We'll burn her along with her goat, with that *cornuto* husband of hers!

—She's your whore. Even the stones know it. Hand her over to us, it'll be better for you. We want to drink her blood!

Federico protested indignantly. Although he did not tremble, he was as pale as a corpse.—I tell you that there is no one here.

—We knw she's your concubine, that's why you're hiding her.

—Liar! Deceiver, exploiter of the poor! Clown, *tragediatore,* charlatan, crook!

Amid the insults there flew a rock which hit the padrone in the chest. The bestial crowd moved to attack his house.

Federico had barely time to move back when there sounded a salvo of rifles. The field guards, who had come to the door without waiting for any order, fired. And after the first shots in the air they pointed their guns straight at the most inflamed members of the mob.

The crowd ebbed, disbanded, dispersed. All the same, from the attitude of the most violent it was clear that they were running away only to return to the attack

When Federico had reached the top of the nearest hill in his frantic flight from his estate amid the escort of his armed field-guards, he turned backward. At the sight of the plume of smoke waving over his house, with a powerful pang in his heart he had the clear sensation that his dream was being ruined forever and that a second life was beginning for him.

The company rode close together and at a good pace toward the town. The weather had turned into rain. Although it did not rain thickly, but in fits and starts—a shower that seen against the light pierced the heavens with a thousand silver needles—the paths sank in the mire. The mud stuck to the horses' legs, which here and there were swamped in the holes, and made it difficult to put one step after another, in a constant splashing of lumps of mud. They were aware of nothing but the thud of their hooves in the desolate silence of the countryside. None of the travelers spoke except to encourage the animals with some brief word.

The darkness was thick when they reached the outskirts of the town. Suddenly a flash of bluish lightning illuminated the skeletons of the first trees and the roofs of the tallest houses. A crash, a crackle, a dark echo rolled from valley to valley. Then nothing more.

The town was dead. Some pale and rare lights at a window, some ribbons of smoke silhouetted from a chimney.

Turning into one of the many little slippery side streets which converged like the ribs of a fan on the inhabited center, the little brigade stopped before a door raised above ground level by two flintstone steps.

When he had dismounted Federico handed the reins of his horse to one of the guards and knocked with the knocker attached to one of the double doors. A long howl of dogs answered, scratching behind the door as if they there were on guard, ready to hurl themselves on the nocturnal disturber.

At the third knock a little high window opened a crack and a woman's voice, annoyed and angry, asked:

—*Cu è ddocu?*

—Friends—answered Federico.

—Friends who?

After the spplicant had given his name the woman disppeared behind the window. After a bit she reappeared there.

—*Aspittassi*—wait, she said with a more polite, indeed ceremonious tone—I'm coming down to unbar the door.

A slow clatter of wooden shoes, the sliding of metal through the rings, the squeak of a double lock, then the labored flicker of a tiny flame trembling on the mouth of a little shepherd's lamp.

—*Trasissi*—come in, she invited—I'll go ahead to give you some light.

A stairway of slate with over-high steps led to a landing; on the left, an open door.

A deep voice, roughened by smoking, called back the mastiffs who were still giving tongue:

—Come here Leone, here Malandrino! Lie down! They're friends.

The massive gladitorial figure of don Salvatore Calò stood out from the shadow of the doorway. From the groping motion made by his hand—an enormous hand of vigorous shape—to extend it to the visitor, it was apparent that he was blind. With a bit more light two whiteish balls, veiled by a membrane like the eyes of nocturnal birds, could be seen swimming in his eye sockets. The mask of his face, with a powerful and sensitive bone structure, was wreathed at the cheeks by a short beard, unkempt and bushy, of ebony inlaid here and there with silver arabesques.

—Good evening, don Turridu.

—*Baciamo le mani,* cavaliere. Clasp these four weak bones (Federico's fingers were almost crushed in the mountaineer's iron fist). To what do I owe such honor this evening?

—Honor? rather say disturbance. The honor, if any, is all mine.

—Let's not speak of such things...

—I know that this is not the hour for social calls. But what would you have, necessity obliges us to take advantage of our friends.

—Don't say that, cavaliere. Your Excellency is the master here. Pardon me if I lead the way.—And the blind man, feeling the ground with his rustically inlaid cane, led his guest into the next room, a vast chamber with whitewashed walls, simply furnished: a round table and an old divan whose stuffing poured out from its unsewn sides, an old credenza, and a few chairs around a brass brazier where a little fire of cherry-wood smoldered.

—At your service—said don Salvatore, when they had sat down.

—Humblest thanks. So. Hear me, began Federico, passing his hand over his brow furrowed with premature wrinkles.

—I'm all ears. But be patient for a moment—said the old *capomafia*, understanding the importance of the coming conversation—the walls have no ears, and yet they hear.

Having made sure that the door was well closed by giving the handle a shake, don Turriddu returned to his seat.

While Federico spoke excitedly, the old man sat with his chin on the handle of his staff, in thought. Occasionally he awakened from his seeming lethargy, proudly raised his head, and searched the void with his eyes, which seemed suddenly to regain the power of sight. In his expression there was something solemn and majestic, like an Homeric king who administered justice under a tree or up against a column.

For fifty years he had given law, above any other law, in his kingdom, and his moral authority was such that often people came to him from outside its borders to hear his wisdom in questions that involved the whole island. He did not boast a family tradition in the Mafia, he was in fact the founder of a new dynasty which had forced out the previous one. Rising through all the ranks of the invisible hierarchy by his courage, his resolution, his love of risk and his contempt for every authority, he had earned his baton of command. Having gone into hiding to avoid a heavy prison sentence for killing his father's murderer, he had lived for some time the life of a robber: a kind of robbery *sui generis* exercised not without a spirit of justice and chivalry, unyielding with the powerful, generous with the weak. Sought by the police, one day he had decided to give himself up to spare his family from reprisals. Having served a large part of his sentence (the rest had been remitted as a reward for his good behavior), he had returned to his town surrounded by great prestige. He no longer belonged to an active role in criminal life because in prison he had lost his sight through glaucoma. But he preserved an unquestioned authority in governing circles, an authority which was constantly increased and consolidated so as to make him the *capo dei capi*, the generalissimo of the association. Although blind, he saw everything; confined to his house, he was present everywhere. His justice was infallible, every one of his judgments was irrevocable. There was no quarrel between families that was not settled by his intervention, no wrong committed that was not righted just by a sign from him. There did not exist a poor man, a widow, an oppressed man who did not find in him a stronghold. No bounty or contribution was imposed on the rich landowners except with his consent. No one went to the police without his 'nulla osta': in short, not a leaf of a tree moved in the province without either his authorization or his permission. It was enough to speak the name of don Turiddu (and no one dreamed of taking it in vain) for things to go as they *had* to go.

Before this authoritative personage Federico began to retell the history of Astrea, from the time that it had emerged from his mind until its full realization. His account was clear and precise, only interrupted by a pause when he had to catch up again the thread of a memory that was escaping him.

—*Appresso, appresso,* Stick to the facts—the blind man interrupted from time to time, just as professors do, when the narrative got off the track and became verbose.

Federico had just finished telling the whole story and remained waiting for an answer, when the blind man, who was well known for his frequent insertion of popular proverbs into his conversation, said:

—*Vossia,* excuse me. Can I say a word? *Cu fa ligna a mala banna 'ncuoddu di li porta,* If you choose the wrong place to gather wood you must carry it on your back. Proverbs are never wrong. Vossia *avi la littra,* you are educated, I am a poor ignorant man. These eyes have seen so many things before Jesus Christ took the light of the sun from them. They have nothing more to see, I would say. Even now that they are buried in night, they know how to tell right from wrong. What do you wish? If Your Excellency had done me the honor of asking my opinion before embarking on this enterprise, I would have told you, watch out for missteps. Now that the step has been taken, we're on the edge of the *sdirrupu,* the abyss.

—I was mistaken. What can I say? Everybody can make a mistake.

—Satisfy my curtiosity, *Voscenza.* Who put this wonderful idea into your head?

—No one. I reached it by myself. One day my conscience suggested to me: You must do something for the poor, it is right they too should have their part of the earth that today is possessed only by the rich.

—*A cuscienza è du lupu,* Conscience belongs to the wolf—moralized don Turiddu bitterly.—My seventy years teach me that it is useless to speak about conscience to men. Everyone says, This belongs to me and I'm taking it, that belongs to someone else and I'm taking that too.

—But I wanted everyone to have his own portion of happiness.

—Happiness is in heaven—said the blind man, raising his finger—it's up there. Down here we are all unhappy. Some more, some less, but everyone. You want to make the peasant happy. Madness! Have you ever heard a peasant who was content with the weather that the Lord God sends him? If the weather is dry and sunny, he wants rain. If it rains, he longs for fair weather. If heaven gives rain and sun when he desires, he quibbles about the amount—only a bit less, a bit more, what a rich harvest! And he ends up complaining all the time. Give him the earth. Do you think you have made him happy? But the land, since the time God made the world, has always belonged to the padroni. Only the master can find work for everyone. You have given the land to the peasant. He will never appreciate the good that you have done him. He will say that it's his right and he will hate you, because the benefited always holds a grudge against his benefactor. So it is written. But it is also written that the peasant should be treated like the wild thistle: first you stamp on it, then you weed it out. If not, what thorns you will feel! Let me say, my dear *Cavaliruuzu,* that you have divided up the earth, an estate like gold, among all those *piedi di pelo,* those shoeless peasants, dismissing so many gabelloti who, I don't doubt, said openly that they held Your Lordship's estate in the palm of their hand. What have you gained?

—Nothing at all—sighed Federico.

—You have created a bunch of freeloaders! And what arrogance, what pride! They saw you go by and looked down on you, they were ashamed to say 'your servant,' not even as if the dog were passing by. Word of honor (and here the voice of don Turiddu took on a cavernous tone of contempt), if it were not for our repect of your family, my boys would have made those unfortunates smell *u ciaru da pruvuli,* a whiff of gunpowder. What a lesson they would have given that lousy bunch! But don Turiddu Calò (at this point the elderly mafioso struck his breast with his great hand, raising the dust from the fustian of his waistcoat, which had been a stranger to a clothes brush for who knows how long), who is older than them, said, Patience, my boys! Time is a gentleman. He has no hurry but he arrives at everything. My late father used to say, *Dissi la vurpi a li vurpotti, ntu lu nguantaru nn videmu tutti,* Said the vixen to the fox cubs, we'll all meet at the glovemaker's.

—And now what's to be done—interrupted Federico, impatient to reach a conclusion.

—Indeed, Eccellenza, you find yourself, as they say *nto peri du nigghiu,* in the claws of the eagle.

—Is there a remedy to free oneself from the eagle's claws?—asked Federico, repeating the metaphor of his interlocutor.

—There's a remedy for everything except death.

—How do you think I can get out of this mess?

—I have my plan—answered the capomafia, closing his eyes and leaning his chin on the handle of his cane, as if to concentrate his ideas.—It is understood that Your Excellency must give us *carte blanche.* You will see that in less time then it takes to say it, your estate will be cleansed of serpents. *Voscenza* must pledge your word...

—Speak. Everything necessary will be at your disposal—said Federico, reaching for his wallet.

—What are you doing?—interrupted don Turridu, restraining Federico's hand, whose gesture he had guessed.—Some things you don't joke about. One does not sell one's help to friends. Are we Jews?

—Pardon me—Federico corrected himself.

—I wanted to say—continued the blind man—there is one condition: That the law must know nothing of what has happened and what will happen. Let's do things *belle assistemate*...a *taci maci*..., well arranged, on the sly between ourselves, like serious people. You silent and me silent. Are we understood?

—Agreed. Can you have any doubts? But if the law already knew about it?

—I'm the only law here—smiled don Turiddu with all his thirty-two teeth.—For the rest, deny, deny, keep on denying. The only thing you can't hide is a corpse. And thank God, there are no corpses here.

—What if the others talked?

—No one will breathe a word—declared don Turiddu firmly.

—What must I do?

—Nothing. Nothing except return to your house.

—Return! But they've driven me away from it!

—Say rather that Your Excellency has left your property. Don't give those *mascherati* that satisfaction. Meanwhile...I wanted to say...it would be better if, while we are working, you went on holiday to Palermo... No (he corrected himself after a moment's thought), *Voscenza* will stay here in my house. May I have such an honor?

—The honor is mine.

—What are you saying? This is not a house fit for the *signoria*...a house of the poor...but you will lack for nothing. Surely Your Ecellency has not eaten.

—I have eaten bile, don Turiddu.

—I'm not offering you a dinner. You will eat a plate of pasta with me. It is not equal to your merits, but it is offered with all my heart. Will you permit me?

The blind man stood up and left the room, finding his way with his staff, until his steps were lost in the silence. He was heard conferring with his women.

He returned with a jovial and satisfied air.

About three quarters of an hour later came a light tap on the door.

—Supper is ready. Come and do penance with your servant—said don Turiddu, inviting his guest to precede him into the dining room. The table was set for two. Following the custom of the island countryside, when the master of the house has men to dinner woman are not included among the guests. Their role is limited to serving the diners, rapidly appearing and disappearing, visions almost imperceptible to the eyes of the beholders.

In the circle of light that poured on the tablecloth from an oil lamp hanging from the ceiling, there smiled the vermilion of a jug of wine, and a golden loaf of pure wheat shone.

Veiled by the smoke of two plates of minestra which she was balancing in both hands, there entered an olive-skinned girl, a real Arab with a noble profile (a pity that two scars under her cheeks, the sign of childhood scrofula, disturbed the purity of her features).

—The smallest of my daughters—introduced don Turiddu, while the girl chastely averted her glance.

The Pantagruelic appetite of the master of the house contrasted with the lack of hunger of Federico, who unwillingly nibbled at the savory lamb thigh on his plate.

—Your Excellency is not eating—said don Turiddu, observing that his guest was struggling to take the meat off a bone with his knife.

—Do like me.—Grabbing a rib, with his strong teeth he tore off chunks of red meat, coating his face with grease.

Two dogs lying at his left and right greedily awaited the leftovers. Losing patience, now one, now the other lifted its paw from time to time to tap on the edge of the table.

—I can't see. But I feel that Voscenza is not eating. How can you have an appetite if you don't drink? *Mangiari senza viviri è comu trinari senza chioviri,* Eating without drinking is like thunder without rain. When this is over we will raise our glasses together to toast your health and defiance to the envious.

When the meal was finished, don Turiddu lighted his pipe, scratching the sulphur match on the floor. Then he rose, and by the light of a candlestick he accompanied Federico to his bedroom, which was already nicely prepared.

—Sleep well—he advised—and don't think about anything. God is great!

The following Sunday—barely three days had passed since the conference between the two men—while the peasants were gaily gathering after mass on the square in front of the Mother Church, the great tidings spread.

—Do you know the news? There's no longer anyone on the estate. Everybody cleared out. General eviction. The freeloaders *Si cogghinu li pezzi e si nni vannu,* They got their stuff together and scrammed. By whose order? For heaven's sake, don't speak. No one must know anything about it. Nobody has seen. Water in the mouth, otherwise there's trouble. It was Saturday...

On Saturday a brigade of mounted men, no more than a dozen, armed to the teeth, had appeared at the settlement and having assembled the elders and the leaders, with a masterful manner that did not admit of comments or replies they had delivered the sentence:

—By order of don Turiddu, before the sun sets nobody is to remain here, not even the cat. Clean sweep. Everybody go back where you came from! If anybody asks you, not a living soul has come here, you haven't seen anything. You left the estate because it no longer suited you to stay here. Understand?

By evening there was no trace of a human being in the estate. The land was deserted, the farmhouses empty, every light extinguished. Only a few whining lost dogs, looking for their masters. *Astrea* had disappeared in a flash, as a transformation scene in the theater. Like a prehistoric Destiny, intact and mysterious, the latifondo returned to dominate in its splendid loneliness.

The year was 1852.

Chapter 4

TEN YEARS. The face of the estate was changed. The soul of Federico was changed still more and irreparably twisted out of shape. The youth of the earth is eternally renewed by the changes of the seasons, the smiling green descends again like a symbol on an earth devastated by the winter and dried up by the summer. In the life of man what passes does not return, what dies is without resurrection. It is not possible to step twice into the same river when the water flows without pause. Federico was no longer recognizable. Grey and bent-over before his time, his brow furrowed by deep creases; with his drooping cheeks and his beard, which had grown long and unkempt like that of a Capuchin, he showed in his whole body the signs of precocious decay. How many and what kinds of events had passed over the world since he had come to his estate in the full excitement of faith and enthusiasm to realize his project of social renewal! In 1850 the execution of Nicolò Garzilli and his companions; in 1856 the attempt on Ferdinando II, followed by the execution of baron Bentivegna at Mezzouiso as a retaliation; in 1857 the martydom of Salvatore Spinuzza and the massacre of Carlo Pisacane and his expedition at Sapiri; then the death of the perjured king; the attempted murder of the terrible Maniscalco in Palermo; the unfortunate insurrection of 4 April and the execution of the thirteen heroes in piazza Castello; and finally the landing and the glorious march of Garibaldi and the Thousand, followed two years later by the sad episode of Aspromonte... Names, dates, circumstances, paraded like a moving scene in Federico's memory, surrounded by a cloud of fog that softened their outlines and drove them back into a distance beyond recall. Between a 'yesterday' that every day retreated farther in his memory, and a 'tomorrow' that refused to take form in his desire, Federico was isolated, an anchorite of time, in the brief space of 'today' as in a hermit's cell without doors and windows. He did not see and did not feel anything but the life of every day, in some good work that he happened to carry out. He had begun finally to understand that the world has more need of mercy than of justice. There is perhaps already too much justice by comparison with the little charity that abides in the heart of men. That small bit which exists would be sufficient if men remembered to be merciful before being just.

That evening Federico was returning from one of those works of mercy that he practiced with discreet humility.

Someone had died in the cottage perched on the edge of the village, near which he found himself passing while taking the road back to his estate in the late afternoon. He guessed it from the desperate cries which issued like mortuary birds from the black and scabby walls of the hut. In the doorway some poor children with hollow cheeks were crying.

—*Arripetino,* they are mourning the widow Anna's baby—said a poor woman who was coming out of the house of sorrow, wiping her eyes, when he asked.

Federico crossed the threshold, accompanied by his armed guard. At his appearance in the doorway there arose a piercing scream, followed by heavy weeping that subsided into a funereal lament. The lament was echoed by a chorus of women who shared (or pretended to share, according to the custom of the Sicilian countryside) the mother's disaster. On a bed of rags a disheleved old woman alternated her slow-witted glance between a little corpse and the faces of the bystanders and laughed, scraping the bottom of an empty bowl. Within a *madia,* a kneading trough for bread, transformed into a coffin, the little body of a baby was stretched out. Its almost bald head with a tuft of rough hair, its cheeks violet, its eyelids white as paper. Crowds of flies, like bees around a hive, buzzed over it and rested on the misshapen face, an offence to the poverty of death. A mangy yellow dog of a thinness that was the ghost of hunger mounted guard over the little corpse, his eyes fixed on it. He did not move except to chase away the flies which were stinging his sweaty and wooly ears. At the sight of her visitor, the mother burst out in a convulsive and frenzied lament. Federico informed himself about the illness, about the death, made a rapid inquiry into the conditions of the family, offered words of consolation, and left a considerable sum of money in the hands of those abandoned people. He gave orders to procure a veil to protect the little angel from the stings of the winged insects. A hundred blessings accompanied him to the threshold of the poor house that had been visited by the Relentless One.

When he had returned home, even before he entered the courtyard of his country house he knew that someone from Palermo was waiting for him.

He suddenly found himself face to face with his nephew. They embraced. Goffredo handed him a letter from his grandmother, which Federico read, not without effort owing to the fading daylight.

When he had finished reading (donna Ortensia, after describing Goffredo's adventures in her biting and caustic style, begged her son to welcome him and shelter him until the storm had blown over), he clapped the young man on the shoulder and said with a smile between irony and sorrow:

—You too, me a second and you a third Don Quixote, have fallen from your horse...from the Ideal. Thrown from the saddle, with your lance at rest...it's funny and humiliating, isn't it? We will console one another, dear boy...In the meantime you will need to eat and to rest. You must be tired from your journey.

—No, uncle. I feel as fresh as if I'd just come out of a bath.

—A strange sickness, youth. Fortunately I've been cured of it for a good while.

—You're not old, uncle. Quite the opposite!

—Yes, to console us old people they usually say that if the body declines the spirit is always lively and bold, *Spiritus promptus, caro autem infirma.* Lies, my dear boy. It is the spirit that languishes and decays before the body does. The body only follows it, like the donkey follows its master. The patriarchs lived so long because they did not chase after impossible fantasies, deceptive illusions, as we do. Come. While our meal is being prepared, let's take a walk through the vineyard. They're already harvesting the grapes. The excessive heat this year has hurried their ripening. There is not a bunch that is not already golden. Nothing at all that one expected, the sun will finish by cooking even the last grape. You too must begin to interest yourself in these things, now that you are about to become a countryman like your uncle.

—True, by the necessity of things.

—Say instead, by your luck. The countryside is stillness and peace. It is a friend who does not betray you. If only humanity resembled it!

They had already reached the vineyard. A bustle of barefoot men, of women with their skirts kilted up around their waists. Joviality spread in the air, which was ringing with shouts and cries, a bit intoxicated from the strong odor of the wine must. Some went back and forth with baskets filled with bunches of grapes between the rows of the vines and the clearing where they began the treading; some emptied the grapes from the baskets into the treading tubs; some gathered up the bunches that were scattered on the ground; some handed the empty baskets back to the women vintagers.

Their leader was *zio* Damiano, a little old man with a face like a *focaccia*, prominent cheeks, a snub nose between two laughing eyes with a mocking faunlike expression.

In a tub a peasant was mashing the grapes, straining to crush them with his legs shod in leather boots, swollen with muscles that rippled like snakes. The trodden and squashed grapes danced, dived, remerged in the grape crusher, until a cloudy liquid in which there floated mashed grapes, seeds, and stalks foamed on the surface of the tub.

—Do you hear what a fizzing noise?—said Federico.—It is a kind of grape that no one except me possesses around here. Do you want to try a sip of must?

—No, uncle. I don't drink. Just the smell makes me dizzy. Let's walk.

The peaks of the Madonie were colored rose pink by the setting sun. The heat was dying down, and a delicious breeze descended from the heights to the earth like a pardon. Under their steps the dry grass rustled with a light whispering.

Encouraged by his uncle, Goffredo broke his silence and spoke of the adventure, or rather the misadventure, of Aspromonte. And he bewailed the fickleness and ingratitude of men. Who would ever have said that Garibaldi would end up like that? Treated worse than a criminal! Was it for this that we would have made the revolution?

—Every revolution has its sorrows—commented Federico.—You would like to be a Prometheus without the vulture, my boy. You cannot attempt peace for the world, even if this peace stinks of rot, without someone eating your liver.

—Indeed, to cleanse the world of the rot, every so often you need a revolution. And we'll have one soon in Sicily.

—Has some sibyl foretold this ?—joked his uncle.

—It just could be. Anyway, I don't think that one would have to be a prophet to foresee something similar. There are too many signs...in the air.

—I really dislike the prophets, the augurs, the haruspices, and all those who claim to read in the book of the future. They're malevolent beings when they're not just charlatans, impostors. Think what kind of hell life would become if the future were as clear as a sheet of glass. We would torture ourselves about evils to come and would not enjoy the good things of the present, whose end would seem certain, perhaps imminent. Belive me, the ignorance of the future is a necessary and good thing. Ignorance gives us unawareness, and unawareness gives us happiness. The man who knows the future is an unhappy man. And God has willed for our tranquillity, if not for our happiness, that we should know nothing about ourselves and about others. Do we know what we will be in a year, tomorrow, even in an hour? Everything is dark and the spirit is in a condition of perennial blindness, worse than a man born blind. Perhaps that is why it is said, Blessed are the poor in spirit.

—But we can't be fatalists and resigned. When things don't go the way they ought, only one course exists, to revolutionize them.

—We are always in a state of revolution, my boy. Doesn't the earth have a constant movement of rotation and revolution? And yet we feel as if we were not moving. We believe that all men are motionless with their feet on the earth, and instead the inhabitants of the Arctic zone have their feet where those of the Antarctic have their heads. Our planet turns and re-turns without a single man flyng off its surface, like a grain of rice falling off a ball that we twirl in our hands. Revolutions! They serve to enrich the glaziers, who install new glass after the old is broken; or they benefit the dyers, who dye old rags in new colors. For the rest, they leave everything as it is. I have seen three revolutions (aside from the French one of

'89 of which my mother still preserves some memories): those of 1812, of 1848, of 1860, and I don't know whether the world came out of them better or worse off. Riots, disorder, destruction; changes of programs, of slogans, of institutions...in the end, men remained the same: with the same merits, if they have any, and the same identical faults. Was it worth the trouble to make such an uproar for nothing? To be optimistic, you could say that revolutions obtain with violence and bloodshed in a few months or a year those same conquests that would have been obtained peacefully in ten. A small loan of time, when life is so long, when with respect to infinity all finite things are equal to zero. My boy, believe instead that the game is not worth the candle. But men are in a hurry. And who knows why? Time is so long in passing. As to wisdom, the woodworms possess a thousand times more than we do. They accomplish their destructive work, their revolutions, they dig immense underground tunnels, they split massive tree-trunks into fine powder, without heeding time. Do you hear? Here too we have a 'death-watch beetle.' It is called that because the dead are timeless.

Goffredo pricked up his ears (in the meantime the two men had returned to the house after their walk in the fields) and heard the gnawing of the woodworms, which punctuated the silence of the dying day.

The following day, appointed for a visit to the estate, uncle and nephew were up and about at an early hour.

—An ungodly hour for you city people to get up—said Federico, greeting the young man, who was quite ready, before daybreak. —For us country people this is everyday life. You city dwellers lose the spectacle of nature, which is all freshness and innocence, I almost said virginity, in the first light of the morning. Afterward it is as if everything were profaned and touched by the sins of mankind.

—You forget, uncle, that I have been to war. Then there was neither day nor night. Always on the alert, always on our feet, at every hour.

—It's true. I am forgetting everything. When I have gone to the other world no one will say, Poor Federico of happy memory...And when did you stop being a soldier?

—*O bella*! the day right after Aspromonte. I went from the field of battle to the jailhouse.

—Come, I'll give you a good cup of coffee. Confess, you didn't drink anything like this during the war.

—Our only coffee was the putrid water of some brook. And God was to be thanked when there was that.

Federico went into the kitchen and returned with a cup full of coffee heated on a little spirit stove.

—Taste it, it's my own work—he said proudly.

—There's no one to make it for you?

—No one. And if I gave the machine to some maid to work it, you'd see what dishwater! The first duty of a bachelor toward himself is to know how to offer himself a good coffee.

—Why didn't you marry, uncle?

—And why haven't you done so?

—I'm too young.

—And I'm too old.

—Is it a good thing or a bad one, not to marry?

—Socrates said, Whether you marry or whether you don't, you'll regret it all the same. One always regrets both what one has done and what one has left undone.

—All told, I think the regret of not having done something is worse. A life full of errors is preferable to a completely empty life. The void is horrifying, especially when we are born to act.

—You are repeating the dictum of the ancient philosophers, *Natura abhorret vacuum,* Nature abhors a vacuum, without knowing it. And yet everything all around us is empty, so empty: perhaps even within ourselves...

The horses were waiting in the courtyard. Fresh, saddled, well fed, they were pawing the ground with impatient hooves.

The two mounted, balancing their guns on their saddlebows; they gave a light twitch to the reins and set off. Rather than leading they let themselves be carried at the whim of the animals, who knowing the places, ears up and manes to the wind, devoured plains, scaled hills, forded streams, as if they were proud to communicate their joy to their riders.

Leaving the valley behind them, the two men entered a transverse path climbing the side of the hill and found themselves in the endless expanse of the estate.

The lonely yellowish sea of the earth at rest was punctuated in the distance by a sparse flock of houses.

—What are those dwellings?—asked Goffredo.

—There arose Astrea—Federico was about to answer. The words died in his throat, while in a burst of sadness distant ghosts emerged in a sinister procession on the edges of his memory.

Since the eyes of his nephew were still watching him intently, anxious for an answer, he asked:

—Have you ever done foolish things?

—Many. But I don't regret them, I'd do them again.

—Then they are not foolish.

—Doesn't it seem to you, uncle, that all our mistakes, at the moment we are committing them, appear to us as the flower of wisdom? Otherwise we would not have fallen into them. It's clear. But to persist in an error, with the full knowledge that it is wrong, is impermissable.

—It should be like that, if man were a reasonable animal. Quite the opposite! Look, you will know my story. Nor do I want to tell it to you now, it would be too sad. Do you believe that I can forgive myself the greatest mistake that I ever committed in my life? Not one but many. I was wrong about the end and about the means.

The first mistake (which concerns the end) is to have believed that you can bestow happiness on mankind. Good luck! How can we want to give to others what we can't manage to achieve for ourselves? Man, even if you put him to swim in a sea of gold, will always be unhappy...To suppose the contrary means to be able to usher in paradise on this earth, to believe in a temporal, present paradise. Or in a future paradise that can appear here tomorrow, or the day after! Folly, my dear boy. In other words, it would mean exterminating evil from the world. Can you imagine anything more absurd? Evil is within mankind, it is man himself. A shirt of Nessus, a poisoned shirt, from which the flesh can free itself only by death.

To my mistake about the end add my mistake about the means. That is, believing that happiness can be attained on the economic level by working on the material goods that surround us. We say, let us transform the social order, let us distribute material goods better, with standards of equality, let us assign to each an equal portion of the riches of the earth, and we will have made mankind happy. In short, let us change the outside world, and—hey presto!—mankind is reformed. Let us unchain the economic revolution and the new man will replace the old one. No, my dear.

You must reform mankind first, and then the world. What will you make of a world transformed in the best of ways, according to your opinion, if man remains the same, with his second-rate vices, his insatiable appetites, pale with envy and yellow with hatred for his fellows?

Talking like this, they had stopped under an ancient Saracen olive that twisted its earthy trunk like a Laocoön.

—Humanity writhes like that in its eternal sorrow—said Federico—in the pain of its unsatisfied desires. And it does not know how to attain even the peace of this olive tree, which for centuries has lifted its prayer to God, happy for the rain and for the sun alike.

When they returned home in the late afternoon, the news had arrived from Palermo that the Ratazzi government had conceded an amnesty for the events of Aspromonte.

—So, from today you are free—said Federico.

—I don't accept the amnesty—Goffredo answered, scornful and bitter.—It's a handout that I don't need. Cowardice offering an anmesty to bravery! Shame pardoning honor!

The skies had darkened and had released a short and violent burst of rain. Calm returned and the countryside appeared clear and shining like a picture under glass.

PART III

Chapter 1

—You SEE that stump of a dagger up there, stuck into the right shutter of the main entrance? It's the weapon with which in 1160 Matteo Bonelli stabbed Maio of Bari, the chancellor of William I, who was tyrannizing the people. God uses madmen to punish those who transgress his laws.

Thus spoke a three-cornered hat perched on the twisted shoulders of a little hunchbacked priest (his head disappearing into the shell of his collar like that of a tortoise) to the hood of a beanpole friar, who raised his nose as if he wished to reach the butt of the knife blade nailed to the door of the archiepiscopal palace. He chanted in approval, *Supervenit interitus exercentibus tyrannidem,* Destruction has come upon the workers of tyranny.

A solemn meeting at the Bishop's Palace. A few at a time, or in flocks, or lined up by their respective communities, priests and friars entered via Matteo Bonelli and disappeared into the entrance of the palace. Seen from one of the spires of the cathedral they would have looked like streams of ink sucked in and swallowed by some aperture of the historic edifice.

They mounted the stairway, jabbering, scratching, spitting into their red and blue handkerchiefs; canons, beneficiaries, parish priests, archpriests, chaplains, seminarians, as well as a dense crowd of friars, pouring down from all the churches, abbeys, cloisters, and convents of the diocese. Cassocks that were faded and green with use, black and purple robes, tricornes both shiny and mangy, with black, green, and violet cords; gowns, hoods, and scapulars of every cut and color; feet roughly shod in leather and rope or tripping along in little patent-leather slippers adorned with fine silver buckles. They climbed the vast stairway of red marble and poured into the vestibule, a fine rectangular chamber frescoed by Borremans, the wizard of perspective and chiaroscuro. Rampant arches, foreshortened columns, rich capitals, cornices, cymatia, mouldings, festoons, volutes—all as if they were in full relief—ran across the ceiling, miraculously suspended from the blue of a painted heaven filled with golden clouds.

At the head of the room there played a jet of water irradiated by the sun like a soap bubble. Under this a small table, and under that a platform covered with a flowered carpet. On the near side the white flock of chairs. To the right of the platform a canopy of crimson velvet enshrined the great gilded baroque throne for His Excellency the Archbishop.

The prelate made his entrance with a rustle of silk and a buzz of voices, followed by his long train and by a mob, not less long, of the great men of the Curia. The amethyst of his ring flashed on the prelate's hand as he blessed from right to left with the pendulum of three pale fingers.

When Monsignor Naselli was settled into the violet cloud of his cappa magna, the speaker—the abbe Melchiorre Galeotti, Prefect of Studies as well as Reader in Patrology in the seminary—mounted the platform, and drew out a sheaf of papers. Having dispatched the required reverences by swinging the thurible of his bald head in every direction, he launched into his homily. It was a text for public discussion, mobilized by vast erudition, by virtue of which he was pardoned the frequent slips of the tongue which punctuated his discourses, in part from faults of pronunciation, in part from distraction. His unclear diction, which broke up syllables and swallowed word endings amid a rise and fall of high and low pitches, imposed on his audience an unusual effort of attention. Since not everything reached the ears of the bystanders, from the last rows of chairs someone occasionally called, 'louder.'

Only a few parts of his long harangue were clear enough to be heard:

'The sacrilegious idea of the secularization of the goods of the Church could only germinate, like a flower of evil, from the French Revolution. Two traitors promoted it before the National Assembly: Charles Talleyrand de Périgord, apostate bishop and concubinist, who was stabbing the

Church, his mother; and Gabriele Riquetti count of Mirabeau, a deserter from the nobility, into whose bosom he had been born...

'Mortmain, *manus mortua*, a bugaboo with which to raise goose pimples on the simple-minded: goods withdrawn from circulation, from their social function, destined to non-productivity, the ruin of the economy! Lies, gentlemen. The religious orders were the first tillers of the soil, the first reclaimers of the earth, after the devastations and derelictions of the age of barbarism...The Church has drawn on these goods to finance its universal organization, to nourish, as well as its worship, its works of charity, of education and instruction, of civilizing. From there she stretches out her pitying arm, which alleviates so many miseries and so much human suffering...They forget that not only the clergy but also hundreds of families live from the estates of the Church: the families of the bursar, of the porter, of the accountant, of the sacristan, of the doorkeeper, of the peasants who work the land...By confiscating these goods you will have thrown out onto the street and condemned to hunger more than just the friars and the nuns, who live by poverty, but also their innocent little children...I meant to say (*sit venia verbis*) the little children of the numerous families who depend on the nuns and friars...

(At the unexpected *gaffe*, the audience burst into laughter. The archbishop, who was foundering in a theological torpor, shook himself. His well-combed aluminum-colored hair was disarranged, and the black earthworms of his thick eyebrows met at the top of his nose in a grimace of dislike.)

'...How many slanders there are about the origin of ecclesiastical property! They talk of bargaining for the forgiveness of sins, of donations and testaments extorted from the rich with the threat of Hell, of expropriations to the detriment of the debtors of tithes. What a distortion of history! Above all, our Divine Founder allowed the Church to rely on the offerings of the faithful to render her independent from secular sovereignty. But in Sicily the ecclesiastical alliance boasts purer origins. It goes back to the Normans...

(A voice commented, In Sicily everything good goes back to the Normans, who after all were foreigners. Always toadying to foreigners, that's us!)

'Roger de Bouillon, when he had freed our noble island from the Saracens, divided the conquered lands as fiefs among his fellow-soldiers and the Church, which had aided his holy undertaking...With what right does the atheist and liberal State now come to rob us of these fiefs?...

'That is the State which the great vicar of Christ Pius IX repudiated and unmasked two years ago, 8 December 1864, with his *Syllabus*, condemning its errors...

'It is true that the enemies of Christ lie ever in ambush. An attack by the so-called Reformed Christianity ravaged the whole kingdom soon after that event. It was not so long ago when here, in our Sicily, the stronghold of Catholicism, Valdensian missionaries descended to spread among the people the error of their heresiarch Pietro Valdo. But their insane attempt at evangelization found in Palermo a barrier as solid as the granite of its mountains: the most excellent archbishop monsignor Giovan Battista Naselli, here present (the archbishop nodded his head in sign of assent, cracking the wax of his inattentive and inexpressive mask), with canon Turano and your humble servant as his collaborators, gave the excommunicates something to chew on...

'What would you have, my sons? Was it not signor Garibaldi who wrote on 20 January 1854 his famous letter to the Palermitans, in which he exposed the religious corporations to public hatred as a foul plague? To whom, if not to the Garibaldini, do we owe the campaign of anti-clericalism and anti-monachism on our most Christian island?

(Murmurs among the public.)

'What had to happen has happened. Today the great sacrilege is complete. *Consummatum est.* The law for the suppression of religious corporations was approved on 19 June with one hundred seventy-nine favorable votes and forty five against. Among these—an invincible Ajax—stood our own Vito d'Ondes Reggio, who demonstrated that the ecclesiastical possessions of Sicily have an origin and a function different from those of the other regions of Italy, and that mortmain, if it must be abolished, must go in favor of the people and the comunes of Sicily. Instead, the landholders and the speculating middle class are waiting to hurl themselves like vultures on those goods, to acquire them cheaply and to enrich themselves at the expense of the poor.

(Prolonged applause.)

'Does there not exist the law of 10 August 1862 for the concession in perpetual lease of the ecclesiastical and governmmental estates in Sicily? Well, this law, which would have been a relief to the Sicilian population, has never been applied. Why has it remained a dead letter? Because since that time they have been planning the expropriation of the ecclesiastical alliance by using the law of insurgency. But the height of illegality was reached with the order given by the government to occupy monasteries and convents under the pretexrt of assigning them to civil and military uses...

'Churches razed to the ground, damaged, desecrated, or worse: degraded into barracks and stables; convents and monasteries turned into hospitals and madhouses; sacristies transformed into taverns, collections of works of art scattered and destroyed, precious libraries broken up and dispersed; elderly nuns thrown out on the streets, venerable old men wandering through the world, sinful virgins (no, no I meant virgins abandoned to the sinful dust of life)...

'But we are a force, an unbeatable army without weapons. In Italy there exist eighty-four monastic orders: eighty property owners, four mendicant orders. Do you know the consequences of the abolition of the religious orders? 2,382 convents will remain deserted, forty-five thousand monks and nuns must leave their cloisters: precisely: 16,000 friars, 18,000 nuns, 8,000 lay servants. To these must be added some 5,000 lay people who live by serving the religious houses. In Sicily, of a population which does not amount to two million souls we constitute about sixty-three thousand between priests and friars, without counting the nuns. Embracing these as well (the new *lapsus* aroused a burst if laughter, which fortunately lowered the tension in the room), we reach about one hundred thousand. My brothers, we are therefore a force, and being as united as an army we can hurl a challenge to Satan: you shall not conquer. *Portæ inferi non prevalebunt...*, The gates of Hell shall not prevail...

'The Church has overcome more tragic and terrifying tribulations than this, and she has continued her forward march, ever victorious. *In mundo pressuram habetbitis sed confidite, ego vici mundum,* In the world you shall have tribulation but trust, I have overcome the world, we read in John XVI, 33. Through all her adversities and persecutions the Church continues her earthly pilgrimage, until from the Church militant and suffering she will be transformed into the Church triumphant, the heavenly Jerusalem, where neither death nor weeping will echo forever, but songs of glory and everlasting blessedness...'

When the discourse, which had lasted a good hour and a half, had ended, the applause was thunderous. The strongest emotion in the air was the feeling of finally being liberated from bordeom and fatigue. Around the table of the orator, who was being complimented by the archbishop, an enraptured crowd was waiting to congratulate him. The usual flatterers and sycophants elbowed each other to arrive first, intent on making a career and keeping themselves in the good graces of the abbate, who was well known for his high prestige in the Curia.

The names of great preachers like Bossuet, Bourdaloue, Lacordaire, Lamenais ran and danced on the lips of the fawners like small change.

—Stupendous! Marvelous!

—He has surpassed himself!

—What splendor of Biblical style!

—Will we see it in print soon?

—The end! The closing! Where he refers to the ascent of the Church through its tribulations! What dramatic power, what apocalyptic spirit! It makes you want to hear it again.

The abbate, moved and elated, picked up his papers and began happily to repeat the closing for the benefit and consumption of the little crowd of incense-bearers who hedged around him.

Contrasting opinions and evaluations were however being formulated, overlapping, crossing between the groups and onlookers of the religious, both furtively and out loud amid the noise of the chairs and the rustle of steps on the pavement of the room as it slowly emptied. The *concordia discors* of the sentiments, of the passions, of the convictions, of the various parties, of the schools crackled in their assenting and dissenting remarks.

—A masterpiece!

—Unparalleled mush!

—A richness of original ideas, you can't deny.

—Poor, outdated stuff, nothing more.

—Bits and pieces clipped out of the newspapers.

—And so, what are we to conclude? That we should rebel? Or that we must bow our heads to the *fait accompli*?

—We must rebel. Did we come here to hold an academic seminar?

—Let Divine Providence act. God doesn't pay only on Saturday, His mills grind slowly.

—I don't agree with the opinion that we must not resist evil. This might be good advice for Christian perfection. In everyday life we can't let evil triumph. All life is a struggle against Satan.

—Legitimate defense is an inviolable right: *Vim vi repellere licet,* It is permissable to repel force with force.

—But only when it's a question of defending your life, not just your property. It is not legal to kill a thief.

—The goods of the Church are her life.

—Gentlemen, let us not create confusion, let's not beg the question. Here it is not a matter of life and goods. Do we or do we not have the right to react against tyranny? This is the point. A wave of diabolical tyranny has been unleashed against the Church of Christ.

—We have the right to suppress the tyrant, when his yoke is unjust— said a Jesuit.

—Tyrannicide is a sin.

—Let's not use strong words. We don't want to kill or massacre anyone. But no one can question our right to repel force—unjust force, understood—with just force. Violence with violence. The revolt that raises the banner of justice is holy.

—Are you intending to prepare a new disaster for Italy? The defeats of Custoza and Lizza are just a few days old. Shame on you. Don't you have any Italian blood in your veins?

—We are Christians, not Italians. Welcome to a hundred defeats, as long as the liberty of the Church is safe.

Things were going badly. The disputants, heated up, flushed, shouting and carrying on as if obsessed, had descended the staircase from the hall into the courtyard. They were in great part young, but a few florid old men, peppery and quarrelsome, mingled with the litigants and were raising a great deal more disturbance. The discussion threatened to degenerate into a quarrel and perhaps even a fistfight, with little edification to the bystanders and no respect for the holy place. A voice of reason was lifted up:

—Peace, calm, gentlemen. What good does it do to squabble among ourselves here? With so many conflicting opinions, I propose taking the controversy to the judgment of a theologian who is a holy man as well. For example, father Benedetto di Castellammare.

Some smiled, some launched an ironic witticism. Many, feeling humiliated by the idea that there was one of greater authority in sacred theology than themselves, slipped away in scorn. Only a group of young priests and friars, in perfect good faith even in their irreducible fanatacism, flocked onto the road that led to the convent of the Capuchins.

When they arrived at the convent piazza, which was watched over by two leafy plane trees, they knelt at the foot of the rough and imposing wooden cross which stretched out its shadow on the stony ground and prayed.

They knocked at the convent and asked for father Benedetto.

A lay brother answered that the father had just come out of choir and was in his cell. That they should wait while he carried their message.

The father did not keep them waiting for long. He entered the sacristy with a light and active pace: an almost youthful step, which his mature years, bordering old age, had not yet made heavier.

In his face there shone an innocent cheerfulness, which transformed the signs of encroaching age into an harmonious and rhythmic energy of life like the convolutions of a seashell. In a transparency like spring water his eyes emanated the tender pale blue with which Perugino painted the mantles of his Madonnas. On his well-formed red mouth, in contrast with the silver of his beard, the words were formed before they were pronounced, and they vibrated solemnly, punctuated and measured by the habit of chanting psalms.

—To what fortunate circumstance do I owe the joy of this rosary of youth?—he said.

The young group crowded around him in a semicircle, talking confusedly. Everyone wanted to express his own opinion.

—One at a time—the friar begged—otherwise we'll end up with the confusion of tongues. No Babel!

One of the oldest spoke for them all. They desired some light on the problem of the suppression of the religious orders after the recent law voted by parliament. Fresh from a speech by the abbate Galeotti, they had found themselves in serious disagreement about its conclusions. A word of peace could come only from a theologian and from a man who stood outside, above parties.

Father Benedetto's face darkened, he stroked his beard with his slender and spiritual hands, he reflected for a few seconds and said:

—*Quis me constituit iudicem aut divisorem super vos*? Who has appointed me judge or distributor over you?

The severe response spread a feeling of perplexity among those present. It seemed that the holy man wished to escape from the responsibility of an answer. A dull murmur ran through the group, and some of them looked so irritated that the friar felt the need to explain himself better.

—Listen to me, my children. If it helped me to entrench myself behind a convenient and calculated silence, I would tell you without doubt that the Master forbids to each of us the faculty of judging. *Nolite iudicare,* Judge not, that ye be not judged. I tell you, instead, that in truth I lack the competence and the authority to participate in such a question. When you ask for a judge, do you want one partial or impartial?

—Impartial—answered his questioners with one voice.

—All right, you will understand that I cannot be impartial in a controversy like the one you submit to me. How can you claim that a Franciscan, a friar bound by the vows of poverty, who has sworn to despise all riches, should judge impartially in a question...of goods...of riches?

—No, no!

—Reason with me a bit. If you want an opinion on a picture or a statue, whom do you turn to? To a painter, a sculptor. And if you want to hear an opinion on the solidity of a house, whom do you call if not an engineer? And if you need advice on the best way to cultivate a field, will you consult the work of a philosopher, or a sailor, or a soldier? The answer allows no doubts. Now does it seem to you that the question of the property of the Church can be decided by one who is poor by choice, I almost said, by definition? The poor man raised to be the judge of the rich cannot but be unjust.

—We don't want your personal opinion, father, but that of Christ.

—And for that you come to me? Are you not yourselves priests? Do you not have the Gospel?

—Indeed we do. But we want someone who is higher than us, to reveal the deep meaning, the hidden spirit, one who speaks for Christ.

—And has the Church not spoken? Would you want to place a poor friar above her? My sons, listen to the Mother of the saints.

—But the problem of riches is not confronted and solved in a clear manner by any interpreter.

—If you have doubts, read and re-read the episode of the temptation... where Satan, having abducted Jesus up to the pinnacle of the temple, promises Him all the treasures and the plenty of the earth...Meditate on any passage of the Gospel, which is the total devaluation of riches. Christ is, and wishes to be, the true poor man, the absolutely poor man. Born in a stable, on the straw, between two beasts, He dies on the cross, the execution reserved to slaves, between the two thieves...He was poor in goods, in friends, in protectors, in power, in authority...Teaching us to care for the poor, He never promised riches to the poor...on the contrary, He wants the rich to make themselves poor for love of Him. Whoever lives to enrich himself, and worse, misleads the poor, deluding them with the mirage of prosperity, is not a good Christian...You cannot become rich except by selling the body and blood of Christ. Every man who enriches himself is selling Christ. Here is the clear distinction between us Catholics and the Protestants. The Protestant considers earning money as the purpose of human life, and not merely as a means of satisfying material needs. 'Making money,' is the Alpha and Omega of the Protestant ethic. In Luther, the concept of 'vocation' is nothing but the the performance of worldly duties, the attainment of material success. Luther and Calvin join hands. From this comes their hatred for monastic asceticism, their incomprehension, indeed their contempt for the mendicant orders...We instead hate and condemn the worship of Mammon under any form whatever. For us is it easier for a camel to pass through the eye of a needle than for a rich man to be saved...

—But how are we to act in facing the concrete problems that life poses us? This is the heart of the question. If the solution of a problem given by the constituted authority does not seem to be in conformity with the teaching of Christ, must we stand by passively, or do we have the right, and perhaps the duty, to disobey, to protest, to rebel? Must we resist evil?

—What did Saint Paul teach you? *Noli vinci a malo, sed vince in bono malum,* Do not be overcome by evil, but overcome evil with good.

—And if evil threatens to overcome us? If the political power tries to supplant the Church, to despoil her of her rights, what remains to do to defend them?

—To pray, to pray, my children. The rest will be given to us as a surplus. What profits us to save life and riches, if the soul is lost? For goodness' sake don't drag me into the field of politics. Don't disturb my peace and yours. Religion knows only one means of influencing politics: staying out of it. Politcs is an unclean thing, the work of Satan. The only politics allowed to a cleric are those of working for the good of souls. *Qui habet aures audiendi audiat,* He who has ears let him hear. And now kneel and say the *Salve Regina* with me. May the Madonna enlighten us in our harsh pilgrimage through this vale of tears.

The sound of knees on the bare earth, a low rustle of lips. The Spirit was present.

Chapter 2

WHEN THE marchese entered his study, don Assardi was washing his hands with the irridescent foam of an imaginary soap (perhaps the only kind with which he cleansed his hands, which were strangers to water). He had the air of saying, as if offering a gift, 'Dear boy, today you deserve a ten for good behavior. Well done, Bastiano!'

—The bird has flown—he announced point-blank to the marchese, without giving him time to ask.

—Already?

—Yes, dear don Fabrizio. And not through the merit of this poor little priest who stands before you. All the praise goes to those big guns that your humble servant can fire off when he wants to. You light the fuse and ...boom!

—So?

—His Eminence has had just this morning the news from the Ministry of War that our little lieutenant Don Giovanni is going back up to his hamlet of Asti. *Acqua davanti e ventu darreri,* Water before and wind behind. Amen.

—You're worth all the gold in Peru—said the marchese, warmly clasping the priest's hand, shaggy with red hairs.

—I'm not worth anything. But I knew how to act with prudence, without noise and uproar, to avoid raising a scandal in your family and throwing a shadow on the honor of our party.

—Are you sure no scandal will break out?

—Absoutely none. Who would speak? We are all interested in silence:

He on one side and *we* on the other. Everything ends there, a little affair of ordinary business. Would it be the first time that an officer is transferred from one garrison to another? Reasons of service. One *frusteri* less in our city...God be praised.

—God be praised—echoed don Fabrizio.—As for *him*, I'm sure he'll resign himself. After all, someone from the continent is happy to return to his own parts. In Sicily they live uneasily. But *she*?

—She too will not become desperate. Do you know how women are? They fling themselves body and soul into amorous adventures, they love their little extra-marital vacations, let's call them that...as long as they have nothing to lose. But when the stakes of the game become high, when it becomes too risky...they pull in their horns like snails. 'My treasure,' 'I'll love you for my whole life' 'no power on earth can separate us' (and here the priest imitated a female voice in a mocking tone)...but as soon as they hear the clank of chains, 'feet, do your stuff'...some flee from here, some from there...goodbye to love, passion, and all the rest. In short, love is pleasant when it's cheap, but no one wants to buy it too dearly!

—You don't know Teodora—the marchese objected.—She is a proud and stubborn woman. I don't know what she would be capable of out of pure obstinacy.

—You'll see. She will be the first one to accept this solution. We'll present her with a *fait accompli*. And the marchesa, who is a sensible woman, will accept it without a word. She will react...by silence, pretending to believe it the most natural thing. And she will come back to the fold like a lost sheep. With the help of God.

—Of course. With the help of God—repeated don Fabrizio, with more devotion than conviction.

—And now that I have done you this service, let me return to my job. *Dimitte servum tuum, Domine,* Lord, now lettest thou thy servant depart in peace...

A few hours after this conversation, don Ciccio the gate-keeper came up carrying a letter.

—I have to hand it personally to the marchese—he said, refusing to give it to the footman, and the syllables crunched in his throat like crushed pebbles amid the oscillating of his Adam's apple.

—Who brought it?—asked his master, observing that the letter was unstamped.

—A *gentleman,* advising me to give it only into Your Excellency's hand.

—Is there an answer?

—Excellency, no. The man did not *say* anything. Except that it was very urgent.

With trembling hands, gripped by the presentiment of something unpleasant, the marchese opened the envolope, took out a sheet of paper, and even before reading the contents skipped to the signature. 'Lieutenant Sergio Spada.' The text read:

'Most Esteemed Signor Marchese (the mocking flavor of that superlative!), I have just received notice of my transfer from Sicily to Piedmont, and I reason thus. The possibilities are two: the transfer has either been decreed officially or it has been requested by someone. Excluding the first hypothesis, the possibilities are two: the request has come from someone who wishes me well or someone who wishes me harm. I discard the first solution, and then the possiblities remain two: either the person who wishes me harm is a madman or he is a scoundrel. Refusing the first horn of the dilemma, there remains the second: that the author of the request is a scoundrel. Here there are two hypotheses: there are intelligent scoundrels, and there are idiots and boors. One who has intended to act to my harm is not intelligent. Wishing to damage me, he has rendered me a great service, he has satisfied my desire to leave as soon as possible this land of Lotus-eaters and flesh-eating Laestrygonians, from which even Ulysses felt the need to flee. Decide to which category among those I have indicated that you wish to belong and give me an answer. I have already classified you.'

On reading so insolent a letter don Fabrizio felt rushing to his head all the noble blood of Greek tyrants, Arab emirs, Norman counts, Spanish hidalgos, which circulated like a complicated and bitter mixture in his veins. His heart swelled with wounded pride, offended dignity, and immediate instincts of revenge. He remembered that he was a gentleman first and a man second. If as a man he could not allow himself to understand insults which did not touch him, if as a Christian he could even pardon, as a gentleman he was bound to the all-powerful laws of honor, which did not allow him to let the outrage pass without an appropriate reaction.

This was the first time that he had found himself in a similar situation. Haughty, arrogant, proud of his family, jealous of the reputation of his ancestors as people without stain and without fear, nonetheless thanks to his rare sense of balance, of measure and discretion, he had succeeded in living for more than sixty-five years so as to avoid misunderstandings, frictions, collisions, and conflicts with anyone. Moving straight forward with tact, integrity, and nobility, not unaccompanied by dignified firmness, he had the rare ability of getting along with everyone and of not haring off after chivalric disputes at a time when these were frequent in Palermo, one of the cities most afflicted by the mania of dueling. The exaggerated sense of honor, the heat of the social life, the disorderly ferment of political passions, led men of good society onto the field of honor, often for no reason at all. Since the chivalric spirit was deadly serious, such encounters often ended with mortal results. Nonetheless, although marchese Fabrizio was obliged to live in so Dartagnanesque an atmosphere, with his *savoir faire* not only had he avoided playing the role of challenged or challenger, but by elegant subterfuges and sophisms he had even succeeded in avoiding the unquestionable duty of every gentleman to act as emissary, sponsor, or second in the frequent affairs of honor among his friends and relatives. Now, all of a sudden, he found himself in the jaws of a dilemma which was difficult to escape: either swallow an offence or demand satisfaction by arms from the offender. The choice was hard. He felt himself crushed between the anvil of his personal honor and that of his family, and the hammer of his Christian convictions. As a Christian his conscience was clear: no one could blame him for having maneuvered to send away a womanizer who was disturbing the peace of a respectable family and threatening the fragility of a good woman. But as a gentleman and the bearer of a great name he could not resign himself to an insult and unspeakable rudeness. Would he offer the other cheek to the man who had slapped him? Would he react? And how? By legal or by chivalric means? He would have to choose, and that immediately.

After a short debate with himself, he ordered his majordomo to go find don Assardi and to beg him to come to the palace as soon as possible.

The priest did not delay. Letting his duties as coadjutor fend for themselves, he quickly covered the short distance between the parish of the Catena and via Alloro and arrived in sight of his friend out of breath.

—What news?—he asked, wiping the sweat which was dripping from the hairy cornice of his eyebrows.

Don Fabrizio simply passed him the letter, which he was still holding. Then he added:

—Read it. The scandal, which you said was impossible, has broken out.

—*Oportet ut scandala eveniant,* It must be that scandals come...—the priest quoted piously, raising his eyeglasses above his brow after reading it.—The Lord allows this to put us to the test.

—A harsh test, you will agree. And now, *quid faciendum,* what is to be done?

—Nothing. Let it go—said the priest, in a superior tone.

—Just, 'Let it go'! And the offence?

—Our Lord was more offended than you. He bore shame and spitting.

—But Our Lord did not find himself in this kind of mess, dear father.

—Don't blaspheme. Aren't you a Christian?

—A Christian, yes, but also a gentleman.

—So, for your gentility you would like to put yourself *en garde* and make *za za*?—and he gestured like someone thrusting a sword.

—So, according to you, I should swallow an offence without saying a word! Really good advice!

—Do you know what I would answer to such a provocation? 'If you have an itch for duels...descend to the dueling field and fight by yourself. When you have relieved yourself come back to your senses. I'm not following you in your ridiculous folly.'

—Your are joking, you're amusing yourself.

—Well then, sue him for slander. It will be the finest lesson for a conceited man, who by crossing swords with you wants to become the hero of a novel...a comic-strip novel. Everyone will admire your patience and will say 'marchese Fabrizio is a man with seven pairs of...underpants.'

—And the law! the justice of the State! This was worth something in my grandfather's day, perhaps even in my late father's, when it was administered by the nobility, and any jumped-up boor who dared to insult a nobleman had his ribs flattened by our footmen. Now it's all democracy: *The law is equal for everyone.* The revolution has overturned every social order. Some satisfaction I'd get from suing him! My abuser would be punished with a few days in prison, with a simple fine...And my peers, those of my own rank, would laugh at me behind my back.

—Let them laugh. *Risus abundat in ore stultorum,* Laughter abounds in the mouth of fools.

—A priest does not know the rules of chivalry, of honor. I'm not criticising you. I see that it is difficult to for us understand one another.

—That is certain, commented don Assardi, with a sarcastic grimace on his fleshy lips—I am only a poor pedestrian: to you is reserved the honor of going to hell on horseback. You'll get there all the sooner.

And turning on his heel, with a deep bow, he slipped out through the door by which he had entered.

The departure of the priest struck a certain superstitious terror into the skin of the marchese. No, you don't fool around with Hell. But the purgatory of gossip, of malicious remarks, of accusations of cowardice, which loomed up in his clairvoyant imagination, was also nothing to joke about. If there were only possible a middle way, a loophole, an accommodation between his conscience and the customs of society, so as to avoid the Inferno without falling into Purgatory! Even the laws of chivalry, like all the laws of this earth, offer weak links, unexpected loopholes, through which with a certain cunning one can excape. Everything depends on putting oneself in the hands of a specialist in such matters! An unexpected thought, prompted by fear, spread through the confused and dulled mind of the unlucky man. And the thought turned into action. Without calling his servant, don Fabrizio slipped on his dove-grey redingote, pressed his top hat of the same color on his head. Swinging his cane to give himself a courage which he did not feel, he set off for the club-house of the *Sette porte* in piazza Bologni to consult some expert on matters of chivalry. If possible, the baron Turilla di San Malato (despite the fact that he belonged to the liberal party), a famous swordsman and consummate connoisseur of the laws and customs of honor.

While stroking his fine blond Nazarene beard, the baron gave his answers to the convoluted list offered by his questioner.

—A serious offense...of the fourth degree...not only was the personal honor of a man or of his family damaged, but that of the social class to which he belonged and of his country...he intended to insult Sicily and all

Sicilians...what to do? Nothing but one's duty...everyone who had a drop of real blood in his veins would feel obliged to demand satisfaction with weapons...in the most serious conditions...Avoid the duel? there was only one way of escape: age...no one is required to fight after the age of fifty... and the marchese had passed sixty...but to hide under the excuse of age, as long as one is able to grasp a sword or a pistol, is always an expedient that smells of cowardice...The remedy: substitution...dear God, did there not exist some near relative willing to descend to the field to defend the honor of his kinsman?...A son, a brother, a brother-in-law, a nephew can substitute for the respective relative who was the victim of the offence... don't you have a brother?

—Yes, but he's a dreamy philanthropist, a foolish ascetic...steeped in socialistic and humanitarian ideas...Not to be depended on. And anyway they had not been on cordial terms for years.

—You have a nephew.

—I have no nephews—said the marchese, firmly and darkly.

—And so...nothing can be done! What do you want me to tell you? Have recourse to the legal authorities to defend your honor. But that is none of my business. For everything else I am always at your esteemed service.

In town there was general surprise when the news spread that Goffredo had accepted the offence given to his uncle and had sent his seconds to Sergio Spada, demanding satisfaction by arms.

A messenger (sender unknown) had arrived at the estate to deliver an urgent letter for Goffredo. The young man was overseeing the threshing in shirt sleeves and an old straw hat which threw golden reflections on his little blond beard.

On the threshing floor the air was vibrating with bits of golden straw. Two pair of blindfolded mules were trotting in a circle to the encouraging cries of the mulateers, who were themselves running, splashing in the chaff with their bare feet. Under the measured pace of the animals the stalks peeled and husked themselves while the chaff flew away in a dazzle of shining motes. The bundles of grain carried on the shoulders of the peasants fell one by one between the legs of the animals: they were raked by pitchforks and quickly pulverized amid the measured thuds of the hooves of the patient mules. Other peasants, with their white shirts outside their trousers, were working to sack the grain and carry it into the storehouses. Jars of wine mixed from a barrel fixed on a trestle came and went, guzzled by the threshers,—already intoxicated by the sun,—who drew new strength for their work. Boys coming from nowhere, seeing the chance to play, threw themselves into gathering the grain scattered from the threshing floor. Dogs with their tongues hanging out from the heat circled around between the legs of the men. Chickens scratched and pecked at a distance, following a rooster with an arrogant crest and eye. The foreman with his terracotta arms outside his rolled up sleeves tallied the number of sacks filled one by one by nicking a branch of elder with a knife.

After reading the letter and exchanging a few hasty words with the foreman, Goffredo quit the threshing floor and headed toward the houses.

Soon after he left the estate on horseback.

The conditions of the encounter were serious, equal to the bitterness of the offense. The choice of weapons was an object of discussion among the seconds. According to the rules of continental Italy this would belong to the injured party, while by ancient Sicilian custom it belonged to the one challenged. Since the two contenders were from different regions the problem was not an easy one to solve. The seconds of lieutenant Spada, who was an excellent swordsman, proposed cold steel, the representatives of Goffredo insisted on the pistol. The dispute was decided by lot, which fell on the latter weapon.

The conditions of the encounter were defined thus. Weapon: the pistol. Place and hour: Villa d'Aumale at seven in the morning. Procedure: advancing, firing on command. Initial distance: twenty meters. Advance: not more than twelve meters. End of the encounter: the absolute impossibility of continuing, according to the judgment of the medical men.

The next morning at six, two *landeaux* passed at a walk through the gate of the splendid park. When they had reached a clearing, there descended gentlemen impeccably dressed in black—tailcoat and top hat—except for their gloves, in shades of red and canary yellow according to the fashion of the time. Principals, seconds, director of the encounter, doctors, greeted each other and ceremoniously divided into two groups, to the left and right of the field, to consult together. While the surgeons set up the first-aid station, the seconds proceeded to examine the field.

The conditions of light, of wind, and horizon were studied to guarantee identical situations for the two duellists, so that each of them had at his back a curtain of trees instead of being silhouetted against the open sky, an easy target. The respective lines of fire and the stages of the advance were marked out with pebbles.

The director of the encounter showed the case containing the weapons and the ammunition to the witnesses, confirming that the seals were unbroken. Proceeding to the loading of the pistols, he took the weapons one in each hand and invited the offended party to choose. Goffredo chose the left, the other was given to his counterpart. They drew straws for position and Goffredo got the disadvantage of the light, barely broken by the leafage of the trees, which struck his face sideways. The seconds announced that they agreed to waive the customary examination of the two duellists to ascertain if they were wearing any body protection, certain that they would behave like gentlemen according to the rules of chivalry and were ready to obey the orders of the director of the encounter.

The two duelists took their positions in profile, facing each other. Pistols in hand, pointed at the ground.

At the command 'To you!' they simultaneously cocked their weapons.

—Aim, not more than ten seconds!—ordered the director.

The two raised their weapons to eye level.

—Ready? Fire!

Two shots were fired with a barely perceptible interval between them. The smoke of the black powder employed as a charge raised a thick curtain between the shooters.

Amid the witnesses, who had immediately run to him, Goffredo touched his forehead.

—Nothing at all—he said calmly.

The bullet had grazed the top of his hair.

The duelists advanced five paces, marked off out loud by the director.

—Aim. Fire!

At the same time as the explosions, lieutenant Spada crumpled over, bent his knees like an empty sack, and collapsed face down on the ground.

—Halt!

The seconds came running, they lifted him up, hauled him by his arms to the medical station. When they had stretched the wounded man out on the grass, with their hands drenched in blood they helped the doctor to undress him. The bullet had lodged in Spada's right side, stopping between the muscles after breaking a rib. After the wound had been probed and the bullet extracted they stemmed the bleeding with a tourniquet and a bandage.

It was not a serious wound, but it was prudent to transport the wounded man as soon as possible to a place better suited to a more complete medical treatment.

Revived from the shock, the lieutenant opened his eyes while a sip of cognac was poured between his bloodless lips.

The seconds asked the duellists if they wished to be reconciled. Goffredo bent over the wounded man and sincerely offered him his hand, which the other shook weakly.

Creaking on its hinges, the gate of the villa closed behind the two carriages, which exited slowly with a brief interval between them.

The evening of the duel, Goffredo, coming up in incognito by the service stair, plummeted into his grandmother's room.

With youthful enthusiasm, the old woman lept from her chair and threw herself into her grandson's arms.

—Here I am, grandma, safe and sound.

—Let me hug you, my child, let me touch you. Are you really unharmed?— said donna Ortensia, embracing the young man's strong torso.

—Are you looking for holes, grandma? Not even a scratch. The only hole was the one I made in my opponent.

—If you knew what I suffered, what palpitations! I had heard that the lieutenant was a crack shot.

—Everything is luck. I swear that I would never have fired if my opponent had not done so deliberately. His first shot grazed my forehead. One centimeter more and I would never have come up these stairs again.

—Don't say it. Do you think that I could have to survived you? Don't let's talk about it. Anyway, what's done is done. You behaved like a gentleman, you saved the family honor. That's why I asked you to come. Your uncle's refusal! It would have been the first example of cowardice in our family.

—But believe me, grandmother, it's not amusing to fight without hating. Like that, by proxy.

—By proxy for your grandmother, not for *him*. I promise you that if I had not been a woman, and an old one, I myself would have fought in his place. When it is a question of honor...

—All the same, this honor is a funny thing! The name of Spada is honored because, having compromised a woman's reputation and insulted her husband, he descended to the field of honor...I am honored because, without the excuse of personal resentment I put a bullet into his chest. Uncle Fabrizio is honored because, while a half-witted nephew was risking his life for him, he was wandering around the house in his bedroom slippers. And with whom does the dishonor rest in this business?

—With common sense—the old woman concluded, smiling joylessly.

—Perhaps if God had had a bit more common sense, He would have done better not to create this stupid and clownish world tumbling about in the void.

Chapter 3

THE ACTING Public Prosecutor of the King, don Prospero Camarda, lived in a little old house in via Gioiamia, one of these elderly and dignified houses with an air of impoverished nobility whose old-fashioned *petto d'oca* balconies are decorated with a pot of basil, which have a cobbler as gatekeeper, and a slate stairway with very high and not too clean steps.

Up this stairway one morning climbed don Assardi, rather out of breath, with his breviary under his left arm and a pinch of snuff between the index finger and thumb of his right hand, which he constantly held under his nose to counteract the piquant odor of cat which assaulted it in waves.

When he had reached the first floor landing the priest paused a moment to fill his emphysemic lungs and gave a polite tug on the dark blue rope, with a tassel at the end, of the bell-pull.

Preceded by a lazy clatter of wooden shoes, two eyes darted out from behind the peephole.

—Who is it?—said a woman's voice.

—Is the cavaliere at home?

—But who are you, *Vossia*?—insisted the woman, who had orders to open to no one.

—*Benedicite*. I am a servant of God.

At these words the door opened and the maid apologized for not having done her duty sooner. If she had seen that it was a priest... (how could she have seen him, since the priest, with his tiny stature, remained below the level of the peephole?).

Ushered through a flight of rooms into the magistrate's office, don Assardi remained standing, fanning his face with his handkerchief. The place was not new to him. Its wide balcony opened onto one of the so-called *cortili,* a blind alley flanked by a jumble of hovels which exuded poverty from their scabby walls. Inside a smell of old rubbish. On the ceiling a globe of gold-colored glass, encrusted with fly-specks; on the walls faded wallpaper, torn here and there into rolled-up strips; old bookcases closed from time immemorial, where thick *in folio* volumes bound in parchment were lined up. Above the back of a torn divan two oleographs—Victor Emmanuel II and Giuseppe Garibaldi—on either side of an ivory crucifix expiring in agony on a tortoise-shell cross (which picture was the good thief, which the bad one?). In the corner, a little table half-buried under mountains of paper.

The priest bowed ceremoniously and most respectfully before the Prosecutor, who was entering at that moment.

—What is it, father Assardi?—asked the magistrate, playing with the green tassel of his dressing gown—what good wind brings you here? But why don't you sit down? You're out of breath.

—Indeed. Your stairs are a bit steep. At least for an old man like me. What would you have? Past six decades on my shoulders.

—Unfortunately, it's a terrible stairway. But what can one do?

—After all, they are the stairs of justice. Harsh to climb. *Per aspera ad astra,* Through hardships to the stars...But you must excuse me, illustrious sir, for turning up at your home so early in the morning. I ought to have come to your office. A magistrate should be sought in his kingdom. But I have presumed, since it concerns a friend.

—I am honored by your friendship. And my house is always open for a man of the cloth.

—A lot of work, eh?—said the priest taking in with an eagle eye the dossiers and piles of paper which encumbered chairs and divan in additon to the little table.

—Justice is at work. She never tires. Law cases are pouring down from every side. As if the common ones were not enough, now there are also the political ones. A flood, my dear father. Luckily I have strong shoulders.

Family shoulders. My father was also a judge (and don Prospero pointed to an old portrait leaning against the oil lamp, depicting a magistrate in bonnet and gown, with an austere expression) and he rendered outstanding services to his Bourbonic majesty. In our family the passion for the law descends through its branches. A question of vocation.

—*Dilexi iustitiam, odivi iniquitatem,* I have loved justice, I have hated iniquity—mumbled the priest, remembering the words of pope Gregory VII (minus his addition, 'therefore I die in exile')—So should it be. And it redounds to your honor.

—Today I serve Victor Emmanuel with the same zeal with which yesterday I served Ferdinando—the prosecutor assured solemnly, rolling his sword-shaped papercutter around on the palm of his hand.

—And tomorrow...

—Tomorrow I will serve Francesco II, God bless him, with unchanged loyalty if he should return to his throne. I make legal briefs, not politics.

—He will return, he will return—the priest crooned, with the air of one who sees into the future, drumming with his fingers on the lid of his snuffbox.

—You see, when it comes to political opportunism they talk a bunch of nonsense. How many slanders have covered Liborio Romano, the last prefect of police and then minister of the interior to His Majesty Francesco II! What had don Liborio done? He served his king as long as it was possible. But when Garibaldi was already marching on Naples and the court had taken refuge in Gaeta, he telegraphed to the 'unconquered dictator,' the 'redeemer of Italy,' placing himself at the latter's complete disposition. Was he a coward? No, he was a prudent man. What would you have done in his shoes?

—I ask instead what *you* would have done.

—I? Neither more nor less than what don Liborio did. This is little, but certain. I serve the one who pays me. I have only one god (don't excommunicate me for my idolatry), my career. I have the right to rise. I have no desire to rot, to become a mushroom, in the rank of substitute Prosecutor. Do you understand?

—And what are you doing in order to rise?

—This: for the moment I am against the Garibaldini, since the government opposes Garibaldi to the death. Don Peppino's stock is down. The police have only one order: Give it to the red shirts! Cases are being prepared against them, anything goes. It's enough for someone to shout 'Viva Garibaldi,' or just to whistle, 'Get out of Italy, get out, foreigner,' to throw him into jail. The police make the arrest. Then it's up to the judiciary to *put a face* on the evil deed, that is, to find how the action committed by the accused *stands in the law* (article such, paragraph so-and-so) and open the case. Ah, you can only say, life is funny. I move or I stand still, according to circumstances. I am reactionary and progessive, revolutionary and conservative, according to which way the wind is blowing. *Vulgus vult decipi,* The crowd wants to be deceived.

—*Ergo decipiatur,* Therefore let it be deceived—completed don Assardi, as if he were reciting an antiphonal prayer.—But listen. I will propose a problem to you. If, as things are today, there fell into your hands someone—let's call him X—who was seriously compromised by the events of Aspromonte...

—Nothing to be done. There is the amnesty. Plenary absolution for everybody. What can you do? Maria Pia of Savoy, daughter of Victor Emmanuel, is to marry don Luis of Braganza, king of Portugal, and out of joy our Sovereign throws open the jail gates to all the criminals.

—Excellent—approved the priest.—But suppose that signor X, having taken part in the childish stunt of Aspromonte, continued to fish in troubled waters, to plot against the institutions of the State, to prepare uprisings and revolutions...

—If I am not mistaken, you also want to make the revolution, don Assardi, you and your Bourbon friends—interrupted the Prosecutor, giving the priest's paunch a slap.

Distinguo, signor Prosecutor: *we* do not want a revolution. We look to restore the *status quo ante,* to return a legitimate sovereign to his throne... There's a great difference. But let's move on. I ask you, *exempla gratia*: Would signor X be committing a crime?

—Certainly. The crime of conspiracy.

—And what would you have to do?

—To proceed, naturally. Always assuming there was proof, you understand. Are we or are we not honest magistrates?

—And what do you mean by 'proof'?

—Come, come! You are too intelligent a person to ask me that. Writings, witnesses, other indications...

—And personal confidences...would they be sufficient?

—As simple indicators, yes. Especially if charged to dangerous persons, those who, according to the procedures of the Bourbons, were 'to be watched.'

—And there we are. Because signor X is a dangerous person.

—Let's not beat around the bush, don Assardi. Have you come here to make a formal denunciation to me?

—God forbid. A priest make a denunciation? And where would Christian charity end up?

—So who is this dangerous person?

—You would not believe it—said the priest, lowering his voice mysteriously—nor am I sure I'm right to tell you. But I'll tell you all the same. It is...it is...someone that you know: the nephew of marchese Fabrizio, of the excellent marchese, your friend and mine.

—Him?

—Indeed him, it seems.

—Seems or is?

—Seems, I tell you. It could be him. *A posse ad esse non valet consequentia,* From 'might be' to 'is' does not require logical consistency.

—But what difference does this make to you?

—To me, nothing, nothing personally. I do not judge. *Nolite iudicare,* Judge not—said the priest unctuously—you understand, Christian charity...But sometimes the facts speak louder than the persons. As you know, this awful boy, the son of a rabid Garibaldino, was kicked out of his house by the marchese, who had received him like a son. The arrival of Garibaldi in Palermo drove the boy crazy and he followed the scoundrel to Aspromonte.

—The deed was amnestied, I told you.

—It's not that, I repeat. The fact is that this young man, certainly not evil, but overstimulated, when he returned to Palermo was still tied up with that gang of crazies who want to turn the world upside down, they dream of the revolution, they long—I don't deny—to hang us priests from a lamppost...They have Garibaldi, Mazzini in their heads...and other devils as well. In short, doesn't seem to you that in a delicate, indeed serious moment like the one we are now going through, it would be prudent to put such tools out of circulation?

—This is the business of the police, my excellent friend. Why do you want the magistrature to get involved?

—But isn't the Prosecutor General the head of the judicial police? Isn't everything that concerns the law reported to him?

—Always assuming that it's a question of crimes already committed. But according to you, here we are discussing preventive measures. Satisfy a curiosity of mine, don Assardi—asked the magistrate, halfway between the serious and the facetious, drilling his great inquisitorial eyes into those of his interlocutor—explain why this business matters so much to you? Seriously, I have never seen you so impassioned for a case of justice or rather...reasons of State. One must say that you nourish a special affection for this young man—and here the magistrate's voice took on a diabolically sarcastic tone—to be so interested in his fate.

—Well—the priest spoke resolutely—one must tell the truth to magistrates as to confessors. There exist higher reasons to explain my zeal in these circumstances which otherwise would be misplaced. You know, and if you do not know I will tell you, that marchese Fabrizio, estranged from his wife and his only nephew, has left in his will all his possessions to a good work, a charitable institution, in which I have an interest. A work which is dear to a very highly-placed person whom I do not feel allowed to name, at least at present. At one point this testament ran the danger of being revoked or modified. It was when the marchese, seized by affection for the nephew whom he had welcomed into his house, had almost decided to adopt him. Fortunately the wildness of the young man and his flight from the house intervened in time to put an end to that insane project. The danger of a change in his last will and testament seemed averted. But now...

—Now?

—There are new developments. Old don Fabrizio has resumed his affection for his nephew. Do you know from when? From when the nephew fought for him. For a duel! An action condemned by the Church! And adoption is again being discussed. The matter of the will, as you can understand, is again all at sea.

—So?

—So, this adoption must not take place.

—And to impede it you think that the arrest of the nephew is sufficient? Excuse me, I don't see the connection between the two things.

—There is a connection, signor Prosecutor. You understand that, if not a conviction, an arrest, sending the boy into confinement, would make him seem incorrigible in his uncle's eyes and would douse the fire of his affection. A supporter of the Bourbons of that type will never be so weak as to give his name, his titles of nobility, not to mention his entire inheritance, to a degenerate and unredeemable son of the revolution.

—You are a Machiavelli, my friend—exclaimed the magistrate, clapping the priest on his shoulder—. Your goal is not wicked...

—And neither are my means wicked—observed don Assardi, to purge himself of the charge of Machiavellianism.—After all, another little slap on the wrist of that misguided boy would help to bring him back to the right path. Infinite are the ways of the Lord.

Don Prospero remained in thought, as if an unexpected idea had crossed his mind. Then he asked suddenly:

—And what does the marchesa Teodora think of all this?

—What should I say? It is easier to penetrate into the horn of an ox than into the heart of a woman. Speaking objectively, the adoption of the nephew should not please her, it is against her interests. Subjectively, she would suffer from the new political persecutions against the boy. She has her weak points. After all, she's a woman.

—They say that she had a weakness for the young man.

—They say so many things. We must refrain from rash judgments. God is the only judge of our consciences. In short, I think that she might perhaps agree with us on the goal, to prevent the adoption. She would not agree with the means: when one has a liking...

—Only a liking?

—Nothing but a liking, I think.

—Do you insist that donna Teodora is really a *turris eburnea,* a tower of ivory?

—Please—said the priest, making the sign of the Cross—don't soil a term that belongs only to the Madonna. Let's not mix up the sacred and the profane.

—Leaving ivoryness aside—don Prospero retreated—do you believe that there exist unconquerable towers?

—Excuse me, that is your affair. The art of war is a field prohibited to us clergy.—And with these words he took his leave of the magistrate.

The latter accompanied him ceremoniously out of his office.

In the entrance hall, on a mahogany tripod a filled crystal bowl flirted with a thin ray of sun, displaying its finest rainbow garb. Within the vase, which was narrowed in the middle like an hourglass, two goldfish diminished and enlarged alternately while swimming with their dark fins, now in the concavity, now in the convexity of the glass, which served as a lens: the only note of gaiety in the old house inhabited by spleen and dust.

Chapter 4

IT CANNOT be blamed on don Prospero, a most upright magistrate, that if while talking with the priest he conceived a diabolical plan. It is true that the proverb 'the occasion makes the thief' is not provided as a justification in any law codex or digest. But where is it written, on the other hand, that man must be such a fool as not to seize the passing moment?

The Prosecutor Camarda was mulling over thoughts of this type as he made his toilet in front of his mirror with more care than usual. When he had finished wrapping his black necktie with the little green dots around his vast collar and had fastened the knot with a golden pin—a fine tetradrachm from Selinunte, a chariot with a warrior urging his horses—he was invaded by a sense of excitement. He was not young, but like this—glossy, spruced up, cravatted and gloved—he could still make an impression on the imagination of a woman. He had a bold head, made still more masculine by the thick muttonchop whiskers which joined his mustaches through two rivulets of black hair, and a proud steely glance which was difficult to resist. And then, you know, women are more sensitive to the fascination of power and the prestige of social position than to mere physical beauty.

How bizarre life is!—he soliloquized—standing stiffly before his mirror—how chance suddenly puts within our reach the happiest situations, beyond the limits of the predictable!

His conversation of a few days earlier with don Assardi, intended to infervorate (as they say in legal jargon) his powers as a public minister, had provoked in his old libertine flesh an exquisitely erotic arousal, to call it by its right name, reactivating old longings for a woman who was desirable if not exactly embraceable. Not (God forbid!) that he considered himself capable of betraying his duty as a firm guardian of the law for his own private interests. But if he happened to serve the interests of the State and at the same time to fulfill a sensual whim, what damage would justice have suffered therefrom? A few friends called him vicious, in private. Vicious, he? Slanders. Nameless hypocrisy. His rectitutde was known even to the mice. Everyone spoke of the exemplary severity of the magistrate Camarda in repressing the *delicta carnis,* the crimes of the flesh. It was a susceptibility, a radical idiosyncracy, indeed innate.

—My program—he used to say—is to cleanse society of the dissolute, the libertines, the erotomane apes, of the don Giovannis and the Magdalens (repentant and unrepentant), of the lecherous, the seducers, the temptresses, the flirts...To those who pointed out that this would mean the end of the world, he replied—And where is is written that this evil world is not to disppear? Better to perish by excess of purity than excess of depravity.

It was no mystery in the circles of polite society that the dauntless womanizer don Prospero Camarda had fixed his eyes on the green-eyed marchesa Teodora. The young wife of an elderly husband is always a magnet which attracts masculine desire. What to say, then, when the magnet has begun to drift down the inclined plane of the first unpardonable favors? Then all the iron filings of those who undermine female virtue, professional and amateur, rush toward the magnet, sure of finding easy and immediate welcome between its two forks.

In truth, during her marriage, Teodora had appeared to the many men who passed close by her as desirable, yes, but not easily approachable, and even less corruptible. If she had made some little rift in her pure nuptial veil she would render accounts to God, not to men. But her adventure with lieutenant Spada had suddenly opened her heart to the numerous suitors who swarmed around her, restless to climb the stair to the wedding chamber of the ancient Ulysses. When a woman has fallen for the first time she has lost the privilege of weaving and unweaving her tapestry like Penelope in order to hold off the crowd of suitors that surrounds her, besieging her chastity. It is difficult for the first act of weakness to remain the only one. If one man has leapt the ditch, why should not the others who are lined up before it also climb over?

This idea, so foolish as to be impractical, had for some time become an obsession in the mind of don Prospero, one of the most lecherous of her suitors. With the cunning of the perverted, he reasoned: If the precious Teodora dropped like a ripe plum into the arms of the first little officer who courted her, so much the more will she give way to the authoritative graces of the Prosecutor General. And it did not pass through his foolish mind that the wife of an old husband, still embraceable, has no desire to repose on the knees of a senile lover. He was unaware that the marchesa, athirst for youth, had become the scandal of her palace when, consumed by her desire to rejuvenate the decrepit barracks on via Alloro, she had sold the ageing horses in the stables, exiled the old dogs to the countryside, and poisoned the parsley of a Peruvian parrot (it is said, but without proof) who had monologued and dialogued for more than a century with the inhabitants of the ancient house. If they had allowed her, she would have exchanged the darkened canvases of bewigged ancestors for colorful and festive oleographs. But here 'reasons of State' opposed her, and she could only avert her glance from those old daubs whenever she was obliged pass before them.

Now the magistrate was constructing a new plan of battle.

The priest's suggestion of laying hands on Goffredo had opened up a new horizon to don Prospero. He could barely keep from leaping with joy, shouting *Eureka*. Here was the famous Archimedean point to stand on, here was the wonderful lever to lift the world and to subject it to his reinflamed eroticism. The point to stand on was this: Teodora has a weakness for Goffredo (which he suspected and which had now been confirmed by don Assardi). With that premise, the argument ran like a train on its track. Teodora loves her nephew and I love Teodora. If I put the nephew in jail, his aunt will take pity on him and will not refuse to save him. And she will also have a bit of pity for yours truly, who is madly in love with her. In cruder and less sentimental terms: By arresting the young man (always, it is understood, according to the law) I will have a precious hostage in hand, which will give me the means to pose a final ultimatum, *aut-aut*, either-or. The rest will come by itself. Naturally, the matter will be conducted with great tact (leave it to me, since I understand women), with every nicety. It must not have an air of intimidation, of blackmail...God forbid. To a woman, and a woman of class, the illusion of her freedom, of her initiative must be left complete...What pleasure, what glory is there in taking a woman by force, like a creature reduced by fear *perinde ac cadaver,* like a corpse? To embrace, I won't say a corpse, a dead thing, but a statue, what prowess, what satisfaction is that? A woman like Teodora must fall, not from fear, but from gratitude, from thankfulness, from intimate persuasion. Not different from the way a billiard ball rolls softly into the pocket, gliding on the velvety table, barely nudged by an imperceptible stroke of the cue. A trap, certainly, but a golden trap, polite, sweet, nothing resembling a vise...

Carried away by such meditations, the Prosecutor General took his bronze bell, whose handle imitated the beam of a pair of scales (the useful scales of justice) and rang.

—A secretary—he ordered the usher.

There entered a skinny little man with brush-cut hair, his pen balanced on his ear, which blossomed with thick tufts of hair.

Becoming aware of the presence of the secretary, the Prosecutor dictated coldly his order for the arrest of Goffredo...as being involved in the charge of conspiracy to change violently the constitution of the State and the form of government, as well as raising the inhabitants of the kingdom in arms against the constituted powers. A case in which inquiries were being made, etc. etc.

—Send it immediately to the chief of police for execution—he aded imperiously.

Then he dictated, on the appropriate printed form, an order which obliged the marchesa Teodora Cortada, *in the name of the law,* to appear before the Prosecutor General of the King to be heard on a legal matter.

—The invitation must be delivered within the day tomorrow—he ordered as head of the inquiring magistrature of the district.

The invitation was for five o'clock, a rather unusual hour in juridical practice. Teodora was not surprised. Rather, she interpreted the matter as a special regard owed to her person, which would not be exposed to public curiosity, at an hour when juridical offices began to empty. That did not keep her from being somewhat disturbed. Even the most upright person is upset by a call from the law, which can often conceal an unfair trap. Teodora well knew that she needed to render no account to the judges. But you never know! And didn't that invitation from the highest magistrate of the district have something strange about it?

A bit before the appointed hour she left her house and set out for the office of the Procuratia by the most torturous and narrow streets, with a thick veil lowered over her face. She was annoyed by the idea of being seen as she entered the Hall of Justice, where she had never before set foot. Who knows what the people who knew her would have thought?

Just inside the entrance hall of the palace, she felt lost, disoriented. Fortunately, the doorman, who must have been notified of her visit, came forward politely and offered to accompany her to the Prosecutor's office. The rooms were deserted, and the vast halls echoed with the sound of their footsteps on the pavement. Only one man, with a stack of greasy papers on his shoulders, crossed their path. Then no one further. In the waiting room, where she was asked to sit, the framed likenesses of many generations of Prosecutors General made a fine display all around the walls. Some in robes and bonnets, some without, some in wigs, some with their own hair, and even some without. Intelligent and strong-willed heads or faces that betrayed a complete imbecility, puffed up with conceit and authoritative arrogance; faces menacing, dull, ferocious, jolly, boastful. A shop window display of splendors and miseries, of high noons and sunsets, of victories and defeats of that ambiguous and two-faced goddess that humans call by turns justice and injustice.

The distracted eyes of the waiting woman were wandering around the colorful gallery when she was asked by the usher to enter.

The revolving door, lined with green cloth faded and smooth at the edges, screeched on its hinges and revealed the Prosecutor standing on the threshold, impeccably buttoned up in his stiff black frock coat.

The magistrate bent low in a ceremonious bow, kissed the hand of the veiled woman, and begged her to have a seat on the mahogany divan upholstered in crimson velvet which occupied an entire wall in front of his monumental deak. In the corner behind the seat, invading the discreet shadow of the room, there glowed a monumental marble bust of king Victor Emmanuel II, placed there to terrify visitors with the tangle of his curved moustaches and silky topknot. A crystal vase (an unusual sight in the office of a magistrate) overflowed with a bunch of roses.

—What an honor—don Prospero declared gallantly—to receive a noble and charming lady, a lady of such high lineage. I thank you, and at the same time I ask your pardon. To begin with, you can raise your veil…there is no one here but us.

The woman raised her veil lazily. Her emerald eyes set in their blue orbits shone (bathed in worry? suffering?). In her features could be read impatience and her anxiety to be informed.

After several beats of silence she asked:

—You see that I have come…punctually. I am at the disposition of the law.

—No law—said the Prosecutor, with a gesture of his hand as if shooing away a fly.—You are in the presence of a friend and devoted admirer. A beautiful and noble lady like you has no account to render to the law. Can you believe such an absurdity?…But give me news, I beg, of your family. The marchese, my great friend the marchese? and your esteemed mother-in-law?

—They're alive.

—I know they're alive, they're certainly not dead—chuckled the magistrate.—That's not what I was asking you.

—Isn't it already a great deal to be alive? To be alive in such thankless times?

—God be praised. Yours is a great family, I'm not just saying so. A true pillar of our social order. If only there were many houses like that of the Cortadas!

—You are very kind.

—Not kind. Sincere. I am singled out for my frankness which—they say—sometimess borders on brutality. Brutal, Prosecutor Camarda? I do not think that I have ever failed the obligations of humanity, of chivalry, of kindness, even when I have had to carry out painful duties…And now, you will wonder why I have dared to disturb you, why I have made you come here, to my office…It is a legitimate curiosity.

The woman assumed an an interrogative air.

—Well, I will tell you—continued the magistrate—savoring the effect of his words on the woman's face—you have a nephew…

—I do not know which one you mean. I have several nephews.

—I am referring specifically to a nephew of your husband.

—What have I to do with my husband's nephews?—she burst out, visibly annoyed.

—I am speaking of Goffredo... whom you know well. He lived in your house like a son. Indeed they say that the marchese wishes to adopt him... or wished to.

—I do not mix in my husband's affairs. They do not concern me, she said cuttingly.—His intentions, his proposals, near or far, interest me even less.

—So. That Goffredo! I'm not saying that he is a bad sort, indeed he may have some good qualities. But his too lively blood, his bad companions, the corruption of the times...Sometimes they commit foolishness, childish things, without wishing to...A restless spirit, fiery...Not long ago he wounded an adversary in a duel.

—And for this you have summoned me?

—Not for this. Even at the time the Law, which is aware of everything, was informed of the fact. It should have proceeded, because dueling is a crime. But through my intervention the matter was silenced. You understand, a great scandal would have broken out, harmful to a respectable family like yours. And then...I considered the displeasure that you (and he stressed 'you') would have received from it...For you, I forgot that I was the Prosecutor General of the district.

—Thank you. And now?

—Now the matter is much more serious. Conspiracy, you understand, conspiracy! A crime against the State. A bunch of insane heads, of idiots, of madmen are conspiring to unhinge our institutions. Some to send the king packing and introduce the republic, some to put the Bourbons back on the throne, some to detach Sicily from the kingdom of Italy. A real wrath of God. And unfortunately the boy is part of this gang. The inexperience of youth, the excess of imagination, fanaticism of party, call it what you will. But the fact remains what it is, an attack against the safety of the State. A branch of noble ancestry (here the magistrate slipped in a bow between his words) becomes a rebel, a thug, he slides into the criminal code, he flirts with prison...What do you think of it?

—What do you want me to say? They are young. Youth is a gift of God, but it is also something resembling a sickness. Blessed are those who begin to recover from it...like us.

—For goodness' sake, marchesa, do not slander yourself. You are a fragrant flower of youth, the most beautiful flower of the Conca d'Oro.

—But what can I do then?—she interrupted, at the utmost limit of her patience.

—Woman always has a magic power, when she is beautiful and gracioius.

—Thank you for the compliments. You have already made me so many. Now it is time for me to know why I am here.

—Don't you care for your nephew?

—Certainly. He's a fine young man and I am sorry that he is in trouble, even through no fault of his own.

—Don't say that. The fault exists and it is serious. But there exists no sin that cannot be redeemed, pardoned...through an influential intercession. Justice is firm but not inflexible. There is no law that cannot be bent... Everything depends on the authority of the intercessor.

—And who might this intercessor be?—asked Teodora innocently.

—You, for example.—And having fired off the words, don Prospero paused, gloating to observe their effect on his interlocutor.

—And what authority could I have? A woman?

—Immense, incalculable. Greater and more decisive than you imagine.

—Do you think so? You are joking.

—Confronted with a word from you, the man who has the fate of Goffredo in his hands would say, *Flectere si nequeo superos, Acheronta movebo.*

—I don't understand Latin.

—I'll translate it: If I cannot bend the gods of heaven, I will move those of the underworld.

—Excuse me. And whom must I move?

—Your humble servant.

—Then you are a god of the underworld?

—...who could transform himself into a beneficent god...but only if you wish it.

—And what should I do, pray tell?

From its soft contact with the hand of the marchesa, the hairy hand of the Prosecutor had moved on to a caress. His palm grazed the back of her hand, with its fine silken skin permeated with precious perfumes.

—Oh, nothing—ventured the magistrate, encouraged by the passivity of his lovely guest, who seemed to be willing—that 'nothing' for a woman, which is everything for a man.

The marchesa rudely freed her hand from the one that imprisoned it. Her face assumed an expression of restrained sarcasm.

—Speak then! Is it a question of testifying in his favor, to make me guarantee the young man's innocence? Speak.

—You still have not understood—the magistrate moaned, throwing himself almost on his face and embracing her knees—that here, at your feet, is one who sighs for you, one who is dying for you...who loves you madly?

Teodora sprang to her feet, freeing herself, and remained standing, in control of herself, unmoved, fearless.

—You have lost your senses—she said, surveying from top to toe the man whom she towered over proudly by almost a head.—Sometimes one loses them...even if one never had any.

—Yes, offend me, humiliate me, I am happy. But say a single word to me, only one word...

—Please: I offend no one. I would be afraid of offending myself just by insulting you.

The old satyr did not give up. Full of desire, his eyes shining with lust, he threw himself forward, trying to reach the woman's mouth to steal a kiss from her.

She was strong, rendered even stronger by her repugnance for the inflamed animal. She defended herself with a jab of the elbow that sent her aggressor rolling on the carpet.

—I was mistaken—murmured don Prospero, as he picked himnself up off the floor, breathless and foolish—I was mistaken. Pardon me. You are a monstruously virtuous woman. You will end up as a saint, a virgin or a martyr, glued onto a page of the calendar...I chose the wrong tactic. I should have bluntly given you the choice: Either give in or your nephew stays in jail. But I'm not like that.

—Then leave him in jail. It makes no difference to me. The dirty tricks remain the deeds of their doer.

—I offered to be your friend—continued don Prospero—you have chosen me as your enemy. That's it in a nutshell.

—Calm yourself, dear sir. I am accustomed to choose my friends and my enemies for myself. And I do not choose my enemies from imbeciles like you.

Having said this, Teodora drew on her gloves like a great lady, went to the door, and left without slamming it, indeed sketching a dignified farewell with her head. Never had she felt more calm, more at peace with herself.

But while descending the stairs of the Hall of Justice she brought her handkerchief to her mouth to hold back her sobs, to overcome the thick convulsive weeping that veiled her eyes and blocked her throat.

—How disgusting men are! And after all, what have I done to suffer so? Have I indeed fallen to the level of the lowest creature?

Chapter 5

THE SCANDAL of the duel between Goffredo and lieutenant Spada, which had crackled like a flickering little fire that can be extinguished at the beginning with a handful of ashes, was now burning like an untameable blaze in a field of hay. In the palaces of the nobles, in the houses of the middle class, in the clubs, in the cafés, in the shops and in the sacresties, nothing else was talked of except the bloody encounter and the reasons that had caused it. The discussions and gossip were naturally mostly at the expense of the family, which boasted one of the most notable blazons of the Sicilian nobility.

Every scandal is prismatic. It breaks up the light of public opinion according to both the absorbent and the refractive power of its many facets. The fans of dueling discussed the event according to the forms of chivalry and unequivocally condemned the behavior of don Fabrizio. The moralists blamed him for letting he honor of his wife, which he should have safeguarded jealously, become the talk of everyone. The religious, while they approved his refusal to fight, castigated him for having allowed his nephew to descend to the field of honor in his place. But the most dismayed were the companions of the marchese's own political faith, who feared that the crime could throw a sinister light on the man who held the rudder of the legitimist party and added luster to it by the prestige of his name.

In the midst of such a tumult the most impassive person was its protagonist. Above all, don Fabrizio felt at peace with his religious conscience for having refused a so-called affair of honor, in obedience to the fifth commandment. Moreover, the event had taken place—thus he consoled himself—outside his own will. He had acted within the limits of the permissible and the dutiful by arranging the transfer of a paramour or a uniformed dandy from one posting to another. Could he have imagined that from an action so honest in intention there should spring such disproportionate consequences? As to the Dartagnanesque gesture of his nephew, was it his duty to prevent it? Hot-headed and without judgment like his father, the young man had insinuated himself into the contest of his own accord, unloosing that tiny pandemonium. Reckoning up the accounts, on his honor as a gentleman and in his character as a Christian, Fabrizio had nothing to reproach himself with. And if the frogs of the liberal pond and the republican swamp didn't like it, let them croak until they died.

That does not alter the fact that, deep down inside, don Fabrizio felt the need to justify himself, at least to his mother, whose opinion overshadowed him even if it was not expressed in so many words. Everything had taken place without his having consulted her. And although he was accustomed to do things on his own, if he did not exactly feel remorse about it, the marchese at least became aware, bit by bit, of the unseemliness of the situation. The more so since the view of the old lady reflected more or less the pressure of public opinion, like the mercury in a barometer.

He found her in her room leafing through a superb old edition of the *Télemaque* of Fénelon, one with the beautiful copper engravings of its period.

At his greeting the old lady moved her eyeglasses to her forehead and scanned her son from the top of his head to the tips of his toes, a severely inquisitorial examination of his entire personality.

—Mamma, what do you thnk about what has happened?

The old woman continued to leaf through her book, admiring the pictures.

At her unexpected silence don Fabrizio, to gain some self-control, moved closer to the console table and started to wiggle the head of a little porcelain dog, as he used to do in his far-distant childhood.

—Are you upset, mamma?—he insisted.

—I? Not at all. What should I be upset about?

—I'm talking about the recent unpleasant incident.

—Is it something that concerns me?—donna Ortensia interrupted—Your business. I've never fought a duel...except with my tongue.

—So, in your opinion, I should have descended to the field of honor... and crossed swords with a common gigolo!

—I say nothing. But...

—But what?

—By your foolish behavior you have transformed into a certainty what might have been only a suspicion.

—What suspicion?

Annoyed at not having been understood, for her only answer the old lady continued to read out loud: *A-t-on jamais ouï parler d'aventures si merveilleuses? Le fils d'Ulysse le surpasse déja en eloquence, en sagesse et en valeur. Quelle mine! quelle beauté! quelle douceur! mais quelle noblesse et quelle grandeur! Si nous ne savions qu'ilest fils d'un mortel, on le prendrait aisément pour Bacchus, pour Mercure, ou même pour le grand Apollon...*

—Please say something.

On the wall there suddenly appeared an enormous black hand, from which the index finger and the little finger broke out so as to form two horns.

The effect of that shadow was terrible. Don Fabrizio seemed like a tree that was splitting as if it had been struck by lightning. He staggered, tried to find something to hold on to, turned, straightened himself, and with a heavy tread left the room which he had entered so confidently.

Pursued by the shadow of the two fingers, which branded him as a cuckold (and which, horrible to think, were the fingers of his own mother), the marchese was stung by an irresistible impulse to burst into his wife's room and to make a scene whose consequences were unforeseeable. His will was firm: but his legs? Ah, his legs! They refused to carry him, they went zig-zag, they slithered like snakes, they gave him the sensation that the floor was paved with soap. He could barely reach his study. As soon as he was inside he collapsed like a limp rag on the seat and let hs head drop on the chair back. His ears were ringing, and in the buzz there began to define themselves two voices like words emerging from a confused noise. One voice, on the left, commanded him, 'Right away! there's no time to lose!' The other, on the right, suggested, 'Let time pass! don't hurry!' And before his eyes always that implacable shadow play. Horns! Horns!

The imperative of time won out. We can suppress everything, in ourselves and outside us: time remains. We are made of time. Time is the waiting, the doubt, the desire, the dream, the pleasure, the sorrow... everything that detaches us from eternity and gives us a sense of our own presence, of passing, of living, of existing...we are an imperceptible 'now' that wavers endlessly between a 'yesterday' and a 'tommorow'... Yes, to exist is to endure time, to bear up under it as a grain of sand groans under a mountain, and to be crushed by it...life is a battle against time, a painful and unequal battle, an agony. And the liberation from agony, that is from time, is death. Truth is beyond time. All the rest is only error and anguish.

To live, even without truth, there is no escape other than accepting time. Don Fabrizio bowed to this necessity and put off until the next day the conversation with his wife which he called *definitive*—such as to close the temporal circuit of his suffering. Tomorrow, tomorrow...

Tomorrow came, and the marchese had a long consultation with don Assardi. With his customary bonhomie, the priest first tried to de-dramatize the situation and to lower the feverish agitation of his friend, who was on the verge of a breakdown. On the other hand, he agreed that if they did not wish to give to the episode the importance of the 'case of Sciacca,' that bloody fifteenth-century family vendetta, it was necessary—without violence, naturally, but with decision and energy—to throttle once and for all this story of guilt and human weaknesses which threatened to become a sort of serial romance. Amusing for the general public but little edifying for the persons who were implicated therein, as well as for all God-fearing and well-mannered souls. In short, this story had to be put to silence urgently, with a tombstone over it, suffocated under the veil of oblivion. And to this end the priest did not see any means except that one of the most visible actors should exit the stage at least for a good stretch, should head off prudently into the wings without appearing further. Of course he did not wish the death of the sinner, but rather that she give proof of repentance and reformation...To change her manner of life, a change of air, better yet to lower a curtain of time between herself and the world... this world, this *sæculum,* which is the seed-bed of all evils.

The priest's speech, tactfully imprecise, took on firm outlines in the mind of the marchese, which was heated by a high-voltage jolt of courage. More than his own courage, it was his desire for a doctrine, an ideology and a party, which was acting in him. In certain circumstances a man and his will are only the reflection of his social situation. The *alter,* the other, subjugates the *ego,* the self.

That evening, like an automaton controlled by an overwhelming force, don Fabrizio knocked at his wife's bedroom door.

—Teodora—he said, with a visible display of firmness—I must speak to you.

—I'm listening—she said with a clear and steady voice. Her attitude seemed a scornful security of spirit, but it was instead a preparation, perhaps a resignation, for a fate that must irrevocably be fulfilled. Rumors direct and oblique, both allusive and explicit, had already reached her ears from several sources about what was being 'plotted' against her. The conspiracy—of low and vulgar politics hypocritically dressed up as morality—aimed to eliminate her, to put her out of circulation. Could anything more foul be imagined? How would she react? Would she defend herself? Would she bow her head before the irreparable? When he found herself in the presence of her husband that evening, she was caught between the horns of such dilemmas, seesawing between thoughtless impulsiveness and reasoned wisdom.

—I have to speak to you about something serious...very grievous.

—Can there be anything more serious than what has happened?

—Let's let the past be What has happened has happened. But there remains the future, tomorrow.

—Ah! for you the past does not exist, it is nothingness, even when it has crushed a human being and torn apart a life?

—The pardon of God descends in pity on the past...and also the pardon of the one who has been offended.

—Your pardon, for example!—rebelled Teodora, indignant and aggressive.—This, no. I refuse it. I do not acknowledge any guilt for which I have to grovel for pardon.

—Let's not bring guilt and innocence into play, please. Only God knows who has failed in His sight and in the sight of men. He alone can judge where weakness ends and guilt begins, distinguish chance from destiny, thoughtlessness from criminal folly.

—If there has been a fool between the two of us, it is you.

—I?

—Yes you, who with your rashness have precipated matters, created the irreparable.

—Then I am a fool—burst out don Fabrizio with impatient bitterness—because I have seen, heard, tolerated as much as a husband can tolerate, that I have used indulgence, perhaps blameable indulgence, toward your thoughtlessness, as if you were a little girl, that I have swallowed humiliations and tears for you.

—Go on, what have you seen and heard...I say, seen with your own eyes, heard with your own ears—Teodora challenged him, emboldened by his submissiveness—tell me, tell me. Have you surprised me in the arms of a lover? Have you heard words of unmistakeable guilt on my lips? What real proof do you possess of my impurity?

—I could have had the proofs if I had wanted to.

—Setting spies on me, true? Rewarding informers?

—I have never stooped to such baseness...however much I had to right to do so.

—What right?

—The right of guarding my honor.

—Your honor?—Teodora laughed ironically.—Magnificent! Stupendous! But if you had possessed any honor you would have descended to the field yourself like any gentleman instead of making your nephew fight.

The words fell on the marchese like a hammer-blow. His honor was the most sensitive and painful area of his whole being, like a brain that remains naked and uncovered in some of the most serious lesions of the skull. The stricken man touched his head, the nape of his neck, twisting his mouth spasmodically.

—I could not—he growled, after a bit, with a changed voice—because the law of God forbade it. It is superior, as you know, to any law of chivalry.

—The law of God is valid for everyone...your nephew as well.

—He acted on his own account. Did I force him, invite him, beg him? Can I be responsible for the actions of...an impulsive foolish man?

—As an alibi...it couldn't be better—if you were rendering accounts to a human judge. But you are invoking divine justice. And before Him—she said solemnly—there is no difference betwen the one who does something and the one who allows it to be done. But *your* religion is quite elastic, so to speak.

—May God pardon you. You do not know what you are saying. You are blaspheming. May God have pity on you. My pardon is such a little thing by comparison with His infinite mercy.

—I have need of no one's pardon and pity, even less of yours. It should rather be me to have pity on you, since you are no longer a man, only a plaything in the hands of others.

—Of whom? Tell me.

—Of *your* priests, if you please. Do you think that I don't know everything?

—If I should follow the advice of those whom you despise—he explaimed, gathering courage—I would have only one proposal to make to you. To withdraw from the world, if only temporarily, and to retire to some pious place to meditate on your situation, to return to your senses in solitude, and to expiate with prayer the evil that you have done.

—Withdraw from the world? Do you think that I would fear that? I ask nothing better. I am sick of you, of your house, of your relatives, of your servants, of your spies... Then send me to a convent. I will be calm, I will drop this mask that humiliates and degrades me... In the silence of a convent cell I will be able to shout that I don't love you, that I have never loved you, that I repent to the tips of my hair having married you, that I curse the moment in which I swore faithfulness to you before the altar...Who convinced you that my heart has been yours even for a moment in these fifteen years of prison?

—No one. I have never believed it. I would have been a fool to believe it. A husband has not rights over the heart of his wife... Over her behavior, yes.

—A right! Who gave it to you?

—The sacrament of matrimony itself.

—A sacrament which you transform into a prison. Prison for prison, I prefer the convent. It seems to me a more logical command.

—I do not command. I advise, propose...humbly...for your own good.

—I will go. But leave me alone, free me from your presence...don't you understand that I can't take any more? What have I done that I must bear so much pain? Have I not suffered enough already?

—And I? Do you think that I have been happy all these years?—moaned don Fabrizio.—I know that it is more difficult to be just than to be good... At least have the goodness to understand that no greater disaster could befall a man... an old man, who has few years to live.

Don Fabrizio made an effort and left, dragging his feet, having transformed the grief that tightened his throat into a coughing fit.

Teodora, bright, cold, unmoved, as if she had been changed into a block of rock crystal (never had she felt in such a state of wilful decision and perfect mental lucidity) did not even turn to look at him.

Upright, motionless in the middle of the room, she is completely calm. Locked in the immobility of a statue, she pauses in front of her mirror, the faithful three-winged mirror that is the confidant of her beauty. A gesture of her nervous hand. First the dressing-gown, then the *dessous* slides down her body. They lie on the ground like a basket of flowers. The lace and the embroidery of her fine underwear foam around her feet. The mirrors compete between themselves for the reflection of her nakedness.

Lazily she unclasps her pearl necklace from her neck. She frees the small lobes of her ears from the weight of her earrings, the gift of her husband, and throws the precious jewels contemptuously to the ground.

A shiver is released from the three images reflected by the mirrors.

Is it still the former Teodora? Or has age not passed in vain over the sculptured harmony of her mature flesh?

The first wrinkles of autumn are already descending on her temples.

The sunset of youth and joy.

What a sad thing life is!

No matter however they had agreed to surround the matter with the greatest secrecy, the news quickly spread that the marchesa Teodora, having left the palace on via Alloro, had retired to the convent of the Stimmate, under the rule of Saint Clare.

The monastery stood near Porta Maqueda, at the extreme northern limit of the city, enclosed in the small cloister of its walls. Constructed in 1603, it had a glorious life, along with the splendid church that flanked it, until 1875, when the whole area was gutted to make room for the Teatro Massimo Vittorio Emanuele.

Another monastery was backed up against the Stimmate (a not

infrequent example of rivalry and emulation even in the field of religion): San Giuliano, whose immense green cupola had been vaulted over the robust walls of its church in defiance of the the modest blue cupola of the Stimmate. In the the Stimmate the Clarisse lived and did penitence. In S. Giuliano the Theatine Virgins of the Immaculate Conception prayed and arrayed themselves for the joy of Paradise, which nonetheless did not prevent great jealosies, quarrels, and rivalries between the two communities. The reason was that S. Giuliano, by constructing convent and church, had blocked the Stimmates' view of Monte Pellegrino: a motive that survived from one century to the next and served to justify before God and man all the spite, the rudeness, and the *stizzoserie,* the irritations, that the two orders believed it their duty to exchange. When they could do nothing else, the good sisters annoyed and tormented each other by ringing their bells. The common people, accustomed to the periodic duels of the sacred bronzes, commented while shutting their ears with their hands, *Sunnu i du' batissi chi si sbattuliano li corna,* It's the two abbesses locking horns.

That donna Teodora had chosen for her retreat a monastery of strict enclosure and without great aristocratic traditions, perferring the Stimmate to S. Caterina, could surprise some, but not those who had not known her in her early years. Between those walls she had passed the first part of her adolescence, from nine to fifteen years, as an *educanda,* a convent student boarder. There she had received her first religious instruction, her earliest education, and the first rudiments of culture which, to tell the truth, did not exactly sin by excess. It was the *non plus ultra* when a girl of good society in those days could just manage to read and to write without gross blunders.

At a bit more than nine years old, Teodora, dressed as a miniature Clarissa, had crossed the threshold of the convent, welcomed with all the honors that the community was accustomed to bestow on *educande* coming from noble and monied families. The little girl was enchanted by the magnificence of the garden more than by the damp kisses of the old nuns. Within the enclosure of the high walls, suffocated by thick blankets of ivy and reddening with bouganvillea, the tall monkey-puzzle trees stood out against the sky, proud palm trees shed their leaves, and in the fields edged by box hedges there shone endless species of flowers, a many-colored palette. In the middle, a fountain with a jet that spurted from a clump of papyrus into a pool in the form of a four-leaf clover, whose stagnant green water was the only mirror allowed to the vanity of the novices.

Behind the grill of the little choir, the girl was sweetly lulled by the mystic languor which breathes from the chants and the prayers, rises saturated with incense from the altars, and evaporates into the air from the liquid surface of the holy water stoups. Dazzled by the images in her prayer book, Teodora had dreamed that the Good Shepherd gave her the little lamb that he had taken from his shoulders to carry in her arms, and that the baby Jesus played hide-and-seek, disappearing and reappearing without letting himself be caught, in the darkest corners of the convent.

There in the choir she had experienced her first boredom with the long prayers, and the pleasure of confession. When they did not act on her as a sleeping draught, the rosary of fifteen stations, comprising the mysteries and the litany of the saints, exasperated her and made her impatient, tugging on the tight cord of her nerves. The holy readings during the meals in the refectory induced a playfulness, they gave her an irresistible itch to laugh, for which she often received solemn scoldings. The Evil One was using her to distract the pious community from its holy meditations.

On the other hand, she went willingly to confession. She took pleasure in kneeling before the grate of the confessional at the feet of an unknown confessor, opening her conscience to him, blurting out her little venial sins and those which in her limited childish perception she considered serious and unpardonable. The fatherly and anonymous voice of the invisible priest put her in communication with the Mystery. And the Mystery thrilled her, especially when it was translated into stern warnings and reproofs. She enjoyed being represssed and mistreated. A bitter voluptuousness was released by the severe reprimands and threats of eternal punishment. In the depths of her being there stirred a strange desire for suffering and humiliation. Falling again into sin filled her with remorse, with hallucinatory fears, nonetheless her remorse often turned into a shudder which was not terror alone. It acted like an electrifying spark, accompanied by a not completely painful flash of lightning. Isn't suffering, dying of unrest and languishing from nebulous worries, a way of living? She envied the sisters, who on the Friday of every week submitted to the discipline, whipping themselves with bunches of knotted cords in the dark while singing the *Miserere* psalm. She eavesdropped, hidden behind the door of the hall where the flagellation took place, she heard the simultaneous blows of the ropes on living flesh and thought that was real penitence. If sin is an evil, it must be driven out with pain and not with the little prayers imposed by confessors for the forgiveness of mere failings. God can take into account only real suffering to to render the fragile creature worthy of His pity.

These and other such memories crowded into Teodora's mind while she set foot after so many years in the places where she had spent her first childhood. The memories of former times blossomed again, still fresh in the soul worn out by her experience and suffering. But the well-known places did not speak to her as they once did. Everything seemed to her changed, diminished, patched up. The long and spacious paths now seemed to her narrow and suffocating, the cells like the holes of a dark prison, the vaults of the refectory crushed her. To her eyes the garden faded into a common badly cultivated field gasping between the high walls, with a few dwarf and struggling trees and tufts of wild weeds on every side. Everything was the same as in the past, and at the same time everything was transformed and distorted.

In her new surroundings, Teodora felt disappointed, disenchanted. A new disturbance and a new disquet, quite different from the previous ones, assailed her. Her agitation, which in her early years had been only mystical, was now stripped of any transcendence: it had the flavor of earth and slime. It no longer came from within, but from outside like an evil-smelling and suffocating smoke which rises into the air from the burning of things which are impure or close to rotting.

In the course of a quarter century the community too had changed appearance. Most of the sisters who had seen her grow up were gone. They slept in the convent cemetery, under the old marble slab which her childish feet had jumped over rather than stepped on, for fear that the souls of the servants of God, wrapped in their shrouds, would jump out to give her a beating. Of the surviving sisters, some with dull and half-spent eyes dragged themselves along, scrabbling with their scrubby hands on the walls, the corners of their mouths drooling a little stream of saliva. Others, infirm or injured, no longer left their cells and waited for the Angel to offer them a pair of golden crutches to climb Jacob's ladder up to paradise.

Even the two lively Angora cats who had once romped with the little boarder, rubbing themselves with dainty nudges against her legs, had passed, already decrepit, to the other world, a little world consisting of a hole under a rosebush.

Alas, the new community did not resemble the former one. The devil of politics had inserted his tail among the nuns, who were distracted from their recollection in prayer, and had divided them into two groups. On one side the reactionaries, on the other the progressives; here the Bourbonists and papalists, there the Garibaldians and the republicans. Plots, rivalries, diatribes, quarrels which sometimes escalated into blows, raged in the Stimmate, as in most of the male and female convents of Sicily. From the clash of passions, from the churlish behavior of factional hatreds, the seamless garment of Christ emerged torn and disheveled.

The ferment, which the abbess, mother Airoldi, vainly struggled to tame with a patient effort of impartiality (but the malicious claimed even she, an exemplary bride of Christ, had contracted a second secret marriage with the revolution), boiled over on Theodora's arrival. Such was at least the opinon of the youthful element, restless and seditious if nothing worse. The arrival in the convent of a lady of the black and Bourbonic aristocracy rekindled the haughtiness of the reactionary party, which saw in the newcomer a powerful ally. But the faction of the *ultras,* who prided themselves, owing to their contacts with the outside world, on knowing the 'life and miracles' of the lady, objected that a woman on bad terms with the world for her rebellious spirits could only align herself with the champions of the revolution.

To silence the tumult, the abbess decided to remove the 'stone of stumbling' from circulation. To raise a screen between the marchesa and the community she banished her, with all the honors due her rank, to a lonely apartment in the most distant corner of the great edifice.

To those who murmured against such draconian measures on the pretext of commiserating with the marchesa, the abbess answered *sotto voce*:

—My sisters, it is the archnbishop who has decreed it. We can only obey. *Nun pò truzzare 'petra cu 'a quartara,* You can't break stone with a clay jug.

In fact, as far as Teodora was concerned, she did not make a fuss about the beneficial screen erected to protect her solitude. Tired, disillusioned, bored with the world, eroded by a deaf resentment against everyone and everything, in the slow but fatal withering of every desire and every hope, she accepted her isolation with good grace and was not prompted to escape it. Fed up with existence, she abandoned herself to the flow of an impossible life, which she wished to be a slow death.

Chapter 6

THE PALACE, what a cavernous hole! There remained only a few scattered relics of its ancient family of grandees, a tightly closed phalanx which had resisted the storms of three centuries, always managing to keep on their feet. The best part persisted in the dusty canvases of the gallery, where the haughty ancestors seemed to blush with shame if an irritating ray of sunlight descended to draw them out of their shadowy nests. The painted figures hung there in reproof of the living ones, who were impoverished in their ancient blood and dragging on in the wretchedness of their mediocre existence.

Teodora was languishing in the cloister, oblivious to herself and forgotten by the others. Federico, a lay hermit, was vegetating, having returned to the woods and reverting to nature in the country. Donna Ortensia, old, somewhat infirm, and sulky, dialogued with her favorite books or soliloquised in the solitude of her room. Only don Fabrizio was apparently master of the situation. In reality he had abdicated the absolutism of which he was once a fanatic. He reigned without ruling, since he had handed the reins if the house over to his domestic bursar don Vincenzo Marvuglia, satisfied with his bit of glory as head of the legitimist Bourbon party.

The palace, without youth, without affections, without domestic harmony, without a smile, had become the realm of Dullness. No more dinners, receptions, meetings, and social conversations. It could have been called the house of the dead if it were not for the frequent secret political meetings and the cautious coming and going of informers and emissaries from high and low—that is, both notable personages and the basest classes of society—who were weaving the threads of the revolution.

The linchpin of the situation, the axis around which the whole complex mechanism turned, was naturally don Assardi. The managing and politicking priest buzzed around the palace at all hours, went up and downstairs without being announced, brought and returned messages, shuttled between friendly parties and supporters, served as legal advisor and minister plenipotentiary, always acting in the name of the marchese, of whom he held 'both the keys of his heart,' as Dante said of the emperor Frederick II's favorite.

—You are the Pier delle Vigne of this Court—said don Fabrizio as a joke.

—Away with certain comparisons—protested the priest—I am a poor ignorant man...And I don't like certain little vices...the shepherds Alexis and Corydon...puah! Instead call me *'a cuchiara di tutti i pignati,* the spoon for every pot...yes, that I like.

He protesed in the same manner when someone, referring to the influence he exercised over the marchese, gave him the title of 'dictator.'

—God forbid!—he answered—do you want me dead? Every dictator ends up by being killed, and I intend to remain in the world a long time more. If I were a dictator, in any case I would have the good sense to retire in time, like Silla, the only one of the bunch who saved his own skin.

He preserved diplomatic relations with the old marchesa. There was no love lost between them, but neither did they detest each other. They had enough inteligence, the one through cunning, the other through a native spirit of tolerance, to understand that peace between people who hate each other is worth more than war between people who love each other.

But the meetings between the two, now that the house was closed to society, had become very rare.

One day that the priest met her by chance outside her room, he said:

—Marchesa, is it going to rain? You never come out of your shell, *comu 'u babaluci,* like the snails, except when rain is falling or about to fall.

—I prefer the snail to the devil—she answered—although both of them have horns.

Meanwhile it was not difficult to notice that the old lady was declining visibly. She was burdened with so many physical and spiritual ailments that to enumerate them all (as she herself said) it would take not just the *Dictionnaire* of Voltaire, but an entire encyclopedia. Above all, the affliction of asthma weighed on her so much as to pin her to her armchair, denying her the repose of her bed. Lying horizontal cut off her breathing and drew a pitiful wheezing from her poor bosom.

—Don't you understand—she said to her doctor, who was persuading her to stretch out on the sofa to examine her—don't you understand that the time of being *l'horizontale* is quite finished for me? The women of today are different. They say that is easier for men to lay them down than to keep them standing upright...I am cast in an old-fashioned mold. To the end my motto will be, Ortensia, on your feet! I will rebel against being stretched out even after I'm dead. For that reason I have ordered in my will that my mummy be hung on a wall in the Catacombs of the Cappuccini.

Her doctor was don Saverio Gorgone, a simple man without medical arrogance, the declared enemy of all the quackery of modern science, always quarreling with the high priests of Æsculapius who pontificated from the height of their academic chairs and university professorships. He believed in only a very few remedies, drawn from rare miraculous herbs, and he proclaimed himself a *naturist*. The only curative, he said, is nature. Medicine exists only to damage her. How many ailments would be cured if doctors didn't get in the way! Air! Good air! Also water, naturally, but not too much, and also earth with its finest products, wine, for example. But above all air. Why did Adam and Eve die without illnesses and at so late an age that the memory of it is lost? The Bible speaks of the longevity of the patriarchs, but not a word about the life span of our first parents. Do you know why? Because they went naked.

—Tell me, don Saverio, where is the seat of asthma?

—In the bronchial tubes, in the bosom.

—Well, no womanly bosom, not through my own choice but because of fashion, has been uncovered, *exposé au grand air*, as much as mine. How can I be ill just there? There is an organ inside which whistles with all its stops out and takes my breath away.

—Absolutely right—says the doctor with triumphant logic—but then you were young. And as a young woman you were healthy as a fish. How many years now is it since you have worn low-necked (*décollé*) dresses?

—You are right, doctor. But you are forgetting that for some time I have been completely *décollée*, unglued. Now it would take a carpenter to glue my body back together with my soul.

In the depths of the armchair to which she was condemned she suffered from attacks that tore her to pieces. Sometimes the crises were so violent that her heart threatened to give way. When she regained consciousness after a barrage of reviving medicines, she seemed to have returned from the kingdom of the dead. When she had come back to her senses, she said as she opened her eyes:

—I arrived over there, in the Elysian Fields, but they didn't want me. They have put me under house arrest for now.

Perhaps for that reason she spoke serenely of death, as if it were familiar to her.

One day when some of her visiting young women friends were talking about their fear of death, since she felt herself strong she made this little speech to one of them who was depressed.

—I, instead, am afraid of life. You will say, Because I am ill. No. I'm fine. What is sick is the world, which cannot be cured, although it never dies. It lives on in order to become ever more evil.

She had gained the reputation of being a pessimist and a cynic, but she was merely wise. From pessimism and cynicism she had constructed a screen to wall herself off from the world, to defend a corner of purity and tenderness from its profane eyes, a corner where she lived with her dearest images, such as her dead son Ramiro and her nephew Goffredo, who was alive but torn from her failing life like a branch from a tree trunk. When she privately kissed the faded photograph of the former and wrote to the latter in secret, her harshness dissolved, her usual *persiflage* gave way, and warm tears of tenderness ran down her cheeks.

Goffredo's absence had now lasted for years. The old woman was consumed by it, but she appreciated the reasons that discouraged the young man from setting foot in the house whence he had been turned away, reasons of justice and pride. Fabrizio, unrelenting in his feelings, had never pardoned his nephew, nor would the nephew for his part ever have accepted the condescension of such a pardon. The antipathy between them had been exacerbated rather than smoothed over with time. A meeting between the two became ever more impossible, it would have been a clash with dramatic results. Therefore the young man, on the rare occasions that he came to town, entered the palace almost furtively like a thief in the night, stayed with his grandmother for a few hours, and left early in the morning unseen by anyone.

For those few hours donna Ortensia felt happy. And feeling her end approaching, she spoke of the day in which the Lord would be pleased to call her from this world into His peace.

—I hope—she said to her nephew, holding his hand tightly—that you can arrive in time, when I leave for my *villeggiatura*, to close your grandma's eyes. Remember: my eyes and my mouth (she spoke with a certain coquetry of the one and the other, which she knew had been beautiful)... so that my eyes do not long remain open facing death, as if out of fear, and that my mouth stay indecently open as little as possible...Oh God, what horror! You will find a black veil in that drawer...I have prepared it just for this...you will tie up my jaws with it. It is the final vanity. I don't want to arouse repulsion and horror in those who will see me for the last time. Perhaps in gratitude to you, my lips will still try to sketch a smile... a smile, for you, my child.

Goffredo arrived just before she died.

They met for the last time on that short mysterious bridge thrown between time and eternity by the final flash of consciousness.

—She is still breathing—said old Marco, in tears, as he greeted the young man on the landing of the stairs—it's as if she wanted to wait for you...

That morning the little bell that had rung for sixty years had remained silent. After an hour and more her worried maid had knocked on the door. No answer. The servants come running...they force the door, locked from the inside as usual.

The room is almost dark. On the back of the armchair a white head, nothing but a head, since all the rest of the body, dressed in black, is absorbed by the dark green of the chair. When they call her, she gives no sign of life. But death has not yet taken her. A slight flutter of her eyelids, a rattling sigh from her bloodless lips.

Quickly the news spreads through the palace: the 'old marchesa' is dying. The house is in an uproar. Don Fabrizio, in dressing gown and slippers, rushes into his mother's room. He calls her by name, uselessly. He takes her hand to kiss it, but it falls heavy and inert on the dying woman's lap.

The doctor is sent for. His answer is without hope.

—An apoplectic stroke. Little or nothing to do. Move her to her bed, avoiding jolts. Put ice on her head. Leave her in peace. A question of hours. The only thing to wish for is that her suffering be short...It is a lamp which is going out.

Goffredo arrives before evening. He leans over the bed.

—Grandmother, it's me, it's Goffredo. I'm here. Do you recognise me?

She gives a slight quiver of her whole body. An unspoken word dies on the the edge of her lips. She feels the desperate effort of her tied tongue. Only her poor tired hand (the left one, not immobilized by the paralysis) curls up her fingers, as if she wished to say 'Ciao.' Her eyes, sightless, glassy, seem still to see the corner of the room where an oil lamp is burning out before the portrait of Ramiro. Goffredo kneels and leans his brow on the edge of the bed. Then he rises, bends over the dead woman, and with a light touch he lowers the still warm violet eyelids; he frees her brow from a tuft of tangled hair, he joins her hands in a cross on her breast. He moves quickly to the wardrobe, opens the well-known drawer and takes a veil of black crêpe out of a cardboard box, he wraps her head, knotting it under her chin, after closing her mouth. The tiny mouth, which while she was alive uttered biting words and sparkling epigrams, seems to smile sweetly in death.

If it were not for her black dress and bonnet, her old body, lightened from the weight of existence and later composed on her catafalque, would seem transformed by the miraculous fingers of youth.

It was certain that donna Ortensia had made no public testament. But it was equally certain that there must exist some dispositions of her last wishes since she often spoke of them, even about the manner of her burial. When her cupboards, her desk drawers, her workbasket had been ransacked, no writing was found. Finally, when the books that she read most frequently were leafed through at the suggestion of Goffredo, there slid out of the yellowed pages of the *Profession de foi du vicaire savoyard,*

Rousseau's private statement of belief, an envelope with 'To be opened on my death' written on it in a firm and decisive hand.

The envelope was handed to don Fabrizio, who wished to proceed directly to the verification of the testament and its reading in the presence of the notary. Goffredo and Federico, who in the meantime had arrived from his estate, insisted, except for fulfilling legal formalities later, that the document be read immediately to know the last wishes of the deceased concerning her burial.

When the marchese had removed the writing from its envelope he passed it to Goffredo, asking him to read it.

'Today, 27 June 1862, being of sound mind, I have decided to put down on paper the following dispositions of my last will.

'May the eternal God pardon me if I put my hand to this testament without invoking Him, as is customary. Let not such an omission be interpreted as an act of impiety. Born in an ironic and libertine age in which it was elegant wisdom to ignore or deny the existence of the divinity, I have never ceased to repeat with Voltaire, *Si Dieu n'existait pas il faudrait l'inventer,* If God did not exist it would be necesary to invent Him. Let all the blame fall on me if I have invented a god in my own way. I confess that if I have sometimes doubted the existence of God it has been so as not to burden a perfect Being with the guilt of all the stupidities, the malice, and the evil designs of mankind. I have felt some sympathy for the devil, who, if he does evil, is at least obliged to do so by professional duty. Perhaps one day the spirit of evil might repent and turn friar, but mankind will remain perverted until the end of time. As a little girl I was afraid of the devil. Now I think that, insofar as I belong to the human race, it is rather the devil that should be afraid of me. All things considered, he is a coward. How often, finding myself on the edge of a good deed have I heard his voice: "So, would you have the courage to be good?"

'I have not claimed to have invented God. But I swear that I would be very grateful to Him if He had not invented me, if He had not dug me out of nothing, where I would have preferred to remain. They talk about the "joy of living." But believe me, the joy of not living, of not existing, must be infinitely greater. We come from nothing. Do we return to nothing? I do not know. The pleasure of "nothing" leads many to have themselves cremated after death, and some order that their ashes be scattered to the winds. I do not feel like requesting this treatment for my body, as my father and grandfather did. But neither am I reconciled to the idea of ending up under the earth as a Pantagruelian meal for the worms. Even in the life after death I need air, freedom, light. The ancients believed that the spirits of the dead remained here below, free to wander through the earth. In my uncertainty whether this fate is reserved for me, I express my attraction to the system of mummification in which the friars of Palermo vie with the Egyptians.

'I therefore dispose that my body, essicated and mummified, be placed in the most airy corridor of the Catacombs of the Cappuccini. As a woman and as a noble, the most appropriate place would be in the similar catacombs of the Cappuccinelle, where there rest so many gentlewomen of my rank. But I do not like the rigid clausura of these good sisters, imposed even on the dead. A lover of freedom, as I have always been, I prefer to inhabit democratically an underground tomb open to all and visited by foreigners, by the curious, and by other time-wasters. I smile at the idea that some crazy little thief might steal one of my tibias and make it into a flute or a whistle. How wonderful to be able to whistle in contempt, through the mouth of some nameless person, at the idiotic comedy of this ridiculous world!

'I pardon everyone.

'I pardon my firstborn son marchese Fabrizio his asinine projects, among which the greatest is the illusion of restoring the kingdom of the Two Sicilies, which, after one-hundred twenty-six years of existence, collapsed through the foolishness of its last rulers, one more cretinous than the next.

'I pardon my second-born son Federico his proud proposal of bestowing happiness on the human race (if he is not already cured of it), by calling everyone to participate in equal portions at the banquet of life. Philanthropists always have an evil fate. They end at the hands of their beneficiaries.

'To my poor Ramiro I pardon his pure and innocent idealism, which led him to die for the independence and the union of Italy. I am afraid that he wasted his powder and shot. The Italians are perhaps destined to remain forever disunited and enslaved. Prince Metternich said it well:

When they are lucky they will be envied, when they are unlucky they will be cursed, always in disagreement, winners or losers.

'I pardon my nephew Goffredo his thoughtlessness and inexperience, which make him throw himself headlong into lost causes and often impel him to take on the difficult mission of helping lame dogs over stiles. Let him know that lame dogs love their stiles and men love their twisted ideas. Woe to you if you touch them! There is a conflict in life between poetry and prose, and poetry is always defeated. But poetry remains, after all, the only divine thing on the earth.

'I forgive myself for my wit: which, if it has sinned by biting, has never been stained by frivolity or vulgarity. I know that no one else has pardoned me for it. The world lives too contented in its *platitude* to look favorably on any impulse toward the heights. And since no one has pardoned me for it, at the point of death let me absolve myself.

'A few words about my possessions.

'My sons know that I do not dispose of a great fortune. Their father married me without a dowry, and all my goods begin and end with the widow's dower which he, like all noblemen, established in my favor. I was pretty and had great wit, these were my only riches. Unfortunately, they are the only ones that cannot be transmitted to one's heirs.

'Of that which does belong to me I dispose in the following manner.

'With the exception of the obligatory bequests to my sons Fabrizio and Federico, I leave the remainder of my goods to my nephew Goffredo, both for himself and as the only descendent of my deceased son Ramiro. That is valid, naturally, for real estate consisting in country and city properties. As to moveable goods (money, clothes, jewels etc.) I desire them to devolve upon the poorest religious community of the city, the Capuccinelle. I further dispose a legacy of one hunderd *onze,* chargeable to my heirs, to the beneficent and charitable institutions of Palermo, with the exclusion of the orphanage of Santo Spirito.

'I wish my exequies to take place in the most modest form, without display and without extravagance. If possible let my journey toward my final dwelling occur in the early morning, avoiding crowded streets. The curiosity of others would annoy me even after my death. I have yearned for peace for so long, I want no one to disturb it. No flowers, no expensive funeral, no laudatory obituaries. Pray, as I pray, for my peace.

'P.S. Among my books there is a small Gospel in French, bound in morocco with gold decorations. It is a souvenir of my childhood. Let Goffredo keep it and read it from time to time. When my story is written or told, perhaps people will be amazed that the Jacobin, the sansculotte, the revolutionary Hortense Duplessis possessed a Gospel and prized it. Why should they wonder? On the eve of my eighties I discover that the most revolutionary book that exists is the Gospel of Christ, and that the last, the true, the definitive revolution is the one that men will dare to make in His name.'

Chapter 7

THE LITTLE café Indipendenza, kept by Nunzio Ingrao in the vicolo Conte Cagliostro of the rione Albergheria, was the headquarters of the malcontents. Not all malcontents are revolutionaries, but all revolutionaries are malcontents. They comprise the race of the restless, the failures, the rumor-mongers, those who always find something to criticize and reform, and they resemble termites, who gnaw under the earth at the roots and the capillaries of a tree until it crashes to the ground at the first gust of wind. Woe to the ruler of the State who cannot discover in time the angriest of these chewers and throw them at least a bone to calm their restlessness and their inborn instinct to gnaw!

In every prereolutionary period the discontented seek each other out and find themselves by smell, they sniff each other, they sense each other; they congregate almost automatically in the cafés, the pharmacies, the clubs, the sacristies, and they conspire without knowing it. Everywhere like mixes with like: ants in an anthill, frogs in a pond, bees in a hive.

On the eve of the insurrection of September 1866 one of these meeting places was the tiny café of which we are speaking. Named Cagliostro until 1859, it had been closed by the police under the pretext that it was the resort of people of ill-repute, most of them on the list of those 'to be watched.' The immediate cause of the precaution was found in the attack on the life of the chief of police, Salvatore Maniscalco, a pillar of Bourbon absolutism. With the triumph of the revolution, when Garibaldi had entered Palermo the little café had reopened its doors with the significant name of Indipendenza. The evening of 10 May 1864, when the news of the death of the famous head policeman in Marseille had just reached Palermo, two great globes of colored glass, usually dusted off and set out only for the feast of Santa Rosalia, shone to the left and right of the inn sign. To the passers-by, surprised at the unusual illumination, who asked, *Don Nunziu, chi è u' fistinù?,* Don Nunzio, is it the Festino?, he answered, 'It's to refresh the soul of don Totò (Salvatore). He broke our balls while he was alive, and I put them up outside now that the dear departed has kicked the bucket.' In fact everyone remembered how the terrible head of the police, followed by his men, went around the city smashing with his whip the bright lamp-globes that appeared on the shops of the 'liberals' on patriotic events such as the Festino of Santa Rosalia.

The extremely modest shop of Nunzio Ingrao was hidden in a corner of the most working-class and revolutionary quarter of the city. Outside, a badly-painted brown wooden sign, lined like the face of an old man by bad weather and pock-marked by the stones with which the neighborhood hoodlums targeted it to relieve their warlike impulses. Inside, four little marble tables, once white, now yellowed and greasy, cracked at the edges, decorated with the board-lines for the game of *marrella* and with political caricatures, the work of amateur artists. The owner excused the insufficient cleanliness of the marble slabs by the necessity of preserving these graphic relics, which alternated with the drink-rings of ill-washed saucers. According to him, the brass sugar-bowls marked by the traces of myriads of flies, regular customers of his business, were sufficient to conceal the dirt. On the walls, hung with faded paper and with grease stains at the height of the chair-backs leaning against them, were enshrined on one side the portraits of Garibaldi and Mazzini and on the other the didactic oleographs illustrating the two maxims, 'I sold for cash' and 'I sold for credit.' Commenting on the pictures, the coffee maker added, 'I give my political ideas on credit (in politics, even God doesn't pay on Saturday). Drinks I sell only for ready cash.'

Off beyond the first room a little chamber, separated from the rest of the premises by a small door, lurked in the shadows: a back room reserved for the close friends of the owner, the *sancta sanctorum* of conspiracies and plots.

The customary group of malcontents who hung around the café consisted of some twenty people, more or less. The greater part were confused, outside the law, each forming his own party, solitary wanderers of politics. Others belonging to a faction, but quite uninvolved, unprejudiced and cynical, saying and allowing to be said the worst about their friends.

It would have been interesting to observe at a peephole one of the secret nocturnal meetings in the little back room of the Indipendenza on the eve of the September revolt, to get some idea of the Babel reigning in everyone's mind.

An evening of scirocco, between the constellation of the Lion and that of the Virgin, 1866. Despite the fact that it was about to chime midnight, people are gasping with the heat. The air is thick and weighs like syrup, something sticky which gums up the skin and attacks the joints. A hissing of flies beating their wings like a ventilator. Even Garibaldi and Mazzini are suffocating in their picture-frames. On the table a straw-covered bottle of '*surdo*' wine, which shrinks before one's eyes. *Nunc est bibendum!*, Now is the time to drink, the four men in conversation seem to say, drawing their eloquence from a glass which abhors a vacuum.

Placido Battaglia, law student, permanently 'off course,' with his head leaning back on the chair cushion, his hair plastered down by sweat, tongue-tied by too many libations, pontificates:

—In short, dear sirs, I'm fed up, totally fed up with the questions that they ask me every moment: And you, what are you? what party to you belong to? To none. I am a revolutionary. I am for total revolution, without qualifications, without precedents!

—And yet there are precedents—solemnly asserted the attorney Pancrazio Naso, a fanatical proponent of Sicilian autonomy: a dry little man lean as fishbait, constantly rolling the sparse wool of his goat's beard with his nervous fingers.—In one century the people of Sicily have already risen three times.

—Three, and even four revolutions...too many and none at all—said Battaglia, gulping down a glass.

—None? What about the forty-eight?

—Yes, you defend that revolution. The forty-eight is all yours. You are a separatist, a regionalist, a federalist, and I don't know what else. You would like to make the island into one little state in a federation, something like the mushroom in a mushroom farm, or the mangy sheep in a flock under the staff of a single shepherd, the pope.

—Don't touch the pope—protested don Assardi—whoever eats the pope dies of it.

—Calm yourself, don Assardi. I have none of these desires. I am abstemious...indeed vegetarian. And, as to the pope, I ignore him. *Ignoti nulla cupido,* You can't want what you don't know. You know that I am an atheist...An atheist by the grace of God.

They all laughed, while the priest made the sign of the Cross.

—Don't get me off the track—continued Battaglia.—I wanted to say just one thing. If we are to do something serious, let's kill the forty-eight... and also its son, the sixty. Let's murder the moonlight, my friends. In other words, the morbid romanticism. The forty-eight was a romantic revolution. It has some unpardonable flaws. Above all, it was copied from France. It was sick with graphomania, it didn't know how to do anything except write constitutions. It was made for the use and consumption of the middle class and not of the people. It unloosed national feeling and flooded Europe with wars, terrible wars, of which we are only at the beginning. It awoke in the people the sense of freedom and made them restless and unhappy...

—Wonderful!—interrupted Naso—you would like a revolution without freedom?

—I say that political liberty is a mockery when it leaves the people with an empty belly. You tell the people: you are free to vote, to express your opinion, to choose a government for yourselves...but you're also free to starve to death. A revolution must first of all abolish poverty. What does political equality mean, equality before the law, without economic equality? We are still at the same point as the French revolution, which was and remained exclusively middle class. Only Robespierre understood that it is useless to give people political power without economic power. But his Jacobin republic was smothered in the blood of the Brumaire. The revolution of the third Estate is the one that was made. The revolution of the fourth Estate is the one that is now to be made. We will make it, or rather it will make itself. Will blood be shed? What does it matter? Blood produces order, the new order. After all, in every revolution the rebel is not the people, but the king.

—You have to specify which king you mean—interupted don Assardi.— For Victor Emmanuel of Savoy, you're right a thousand times. He is the usurper. As to Francesco II of Bourbon, the only legitimate king, you are dead wrong.

—One is the same as the other. From the day, 28 January 1850— I cannot forget it, although I was just a boy—when I saw the university student Nicolò Garzilli, with five others, fall under Bourbon machine gun fire in piazza Fieravecchia, I swore hatred to all the rulers of the earth. To hang the last king with the guts of the last priest, that is my creed.

—Bravo, my Marat of the sixty-fourth!—You speak so well that they would give you a kiss, a kiss that could be a bite—and the priest took him by the cheek, pulling the youth toward himself. *Dio nni scansa di muzzicuna du parrino,* God save us from the bites of the parish priest. You will all burst with rage, but you will soon see Francesco of Bourbon, by the grace of God, on the throne of the Two Sicilies.

—There is only one Sicily—Naso affirmed solemnly.—Return to the Neapolitans? Never.

—Then keep your great king Victor Emamanuel, the 'gentleman' king, the most gentlemanly of kings—and the priest raised his tricorne, lowering it to the ground with the most sarcastic of bows.

—The Savoias!—said Naso, with a grimace of disgust.—I love them so much that I don't even eat 'savoiardi' biscuits, they stick in my teeth…I give them to the unitarians. But there's one thing they don't know…That the house of Savoy did not even want unification. Their great king, through Cavour, was already plotting a secret agreement between Piedmont and the Neapolitans, leaving out all the rest of the peninsula. The plan angered the exiles. It was then that Mazzini launched the watchword, 'The unity of Italy must be made beginning from the south.' And to hurry things along he prompted Pisacane to his unhappy expedition to Sapri.

—Hurrah for Pisacane—cried the student Battaglia, half dizzy with wine—the first Italian socialist.

—*In vino veritas*—concluded don Assardi—and here the truth is that among four cats, as we are, there are no two in agreement.

—Who says so?—cried Battaglia—there is one thing in which we all think alike, that this revolution must be made!

—It will get made, it is being made. Hurrah for the revolution!—they cried in unison.

—But, gentlemen—added Naso, with legalistic scruple—there is one here whose opinion you have not yet heard, our don Carmine. It would be an offence to healthy democratic custom not to hear him.

—I am a barber-surgeon—the gentleman in question observed modestly.—I shave, I remove a few rotten teeth, I apply leeches, I make clysters, I draw blood...

Excellent!—approved Battaglia—you will draw the blood of the tyrants.

—As a result I have no other opinions except those of my clientele—continued don Carmine.

—What would that mean?

—It's clear. I have no opinions at all. I am always ready to change them. I go with the wind.

—But what are you today?

—At your service. I am a liberal-conservative, monarchist-republican, Bourbonist-Garibaldino, legitimist-anarchist, papalist-atheist...Do you want more? I'm always undecided between yesterday, today, and tomorrow...you never know. This way I preserve my clientele, my tranquillity, and my skin.

—But not your consistency—someone reproached him.

—Listen, dear sirs. Of revolutions, *N'haiu 'a vozza china,* I've had a bellyful. I have four or five of them (and he started to count the fingers of his left hand with his right, as if he were reciting a rosary without the beads). In '12 they were shouting, Down with the Bourbons, hurrah for the constitution, hurrah for the English! Came the '20. Hurrah for the Spanish constitution, hurrah for the Carbonari, a great show of red and yellow rosettes...The '48 brought us the intense love for Pius IX, Here's to the pope-king!...Now the '49: return of the Bourbons on the bayonets of general Satriano, acclamations of Ferdinando, king Bomba...Finally the '60. Everybody from the saints to the dogs dressed up in red shirts...Today, not six years later, down with them all, a new revolution is preparing...The times are changing, the flag changes, and I see one thing only: always the same *strafalarii,* the same scoundrels, coming to the surface..."Flood time,

Tempo di diluvio"...with what follows, says our proverb, "*tutti gli stronzi salgono a galla,* " "all the turds float up to the surface." Enjoy yourselves.'

Every revolutionary cycle is articulated into two periods: the first weak, the second strong. First the Idea governs the deeds, then like unbridled horses the deeds sweep away the Idea.

In Palermo the revolution, which had long been latent, was galloping toward this last phase. It was an Idea derived from the events, which were imposing themselves with overwhelming power. Foreseen by the wise almost with fatalistic resignation, wished for by the discontented, urged on by the violent and the thoughtless, the Idea was now marching on under its own power. To slow it was rashness, to stop it was madness. The anxiety, the disquiet, the agitation, at first fluid and diffuse, grew more solid from one day to the next, they defined themselves, they became localized. The nerve centers were the most working-class quarters of Palermo: the Kalsa, the Capo, the Albergheria. If the agitation boiled more briskly in these centers, elsewhere it spread with greater menace. It reached the outlying *quartieri,* it overflowed into the suburbs, it rose like a muddy and murky tide through the hinterland above the Conca d'Oro. And when a movement has infiltrated into the countryside the attempt to channel it is almost hopeless.

One of the warning signs of revolutions is the collapse of authority. Order constitutes the connective energy of social life, and order, in turn, rests on the respect for the public power. If this is not felt by the community, there is no material force that can prop it up. When one of its principal links is broken the protective belt of the social aggregate wears out and gives way. The revolution is at the gates.

The disregard for public discipline (an innate defect of the Southern peoples) in these days was turning into a bitter and scornful neglect, sometimes insolent and provocative. The citizens, especially those of the lowest classes, vied with each other in disobeying the commands of authority. They openly challenged authority with an air of 'the hell with it.' Price controls were no longer observed, the ordinances of the urban police were shamelessly broken. Carts circulated through the principal streets at all hours alongside the coaches of the gentry; vendors blocked the sidewalks with their baskets; housewives dumped their garbage cans on the passers-by; the coachmen drove crazily, running over hapless pedestrians. If the *pontonieri,* the municipal police, intervened, there were quarrels, insults, violence, in which the guardians of order had the worst of it. The rabble came running, appearing from nowhere to lend a hand to the rebels, shouting 'give it to the cops.' The result was that the guards appeared as little as possible and sneaked off, never mind that the law was in danger. In consequence the malefactors abounded, and they dared raids of the most reckless boldness even in the heart of the city. In the countryside the roads were unsafe and brigandage ruled openly, its various bands competing in robbery, kidnapping, and murder.

The judicial prison of the Ucciardone itself reported a strange ferment within its massive and insurmountable walls. Something was being plotted there which escaped the most sharp-eyed surveillace of the jailers. 'Buckles' (clandestine notes, in criminal slang} circulated among the inmates; at night the walls of the cells spoke through tapped alphabets; 'damages' (a criminal synonym for knives) and other weapons penetrated into the dormitories, concealed in the laundry and in the loaves of bread brought from outside. During their 'breaks' the detainees exchanged rapid and impenetrable conversations accompanied by passwords, despite the prohibition of forming groups and gangs. They were heard to ask, *Picciotti, siti a cavaddu?* (Boys, have you got a horse=are you armed?) or to mutter, 'watch out for the *cascettoni*' (spies), 'it won't be long now until we're at the *cuba* (home).' The watchword circulating therough the whole Vicaria was that at the outbreak of the revolt the gates of the prison would be thrown open, and the name of therir liberator ran from mouth to mouth: Turi Micheli, *uomo d'onore,* the well-known *capo* of the Monreale underworld, who had solemnly promised to *allibertare* his companions, to free the victims of injustice, when he came out of jail. '*U turcu* (Turi)—he had said—took seven years to give an answer, and I'll give it first to all the scoundrels.'

In town the atmosphere was overheated. Everywhere meetings of conspirators, gatherings, encounters which seemed accidental and were prearranged and programmed. In the markets, at the crossroads, in the courtyards, in the sacristies, in the convents, persons of the most diverse classes approached each other, they gathered together, they consulted together, they asked each other cryptically, 'what do they say?' 'what quails are passing?' 'when will it rain?'

Those who had an urgent family affairs to take care of made haste. Those who were about to conclude a deal put it off until a better time. Householders were burying money and jewelry in some hole or under the bricks. Housewives were stockpiling provisions in their larders. The owners of firearms, even if they were among the most peaceful citizens, oiled them and checked their mechanisms, muttering through their teeth, 'You never know.' In the churches the increased number of the devout prayed to ward off some unknown scourge of God. At evening, thugs went around the buildings that were being demolished, collecting rods and iron bars to sharpen them into pikes. Someone swore that the barrels transported by seeming vendors of salted anchories really contained sal nitrate and sulphur to make gunpowder.

On the buildings, even the most exposed ones, phrases like the following, written in whitewash or painted in oil, appeared every morning: 'Death to the usurpers,' 'Sicily free or death,' 'Down with the despoilers of churches and convents,' 'Hurrah for the republic,' 'To the pillory with the freeloaders, the gravy train is about to stop.' Attached around the neck of the marble statue of Summer atop one of the fountains at the Quattro Canti was found the following printed poetry, the work of an anonymous bard:

Chi liggi chi nni misi stu tirannu/Che ognunu si dileggia lu so regnu./Li chiesi e li batii stanu spugghiannu./Pi quattru sbirri fu stu gran cuvernu./Lu populu si iava rivutannu/Ma si rivota poi tuttu lu regnu./Aspittamu stu iornu e nun sa quannu /Vinnitta si farà, sangu pi sangu.

What law was imposd on us by this tyrant/That everyone mocks his reign/ They are robbing the nunneries and monasteries/This great government was only for a small bunch of cops/The populace began to rebel/Then the whole kingdom rebelled immediately after/Let us await this day and no one knows when/Vengeance will be made, blood for blood.

On the groin of one of the nude statues in the circle around the fountain in Piazza Pretoria, this other garland of *settenari* appeared one morning, used as a fig lesf:

U tempu è fattu niuru/Vinniru arrè li lutti./Comu sipò resistiri/Hannu a finiri tutti?/Sentu friscura d'aria/ lu celi è picurinu./Nun c'è spiranza, populi, /La bufera è vicinu.

The time has become dark /Mourning has returned /How can we resist/If everything must end?/ I feel the wind rising /The heavens are dark./There is no hope, people,/The storm is near!

In the midst of a crowd of people, squads of police mounted on stepladders proceeded to scrape off the writings, to repaint the walls, amid showers of lemon peels and cabbages, and whistles and other obscene noises from the street urchins who had swarmed in from the worst parts of town. Shouts of mockery and provocative cries arose, accompanied by insults and followed by scuffles to arrest the guilty, arrests which were threatened but never carried out. Some of those arrested had to be released owing to the menacing aspect of the crowd, which now had the upper hand. After their first attempts to react, the police ended by pretending to be blind and deaf. The following day, naturally, new and more aggressive writings proudly appeared. The authorities decided not to pay any further attention. One more, one less: at the end the accounts would be added up. And the end, according to many warning symptoms, did not seem far off.

In the surrounding countryside more menacing clouds were gathering. Common criminality was raging behind the shield of politics. Attacks on property and persons were multiplying. The hunger for money and the lust for revenge erupted in the most inhuman crimes. The authorities, powerless and intimidated, had now lost control of public safety. They themselves were openly attacked and forced to remain on the defensive. Armed bands rampaged through the fields, marked out new land boundaries, terrorized the people with kidnappings and murders at the command of the evildoers. The dregs of the jails lorded it flanked by an army of adherents and accomplices who rendered useless any repression by the public forces, even if they had been capable of it.

The government, alarmed by the press and goaded by such politicians as were not corrupted by unconfessed personal interests, sought news of the conditions on the island. The prefect Torelli and the police commissioner Pinna, with that fatuity typical of the rulers of every people on the eve of social collapse, answered from Palermo that the situation was perfectly controlled and presented no cause for concern whatsoever.

On August 31 a poster affixed to the Quattro Canti di città called openly:

'Sicilians, arise: your lethargy, your unspeakable indifference, dishonors you and could number you among the morally despicable: but are you really like that? You, the people of the barricades, the people of great undertakings, who destroyed the throne of the Bourbon tyranny? You are the worthy sons of John of Procida of the Sicilian Vespers, born in the land of the volcanoes, and you cannot shame yourselves forever and drain the chalice of the dishonor and the disgrace of Italy...'

A group of sailors stopped to read it. They were survivors of the recent Italian defeat by Austria in the sea-battle of Lissa, still in the uniform of the marines. Some of them had escaped from the sinking of the armored frigate *Re d'Italia* on that fatal day.

A spark of indignation flashed in their young and unhappy eyes on reading the words inciting an uprising. To what honor did the words appeal, which threw the disgrace on the sorrowing but ever proud figure of the fatherland? Did the reproach of their brothers from every part of the peninsula sacrificed in honor of their common mother not rise from the depths of the Adriatic?

One of the sailors leapt on the shoulders of his companions, pulled out a knife, and set to work scraping off the poster, which fell in strips under his vengeful blade. The small crowd that had immediately gathered broke into applause. Some women, mothers or sisters of the fallen of Custoza or Lissa, wept. The sinister figures who were circling around the place with menacing eyes and mysterious business made off by the nearest streets. There still existed a healthy part of the population in whose hearts the fire of national honor, the sense of the dignity of their own country, was not extinguished. But, as often happens, in the moments of collective disorder and chaos that part of the populace was ovecome and discouraged by the insolence of violent thugs. Bias had so perverted their souls and clouded their minds that many took advantage of the recent military disasters to unleash new hatreds and to incite the ignorant populace to protest. It was not the first time that Italians had rejoiced in the defeat of Italian arms for the furthering of their own low ends. The unhappy days of Custoza and Lissa made it a good game to divide the still-unconsolidated national government, to smash the unifying process born of blood and decreed by fate. The moment was favorable for insurrection. The maneuverers, the *meneurs*, the movers and shakers, the leaders of the various parties, who crouched in the shadows ready to be released, preached, 'Now or never.' The watchword was, 'Let Italy die, provided the factions triumph.' Only a signal was lacking to unloose the revolt.

On the morning of September 15 the first red flag, greeted by salvoes of artillery, was hoisted in Monreale. By night the fires of bivouacs were glowing on the wooded slopes of San Martino. The squadrons of the insurgents were about to erupt into the city.

Chapter 8

SEPTEMBER TWILIGHT. To the west a carnival of light crumbles its last confetti on the crest of Monte Cuccio, sharp as a steel triangle. The shining dust gathers into garlands which sail slowly through a heaven striped with green and fan out scarlet reflections on the city below. When you enter by one of its eastern gates, the peaceful granite giant gives the impression of an erupting volcano.

From the Termini gate something black advances, wobbling on the dusty tracks of the carriageway. Nothing less than a monstrous great box on four wheels. On its night-colored sides emerge ever more clearly the words, 'Charitable Assistance' in white capital letters. It constitutes the final luxury granted to the poor, a carriage ride on their way from the inferno of life to the presumed paradise of the great beyond.

The coachman of the funereal chariot, a red-haired bumpkin with his cocked hat askew on his cropped head, sways like a snake while whipping up his ink-colored horses. He seems to be in a hurry.

Until yesterday the municipal guard was mounted at the customs barrier, along with Bavarian mercenaries, policemen, and carabinieri, to keep the insurgents of the province from entering the city. Instead, now squads of armed rebels are on duty to impede the passage of the forces of order. It is the game of roles, the comic fortune of political life!

The passers-by are stopped, questioned about where they come from and where they are going, searched for fear that they are disguised policmen trying to reach the capital. The vehicles waiting to undergo the checkup are obliged to make long halts, obstructing the passage-way, while their impatient drivers shout, rage, swear, blaspheme, among braying mules and neighing horses. But the people's police are relentless.

The coachman in the cocked hat cracks his whip and makes an infernal noise, claiming the right of precedence for himself. His, he thinks, is the privilege of death, and this renders him 'untouchable' in the sight of any authority.

Two guardian angels of the revolution, bristling with weapons like porcupines, pin him to the driver's box with a fierce malevolent glance.

—Not so fast, *paesano*.

—The dead are in a hurry, my friend. They stink. They don't want to wait for your orders. So, what news today? Are they taxing even the corpses?

—Less talk. Where do you come from?

—Come on! From everywhere, from every place where someone has the misfortune to die.

—How many?

—Fifty years. And I hope, with the grace of God, to live as many more.

—We're not joking. I'm talking about the dead.

—Four, five, seven...As many as the pallbearers load up. The diseases don't even ask permission to kill people. Now all we need is the cholera.

—What are you saying? You're carrying corpses from cholera?

—What do I know? Am I a doctor? But they say the cholera is at Naples. The scourge of God quickly crosses the water. It was like that in '37...In the end, one disease is as good as another. Everything has to end there... At least the cholera works fast. It doesn't give you time to think of death... *Si duna un firriuni e si attanta,* You spin around and drop dead (and the coachman grew rigid, like one struck dead by shock).

—Go, go, and the devil take you...Wait a minute, where are you headed?

—To the cemetery of the Capuchins...If you need any thing down there...—the coachman mocked him.

—Be off, or I'll shoot you—the revolutionary policeman answered back, fingering the pistol inserted in his belt.

Giving his horses a crack of the whip, the coachman set off at a good pace.

When the funeral carriage was near ponte Ammiraglio it stopped before an iron gate flanked by two pillars. Night was falling. The dark was crushng the last remainders of the twilight to the earth like a steam roller. Trees, houses, bell-towers lost their form bit by bit and disappeared into a thick black pulp. Carriage, horses, and coachman were swallowed up by the soft black of the nocturnal scene. Two little points of green light leapt forth low down. They would have seemed bodiless, if the miaow of a cat also swallowed up by the darkness had not reclaimed their ownership.

The scrape of a key in the lock, the metallic squeak of a gate opened by invisible hands, a voice that quietly whispers a password.

Creaking in all its joints, the cart enters a path flanked by low thick lemon trees. It stops in front of a one-story villa unpierced by a single chink of light from its windows. Only the flash of pale lanterns, swung like thuribles, reveals the movement of shadows. The lanterns aim a sliver of light at the interior of the cart, whose doors someone has opened.

—Palermo.

—Republic and Santa Rosalia—answers a subterranean voice.

When the cover had been pulled off from a crate placed at the top of a pile of coffins, there arose a figure, first visible up to the waist like Farinata degli Uberti in the Inferno. Then the whole body popped out, ghostlike were it not for its cherubic head of hair, animated under the lamplight by golden reflections.

—How do you feel, don Goffredo?

—I could be better—said the young man, stretching his numbed limbs amid a rosary of yawns.

—Did you lack air? Were you able to breathe?

—Like a fish out of water...before being fried. Let me take a bellyful of fresh air. What a delight!

—Blessed be Rosalia, our Santuzza—exclaimed several voices together.

—The dead are alive, talking in dreams—thirty one and forty seven, it's the combination to play on the lottery—commented another.

—I'm alive. Think instead about unloading the 'corpses' inside.

—How many?

—About fifty, both good and bad. In a lot of old duds there are some good quality weapons. You'll see.

The shoulders of the bearers were breaking under the weight of the mysterious coffins. Nothing was heard except the scrape of the their hobnailed boots on the dry ground and the gasping of their tired lungs for breath.

—My God, how much these bones weigh!

—There's cast iron inside.

—They're matches to light the fire.

—Light it?! The fire is already spreading.

—What? You still don't know?—one of them answered Goffredo, who was asking anxiously.—In Palermo there's the *Viva Maria,* all hell breaking loose, starting yesterday.

The coachman held out his hands to take the loaf of bread and an enormous glass of wine which were offered him.

—Cherish those—said the giver—In town there isn't a single bakery open, nor even the shadow of a tavern to refresh your throat.

—*Requie materna*—gurgled the coachman, swallowing the last sip of wine.—The dead are dead, let's think about the living.

—And now you can continue your journey. The Lord go with you.

A group of men closed around the new arrival, leading him the way toward the villa. It was one of those vacation houses, frequent in the Palermitan countryside, where the owners spend some months in summer while the houses remain in a state of abandonment throughout the rest of the year. Large rooms with white walls and terracotta brick floors, a few rickety pieces of furniture, some discarded utensils, a few pictures exiled from the town house for old age and decrepitude, rooms smelling of mildew for being closed up so long. Preceded by an oil lantern, the brigade descended by way of a trap door and a circular staircase into a large chamber, probably once used to store wood, which was now a deposit for arms and munitions. In the middle of this improvised arsenal, among piles of muskets, pistols, and revolvers of every age and type, barrels of gunpowder, and boxes of bullets, there was planted a table of rough wood with a few unraveling and spavined chairs around it. Someone put on the table two blond and fragrant loaves of bread and slid out of a yellow paper cone a bunch of black olives, shining and bouncing as if they were elastic. Another brought a fresh caciocavallo cheese and began to cut it in thick square slices from which there emerged a pungent odor.

—This is all—said the foreman of the group.—*Voscienza* will get used to doing penance. But, thank God, there's no lack of wine, he added, pointing to a companion who was coming with two jugs overflowing with a ruby liquor more fragrant than nectar.

—Too much for me—Goffredo thanked him, meanwhile asking news of the uprising. —When did it break out?

—Sunday at dawn. *Iurnata singaliata,* a day that can't be forgotten.

—And how are things going now?

—Full sail. Santa Rosalia is with us.

—Are the royal forces resisting?

—They're holed up in every quarter.

—What forces can they count on?

—A few thousand men at the most. But they're expecting reinforcements from one minute to the next, so there is no time to lose. The city and the province must be in our hands as soon as possible. We have to present the government with a fait accompli, confront them with a provisional administration already completely formed.

—We are *quantu i furmiculi,* as many as the ants—the leader affirmed with a condescending gesture.

—And who is in command?

—Who should command? More or less everybody.

—That means no one—said Goffredo, shaking his head. —A revolt without a leader is doomed to failure.

—All the same...we're winning all along the line. Things are going wonderfully, they couldn't be better...with the help of the Santuzza.

—Today. But tomorrow?

—God will deal with tomorrow. Besides...there is someone who will give you better information than we can.

The little brigade, composed of five men armed to the teeth, set off toward the center of the city by way of Corso dei Mille. The streets were deserted. The street lamps, their glasses smashed, were all extinguished, the night was moonless. A thick darkness like pitch attached itself to all things, which were recognizable only by touch. You had the impression that in the struggle to walk the soles of your feet remained glued to the ground and were unstuck from it only with difficulty. Rare shadows of fantastic beings, more felt than seen, crept along the walls, were swallowed and regurgitated by some mysterious house. Nonetheless the group moved quickly, they were too familiar with the area to lose their way in the night.

At Porta Sant'Antonino an unfinished barrier obstructed their passage. A few smoky flaming torches illuminated a scurrying crowd of shirtless and scattered men, a bustle of workers, mostly boys, who were moving stones, breaking up furniture and piling it in a dark mass which grew in height as one watched. Only a little well-guarded lateral crossing allowed a passage from one side to the other.

—Who goes there?

—Republic and Santa Rosalia.

—You're ours. Pass.

The five advanced along via Maqueda, glided under the arch of the Cutò, emerged into piazza del Carmine; by ducking around back streets and alleys they arrived in via Santa Chiara. A triangle of feeble light announced the presence of a palace gate. The courtyard was swarming with loud gesticulating men: some armed, some unarmed, some in red berets, some in hats or in some strange headgear—tassels, straw bonnets.

On the first floor of the building, an old patrician palace, the door opened into a vast hall immediately recognizable as the seat of a Masonic lodge. On the back wall there winked a handsome sun with a round smiling face, bristling with rays, and a crescent moon in rosy chastity, surmounted by a great triangle with one eye. All around, as recurrent motives in the friezes, were pentagrams, set squares, compasses, plumb lines, interwoven with cordons of brotherhood and collections of hieroglyphics and cabalistic signs. In short, all the implements with which the castle of human happiness is built at the nod of the great Architect of the Universe.

That night, instead of a Masonic meeting the hall was hosting a reunion of the most prominent leaders of the revolt and the representatives of the various political parties. The surroundings had the ambiguous air of something between the Jacobin 'club,' the 'meeting' of political parties, and the seat of a provisional committee or military command. They were all gathered there: the malcontents, the incompetent, the presumptuous, the complainers and the hypercritical, the amateur strategists, the professional rowdies. Everywhere, naturally, a great display of red, the color of blood and fire: berets, scarves, rosettes, sashes of blinding scarlet. As we know, revolutions and republics see red. Unlike the bull, who destests it, they love this color, perhaps because the bull is a constructively working animal, while the revolution is an instrument of destruction.

In one group, one of its most hotheaded members was demanding that the tricolor be replaced by the red flag. Others were opposed, remembering that in France in the '48 a similar proposal had been made after the proclamation of the Second Republic, and that the people had defeated it after a famous speech by Lamartine. The Bourbonists, irreconcilable, were fighting for the return to the white banner starred with golden lilies of their ancient dynasty. The anarchists were for a black flag. It was a romantic tournament of colors.

Another group, more numerous and less romantic, was listening to the pontifications of Giuseppe Badia, a popular and characteristic figure of revolutionary. Formerly a lieutenant in the Sicilian army of the '48, condemned to death by the Bourbons, a Garibaldino fighting at Milazzo and the Volturno, a legionary of the Italian army, broken by General Fanti, re-entered the ranks of the legitimist reaction out of spite, intriguing with every party to grab a leading position. A flushed face, eyes projecting from their orbit like a lobster's, gesticulations of a madman, stentorian voice. Talkative, pretentious, innately incapable of reason, in conflict with everyone and with himself, the perfect mystic of Nothingness, Badia belonged to that category of small-time politicians who live next door to the madhouse. The perfect example of the agitated agitator, the leader in a straight jacket, which was the reason that he enjoyed an immense prestige with the common people.

—Citizen—he crooned in a baritone, noticing Goffredo—be welcome among us.

The young man held out his hand.

—Am I shaking the hand of Marat or of Danton, the hand of the leader of the Jacobins or of the Girondins?—continued Badia, tugging on his Mephistopholean goatee.

—Neither one nor the other. I'm not the leader of any party, answered Goffredo.

—Better so. A revolution needs no leader. It is commanded by the people.

—In theory it is. In practice it's another thing. Without a minimum of organization it won't succeed. Who here is directing the military operations? Who is looking after internal affairs? Who is superintending the construction and defence of the barricades? Who is dealing with burying the dead and caring for the wounded? Who is providing for the grain supply?

—Trifles, dear boy! Every revolution has its star: it is the *star* that leads it.

—Here, instead of a star, I seem to see a nebula, nothing but confusion and disorder. There still doesn't exist a provisional government...we are in total anarchy.

—A government, or at least a provisional *committee* does exist, if it's so important to you. Haven't you read it posted on the street corners?

—But no one knows anything about it.

—The joke is—Badia burst into laughter—that the man who presides over it doesn't know anything about it either: the prince of Linguaglossa.

—What are you saying?

—The truth. Since many people were calling for a leader, they put in any old blockhead. They printed and posted up the name of the prince of Linguaglossa, who interests himself in nothing, who wishes to know nothing...Believe me, it's all the same. He's in charge of the rabble and that's it. Aren't we in democratic times? enough of dictatorships. If I'm not mistaken, they want to dismiss Victor Emmanuel because he is giving himself the airs of a dictator, especially over us Sicilians.

—The dictatorship of the mob is the worst of the worst.

—The dictatorship of the people would not exist without the dictatorship of the princes. That one is dangerous, this one is only disgraceful.

—But you do not scruple to give a strong arm to tyranny now. Aren't you allies of the Bourbon reaction?

—Tactical necessities, my boy! Do I need to explain them to you? We are allied with the Bourbonic party because today it is strong, because it is convenient for us. Tomorrow, when we have won—said Badia, winking an eye and dropping his words slowly into his interlocutor's ear—we'll say the hell with them...we'll be the first to dump them overboard.

—I don't approve of such measures. You can decide not to contract certain alliances, but once the step is taken you have a duty to be loyal to your ally.

—So, you are one of the pure ones. A Mazzinian puritan, from what they say. A moralist of politics...—Badia laughed sarcastically.

—I am, and I'm proud of it.

—But then, excuse me for asking, why are you messing in our business? *Your* Mazzini has declared himself against the revolution.

—Against *this* revolution. He has written fiery letters to dissuade the Sicilians from a separatist, secessionist uprising. His thought is that Sicily must be at the head of the second revolutionary wave, in the context of the whole Italian nation. As in the '60 Sicily was the first to give the signal for the resurgence of the independence and the unity of Italy...

—For the independence, not the unity—Badia corrected bitterly.

—...now she should give the sendoff to the republican movement.

—We too are for the republic.

—But we Mazzinians are fighting for the united republic, for a republican Italy.

—Then I have the honor to tell you, young man, that this is not the place for you. Here we make the *Sicilian* republic, or we die.

—Exactly because people die I have come here, and I'm staying to fight for the *Italian* republic. The revolution has already broken out? All right, we will fight for the honor of the revolution!

A little old man, witness of this dialogue, commented in a corner, 'Who ever made me come here? It's a cage of madmen, of the possessed, Jesus Mary and Joseph!'

Excited voices were crying, Enough chatter! To the barricades!

Chapter 9

By THE eve of September 16 Palermo was writhing in the toils of the uprising. The only one to be unaware of it was the political authority, by its nature slowfooted in following the great upheavals of history. The populace, if it did not know it, felt it, and everyone knows how far intuition surpasses reason. Even a blind man, incapable of threading his dead orb into the needle's eye of world happenings, would have perceived something extremely tense in the air; like the ordeal of glass, not struck but compressed to its maximum resistance, which is about to shatter. When they were not taut from distress, people's faces appeared bewitched, and the customary forms of social life seemed weak allegories of a more profound truth hidden behind them. Dark words, prophetic, Hamlet-like, and menacing, had for some time been circling around an ugly fact, historically irrelevant but pulsing with a more powerful ideal relevance: the truth of that which does not yet exist, but must absolutely exist, because Destiny dictates it. More than words, there were at first confidences, whispers, winks and elbowings, broken phrases, sly jargon (*a baccagghiu*), which passers-by on the same street exchanged in encounters, whether planned or accidental. Then proposals which gained confidence in open speeches, long conversations which broke out into boasting and provocation. Tactical and strategical plans were discussed, places of attack and resistence were located, the zero hour of the 'operations' was pinpointed. The names of the chiefs, the sub-chiefs, and the supporters of the insurrection were all openly revealed.

Mothers were told to keep their children close by, as hens do with their brood of chicks as soon as the weather darkens and a storm threatens. Bakers were advised to provide a good stock of flour in case refurnishing the mills unexpectedly became difficult. The man who had a revenge to carry out rubbed his hands in anticipation, the man who had some bill to pay began to feel a certain fearful palpitation. The poor and the disinherited stared at the rich with unaccustomed sullenness, criminals looked the forces of order up and down without respect, almost to defy them, and pointed out the tools of the police, who were rumored to be the oppressors (*supirchiusi*), as if to say, 'Just wait, we'll give you a party.' Everywhere a state of agitation and over-excitement swollen with anger, resentment, perverse desires, with chilling fears and sinister forebodings. Only the high authorities were swimming in optimism like fish in a lazy pond. Disbelieving the warnings that were rising, they were reluctant to take those wise precautions that every peaceful citizen suggested and claimed would limit if not block completely the imminent disaster. Unfortunately, the optimism of the men of the State is the foolish cunning that fate employs to destroy a regime.

On the evening of September15, to be precise, while the circle of mountains around the Conca d'Oro was dotted with mysterious luminous eyes under a sky veiled by opalescent gauzy clouds, the mayor, marchese Starrabba di Rudinì, and the Bergamasque Major General Camozzi, commander of the National Guard, requested audience of the prefect of the province, count Luigi Torell, at his private quarters in the Royal Palace.

When the servant announced the two visitors, the prefect, stretched out among the cloth poppies which flowered the soft armchair that conforted his lazy and carefree siesta, was meditating benevolent thoughts, like those of every being at peace with his stomach. From his lips, between one puff and the next, there emerged with geometric precision little white circles of smoke, of which their author was generally proud.

Upon seeing the mayor and the commander of the national guard the prefect leapt to his feet. Despite his age, closer to sixty than to fifty, surges of youthful energy coursed through his limbs, contrasting with the gravity of his office and his attire, which, like a stopped clock, remained hopelessly stuck in the year '48. A romantic black redingote enclosed his body of medium height, a great night-black cravat with corners fluttering on the dicky of his shirt confined the wings of a wide white sailor collar. The incipient grey of the ring beard under his chin clashed with the brown of his mustaches, which were badly stained and scorched by cigar smoke.

—What good wind brings you here...at this somewhat unusual hour?—said count Torelli with his usual soothing affability.

—Serious matters, unfortunately, prefect—began the mayor.

—Nothing less? So there still exist serious things in a cheerful epoch like this, in which the Italians, after two military defeats, are amusing themselves by playing at 'political parties,' and are happily turning their coats at every breath of wind?

—The revolution is at the gates—explained general Camozzi, articulating the syllables like a prophecy.

—That is, behind the door—corrected Torelli.—Well, let it wait. It will not be for us to tell it, 'Come in, make yourself at home!' It is not *chic* to play the waltz before the dancing starts. And, my friends, why the revolution? It was logical, necessary, to rebel before Italy was made. But now, well, it would be an anachronism. A disorder at the wrong time. No, let's repeat it loudly, the Sicilians are never late. If anything, they arrive ahead of time.

—Sicily—proclained Di Rudinì proudly—in the '48 began the series of revolutions for independence. In the '60 it was at the head of the revolution for unification. It was the Twenty-four Days of Palermo that in the '48 obliged the princes to concede the Constitutions...

—Excellent—Torelli approved—but let's not forget that the Five Days of Milan, where I was a combatant, confronted and defeated such an army as the Austrian one, among the most warlike, not to be compared with the Bourbon army. If your 'days' had more panache, ours had more method. We are more reasoners, you are more impulsive and improvisatory. And let me express a conviction of mine to you. The Sicilian people are not revolutionary by inclination. Why? Because they do not have a passion for politics. They don't love it. In their souls, politics represents nothing but a flirtation. They prefer to enjoy their lovely sun, basking in their *dolce far niente*, instead of stirring themselves up like madmen to follow the false mirages of an impossible social progress or a change of government. Perhaps this is where their wisdom lies. Or rather, if I am allowed a paradox, the Sicilian does not love revolution because he is *always* in revolt, in revolt against the law. Law and order are his *bêtes noires*. He has the genius of illegality. What do you say, marchese?

—I say that your knowledge of the soul of Palermo is more superficial than deep—observed the mayor, combing his flowing beard, a gesture habitual with him when his irritation began to go to his head.

—I can also descend quite far down, like a deep sea diver, when I wish... you're not looking at a newcomer to the job. I have been prefect here twice. And the first time, in '62, the waters were more troubled than now. This is a good and peaceful people, doomed to be forever tyrannized over by someone. First by the Bourbons, then by the mafia. I admit that today there is a revival of horrifying crimes, of attempts on the property and the lives of private citizens, occasional acts of rebellion against the public authorities. But you need something quite different to allow you to talk about public rage and turbulence...A bold recurrence of brigandage, that's all it is. But the mafia is not sufficient to mount a revolution. And I feel like crushing the mafia like this, Torelli tells you—and the prefect pounded his fist, shaking a peaceful group of porcelain bunnies on the adjacent table.

—But will the forces present in the province be sufficient?—Camozzi asked doubtfully.

—You are right—nodded the prefect—they are not many. For that reason I have turned time and time again to prime minister Ricasoli for an urgent dispatch of troops to reinforce the police. But the man doesn't hear out of that ear. A great and good man, Bettino Ricasoli, but a pigheaded Tuscan. He answers, 'I have no soldiers! Since the war is over, the army is being demobilized. I can't invent soldiers. Fix it yourselves.' Stubborn, but he also has a bit of right on his side.

—There is the national guard—Camozzi interrupted brightly.

—That bunch is called the guard because they have never guarded anyone—quipped Torelli.—Hasn't history taught you sufficiently that in case of an uprising the national guard goes over as one man to the side of the insurgents? But this uprising, may all the prophets of ill omen perish, will not take place. The word of Torelli. And finally, who is to make it? The priests and the friars? They're only good for mumbling paternosters and eating sausages. The Bourbonists? Four nostalgic cats who are meowing for love of their dethroned and eclipsed dynasty. We are no longer in January but in full September, I hope they don't come into heat again. The mafia maybe? But the mafiosi shoot from behind walls and hedges. Anyway, they are great cowards. Listen to this. In '62 two prisoners who were believed to be spies, when they had just returned from the Court of Assises where they had testified, were tried on the spot by a criminal tribunal of the main prisons and were immediately stabbed to death. Naturally, no one had heard or seen anything, *omertà* in high style. What does the prefect Torelli do? Within twenty-four hours he has the whole group where the killing had taken place transferred to the island of Pantelleria. I received an avalanche of anonymous threatening letters, but no one touched a hair of my head. Despite the fact that some newspaper scribblers had defined it sarcastically as a 'torellata,' a typical ploy of Torelli, my lesson passed into history...

—Prefect—the mayor burst out, visibly annoyed—can we leave history in peace? We're here for serious matters. While we're leafing through the pages of history, the house is burning.

—But what is on fire, exactly? May I be allowed to know?

—Do us the kindness of coming to the window. Look up there...all around the Conca d'Oro. Do you see on the crest of the mountains those fires that run down to the middle of the coast? They are bivouac fires of the squadrons ready to march at dawn toward the city, signs of communication between the periphery and the center of the imminent uprising.

—But that is stubble burning harmlessly on the fields. Let's not exaggerate, for God's sake.

—Stubble in mid-September? when the grain has already been harvested for more than two months?—said Rudinì sarcastically.—This is something new! And don't you note, above all, the regular intervals of those flashing signs? Real live semaphores...

—Semaphores! Semaphores!—the prefect began to mutter, and abandoning his staturesque pose he began to pace up and down the room like Manzoni's don Abbondio before the bravos arrived.—As to that, he added, stopping all of a sudden—any moment now we will hear the opinion of the commissioner, whom I have sent for urgently.

Commissioner Pinna did not keep them waiting. He entered looking somewhere between relaxed and sleepy, dangling his hairless ostrich head in the nest of a stiff and sweaty starched collar, under which a high vest, black as the breast of a crow, was buttoned up. Combined with his hairless face, his dress gave him more the air of an evangelical pastor than of a determined and infallible policeman. Chiaves, the Minister of the Interior, who had sent him to Palermo from Bologna, had depicted him as the terror of scoundrels and villains, but at the moment one read in his expression more his annoyance at being awakened and summoned at so tiresome an hour than the ferocity of a scourge of evildoers.

—Here is the man who will be able to inform us about the situation and calm your fears—said Torelli condescendingly.

—What do you want from me?—asked Pinna in a strained voice, rubbing his eyes.

—Give us an exact, objective position of the situation, for these distinguished gentlemen—ordered count Torelli.

—So, you want the position from me...and it should be a dark one, very black. I'm sorry to disppoint you. There is nothing black, at least for the moment. Only a bit of grey. What isn't grey in Italy these days?

—But the indications that are gathered everywhere by the handful, the rumors that are spreading, are more than alarming—said the mayor.

—Rumors are like nuts. They're spreading? Let them spread. The authorities pay attention to facts rather than to rumors. And of serious facts, shocking ones, there is no trace, at least not so far. A state of general unrest exists. According to some, Palermo is already a volcano on the verge of exploding. My answer is yes, a volcano, but an extinct one like your Monte Cuccio, a giant who threatens no one, who doesn't exhale a thread of smoke.

—I smoke more than he does—Torelli commented facetiously.

—After all—Pinna continued—we have the situation under control. The criminals are cornered. A pack of seasoned hounds has been unleashed on the traces of the suspected persons, including the tinpot politicians with their crazy ideas. At every barrier of the city policemen ready to stop the eventual flow of determined insurgents from the countryside into the city form an excellent guard. Armed rounds are patrolling all the inner and outer streets...So we can consider the general situation without any pessimism.

—What do you say about that?—said the prefect, launching one of his most successful smoke rings into the air.

—I say that the uprising is about to break out. Dawn will not be past before we are in the midst of the dance—burst out general Camozzi, who couldn't stand it any longer.

—Boom!—thundered Torelli, unconvinced.—One dead fortune-teller.

—I may die, but it is my duty as a soldier to request that the 'general call to arms' be beaten without losing a minute, and that the guard be assembled.

—All we need is your drums to terrify the citizens! You are seeing red, my friend. You're already dreaming of the bullfight only because you hear a bit of noise from the equestrian circus.

—Let the responsibility fall on whoever wants it. We have done our duty—concluded the mayor.—Let what must happen, happen.

—Nothing will happen—declared Torelli with the veins on his neck swollen and his temples congested.—The people of Palermo will not move. As to the trash from the countryside, the rural mafia composed of deserters and thieves, we'll give them a *mauvais quart d'heure*. They dare to match themselves with the forces of legitimate power! Just try. Torelli is here. Do you know who Torelli is? A mountaineer as hard as the boulders of his native Valtellina, the man who in the Five Days of Milan, under the very eyes of Radetsky's myrmidons, by himself—I repeat, by himself—planted the tricolor on the spire of Milan cathedral. It would take something more than bands of Sicilian criminals to frighten him. Fear, always fear! You know what one does in such cases. You pay in person.

The prefect dashed out of the room and a few minutes later bounced back in, harnessed up like Tartarin de Tarascon: a cartridge belt over a faded soldier's tunic, a big pistol on his belly, and a great Austrian rifle at 'shoulder arms.'

—To us, then! If the dance comes, we shall dance. And what blows you will hear struck!

—It's unheard-of—said the appalled marchese Rudinì into the ear of general Canozzi as they descended the stairway of the Royal Palace—to play the farce *before* the tragedy. God help us.

The first barricade rose in the night at the mouth of the vicolo Giuseppe D'Alessi, which joined via Maqueda with piazza Bologni. Rather than a street, one might call it a passage or an alley, on which circumstances had bestowed a high strategic value. Embedded between the palace of the University and the basilica of S. Giuseppe, it offered the advantages of immediate access to the church tower, one of the highest observation points over the crowded mass of the inhabited area, and of pointing like an arrow at the side of the palazzo comunale, the palazzo delle Aquile, which understandably had been chosen as the first bastion of the city's defence and furnished with arms and armed men. The municipality had its seat permanently there; at first the military command of the fortress also had its headquarters there. The amateur strategists of the uprising reasoned correctly that a column of government troops coming from piazza Bologni could easily take from the rear the first insurgent squadrons organised to storm palazzo delle Aquile, thus seizing the principal center of the resistence. But if the alley were barricaded they achieved the double result of frustrating any attempt of the regular army to break out from the side passage and of protecting the flank of the assault squadrons' first operations of breaking through and eventually laying siege. When the side outlets were closed and the palace was isolated, it could be considered to be virtually in the hands of the insurgents.

Until late on the evening of September 15, the rare passers-by had crossed through the vicolo Giuseppe D'Alessi without noticing anything out of the normal. The narrow little ditch, which runs straight for half its length and then suddenly turns before emerging into piazza Bologni, appeared semi-deserted and silent as usual. Only a few incomprehensible monosyllables rustled through the air, some ghostly beings crept in the shadows and suddenly disppeared as if swallowed up in the wall. Suddenly, when the hour after midnight had rung, a rental carriage with darkened lamps entered from via Maqueda and paused at the mouth of the alley. Ten, twenty arms stopped it, overturned it after unharnessing the horse, placed it so as to completely block the alley. Immediately there began to mount up around the overturned vehicle construction materials, furniture, household goods, soft furnishings, tools—the work of mysterious gnomes the color of night. Objects of neuter gender and anonymous paternity poured down mysteriously. The construction rose up as one watched. It was not a heap bundled up in confusion but an accumulation of things well arranged and joined together, so that each one and all together obeyed a calculated equilibrium of impediment and resistence. Stones, torn shutters and doors, benches and wardrobes, trestles and chairs, divans and matresses, school desks and benches, step ladders, prayer desks, metal grills, were gathered and fitted together skillfully, with a canny use of spaces, geometrical calculation of volumes and weights, in a consistent and massive block interrupted here and there by invisible passages and concealed openings. On the crest of the complex barrier fluttered a red rag, the symbol of revolution.

By dawn the work was completed, and the passers-by on via Maqueda stopped to admire it.

—*Mizzica,* what a mountain!

—It looks like the Chariot of Santa Rosalia.

—Who could manage to climb a fortress like that?

Breathless voices from within the barricade threatened the rabble of children outside who had formed noisy groups and burst into merriment, excited by the novelty.

—Sons of a blessed mother, will you let us work or not?

—Get away, damn it, things will be starting up soon. Any moment now there will be shooting.

—Kids, there are other barricades elsewhere. Go see them, if you want. Here there is *fetu d'abbruscu,* danger!

And indeed, at the most strategic points of the city new barricades were rising bit by bit, as if by magic. One at porta S. Antonio, another at via Schioppettieri, a third at the entrance of via Bandiera, a fourth at the Papireto, a fifth, from the report the most formidable, at porta Maqueda near the monastery of the Stimmate.

Everywhere the excitement was increasing. A species of high-tension current jolted the nerves of the city. A sense of fear and anxiety mingled with an unrestrained Bacchic fervor. But the deeper the sense of fear penetrated into the houses, the more the drunken racket breached the restraining walls of order and civil tolerance. Droves of shirtless boys with their trousers full of holes marched around waving red rags at the tip of a pole. Gallows faces, singly and in groups, paraded the sidewalks and crowded the piazzas as if they owned them. Persons who until that day had been called peaceful citizens boasted scarlet belts and caps, as if to say, 'Here we are, we too are pillars of the revolution. Didn't you know it?'

There was no house where someone did not take the old rusted muskets down from the walls where they had hung for years and years, where they did not hone butcher knives, did not sharpen pikes made of window bars. Palace foyers were transformed into workshops for making cartridges. Alleys and courtyards were barricaded off to be used as deposits for food and arms or to serve as headquarters for the commanders of the *quartiere*. Armed sentinels mounted guard in the most important places and demanded, 'Who goes there?' from citizens who ventured out unaware or curious. Couriers with red arm bands, displaying pistols and daggers, circulated around the principal streets. The forces of order were totally invisible, neither a policeman nor a carabiniere to be seen for love or money. The password 'Republic and Saint Rosalia' was shouted without restraint at the top of the crowd's voices, accompaned by insulting words and gestures aimed at the arms of the House of Savoy on the barracks, the offices, on the signs of the few shops flaunting 'by Royal appointment.'

The insurrection, like a train of powder that rapidly flames up, spread victoriously from one mandament of Palermo to another, from piazza to piazza, alley to alley, from the beach and the port up to the last fastnesses of the Conca d'Oro mountains. The flames flickering on the most distant hearths were about to join into a single conflagration.

The government sat permanently in palazzo delle Aquile, if under the verb 'to sit' could be subsumed the panic, the to-ing and fro-ing, the confabulations, the protests, the gesticulations, the turmoil of the responsible persons who in that serious moment did not know which party to cling to in order to confront the desperate situation. From the news brought by the most recent informers it was clear that half of the forces of insurrection were at the Municipio. The approaching squadrons were marching along many spokes converging toward piazza Preteoria. It was a ring, a circle of iron, that was slowly tightening, and that within a few hours must culminate in a general assault. In the meantime the building was under siege.

A bit before noon, a heavy fusillade of rifle fire took aim at palazzo delle Aquile. They were firing from the University, from the Post Office, from casa Bordonaro, from the bell-tower of S. Giuseppe, which was swarming with insurgents. The terraces, the cornices, the windows, the bell-chamber, the smokestacks all blossomed with heads, with extended arms, with shining gun barrels, and continually flashed with little blue flames. The hail of pellets pockmarked the plastered walls with white dots grouped in strange constellations, while a carpet of plaster flakes spread on the piazza and on the sidewalks. The situation was becoming ever more critical.

The mayor, caressing in perfect calm his flowing beard with his customary gesture, addressed the counselors and the prominent personages of the city gathered together in the palazzo comunale without betraying his agitation.

He explained that the insurgents were attacking the city at numerous points and that the few military forces of the garrison, recruits for the most part, were already seriously engaged, so that the military command found it impossibie to detach a group sufficient to defend the palazzo delle Aquile. At the most they could count on some hundred soldiers, ill-assorted and worse armed, municipal guards, customs agents, and a meager band of national troops. Considering the now obvious maneuver of the insurgents to interrupt communications between the Royal Palace, seat of the military command, and the Municipio, the Municipio ran the risk of turning into a trap from one moment to the next.

—If we don't want to be massacred, let's immediately ask for help from general Righini who is commanding the troops—suggested the prefect.

—I thought of it—said marchese Rudinì—but let's not have any illusions about the amount of help. Now we must rely on ourselves. A proverb says, God helps those who help themselves.

—One word!—the prefect Torelli muttered skeptically, with a shake of his head, which could have resembled a shiver if his courage had not been well known.

—Gentlemen—continued the mayor—here we must above all show no fear.

—Who is talking about fear? We are all courageous here, from the first to the last—said the prefect, casting a glance around those present.

—Well, I propose that we make a show of force...

—Which would be?

—In situations like this you must have the courage to take to the streets. Woe to those who absent themselves, woe to those who stand on the defensive, or worse, hide themselves. I propose that all those here, with the forces at our disposal, drawn up in a single phalanx, confront the rebels, sweeping clean the principal streets of the city. It is an act of daring which could reverse the situation. At the head of the squad will march first myself, the prefect, and the other authorities...

Enthusiastic applause arose from those present.

—No difficulty whatever—observed Torelli—but let me point out that I have left my arms in the Royal Palace, from which we are isolated...and therefore, unarmed...not that I am afraid...but, anyway, it doesn't seem to me...

—Don't give it a thought—answered the mayor—you will be armed immediately, and with good weapons. I surrender to you my Remington repeater.

—That's not what I'm saying. I would not want our defiant action, let's call it that, to be taken by the people as a provocation...That is to say...like adding pepper to cabbage...like putting out a burning fire with gasoline...

Courage is as contagious as fear. It even attacks those in a crowd who are least disposed to catch it. Thus, in the wave of general enthusiasm, the prefect meekly let them gird him with the cartridge belt, put a revolver in his waistband, sling across his shoulders a shiny carbine which seemed fresh out of the gun shop. Then, more confused than persuaded, he found himself impelled, or rather launched by an irresistable force into the front line, shoulder to shoulder with the mayor. So it was his turn. *A tout seigneur tout honneur.*

—Forward, in the name of God, for the honor of our country!—exclaimed the marchese di Rudinì with a stentorian voice.

While the improvised platoon was organizing itself in the courtyard, the prefect was soliloquizing, or rather dialoguing with himself *sotto voce.*

—'Forward, by dindirindina! *Adelante Pedro con juicio,* Forward judiciously Pedro...But our illustrious mayor is very injudicious instead. I am not wrong, no. Not that you are afraid, Luigino. Such a word does not exist in your vocabulary. You have found yourself in much harsher circumstances. The Five Days of Milan, for example. But there was more method in them. You were matching yourselves against one of the most formidable armies of the world, the lansquenets of Radetsky. Here you are going to exchange gunshots with the rabble, with the scum of the criminal class, all of them good for nothing but hanging. No, by God, there is no taste, no style. To make a 'show of force' against the enraged rabble! A boast without meaning, or rather a carnival stunt. So. This mayor, a great noble of the Palermitan patriciate, has a lot of guts, they say. But it's better to keep the guts and all the rest of it in reserve for better occasions. Feudal boasting. These lords of fiefs think they are still in the high Middle Ages, when they held the fury of the plebes and the peasants at bay from the safety of their manors. Now it's completely the opposite. The common people are sheltered in the castles—the barricades and such!—and we gentlemen march on foot in a stupid military parade. Those madmen are shooting as if possessed. And if a bullet makes a hole in your skull, will you take it out, illustrious first magistrate of the city? Heroism is fine. You have it, and I have more of it than you...but it isn't to be imposed on someone who doesn't feel it. Showing off, or rather nonsense. If I did not have the courage that everyone recognizes...I would dump this crowd of clowns and take to my heels, or take French leave.'

While count Torelli, more irritated than not, was thus relieving his feelings, the platoon was nicely drawn up. About a hundred, counting national guards, customs agents, and willing citizens, fifty conscripts who had not yet finished learning to obey orders from the command of the garrison.

As soon as the ill-assorted squad was assembled in piazza Pretoria, the gun volley held its breath. Either the act of courage and resolve had disconcerted the insurgents, or they feared that some trap was about to be sprung behind the bold men ready for the sortie. The fact remains that at the beginning the column could march out without incident.

The spectacle of manly energy encouraged the naturally weak-hearted or timid spirits of the bystanders, the so-called men of order whose fear often made then accomplices of disorder, the eternal horse-flies of success. In an instant windows and balconies burst into flower with tricolored flags: applause to the right and acclamations to the left, high and low, a frenzy of shouts and gestures.

The prefect, encouraged and erect, smiling in the smoke of his large cigar, confided to his neighbor:

—The people are always like that. One act of courage on the part of those who command is enough to make them change completely. You will see that this sortie of ours will act like oil on troubled waters.

—If they're roses they'll bloom—the mayor objected, with elegant skepticism, to throw a dash of cold water on the euphoria of his companaion.—Unfortunately, I see many thorns.

The battalion entered the discesa dei Giudici at a measured pace and marched toward piazza Fieravecchia, the ancient heart of the city. Here the statue of the Genius of Palermo, depressed and frowning—a pensive witness to the revolutions of the Risorgimento—held up a red flag. The statue seemed to say, 'For so many centuries I have sought to keep the foreign serpent from biting my breast, and now I have to witness this too.' A daring man leapt onto the fountain and freed the statue of its red nightmare. The flag passed into the hands of the prefect, who crumpled it triumphantly and rolled it up under his arm as a trophy of war.

Always between two lines of astonished and applauding people, the squad marched from via Cintorinai toward piazza Carracciolo, the site of the largest market of the city, squalid and deserted despite the fact that it was Sunday. During the journey a few insurgents who had peeled off from one of the many bands were taken prisoner.

One of the men they had stopped, a real bearded *pithecanthropus,* looked like one of the most lost and frenzied sansculottes, with the scarlet cockade on his Calabrese hat and a fire-colored belt under his *bonaca* of worn corduroy. He was taken into a vestibule and subjected to a swift interrogation. Entrenched in the most absolute *omertà,* there was no way to get a syllable out of his mouth. Nothing except his name, family name, and birthplace, S. Mauro Castelverde, unless that too was a hoax.

—Why are you in Palermo? What band do you belong to? Who is your leader?

—I don't know.

—But you've come to town to join the rebels.

—Who says so? I'm here by chance.

—And the pistol that you were hiding under your *bonaca*?

—I found it on the ground.

—Why are you wearing these red emblems?

—They told me that today was the festival of the *rippubbrica.*

—Do you know what the republic is?

—*Gnornò,* don't know. Why should I know? *Nuddu 'u sapi,* Nobody knows.

—Who is your king?

—*U Barbuni.*

—But the Bourbons have been gone for six years.

—What do I know?

Everyone laughed, and the anthropoid also laughed into the hedge of his wooly beard. But historians such as Fichte, De Maistre, Burke, Carlyle, Quinet, Ferrari, Thiers could have enriched their theories on revolutions by another paragraph containing a collection of such foolish responses: a paragraph about the perfect irrationality of the great popular upheavals, which are made by a few individuals who reason falsely, followed by countless multitudes who do not reason at all. Where the philosophers struggle to seek more or less ideal motives and interests, there is only a flow and reflux of instinctive forces, of ancestral bestialities, of hatreds and greeds inflamed by a sadistic pleasure in blood.

The armed battalion continued on its way. When it had reached piazza Olivella, it paused to regroup. With the purpose of attempting a pincer movement it divided into two units, commanded respectively by the Prefect and the Mayor, which advanced on the double, the one by via Bara, the other by via dell'Orologio. The heads of the two groups had barely debouched into via Maqueda when—the Heavens open!—an infernal fire greeted them. From the high windows, from the grated terraces, from the penthouses of the monastery of the Stimmate, seat of the most peaceful virgins in the world, as well as from the formidable barricade in front of it, there came a crackle of rifle shots so thick as to seem the Day of Judgment.

—The thrashing is beginning!—exclaimed count Torelli, grasping the carbine that he carried slung across his shoulder.

The first wounded fell. Cries of terror arose. Panic, like an irresistible blast of wind, broke up the column. There was disorder, a stampede, a general dispersal. The Prefect, who was shouting loudly, 'Courage! forward!,' suddenly realized that he too was fleeing, carried along by the frenzied pursuing tide. To save him, someone pushed him into the entrance of a house, one of the few whose doors were not closed and locked. Halfway between fuddled and discouraged, he fell like a sack on a stair step. He was babbling.

—They're all cowards! If it weren't for me, I swear to God, it would have ended badly. But those men up there shoot like devils. It's a hundred against one. Here you need a cannon...Give me a cannon, two cannons...I can maneuver the artillery and blast that trash by myself. We don't have an army, worse, we don't have any military leaders. Carderina...Righini... fine examples of generals! Two stuffed parrots. We need something beside the Don Quixotic antics of Rudinì to save the situation. He thought that he was putting together a kind of Company of Death to get himself killed for the honor of Sicily...And at the first firecracker they all took to their heels.'

One must say, in honor of the truth, that the recriminations of the prefect Torelli against the military command were justified up to certain point. That it was guilty of lack of preparation, lack of foresight, laziness, confusion, there is no doubt. Except that unfortunately the situation was what it was. On the morning of September 16 a few thousand troops, recruits for the most part (the forces present in the entire province consisted in all of three thousand one hundred niney-six individuals) suddenly faced tens of thousands of armed rebels, holed up in convents and monasteries, stretched out in redouts and barricades, masters of the vital nerves of the urban center. Without knowing it, the battalion organized and led with bold Renaissance spirit by the mayor and the prefect had come up against one of the most formidable barricades, the one having as its pivot the convent of the Stimmate at Porta Maqueda.

To avenge the failure of the unfortunate expedition, general Righetti ordered major Fiastri to march with a battalion of the 10th Grenadiers in two companies. A courageous but desperate attempt to break by means of a frontal attack a position fanatically defended by unseen forces.

When the column had arrived under the barricade, advancing at a run, they found themselves exposed to a killing fire. A second volley no less heavy followed the first.

A young lieutenant at the head of the first company suddenly fell flat on the pavement, his arms spread in a cross. The commander, major Fiastri, gasped for breath a short distance from the fallen man. Five, six soldiers, weighed down by their backpacks and cartridge cases, crumbled one after the other with dull thuds in a tangle of limbs lopped off and mangled by the gunfire. The decimated battalion hesitated, ebbed, fell back scattering, a fluid and sinuous mass swallowed up by the silence of the suddenly deserted street.

The uprising was winning all along the line.

That evening the prefect Torelli, who had regained the Royal Palace only with great effort, telegraphed in complete dismay asking the minister Ricasoli to authorize him to proclaim a state of siege. The military command showered the garrisons of Messina and Naples with appeals for the immediate dispatch of reinforcements.

Chapter 10

THE CITY was virtually in the hands of the rebels. Their plan, which consisted of severing the communications between the Municipio, the seat of the city government, and the Royal Palace, the military headquarters, had succeeded.

On the night of September 17 the wretched handful of soldiers guarding the Municipio with the reinforcement of a few auxiliaries—short of provisions, thirsty, discouraged, exhausted, with only some last few cartridges in their belts—evacuated the uselessly defended building. Crawling away in the darkness like a hunted snake, they fell back toward the Royal Palace. Here the royal army was preparing to receive the definitive attack of the rebel squadrons, with the alternatives of resisting until the arrival of help from the mainland or raising the white flag.

On the following morning the red flag fluttered on the balustraded balcony from which on May 27, 1860 Garibaldi had harangued the population in the name of conquered liberty.

The mob ruled unchallenged. Battalions of armed rebels, masses of frenzied men mixed with howling bunches of boys and enraged women of the people, swarmed through the streets, hunting the 'galanuomini,' spreading disorder and terror. Flags and banners of every sort waved above their disheveled heads, over their bloated faces: red rags, banners with images of saints and Madonnas, black pennants, even an American flag with red and white stripes and thirty-four stars on a blue field. They were shouting, 'Hurrah for the republic,' but still more often, 'Hurrah for Santa Rosalia,' the popular cry of the uprisings of the '20, '31, and '48.

Mixed with the invading throng, the worst criminals, sure of their impunity, broke into stores, climbed up into houses to sack, rob, kidnap, rape, and hold for ransom without any restraint. The howls of the mob were interspersed with the silvery noise of window glass and street lamps falling under a hail of stones. Menacing groups assembled under the houses of the nobles. And if someone, curious or frightened, dared to appear at a window or on a balcony, the din became infernal. *'Scinniti, signuruzzi,'* 'Come down, little lords'—they screamed, especially the dishevelled Furies, wilder and more devil-possesed than the men themselves, as occurs in every revolution.—*'Livàti i cappidduzzi, picca nn'aviti,* Off with your elegant hats, you don't have much time, come down, you bloodsuckers of the poor, so we can make mincemeat out of you.'

Few were the shops that did not have the hinges torn off their doors, their shutters gutted, their shelving and counters smashed or burned. In a completely sacked weapon store, a stuffed owl hung from a coat-hanger; two priests' hats and sacred vestments were impaled instead of meat on the hooks of a butcher shop. The sign of a sausage-vendor from which a crazy vandal had removed some letters now read in place of the original 'Mammana—Vella Rosario - pizzicagnolo,' 'Midwife—Rosario Vella—delicatessen': 'Mamm...ella Rosa...-pizzica,' 'that Rose pinches.' To another shop sign, 'Funerals—service at home' had been added in ink 'of casa Savoia.' The mania for renaming streets characteristic of every revolutionary frenzy had quickly cancelled the name 'Victor Emmanuel' from the marble street signs of the Corso, replacing it with the former 'Cassaro.' 'King Frederick Street' had been renamed 'Republic Frederick Street.' The wisdom of revolutions.

When the Municipio had been taken by force and subdued to the possession of the rebels, the inflamed mob needed another objective. Since the fickle popular imagination fed on ever-new myths, the myth of freedom succeeded the myth of command. And the first and most eloquent form of freedom is physical freedom. Instantly, launched by who knows whom, spreading and gathering force, ran the call, 'To the prison, to the prison! Free the poor "mamma's boys"' (as the people indulgently called the prisoners) who were languishing innocent in the cellar of the Vicaria. Every revolution has its march to the Bastille, except that in those days the Bastille of Palermo only yielded up common criminals and political prisoners.

To explain how freeing the prisoners had assumed an almost messianic significance in the situation that we are describing, we must recall the scandalous release, against the law and surrounded by impenetrable mystery, of a certain Salvatore Miceli of Monreale five days before the uprising. Miceli, a previous offender for numerous common crimes and the head 'artichoke' (*caocciola*) of the provincial mafia, was a steady client of the larger prisons, his hands accustomed to 'Cavour's eyeglasses' (in slang, handcuffs). Under the Bourbon government he had been the confidante of Salvatore Maniscalco. When the Bourbons had been replaced by the Italian state, for his diabolical ability as a double agent Miceli had entered the good graces of the police and had become a strong arm of commissioner Pinna. Pinna, in recognition of whatever services the notorious prison collaborator had rendered, on the eve of the revolt had opened the gates of the jail for Miceli, clearly subverting the judicial authorities. On leaving the Vicaria, Miceli had promised their freedom to his companions in misfortune. When the uprising had broken out, his creditors demanded the payment of their bill.

On the morning of September 17 piazza Ucciardone and its surroundings were seething with aroused and excited people, with the town component seeming diluted and overbalanced by those from outside. The province was pouring into the capital in waves, in surges: first the inhabitants of the hamlets and neighboring towns, then those of the villages spread out on the plains or perched in the mountainsides. In carts, on harnessed mules, on foot, armed with old muskets and peasant tools, followed by the boldest of the women, they gravitated toward the center; dressed in fustian, corduroy, in their characteristic tunics, the *bonache*, with their tasselled bonnets (*cu' giummu*). Some were shaved, some bearded like Capuchin friars, some in whiskers, many adorned with gold circlets on their ears according to the ancient custom of the countryside. It was the *calata di' viddani*, the invasion of the peasants, as the real Palermitans said (not without a hint of snobbism).

The crowd was silent at first, but as it thickened bit by bit under the powerful walls of the prison it began to murmur, to riot, to roar like the sea which rises and begins to storm. The women in the front row, the most poisonous and embittered, screamed as if possessed, giving vent to coarse and indecent gestures. From the barred windows of the prison, thick with clusters of men, the prisoners echoed them with animal-like shouts. The sentinels on the fortifications leveled their guns as a threat, enraging the bestial crowd even more. Some shots rang out, some wounded fell in the midst of the crowd. Repeated discharges from the rioters answered the shots. Suddenly the crowd parted and made way for someone to pass. 'Here is Miceli—they cried—hurrah for Miceli, hurrah for our God. Make way for the father of the wretched, for our father!' A hundred arms surged, rose, carrying in triumph a man who waved a red cap in greeting. The jerky motions of his head shook the thick black tuft of hair that hung down his narrow and receding brow, while with his hands he counseled calm. 'Everybody out...freedom for everybody...death to the tyrants' were the few words that could be gathered from his harangue in the general tumult.

A clearing suddenly opened in the crowd. An enormous beam taken from a nearby wood storehouse moved forward grasped by hundreds of arms, supported on the shoulders of a dense group of men. The gigantic and monstrous centipiede marched slowly toward the barred portal of the prison. The beam was flanked by numerous men armed with axes and hatchets. The catapult began its work. The first dull thuds thundered against the doors of the massive portal.

Suddenly a roar, a crash, a second one...what can it be?...A violet flash, the air is torn asunder, a cloud of smoke mixed with the poisonous stench of sulphur...A grenade has exploded in the crowd...then another...the ground is covered with corpses, with torn limbs, running with blood... screams of horror...general flight...

Miceli, the demigod of the day, is lying in the dust with his legs ripped to bits...a miserable pulp of flesh and blood.

The steam corvette *Tancredi,* the first warship to reach Palermo at full speed, is anchored in the Cala. It continues to fire, sweeping clean the plain of the Vicaria.

Dragging the lifeless body of their leader, the insurgents abandon the field.

The revolt, defeated in its attempt on the prison, is repeated with renewed bloody violence in the rest of the city.

From every part they cry, 'To the Royal Palace, to piazza Vittoria!'

The few government troops, disordered and alarmed, waiting for reinforcements from the sea, are in fact drawn up there. The civil and military authorities of the province have taken refuge there in anxious consultation, in prey to increasing alarm.

The outline of the insurgents' plan is now clear.

While the royalists and the few surviving troops take shelter in the Royal Palace, with their vanguard defended by trenches in piazza Vittoria at the entrance of the Corso, the rebel squads have a double aim: to wipe out this principal position by outflanking it at the rear (from outside Porta Nuova), and to establish a solid fortified line at the Quattro Canti to meet the enemy forces disembarking from the sea. The area from this site up to Porta Maqueda defines the hinge of their defensive and offensive preparations. Of the remainder, the entire city is in their hands.

In the meantime, the uprising, victorious and thirsting for revenge for its setback at the prison, is abandoning itself to every sort of excess. Sacking, burning, every type of private revenge is carried out under the pretence of defending the nascent republic. The disbanded soldiers, and especially the policemen hunted down in their houses and hiding places are summarily executed. Poor unrecognizable remains, vilely tortured and mutilated, mixed with animal carrion, lie unburied in the alleys and courtyards and befoul the air. Splotches and rivulets of blood on the piazzas and the sidewalks bear witness to unknown cruelties and unspeakable brutalities.

Emboldened by their easy successes, in the afternoon the insurgents send to the garrison besieged in the fort of Castellamare an embassy with a white flag bearing tthe following ultimatum: 'We appreciate your feelings, but the betrayed fatherland is no longer in time to withdraw, therefore we beg you as true brothers of real equality to hand over the fort to us tomorrow, since otherwise it will be taken by assault with serious losses to both parties.

'It is not true that our movement is not joined by the rest of Italy: Naples, Florence, Genoa, Lombardy as well as the whole island of Sicily are in revolt with one unanimous voice.

'Long live the Republic! Therefore in the name of all Italy we conclude by teaching everyone to shout with us "Viva la repubblica," and tomorrow we will share together the joy of the true sons of Italy.'

Here History becomes confused, as is often its custom.

The prefect Torrelli relates in his *Memorie* that general Carderina was on the verge of giving in. He would have accepted the ultimatum of the insurgents by unconditional surrender, if he (Torelli), summoned to report, had not scornfully opposed such a shameful act. And he adds, with bitterness, that when he had objected that a regular army could not surrender to a gang of robbers, general Righini had observed cynically, 'After all, the insurgents also have a flag, the red flag.'

The counter-memorial of the two commanders disputes this, although admitting tacitly that the lack of food and munitions would have rendered surrender inevitable sooner or later. Which, in conclusion, was put off for twenty-four hours. And that was their salvation. Providence is certainly more honest and bolder than men.

In the meantime their success had inebriated the mob. At evening an atmosphere of tragedy weighed on the city. The crowd ran through the streets like hurricanes, amid a forest of improvised flags, red for the most part. Gigantic bonfires of household goods flung down from the houses burned on the piazzas. Everywhere shots were fired in sign of rejoicing, the crowd screeched, they guzzled, they sang and danced. In piazza Noviziato, the haunt of the worst rabble, a horde of men and women, drunk as monkeys, made a ring-around-the-rosy with piercing laughs and obscene gestures under a lamppost from which hung the body of a famous policeman. The heads of the dancers grazed in turn the naked feet of the corpse, which dangled as if reaching for the earth. The dead man turned slowly like the clapper of a bell. He seemed to be himself the grim leader of the dance.

The barricade at the Quattro Canti di Città was like a prehistoric Cyclopean wall. Intended to meet the shock of the troops pressing in from porta Felice and to withstand the broadsides of the warships anchored in the roadstead, it had been built with dogged obstinacy according to that instinctive military skill which is the inheritance of every rioting mob. A good part of it consisted in masonry, using the uprooted stone slabs of the Corso and great boulders shouldered in from elsewhere. The rest was furnished by the sacking and devastation of the palace of mayor Rudinì, against which the fury of the mob had been unleashed. The noble carriages, magnificent furniture, mirrors, curtains, draperies, original paintings with their canvases slashed, books in rare editions, the finest porcelains reduced to miserable fragments: everything had served to raise the menacing mass whose jagged crest reached the height of a third storey window.

Hinged to the two facing corners of the Quattro Canti, the barricade neatly cut corso Vittorio Emanuele into two sections. An immense violet cloth was hung over the barrier to block the view of the naval artillery up the street toward Porta Nuova—the Holy Week Veil of the Temple, stolen from the church of S. Giuseppe.

Between the Quatro Canti and piazza del Duomo the Corso was blocked by various lines of defence. A barricade arose leaning with its right wing (if you stand with your back to the sea) on palazzo Geraci, immediately after piazza Bologni. Another barrier was backed up with its far end at the archbishop's palace. The intervening doorways and alleys were transformed into workshops for munitions, stores of arms and food for the combatants, medical stations, and centers for gathering the fallen, whether the dead or the untransportable wounded.

Goffredo took command of the great barricade at a crucial moment, when, at the first debarkation of the royal troops, something resembling discouragement was beginning to overcome the insurgents. The optimism of the most fanatical notwithstanding, there was a general conviction that the struggle was about to enter a harsh phase. There was talk of impressive government forces, seasoned and well equipped, under the command of fearless officers, which would land supported by a formidable fleet of the line. They predicted that the most bitter clash would take place in the tract between piazza Vigliena (the Quattro Canti), and Porta Maqueda, which formed the hinge of the revolutionary defence. If that hinge were broken it would be impossible to keep the the forces disembarking at th Cala from uniting with those of the garrison at the Palazzo Reale. Hence the necessity of holding the key position at the crossroads of piazza Vigliena until the last drop of blood.

That night the meeting point of the two principal streets of Palermo was a labyrinth of darkness. Two pale pools of light spread under the Viaticum lanterns fixed at the corners of the massive barrier, their lenses shaded on the side toward the sea.

Goffredo, with the insignia of commander on his right arm, reported, followed by two non-commissioned officers who comprised his general staff. As soon has he had penetrated into the barrier he asked the highest-ranking member of the squad charged with its defence:

—What forces do we have?

—A little less than a hundred men.

—All armed?

—About fifty have good rifles with bayonets, taken from the regular troops. The others have what they can find.

—And how are we for munitions?

—Not too good, commander.

—The men armed with firemarms will stay here. The others will withdraw to the opposite barricades. They would make useless confusion. They will be called into line at need. Sound the order to fall in.

—We don't have a trumpet.

—Then give the order out loud.

—Fall in!—called the non-com, clapping his hands. A squad of armed men poured forth from every side and lined up under the barricade. Faces tanned and pale, faces of men from the fields and city dwellers, clear eyes of dreamers and menacing glances of criminals, high and pure brows and narrow and receding ones under a fringe of wavy hair, noble hands and rough hands attached to hairy arms bulging with solid muscles; students' jackets, blouses and smocks of workmen, peasants' *bonache* and hunters' jerkins; a great profusion of flaming red insignia and badges.

—Fellow soldiers—Goffredo addressed them—a hard day is preparing for tomorrow. We will measure ourselves against the largest part of the royal forces. They are seasoned troops and well armed. Let those who have the will to fight in earnest remain here, those who do not fear to look death in the face. The others will retire to less exposed positions. Men are needed everywhere. Here I need those who are determined, ready for everything.

—We all want to fight.

—Provided they give us arms.

—I have none. Find them for yourselves. Ask headquarters.

—Where is headquarters?

—We'll fight with these.

Pikes, lances, daggers, swords and broadswords stolen from some antique shop, spades, hoes, scythes, pitchforks flashed in the dark under the reflection of the lanterns.

—You will remain in the second line, as a reserve to replace the fallen— Goffredo decided, seeing that they all were eager to fight.—On the barricade I need marksmen.

—We're hungry, commander. We haven't put anything in our stomachs since this morning.

Goffredo conferred with the non-com.

—What can I do, boys? They forgot to bring the second rations. I'll send someone to look for bread. In the meantime we'll serve out the wine.

Siphoned from a barrel, the wine gurgled into the jugs which passed from mouth to mouth.

Gaiety took possession of the squad. They drank to victory.

—Hurrah for our commander! Hurrah for the revolution!—they shouted in unison.

The dawn of September 22 rose brighter than the preceding day. The fog, herald of the scirocco, was breaking up in the east, the shreds of its condensed vapors were edging themselves with pink like the wings of a flamingo. Bit by bit as the sun rose, approaching the horizon with its sphere, flashes of fire set the field of clouds alight. The spreading field of red was interpreted as an omen of victory. It seemed a symbolic acknowledgment by Nature of the revolutionary flag.

—What is the weather at porta Felice?—asked Goffredo.

—The lookouts announce that everything is quiet. The sea is smooth as oil. The trawlers are out fishing sardines.

—That's not enough. Observers must be sent to the highest place, the tower of San Giuseppe.

Not more than a quarter of an hour later, the observers returned out of breath and dismayed.

Warships, surmounted by clouds of smoke, were silhouetted on the horizon. They were hurrying toward the harbor at full steam.

—The music is about to start.

—Do you prefer *Norma* or *Barbiere*?

—Anything, as long as it's not *The last day of Pompei.*

—To hell with the astrologer and his funeral march. Here we're singing *Norma*'s chorus of Druids, 'War, war.'

—I'm afraid we'll hear *Trovatore* first, 'The flames of that terrible pyre...'

The sentries announced that a medium-sized ship, breaking away from the body of the fleet, had moved forward into the harbor, lining itself up exactly with porta Felice.

Even with the naked eye, the lead-colored hull of the ship could be seen in the strip of sea, visible from the Quattro Canti, that borders the far end of the Corso; it seemed almost as it were wedged between the two lines of buildings.

A blue flash suddenly lit up the side of the gunship, followed at a brief interval by a rumble.

—Here the first four-handled pot (that's what the people called bombs) comes flying—shouted the aroused insurgents.—Watch out for your heads.

—To the barricade! Everyone to his station.

After ten shots or so the ship ceased fire.

There followed a long silence that multiplied the anxiety. An attack was imminent. Where would it be launched from? The most varied speculations flew back and forth and piled one on another. The obvious hypothesis was that of a frontal attack by the disembarking troops, advancing like an arrow up the Cassaro from the marina. On the other hand, an outflanking attempt uphill to surprise the great barricade from the rear could not be excluded. A maneuver by the attacking force from outside Porta Nuova to free the garrison besieged in the Royal Palace and to unhinge the defences of the insurgents in the upper part of the Corso by attacking the rear of the Quattro Canti, the cornerstone, would put the defenders in serious trouble. If the attacks were simultaneous, both from the sea and from Porta Nuova, the fate of the barricade was sealed.

While the discussions and consultations were heating up, a lookout notified the commander that an assault column was moving up from the marina in the direction of the Quattro Canti.

—Everyone to his combat post—ordered Goffredo, calm and cold-blooded.—Save your ammunition. Don't fire until your target is at least fifty meters from the barricade. Aim for the officers and non-coms.

—They're coming! They're coming!

A column of infantry of the line, preceded by sappers, was advancing at a quick march.

At about two hundred meters from the redout the order *Halt* was given.

After a few minutes a trumpet sounded the order to load.

The attackers, about two companies, broke into a run. When they were about sixty meters from the front, the entire barricade belched forth an infernal fire.

When the thick curtain of black smoke had cleared the piazza seemed covered with the fallen. Oaths, crashes, blood, cries for help and cries of pain. The very few who tried to scale the barrier were blasted point blank.

The column wavered, broke, disbanded, some disappearing into the alleys, some taking to their heels. Only a few, in the shelter of the corners of the houses, continued to fire kneeling or stretched out on the ground.

The 'Cease fire' was sounded.

A sergeant with a white flag, followed by a trumpet and a drum, advanced toward the barricade to parley.

The action was interpreted as a surrender, and the deafening cry, 'Victory, victory,' rose from the redout.

The parley was limited to requesting a truce to gather up the dead and to succor the many wounded lying on the ground. When Goffredo had accepted their request, the stretcher-bearers started to clear the piazza of the fallen.

Meanwhile the attacking column fell back a few hundred meters along the Corso to regroup.

During the truce the defenders of the redout threw themselves on their rations. A soup of beans mixed with bread crumbs was poured out smoking hot from gasoline cans improvised as kettles into makeshift mess tins and dishes of every shape and color. Loaves of bread of a yellow powdered with dust were torn by famished mouths and disappeared down open gullets. Bunches of spicy purple radishes formed the dessert and were fought over with jabs and punches or wagered in games of odds and evens. The wine ran in profusion, and if some spilled on the ground it was welcomed as a good omen, 'Porta fortuna!' The happy meal was mixed with songs and shouts of joy.

But an atmosphere charged with electricity weighed on the barricade. The leaders worried that the truce concealed the preparation of some strategic move. It was announced that the royal troops, beaten in the center of the city, were beginning a movement of widespread penetration toward the periphery; that little squads unleashed in different directions outside the gate were marching to join together in the area up behind the city; that many secondary barricades had been wiped out; that crack snipers were posted on the tops of the buildings to observe and harass the movements of the rebel squadrons with well-aimed shots.

Goffredo ordered one of the boldest of the volumteers to climb to the top of a water tower in the vicolo Marotta—a *giarra* where only the most experienced hydraulists ventured, using iron brackets fixed in the wall—to survey the movements of the enemy and report them. The observer had barely reached the top of the pinnacle when he opend his arms, made a half turn, and fell, landing with a dull thud and smashing on the ground. A bullet had struck him in the back of the head, crushing his brain, which oozed out in a bloody mush.

An invisible vise gripped the barricade. The hours passed in a strange quiet which instead of calming the spirits of the insurgents appeared ever more threatening. Suddenly, in the late afternoon the rumor spread that the royal troops, already masters of the quarter of Mezzo Monreale, were about to break in from the west, taking the trenches and the barricades on the Corso from the rear.

There was a moment of panic.

—Have no fear!—thundered Goffredo.—We'll fight on two fronts. New fighters are arriving at this moment to reinforce our lines. Courage, boys! You'll see that we'll make it.

In reality, however, a battalion of Bersaglieri was hurrying from piazza Vittoria. The flash of their bayonets and the fluttering of their helmet-feathers in the wind was visible even from a distence.

—Everyone to his post! Fire at close range. Aim! Save your ammunition!

At the same time another attacking column was moving up from Porta Felice.

The defenders were caught between two fires.

As soon as the Bersaglieri were within shooting distance, the whole trench was studded with a mane of lightning.

Some empty places appeared in the assault battalion. A moment of hesitation. Then the mass, passing over the fallen, resumed its course.

The barricade was taken by assault. A furious scrimmage. Defenders and attackers, friends and enemies were alike possessed, united by the same desire to inflict death and to die. Savage hand to hand fighting, tangles of bodies, clusters of body parts, a bloody pruning of arms and legs. They were no longer fighting with gunshots but with the butts of rifles, with bayonets, with pikes, with scythes, with rocks.

Wave succeeded wave, assault followed assault. The barricade is taken and retaken several times, there are no longer winners and losers.

The violence of the assault is such that the barricade has lost its form. Its crest has crumbled, shapeless, and its components, collapsing downward, have formed an inclined ramp on the outer side which now makes it easy to scale.

Nonetheless, as if by an unspoken agreement, a place is made between the combatants of the two parties for a pause in the ferocious scrum. For a moment hatred is overcome by pity for the wounded, who are groaning and lamenting, caught, hooked, suspended from the projections and from the parts of the redout or crushed by the weight of the stones and the collapsed furniture. For a moment there is no longer a barrier that divides them, but a common pity that unites them as brothers. Each one no longer seeks his own dead and wounded, he raises the defeated of the opposing side from their misery, from their suffering, from their abandonment.

On this side of the barricade, that is, on the side of the insurgents, lies a young officer of the Bersaglieri, propelled so far by his determination to scale its height. His half-open hand still grasps the golden hilt of his saber, his chest is torn open by two wounds. As his blue eyes glaze in his death throes, the dying man breathes out in a thin voice the words, 'Water, water.' After he is pulled into the nearest entranceway and laid on the bare earth, someone holds a bowl to his bloodless lips. He drinks thirstily and murmurs his thanks.

With a lump in his throat Goffredo approaches the dying man and leans over to feel his pulse, from which life is about to depart.

The young man, opening his eyes, fixes him strangely.

—But aren't you...?—asks Goffredo.

—Solari—the wounded man completes the phrase, with a distant voice that seems a memory.

—Cesare Solari? Aspromonte?

—Yes, Aspromonte...third battalion...second company...Please...tell my mother...I'm dead ....send her...whatever... you... find on my body.

With the last words his soul departed from his lips.

Goffredo uncovered and ordered the bystanders to present arms.

A savage clamor rose from the barricade.

A non-com burst into the entrance crying, Commander, they're attacking!

A deafening discharge of gunfire.

Goffredo rushed forward, climbed frantically to the crest of the redout, crying, 'Cease fire.' Pulling out a white handkerchief he waved it in the face of the attackers.

The uprising was finished.

Chapter 11

By THE stroke of one o'clock of September 22 the city was firmly in the possession of the royal troops. At first a few flags were hoisted timidly at several windows, then bit by bit balconies, terraces, penthouses, towers were fluttering with a dense forest of tricolors.

The uprising, which had broken out on the night of the 16th, had lasted just seven days, or rather seven and a half. Whence the people had baptised it 'the seven days,' and also the 'seven and a half,' like 'Sette e mezzo,' the name of a popular card game—a telling and pregnant locution. The *insecuritas,* the gamble, which underlies every war and revolution, resembles a game in which the last card, the decisive one, is always in the hand of Destiny.

Between the dead, the seriously wounded, and the deserters, the regular army had lost about four hundred men. Among the insurgents the fallen were uncounted. Several days were required for gathering the dead. They were everywhere: on the edges and at the foot of the barricades, which were not yet destroyed, in the piazzas and the crossroads, in the alleys, in the courtyards, in the gardens, inside the houses, even on the bell towers, where fanciful death had amused itself by shooting its chosen victims. There was an urgent need to clear the city and to purify the air physically and spiritually with all the means provided by intelligence, skill, and chance. The dead stink. And those of wars and revolutions give greater annoyance, perhaps because they are the first to rise again. Conquered today, victors tomorrow.

Crowds of disheveled women with their children hanging on their skirts circled around and crawled among the corpses which were scattered everywhere, seeking to recognize in the misshapen and disfigured faces who was the father, who the son or husband. More piteous to see were the tearful processions of relatives singing psalms behind the vans and the carts of the army, from which there overflowed legs and arms, naked or half-covered with filthy rags, and heads smeared with mire and blood dangled. Poor heaps of battered and crushed flesh which were jostled at every bump in the street and jumbled around, animated by a false and more terrible life.

Here and there groups of street urchins, with the lack of feeling typical of adolescence, rummaged in the garbage in search of a crust of dried bread or a bone that had escaped the hunger of the the dogs. Not finding anything, they beguiled the pains of their empty stomachs by playing with the first things that came to hand: furniture stuffing and bullet shells, stoved-in *kepìs* and riddled cartridge boxes, armbands and cockades abandoned by the insurgents in their flight, masons' and carpenters' tools used to smash and burgle, nails and little sacred pictures, metal buttons and tufts of hair. At the passage of the patrols with fixed bayonets, the crowd of children broke up, hiding. Then they returned to scrabble around in the piles of earth and stones or in the cart-tracks.

Now the insurgents who had fled their command posts with the soldiers at their heels, pursued by the police, who were searching palaces and churches, sacresties, monasteries, convents, threw away their arms and tore off the insignia of the rebellion. Disguised and camouflaged, they escaped, passing from house to house, scaling the walls of the many gardens to reach the open countryside. The people, even those who shunned revolutionary ideas, vied in helping the persecuted and the fugitives, not so much for criminal solidarity as for that sense of chivalrous humanity that often makes the Sicilian scorn to triumph over the defeated.

At six in the afternoon general Raffaele Cadorna made his entrance into the city, taking up residence at the Royal Palace.

His first act was to fire the prefect Torelli.

The count had just returned to the palace, overjoyed at waving the last red flag, which he had snatched from a bersagliere at the barricade of the Quattro Canti, when a soldier handed him, 'without reply,' a letter in the name of the Commanding General of the Island and Extraordinary Royal Commissioner with full powers. The Minister Ricasoli—this was the content of the letter—ordered the immediate recall of the prefect, placing at his disposition a steamship for his return.

At first Torelli (as we read in his *Memorie*) stood there dumbfounded; then he blew up, surrendering to the lump of bitterness that made a knot in his throat.

—Unheard of! impossible! They fire the only officer who has showed some guts in this stinking business, like a dishonest footman! Who saved his country from the shame of the unconditional surrender negotiated with the insurgent rabble by that scared rabbit general Carderina? Who broke out the tricolor on the tower of the Astronomical Observatory while the bullets were whistling by? I, count Torelli. Only a crybaby, only a bigot like Ricasoli, his brain soaked in holy water, only an idiot of a corporal like Cadorna are capable of such garbage. Shame! But public opinion will judge.

Public opinion, in its turn, proclaimed that it would have been better to have in Palermo a prefect less theatrical and oratorical and more serious about forseeing and acting. And as to the flag planted on the very top of the Observatory, they ventured the irreverent opinion that it was a '48 style bluster, a Hail Mary play when the rebels were already defeated and the royal forces controlled the city far and wide.

Whom to believe?

History, written by human beings, is lying truth and truthful lies: a two-faced Herm that weeps at its smile and smiles at its tears.

Now the only truth was the decree of Cadorna, posted up on every corner, in which he denounced the insane movement unleashed by a few violent thugs and stirred up by the religious orders, as well as by the Bourbon reactionaries. A state of siege was proclaimed, general disarmament was ordered, military tribunals were instituted. The arrest was threatened of anyone guilty of robbery and murder who had not handed over the objects of his illegal acquisition within twenty-four hours.

When the last barricade had crumbled and the cause of the revolution was lost, Goffredo thought only of saving himself. He threw himself into the maze of alleys that flanked the Cassaro, popping out of one little street and into another, crushing himself against the walls, almost as if to disappear into them, at every suspicious glance. With the connivance of the common people, quick to advise him of the *puzzo di muffa* ('musty stench,' the presence of the police) who were approaching, he succeeded in escaping from the center of the city to the *rione* of the Capo, thick with the common people. Here it was easy to mingle and get lost in the crowd.

Having plunged into the guts of a dirty courtyard, a hive of mean little houses resembling trogloditic caves, Goffredo asked hospitality at a hovel, something to refresh himself and to repair his clothes and his appearance. He washed his sooty face and his hands darkened by gunpowder in a chipped bowl reglued by the *conzalemmi,* the crockery repairman. He quickly removed his Garibaldian shirt, which he was wearing under his jacket, advising himself to make it disappear. After a glance at himself in a shard of mirror with jagged edges that cut his fingers, he asked for a scissors and a razor to trim his hair and beard. The poor folk did not possess such tools. If he wished, he could use the barber who kept his little shop at the corner, *uomo di panza,* a person whom one could trust until death. In the meantime, Goffredo assuaged his hunger with a slice of bread that they offered wholeheartedly: homemade bread, stale but honest. There was not a single bakery open in the city, even for its weight in gold.

The barber—a little old man of few words, a real white crow among the chatterboxes of his profession—with a few snips of the scissors trimmed back the unruly hair and the unkempt beard which gave his patient the look of a romantic savage. He removed the blond mustaches from Goffredo's lips, restoring to him the smooth and hairless face of a young student starting his first beard. And he did not want to be paid for his work.

Having thanked his benefactors, calmer for having disguised himself as best he could, Goffredo took up his path again without a precise direction. He was fleeing like a hare followed by the hunters. And everywhere the spectre of the uprising pursued him. Everywhere traces of fires and destruction, wreckage still smoking, abandoned weapons, exploded and unexploded bombs scattered among the rags and dust, lumps of clotted blood. Here and there, unexpectedly, a corpse glared with the purple stain of its destroyed face, the eyes staring, round and dull, as if glazed with a layer of mica. A dog with a flea-bitten coat sniffed Goffredo's feet and ran off. A yellow cat, thinner than hunger itself, leapt over the dead and the putrid streams with feline elegance, meowing sinisterly. A spectacle of misery and horrors.

A sort of instinctive and subconscious force impelled the steps of the wanderer toward the convent of the Cappuccini. Perhaps there he would be able to find shelter and a momentary rest. From deep in his inner being, vague and unfocused but insistent, there arose the memory of his grandmother, who had said to him one day, 'I know only one man of charity among the religious, the Capuchin friar father Benedetto da Castellammare. After I have left this world, if one day you need help and counsel, turn to him. Of all the priests and friars, corrupt small-time politicians and shady dealers, that I have seen parade through this house, he alone is closer to the Spirit. What does it matter if I do not believe so many things of the Christian religion? There is one thing in which I do believe: Charity. Quite different from philanthropy, which is a kind of sublimation of the fear that the rich have of the poor.'

Goffredo preserved a faint memory of the friar. He had only seen him twice, and then fleetingly. When he was still a little boy, sent by his grandmother to the convent of the Cappuccini on some errand, he had only exchanged a few words with father Benedetto. But he had carried away an impression of sweetness and friendliness.

The friar was not very visible. He defended himself from the public with an overshadowing sense of reserve and almost of modesty. A zone of isolation and silence had been created around him, from which he did not emerge except when called by the duties of charity. But what did he, Goffredo, need at this moment if not charity?

In his flight he felt hopelessly alone, abandoned even by his past and future life. He had the sensation of having lived forever, and never. Now an endless loneliness reigned over him. He could not explain even how and why he had taken part in the bloody uprising. Out of conviction? No. Perhaps only for a point of honor, for a stab of self-respect, fearful of assuming a responsibility. He had thrown himself headlong into the scrimmage, like a drunk, like a sleepwalker, and he had been wrong. Certainly, one can make mistakes. But if he could absolve himself, as one in error, nonetheless as an active participant he could not flee from the condemnation, *his* condemnation, more unforgivable than that of any other. His intelligence could in some manner be excused (how many others had been deceived like him!); but his *will* appeaared to him inexcusible and guilty. He judged himself. His intelligence *could* be uncertain and vacillating among conflicting motives, all equally plausible. His will *must* refuse itself from a crime. For certainly it is a crime to plunge one's country into a civil war the day after a military defeat, to humiliate the defeated fatherland, to prostrate it even further with betrayal, so that the enemy can better press his knee on its throat. At Aspromonte he had fought for the honor of Italy. On the barricades of Palermo he had made himself more or less consciously the instrument of those who profited from the double defeat of Custoza and Lizza to unleash a useless fratricidal struggle. And here the pale figure and the dying mouth of lieutenant Solari rose up in his anxious and feverish imagination like a an immense shadow, that spread, occupied all the space, filled the world with itself... His world, which was a pitiful ruin. 'Why did you do it? Why ever? Why?'

Obsessed by this voice, like a wild animal pursued by a pack of hounds, moving now at a walk, now at a run, sometimes faltering, he crossed corso Alberto Amedeo, entered via Olivuzza, and by via dei Cipressi, closed between the banks of its sunny and shining high walls, he reached the piazza of the Capuchin convent

If he had been a believer, he would have fallen on his knees before the wooden cross which spread out its arms in pity, facing the peaceful solitary Franciscan shelter. Unfortunately, he did not know how to pray. He was unaware of the comfort of humbling himself, of offering his sorrowing self at the feet of the Consoler. Recalling a vague memory of childhood, he tried to sketch the sign of the Cross. His unwilling arms fell to his sides, refusing to obey his upward impulse. His whole existence was collapsing down into a valley which could not even be called the vale of tears, if tears are a comfort. His hands were perhaps pierced as much as those of Jesus and Saint Francis which were painted at the top of the convent door, crossed, like a symbol of the alliance between the Seraphic saint and the love of Christ.

He pulled the rope of the doorbell once, several times.

Finally a little window high up opened. A great yellowish beard surmounted by the dome of a robust skull covered with skin like a drum (eyes like two slits, and a pug nose disappearing into its hedge of hair) took form in the greenish frame.

—Who's there?

—Please, I would like to speak...

—There's nobody here—barked an annoyed and angry voice, cutting off its questioner.

—I'm asking for an act of charity.

—We don't do charity at this time of day. Come to the church tomorrow.

—I have something urgent to say...

—Haven't you got it through your head that we're not opening up for anybody? That's the order.

—Who gave this order?

—The Father Guardian. Don't you know that the troops are searching, they're turning the convents upside down to hunt the revolutionaries? *Senza mai Dio,* God forbid, if they find a layman here, there's hell to pay. Go away, and may the Lord provide for you.

—Just a minute, be patient. How can I manage to see father Benedetto?

—*U santuzzu,* the dear little saint—said the friar, not without a hint of irony in his words.—Yes, everybody asks for him. You get to paradise by way of the saints, they say. Don't they know that he is no longer here?

—Is he momentarily out of the convent or has he gone away?

—I told you that he's not here.

—Where is he then?

—How should I know? do you know the proverb, *Nunti' mmiscari, nun t'intricari ca mali ti nni veni,* Don't get mixed up in things, don't make complications, because bad things will happen to you. If you really want to know, they say that he's at the plague hospital.

At the plague hospital?—Goffredo asked anxiously—doing what?

—Helping the cholera victims.

—What are you saying? Is there cholera too?

—You bet there is! All we needed was this other scourge of God, and the *furistici,* the foreigners brought it. Every gift comes from up north. Goodbye.

—Listen. Is there some place, some burrow where I can spend the night here?

—There is no room for anybody—warbled the friar, as if he were singing psalms in choir.—How can I get it through your thick skull? *Minnali chi testa di ciaca.*

And the window shut.

Unfortunately, the news was true. From September 18 the first cases of cholera had appeared in the city. And it is also known that the first victims stricken by the Asiatic disease were a captain and three soldiers of the 51st Infantry, coming from Naples and disembarked in the island capital with the troops to reinforce its garrison.

The alarm at the first signs had been such as to relegate even the horrors of the revolution to second place.

It was the third wave of the epidemic on the island. The first two, which old people still remembered, horror-stricken, had fallen like a typhoon on Sicily in 1837 and 1854.

The cavalcade of Death had begun in Europe in 1835, coming from the central plateau of Asia. After two years it reached Sicily. It cannot be said that the dead ride swiftly, as Bürger's ballad of the *Wilde Jagd* sings, but in compensation their harvest was terrible. In the city of Palermo alone, out of a population of about 173,000 inhabitants, in the space of two months the pale horseman took about 24,000 persons on his saddle. On some days the mortality rate was close to two thousand.

By comparison with the previous cholera, the epidemic of 1854, which lasted ninety-five days and destroyed a bit less than six thousand lives out of the 182,000 that populated the capital, was less violent.

The third epidemic, 1866-67, lasted one hundred days with a mortality of a bit more than forty thousand out of 200,000 inhabitants. It was imported, as we mentioned, from Naples by way of the troops coming from that city, which was already infected. Immediately after the first cases were verified among the soldiers, the disease attacked a baby in contrada Castelluccio. It spread rapidly in the suburbs of Cruillas and Aquasanta and in the rione Borgo until it conquered the whole city with an imposing crescendo of virulence and deadly force.

The Sicilians, like all those born of woman, blamed the various epochs of cholera on their fellows and particularly on the government, which (they said) was spreading the poison in order to lower the increasing population. They also say that during the terrible epidemic of 1837 the distingished historian Domenico Scinà, feeling himself attacked by the disease to which he later succumbed, fell at the knees of the city Magistrate, begging him for the antidote. The people, for their part, having no doubt that the cholera was *gettato,* spread on purpose, by the court of Naples, rebelled. They fell to unheard-of violence, torturing and massacring as many as they believed were carrying out the evil instructions from higher up. As his only answer their Most Serene Sovereign Ferdinando II sent punishment in the person of the marchese Del Carretto, who put Sicily to fire and sword as a repression. Always the same story: tormenters and tormented, who in their turn transform themselves into more inhuman tormentors.

In the cholera of 1854 the same excesses were repeated. This time, to give a human face to the disease, it was said that the Bourbon king had given orders to spread the poison to avenge himself for the revolution of the '48. Corrupt small-time politicians played on the credulity of the people to stir up the masses against the public authorities, and the crowd arose, crying, 'Better to die from gunpowder than from poison!'

But sometimes the game turns against its abuser. And in the third epidemic this curious event occurred. In 1860, Garibaldi, speaking to the population of Palermo from the balcony of the Municipio, had come out with the famous dilemma, 'Do you want cholera or war?' The crowd ansered as one, 'War.' Except that they had suddenly found themselves with both war *and* cholera in the house. The public was no longer able to blame the court of Naples and, reasoning on its own, had come to the conclusion that all regimes are more or less the same. The Italian government employed poisons just like the government of the Bourbons, neither more nor less. So why had they bartered the one for the other? The truth is always the same, *'A furca è pu poviru,* The gallows is only for the poor man.

These arguments were discussed (and if the author transcribes them in his own way he should not be blamed) between Goffredo, who had just got rid of his friar, and Scalia, the guardian of the cemetery attached to the convent of the Cappuccini.

Scalia was a fine figure of a man, naturally inclined like all fat people toward benevolence and optimism. His large round head, bald and moon-like, hung like a Chinese lantern on top of his monumental body. This *choinoiserie* was reflected in his eyes with their narrow, slanting slits, like a comma with the tail upward, and it expressed itself in his ceremonious, complicated, and formalistic manner of moving. Even his garments, which were unrelieved black though he was not in mounring for anyone except his clients accommodated in the cemetery, seemed dyed with Chinese ink.

The two met in front of the gate of the Sylva, the cypress-filled burial ground of the monastery. Scalia, who had an instinctive feeling for people, although he frequented only those who had once been such, guessed the quandry, indeed the dismay of the young man and addressed him humanely. Without Goffredo needing to unburden himself, Scalia had already understood his situation as an insurgent fleeing the rigors of the law. Although he knew that military batallions were circulating to round up the rebels and that religious places were the most suspected and under surveillance, he did not seem as rejecting and unapproachable as the fat friar of the convent. Indeed, he offered to do the best that he could to help the unknown youth, who it did not take much to see was in trouble.

—A fine charity of Saint Francis—Scalia commented on hearing what had just happened to his interlocutor.—Are we animals? When someone is *prosecutu,* hunted, you have to help him in every way possible, all the more if you run into a gentleman.

Bit by bit it had come out that Goffredo was an offshoot of the Cortada family. This was enough for Scalia, who from being merely understanding became actively willing to help.

—Oh, the marchesi Cortada, think of that! I helped three generations of their dead to descend under the earth. Shouldn't I go out of my way to hold out a hand to a young man who is healthy and full of life like *Voscenza* (from the less formal *lei* the guardian had switched over to 'Your Excellency'). A few years ago, we settled your grandmother, the old marchesa down here, in the catacombs...what a gentlewoman! what nobility! (Scalia took his cap off as a sign of respect). That gives me an idea. Night is about to fall, and I don't advise you to go wandering around. With my whole heart I would open my house to you. But those damn' soldiers from up north are such *cani corsi,* such mastiffs—dogs, speaking with respect, without a master. I am not afraid...Scalia does not know fear...But I have a family and I have to earn my living. In case of a search...goodbye job! But down in the catacombs, at least for one night, Your Excellency could hide yourself and rest in peace. I don't think that you are afraid of the dead.

—It's the living that I fear.—said Goffredo.

—Exactly. I've lived with the dead for fifty years. All fine people. They've never given me any trouble. Therefore, it's decided.

—Absolutely.

—Good. I'll go get the key. It'll take just a few minutes. But you can't ever be too careful. Instead of standing here in front of the cemetery, go into the Sylva and hide in the shadows of the second group of cypresses to the right of the path. There's a new grave there which you can use as a hiding-place if a patrol of soldiers happens by unexpectedly.

After about ten minutes the gravel of the path squeaked under the steps of someone. The massive outline of the guardian advanced, shaking his keys, amidst the low flock of tombs, silvered by the uncertain light of the stars.

—Pardon me if I've lost a bit of time—he said. I've prepared you a little something to get your teeth into...You must be famished, and maybe also as dry as a punice stone...The dead don't eat, but the living can't survive on air...Good, follow my steps. I'll lead the way.

After looking left and right, they left the cemetery, entered the vestibule of the convent. From there, across a corridor and down a flight of stairs, they found themselves in front of a massive low door. Holding in his left hand a metal lantern with three lights, Scalia inserted a large key into the lock, gave two turns, and passed in front of his new guest.

High steps, a landing, and finally the night of an enormous space that seemed without limits.

The city of the dead. An existence of one dimension only, the past. No future. The present exhausted in a fantastic and almost unreal cohabitation of mummies and skeletons. To the right, to the left, in the distance, a bizarre sleepwalking architecture, whose constructive elements were coffins, sarcophagi, wooden and glass urns, clothed mummies dressed up in the most grotesque fashions, naked skeletons, skeletons wearing caps, miters; shinbones, femurs, ribs, gloved hands and filigreed tissues of bones, ossicles, and skulls—toothless skulls, sardonic, teasing, sniggering, mocking skulls...Nothing left but a disenchanted smile, dazed and chilling.

—Here's a blanket—said Scalia—spread it out on one of the cases and stretch out on top as best you can. It won't be a featherbed, but it's better than sleeping on the bare rock in the open air. Meanwhile there's something to eat in this paper bag. Tomorrow I'll wake you early and it's best that you set out for safer places. This is no place for *Vossia*. All the forces of the law are all in motion, and they've taken aim at the convents and monasteries as hideouts of rebels. People say they want to throw everybody in jail, even the cat.

After having devoured a slice of dark bread accompanied by a few prickly pears and sipped half a bottle of light wine concentrated by the summer heat, Goffredo collapsed like a dead body on the first wooden chest that his knees bumped into as he moved in the necropolis. He couldn't manage anything more. He felt crushed in body and in spirit. The hammering of his emotions, of the surprises, of the delusions, of the disappointments had been so continuous and violent as to make him pass from a state of morbid excitement straight into a condition of dull apathy. A sense of lethargy and despondency which detached him bit by bit from the surrounding life took possession of his being. His brain, which for forty-eight hours had whirred like a top, now became less fevered, mellowed, entered a state of somnolence. His memories smoothed out, rounded themselves, they lost the sharp corners of their articulations, unlinking themselves one from another like the skeletal rings of a snake. It was all a confused flux without highlights and without outlines, like the sliding of a soft mass down an inclined plane...

—Goffredo—called a voice, nasal and dull as if from an enclosed space.

—Who wants me?

—It's I. Your grandmother. Come close to me, because I cannot move.

—But...weren't you dead?

—Dead?—said the voice with astonishment, not without a bit of irritation.—Who said so? What idiot? I'm more alive than before. Rejuvenated, no question about it.

—Rejuvenated?

—Why not? Here time does not move. The clock is stopped eternally. And in eternity there are no distances of years. Young and old, the same age.

From our vantage point we see, unmoved, the endless procession of humanity marching under the arches of the centuries, as you see a flock of bees or ants swarming. We don't even want to feel sorry for humanity.

—Then death is stronger than life.

—Certainly. To live is to suffer, to die is to cease suffering.

—Yet no one wants to die.

—Yes, because they believe that death is sorrowful in itself.

—And isn't it like that?

—Absolutely not. On the contrary, death is a pleasant thing since it frees us from the weight of life. Imagine the joy of someone who has fallen over a cliff, half-covered by rubble, when he sees a pitying hand raise the boulder that is crushing his chest.

—But isn't the moment of passing away an anxious, terrible pang?

—It seems that it should be. But no! Are you aware of the moment of passing from waking to sleep? Up to a moment before dying you know nothing of death, and when you are dead you no longer have an idea of what life was. I will tell you, however. Life withdraws from the body slowly, by imperceptible degrees. The senses diminish, they become deaf bit by bit, like a color fading into white. And this state of sleepiness, of lassitude is perceived, if anything, as a pleasure.

—That can be said about death from old age or slow illness, but not about violent death.

—It's the same. Inside here are those who died by some unforeseen blow, who have been crushed in a landslide, by the fall of a building; those who have committed suicide, those who have been murdered, those who fell on the gallows. Well, talking casually with them about the sensation of their final passing over, some say they did not have the time to perceive it, it was so instantaneous. Others, for example the executed, testify that they went to their final torment so terrified that at the moment the axe fell or the noose tightened around their neck they felt a sense of liberation and therefore of pleasure. But enough of philosophical ruminations. Let's talk about you. How is it that you are down here?

—You don't know what has happened in Palermo in the last seven days?

—I have no idea. Fortunately, the sounds of the world do not reach here.

—A pandemonium, an inferno.

—What's it about, finally?

—A revolution.

—Another one? No, enough, by all the gods of the underworld! I don't want to hear any more about it. I don't want to be bothered down here too and lose my peace by reason of a final insanity of men, a revolution. I hope you didn't take part in it.

—Well...

—You too, my totally scatterbrained boy? Why did you rebel? for example, *voyons,* let us see.

—I don't know. Maybe no one knows.

—Wonderful! And you set out to turn a country upside down without a reason, without knowing why!...Or maybe I'm the fool. If men knew the reason, they would make neither wars nor revolutions. They say, to improve things, so the world will progress. Progress!—and here the skull burst out in a mocking laugh.—The world will keep on going to hell until its destruction is complete. Evil will grow on evil, like nettles on nettles. Without a cure, without escape.

—One cure there might be, grandmother. To unloose oneself from life, before the world dissolves into putrefaction. I swear to you that if I had a weapon here, I'd do it without a tremor. I am so tired.

—Don't go on, Goffredo. Don't make me cry. Remember that the crying of the dead is horrible. It is a weeping without tears.

A scratching was heard from within the casket.

—What's happening?—Goffredo gave a start.

—Nothing—said the old mummy—I wanted to give you a kiss. I was forgetting, forgetful as I am!, that I'm locked up in this glass coffin. Not able to come out, even to embrace you, to be close to you. What sorrow! Think, for that alone I would accept a return to life.

—But you're weeping, grandma! It's horrible, horrible. Now it's I who must console you and I can't. I have no longer any will or strength. I am suffocating.

An energetic tap on the shoulder awoke Goffredo.

—Forgive me—said the custodian—but it's time to get up. What's the matter? I heard you weeping and moaning in your sleep. Don't lose heart. You'll see that everything will end well. Youth is youth. It always wins.

—I was dreaming of my grandmother. By the way—said Goffredo rubbing his eyes to chase away the cobwebs of sleep—you said that my grandmother is here? Where?

—Two steps away.

In the middle of the aisle, leaning agaist the wall on a mound, a sort of tall pedestal, rose a chest of mahogany decorated with the marchional arms of the Cortada, with a glass cover.

Under the transparent sheet of glass a little old lady was sleeping, not a skeleton, but contracted, shrunken, wrinkled into herself as if she felt the cold in her dress of black silk. Her hands on her bosom, intertwined with a rosary, her head clothed in the usual little black cap from which a few strands of faded hair slipped out, not without coquetry. Under the parchmented and darkened skin the fine lines of the face were almost intact. From their half-opened lids, edged with blond lashes, her eyes peeped out with the fixity of enamel. Everything was motionless in the poor old corpse. Only across her lips, thin and a bit drawn back, there played a smile, a teasing smile that did not wish to die. It seemd that it still breathed over the last words exchanged with her nephew just a moment before. It seemed that she had ceased weeping in order to give her nephew a last farewell without sorrow.

Before leaving, Goffredo wanted to ask the guardian for some news of padre Benedetto, which the sullen and cranky fat friar had not wished to offer.

—Is it a mystery, then?—said the amazed Scalia.—But doesn't everybody know that the holy man is in the infirmary?

—Where?

—In the infirmary of the Cappuccini, via Pietro Nivelli.

—Is he ill?

—He's not well, from what they say. Old and sick, he insisted on helping the cholera victims, and his strength gave way.

—Can one see him?

—What can I tell you? I know it's difficult. You understand, everyone wants to visit him, and if they don't put some limits on it, they'll tire him to death before his time. If Your Excellency wants to try...But right now? Wait until things calm down in the city. For now, I repeat, stay away from the places of religion. *Sunnu pigghiati a occhiu di giustizia,* They're watched by the police. Go and take the air...far away, and God go with you. *Biciamu li manuzzi e bon viaggiu,* We kiss your dear hands, and bon voyage.

Goffredo started to put a silver coin into Scalia's hand, but the man drew back scandalized.

—What are you doing? That would be the lat straw. I have served you with all my heart. Your Excellency deserves it. We are not Christians for nothing, good heavens. One holds out one's hand to another as best one can. Today to you, tomorrow to me.

Chapter 12

HIS NIGHT'S rest, although frequented by nightmares and spirits, and the freshness of the morning had restored Goffredo, driving from him his memory of sufferings undergone and his apprehension of new dangers. Free and quick, with a sense of lightness that ran through all his limbs, at first he slid cautiously and circumspectly across the alleys, hugging the houses like a cat slipping through a room. Then he threw himself into the larger streets with indifferent nonchalance, indeed with the self-confident disdain of youth.

It was a bit after six (by Cadorna's proclamation it was forbidden to go out before that hour) and the city was taking up its ordinary life again, not without effort. A few shops were reopening their shutters, a few carts of prickly pear sellers were being parked at street corners, a few vehicles were crossing at a walking pace, almost hesitant to break the silence with the rumble of their wheels. Except for the large piazzas, where soldiers were bivouacked among symmetrically arranged bundles of arms, solitude reigned everywhere. A solitude rendered obligatory by the decree on the state of siege, according to which every citizen was forbidden to associate publicly with any another.

In piazza Indipendenza, a modest hearse, without flowers, drawn by two black horses, was headed toward the Cappuccini. A crested nobleman's landau followed a few paces behind. It was a curiosity, and passers-by stopped to look at it because until the previous day corpses had been transported by wagons. Municipal funeral services, like all other public services, had been suspended during the uprising. Even those who had died of natural causes had to resign themselves to putrefying in their houses for days and days before reaching their final rest.

Goffredo darted a quick glance into the noble carriage which escorted the hearse, and he seemed to recognize don Marvuglia, the household bursar. For a moment he thought of his uncle Fabrizio. But when the carriage stopped because a patrol demanded its *laissez-passer,* he had the impression that his uncle the marchese was sitting on the box with don Assardi beside him.

It was a matter of seconds. Then the cortège set off again and Goffredo quickly continued on his way, not without imagining to himself about what he had seen. Although estranged as he now was from his family, it was difficult to keep from wondering what new disaster had befallen the house of his ancestors. At the end of those tragic days, who was being accompanied to the cemetery with such modesty and reserve?

The pause of his imagination before the mysteries of the other world did not last long. Torn from the past and the future, he felt crushed in the coils of the present, which had him by the throat. Life, even if he did not love or desire it, pursued him with its strangling rhythm. The instinct for survival, not to let himself become ensnared stupidly in the meshes of some new trial, stung him, lashed him to run far away. But the purpose of seeing padre Benedetto appeared to him at the same time as a vow to be fulfilled, indeed as a moral imperative. An inner voice was commanding him: You *must* see him, you must not go back into the dark night of life without drawing a ray of light from that good soul.

He knocked at the door of the infirmary.

Two eyes shone behind the peephole of the door, and a low and slow voice said:

—*Deo gratias,* what do you want?

—Is father Benedetto of Castellammare here?

—Yes, he's ill.

—I am a friend of his. I have something to tell him.

The door opened and there appeared the figure of a robust friar, with thick dark hair and gentle eyes resembling those of a good poodle.

Goffredo, encouraged by the appearence of the friar, kind with a kindness nourished by clausura and silence, asked:

—Is he in bed?

—Naturally. Where should he be, poor man? The Lord still wishes to try him.

—It's not cholera?

—If it were cholera he wouldn't be here but in the plague hospital or... in the next world—the friar smiled.—What can you do? The saints have hard heads. He wanted to go there, to the plague hospital, to help the cholera victims, as he had done in the previous epidemic. Except that then he was still fresh, notwithstanding his more than sixty years. Now eight more years have passed, which weigh on his shoulders, even if God helps him. Not to mention the other infirmities that have reduced him to a different man.

—What illness does he have?

—What can I tell you?—and the friar shrugged his shoulders—exhaustion, fatigue, weak heart, excessive emotions. The events of these last days have really laid him low. Believe me, it is not too strong a word. And yet he has remained to slave away among the sick, as if he were twenty or thirty years old. A sudden collapse with loss of consciousness. When we saw hin arrive here he looked like a corpse. Now he loses ground every day. He is a light that is going out.

—What do the doctors say?

—They say that if he were not as old as he is, if his system were less compromised, perhaps he could recover. But in his present state, consumed by his labors and his penances, they can only commit him into the hands of God.

—Could I see him?

—Go up and try—said the friar sympathetically.—It isn't up to me. The nursing brother is upstairs. Cell number eighteen, first floor.

Goffredo quickly mounted the stairs, crossed the corridor, sought the infirmarian. Since the corridor was deserted he ventured, not without a tremor, to knock on the door of the indicated cell.

There emerged a young friar with a crisp reddish beard rather thin on his emaciated cheeks, his glance directed steadily at the ground.

—What do you wish?

—Might I see father Benedetto?—asked Goffredo.

The friar's face clouded over.

—The doctors have advised us to spare him any effort, any emotion—he said.

—Is it serious?

—It arouses serious worries. Cardiac crises follow one another, they keep recurring...we don't know how to keep him going.

—It would be enough for me to see him just for a bit, avoiding any agitation.

—Is it really necessary?

—I need to. I come from far away. It would be doing me a real charity...

The little friar lifted his eyes, raising them off the ground almost unwillingly.

—You are a friend, yes? Give me your name so I can pass on the message. If the answer is negative, please don't insist. He may even ask you to come in. Don't tire him, I beg you.

Having Goffredo's name, the friar tiptoed back into the sickroom as if he were crossing the threshold of a church and feared to disturb the halo of silence and invisible light on the head of the suffering man.

The friar reappeared in the doorway soon after and made a silent sign to the visitor to come forward.

—For the love of God—he said quietly into Goffredo's ear—don't drop any reference to his 'holiness' as so many do, it would upset him greatly.

The father rested motionless on his pallet with his head and back raised by several cushions. His beard snowy, his face white as if it had been washed by too many tears; his eyes of a calm blue, paler than usual. The cell barely received light from a little high window, which was woven and rewoven by the frequent songful winging of the sparrows. But a great light breathed in the little space above the poor straw bed, either irradiated by a heavenly source or from the body of the sick man itself.

At Goffredo's entrance, a word was breathed without forming itself on the lips of the sick man, which were accustomed to the unexpressed whisper of prayer.

Goffredo forestalled him.

—Don't speak, father. I will talk. Do you recognize me?

—What will you? My memory is a bit gone. I see everything as through a veil. It's so many years now...Let me look at you...yes, I recognize your features, the family resemblance, my boy. You were a few years younger then...like me. Welcome, my son—and the friar clenched his hands to his chest, as if he wished to embrace his visitor. Poor hands, as colorless and transparent as if they were about to grasp to his bosom our sister the Death of the Body.

—How do you feel?

—All right. Almost content, as on the eve of a great voyage toward better lands. But tell me about you. What have you done in all these years?

Goffredo recounted his adventurous life in a swift summary, from his flight from the house of his uncle and from Aspromonte, up to his long stay in the country and his return to the city to take part in the uprising. Of this last episode he spoke with embarassment and almost with sorrow, as if he were making his confession. He breathed out his discouragement and his dispair, ending:

—I have erred. I must pay.

—Who does not err, my boy? All our life is a forest of errors. If we were allowed to be born again to redress the errors we have committed we would fall into others greater than the first. The best that we can hope to do is to pardon each other. What was your error? Making the revolution? You can say that you were not the only one to err.

—A great part of the people were for the revolution.

—Say instead, all humanity. Not you alone, all humanity deserves pity and pardon. War and revolution will never disppear from the world until men turn from error to the truth. And the truth is this: That only evil can be born from evil, violence begets violence, from blood flows only more blood.

—Then what can one say then when the violence has been useless, when the use of force is crowned by failure?

—Useful! Success!—said father Benedetto severely, trying to instill energy into his voice, which was weakening:— Blasphemy! Evil is never useful. You could show that wars and revolutions, when you add them up, represent a bad business for humanity. You lose a hundred in order to win one...Evil is a tragic farce. It appears disguised, camouflaged in fine appearances, and cries, I am Success. No, we tell it, You are Evil!

—That does not alter the fact that the lack of success is a failure of life. And when life fails, there only remains...

—Only remains?—asked the friar, in order to float the speech of the young man off the shoal on which it had run aground.

—There only remain two ways: to become a hermit, or to shoot oneself.

—Neither the one nor the other—said the father with that deliberate harshness that came to him from a long life of discipline and of grief overcome.—All men, when they are about to shipwreck, pose themselves the strange dilemma, God or the Devil. Their anguish makes them talk nonsense. They believe that sorrow is eternal and that to save themselves from it there is no other escape than to flee from life or to throw themselves into the arms of the Evil One. Blind men, they do not know the pity of God...In this world sorrow is not endless, it has a limit. Among our miseries or among our virtues, there is also this: that we are not capable of being unhappy indefinitely. The Lord, in telling us 'take up your cross and follow me,' never lays on us a cross heavier than what we are able to bear. None suffer more than what they have been allowed to suffer...You are too young to be nailed for life onto the cross of your unhappiness... You will see that soon a small light will illumine your path, a light that wil become ever brighter. You will hear a voice that will say, Rise up and walk! Then the fever of life will seize you again. Then you will march, struggle, fight, fall, you will rise again...and you will come to the conclusion that life, rather than being an earthly adventure, is a duty or rather a service, a divine service...

—For a priest—the young man observed.

—Not for a priest, for everyone, my son. Each of us is in some manner a priest, inasmuch as we are called to guard and feed the holy fire. In fulfilling such a mission you are not allowed either to doubt or to despair. To despair and to desert.

—But if life has bceome useless?

—No deed is without meaning, without value in our existence, when it is rightly and nobly directed. Look. What life is more useless, more powerless, than mine, in my present state? Yet all the same a great resource, an immense force remains to me: prayer. There are prayers that please the Lord more than any other form of action. I have prayed to God so much in these days. I have offered Him my poor life in exchange for a bit of peace for mankind. I have said to Him, 'Here is my existence; count all the sins of mankind—brothers, fellow citizens, friends and even enemies—as mine, let me make amends for the others, provided that their eyes may finally see the light.' I have repeated the words of Moses, 'O Lord, pardon their great failure to my people. If you do not, remove my name from the Book of Life written by you.' I feel that God will pardon, perhaps He has already pardoned. My poor offering lies at His feet and is about to be accepted. I see the signs. God wishes better times to come...

—And that the kingdom of justice may come—continued Goffredo—But will it reallly come? Our country is still in turmoil, and while we kill each other like evil brothers, we maul each other, we tear each other to pieces, the foreigner is still camped on our land.

—The kingdom of justice will never come until man becomes just. But enough of struggles, of violence, of blood, enough of war and revolutions. Let us not tempt the anger of God too far. May charity finally triumph. She alone can bring us peace.

—And I, what shall I do?

—Go back to the land. The land is good, if we know how to plow and cultivate it, as we are plowed by sorrow and made fruitful by adversity... Now kneel and pray.

With the last words, the sick man's face changed color and he fell back on his pillows as if he were choking from a sudden lump in his throat. The tension of thinking and speaking had brought on the reaction of an abrupt faint.

Goffredo rushed out of the cell to inform the nurse.

—I told you not to upset him—he said in a voice of gentle reproof, and hurried to the patient's bed. He tried vainly to administer drops to him. Padre Benedetto's mouth refused, his jaws were clenched so tightly.

He remained unconscious for a few minutes. Then he slowly opened his eyes and attempted to speak.

—*A...ria, a...ri...a*—were the only disjointed syllables that he managed to whisper with his bloodless lips.

The nurse made a sign that the window was already wide open. He opened the door to the corridor as well.

The sick man breathed a sigh of relief. It seemed that his suffering had lessened a bit.

—How goes it, father?—asked Goffredo.

—*Vado ad Patrem,* I am going to my Father—he said in a now distant voice, and made a sign that they should give him the Crucifix hanging on the wall.

When he received it he was transfigured. His eyes were veiled with weeping, a soft weeping in which the blue of his pupils was fading ever more.

Letting go of the Cross a bit, he made a sign to the nurse, perhaps a sign they had agreed upon, begging him with beseeching eyes.

—Stay here a moment—said the friar to Goffredo.—He desires Extreme Unction. I'll go tell them.

A priest in a surplice and stole entered with the vial of holy oil. The prayers for the dying filled the religious silence of the bare cell with their murmur. It was the last act of preparation for death, since the dying man had already received the Viaticum that morning.

The priest recited the *Asperges.* The friar's feet, when they were anointed, were so poor and fleshless that they seemed ready to be pierced by the stigmata at any moment.

When he had been anointed, the dying man requested the grace of being able to kiss the hands of all those present (many friars had gathered in the room) to obtain their pardon. He made signs that he was sad and humiliated at not being able to carry out this duty on his knees. When it was Goffredo's turn, the friar's kiss was more tender and longer than any other. The young man's hand drew back bathed with warm tears.

Suddenly the dying man's strength left him. The dark and doubtful weight of material things detached itself bit by bit from the being which was rendered bright and light by the nearness of death. When the last slender thread that bound him to the earth seemed broken, there was no longer room in the cell except for a great light. It appeared that nothing had died there within. A light continued to live in light.

A subdued sound of knees on the bare ground. A few sobs. The rustling chorus of a *Requiem.*

Goffredo returned to the country as if fulfilling a vow.

When he reached the houses, night was falling.

Uncle Federico was finishing reading a letter from his brother Fabrizio, brought him by hand from the city.

—So poor Teodora is dead—he said, blinking in the faint circle of light projected by the hanging lamp—while she continued stubbornly to watch the last attack on the monastery of the Stimmate from the nuns' grating on the terrace...A recklessness that suggests suicide.

Thoughts without words passed like remote veils in the mind of Goffredo.

—'To disappear without leaving behind even one face in tears...It is the death of beings who were never loved...' continued Federico, as if he were re-reading a passage from the letter.

—Uncle—the youth said suddenly—why think of suicide? It is the Lord who has taken pity on her.

—Germantown NY, 2022

GIUSEPPE MAGGIORE: *Sette e mezzo*

Translator's Notes

Giuseppe Maggiore's novel *Sette e mezzo* was published by Flaccovio of Palermo in 1952, six years before the posthumous appearance of Giuseppe Tomasi di Lampedusa's *Il Gattopardo*. Unlike Lampedusa, Maggiore (1882-1954) was not an aristocrat but a member of the professional classes, a lawyer (and a diehard Fascist). *Sette e mezzo* spans the years 1848-1866, centering on 1862-1866. The main action of *Il Gattopardo* begins in 1860 and ends in 1862, just after Garibaldi's defeat at the battle of Aspromonte in Calabria.

The 1866 Palermo insurrection was nicknamed 'sette e mezzo,' 'seven and a half,' because it lasted just over a week, 16-22 September 1866. 'Sette e mezzo' was a popular card game in which the cards from ace to seven were worth one point each and face cards one-half point. A winning hand was precisely seven-and-a-half points; anything more or less lost. Maggiore refers obliquely to this 'telling and pregnant locution' at the beginning of III/xi:

> The *insecuritas,* the gamble, which stands at the base of every war and revolution, resembles a game in which the last card, the decisive one, is always in the hand of Fate.

Verbal coincidences between Maggiore and Lampedusa can be striking. In *Sette e mezzo* the lecherous *procuratore* don Prospero prepares himself for seduction:

> ...when he had finished wrapping the black cravat with little green dots around the wings of his vast collar and had fastened it with a golden pin—a fine tetradrachm from Selinunte with a chariot mounted by a warrior driving the horses...

Lampedusa's prince Fabrizio dresses for the day:

> It was the moment to wrap the monumental cravat of black silk around his neck. One turn, two turns, three turns. His large delicate fingers composed the folds, spread it out, pinned onto the silk the head of Medusa with its ruby eyes.

But the divergences between the two novels far outweigh their superficial similarities. One striking difference is the almost complete absence from *Sette e mezzo* of the replacement of the old aristocracy by the rising bourgeoisie which constitutes a central theme of *Il gattopardo,* exemplified in the mésalliance of the penniless prince Tancredi with Angelica, the wealthy granddaughter of a peasant known as 'Peppe Mmerda' ('Joe Shit').

Both novels have Palermitan aristocrats of ancient families as central characters (they even share the name Fabrizio). But Lampedusa's prince is intelligent, self-doubting, ironic, grudgingly open to new ideas, a detached and somewhat cynical observer of the decline of his class: 'Noi fummo i gattopardi'—'We were the leopards, after us come the hyenas.' Maggiore's marchese Fabrizio Cortada, on the other hand, is imprisoned by class, inherited privilege, and a rigid and uncharitable religion. He is struggling impotently against the erosion of his world, symbolised by the dethronement of the Bourbon kings of the Two Sicilies.

Political History

We have been conditioned to believe that the achievement of Italian unity in the Risorgimento under the House of Savoy (rulers of Piedmont, known as the kingdom of Sardegna and after 1861 as the kingdom of Italy) with Rome as its capital was a smooth and predestined historical transition.

Scholars have gradually dismantled that myth. As early as 1899 the historian Giustino Fortunato declared that the unification of Italy was a sin against both history and geography, and now the conventional narrative is even being questioned on popular television.

In the wake of the Napoleontic collapse Sicily had been deluded into believing she would again become an independent state, but in 1815 France and England forced her subjection to the Bourbon kings of Naples, who became the rulers of the kingdom of the Two Sicilies. Abortive uprisings in Sicily followed in 1820 and 1837, exacerbated by an epidemic of cholera which killed more than 41,000 Sicilians. The first of the 1848 revolutions which swept most of Europe broke out in Palermo.

Piedmont originally envisioned the unification of Italy as being basically the territorial expansion of the House of Savoy. Meeting in 1858, Napoleon III and count Camillo Cavour, the Savoyard prime minister, projected a greater Piedmont created by the annexation of Parma, Modena, Lombardy-Venetia, Romagna; Tuscany plus Umbria and the papal Marche; and the kingdom of the Two Sicilies. In March of 1860 Tuscany united with Piedmont. The following May, Giuseppe Garibaldi landed with his Thousand at Marsala and entered Palermo. In September a plebiscite whose dubious legality is vividly depicted in *Il gattopardo* annexed Sicily to Piedmont. On February 13 of 1861 the fortress of Gaeta, the last refuge of the Bourbons of the Two Sicilies, capitulated, and king Francesco II and his wife Maria Sophia (whose joint portrait figures prominently in Chapter I/1 [see Frontispiece]) went into exile. The next month the king of Piedmont-Sardegna assumed the title of king of Italy as Victor Emmanuel II.

Sicily was ruled by the house of Savoy from a distant continental capital (Turin, then Florence in 1865, finally Rome in 1870) as conquered territory. Instead of simple annexation by Piedmont, alternative solutions for Sicily had been proposed and were being ventilated again in 1864, as at the end of Chapter I/1 of the novel: '[T]he island completely independent; the island united with the kingdom of Naples; the island autonomous but a member at the same time of an Italian league or confederation, with or without the pope presiding.' (Whether or not Rome was to become the capital of a united Italy, it would remain the center of world Catholicism.)

In 1862 Garibaldi began recruiting a volunteer army with the intention of solving the 'Roman question' by annexing the papal city under the banner 'O Roma, o morte,' 'Rome, or death.' He was opposed by the Savoy government and by Napoleon III, whom pope Gregory XVI had been forced to call in as guarantor of papal liberty until the emperor's defeat and capture by Prussia at Sedan in 1870. Garibaldi's forces met their opponents near the hill of Aspromonte in Calabria on 28 August 1862 and a brief battle followed the next day. Garibaldi ordered his forces not to fire on their brothers of the kingdom of Italy, but a few shots were exchanged, and Garibaldi was wounded. His troops were pursued as criminals but were eventually amnestied on 5 October, and Garibaldi returned to exile on his island of Caprera.

The Sette e mezzo revolt against the Savoy government took place on 16-22 September, a parenthesis in the third Italian war of independence, fought in June-August of 1866 between Italy, allied with Prussia, against Austria. On 16 June Prussia opened hostilities and on 23 June Italy declared war on Austria with an eye toward detaching Milan and Venice from the Austrian empire. Two events are referred to frequently but obliquely in *Sette e mezzo*: on 24 June, Austria defeated Italy at the battle of Custoza and again on 20 July at a sea-battle in the waters off the Dalmatian island of Lissa The Italian ironclad *Il Re d'Italia* was rammed and sunk by the Austrian admiral with great loss of life. These setbacks were balanced by the Prussian defeat of Austria at Königgratz on 3 July 1866 and the Italian defeat of Austria at Versa on 26 July. In October, Austria ceded to France its Italian territories of Venetia, Friuli, and Mantua, which were then annexed by Italy, a gain confirmed by another puppet plebiscite.

Sette e mezzo begins on January 16 of 1864, the official birthday of the dethroned Francesco II, Bourbon king of the Two Sicilies. With the arrival of young Goffredo Cortada the time shifts back some two years, and Part I ends before the amnesty of October 1862. Part II centers around the *cavaliere* Federico Cortada, the marchese's younger brother, in a flashback to Austria and Germany in 1848 documenting the roles of Marx, Engels, and Bakunin in the revolutionary movement. It ends with the proclamtion of the Aspromonte amnesty in October 1862. Part III begins in 1866: III/7 is dated 'the eve of the insurrection of September 1866,' and continues until the end of the uprising and its aftermath.

PALERMO

Sette e mezzo requires some knowledge of Palermitan geography. Looking at the city from the sea, on the right towers rocky monte Pellegrino with its sanctuary of santa Rosalia, the *Santuzza,* the patroness of Palermo. Beneath it lie the Colli, the Hills, the site of the summer villas of the aristocracy that figure so largely in *Il Gattopardo.* Behind the city rise the sharp pointed peaks of the extinct volcano Monte Cuccio and other mountains. The coastal plain on which Palermo and its hinterland are situated is called the Conca d'Oro. It once extended from under monte Pellegrino east toward the summer village of Bagheria for about one hundred square kilometers. At the period of the novel the Conca d'oro was filled with citrus orchards, which gave it its name, the Golden Valley, a famous beauty spot.

Describing the geography of Palermo is conplicated by the fact that its main axis runs roughly south-west to north-east. However, maps of the city are conventionally oriented north to south, like the map in the Touring Club Italiano *Guida di Sicilia,* or occasionally even west-east, as in the *Companion Guide to Sicily.* Real compass directions will be employed here.

Palermo was anciently divided by the crossing of its two principal streets into four **mandamenti** or districts, under a variety of names still in use: the Kalsa (NE), the Albergheria (SE), Seralcadio (Monte di Pietà, Capo, SW), and Castellammare (Loggia, NW), named for the fortress on the farther shore of the bay of the Cala, partially demolished by the Piedmontese in 1860.

At the time of the novel the heart of the city was defined by two streets, as it still is. The **Cássaro** (also known as via Toledo, now officially corso Vittorio Emanuele) runs from the main southern entrance into Palermo at the Porta Nuova and the Royal Palace in a straight line through the city to Porrta Felice at the shore. Starting from the Royal Palace, a.k.a. palazzo dei Normanni, seat of the royal government as the residence of the Savoy prefect, the Cassaro passes on the right piazza Vittoria, where in 1866 trenches were dug to protect the palace; on the left the archiepiscopal palace and the cathedral and its precinct; farther along on the right is the church of the Santissimo Salvatore. Nearly opposite is **palazzo**

Geraci, the setting of a key scene in the novel, situated between the salita Montevergini and piazza Bologni. Further down, piazza Bologni opens on the right, connected to via Macqueda by **via D'Alessi**, site of a crucial blockade in the novel. The **Foro Italico** (formerly Foro Borbonico), from which Goffredo and his companions set out to join Garibaldi, is a large open space which runs along the shore of the Kalsa from the garden of villa Giulia to porta Felice.

The east-west axis of Palermo is **via Maqueda**, running across the old walled city from Porta S. Antonio to Porta Maqueda. The place where the two arteries cross is called the **Quattro Canti di Città**, the Four Corners of the City, officially (and confusingly) named **piazza Vigliena**. Modelled on the Quattro Fontane of Rome and laid out by order of the Spanish viceroy marchese di Vigliena in 1608-20, its four curved façades are decorated with fountains and statues representing the four seasons, the four Spanish kings of Sicily, and the four sainted patronesses of Palermo. At the crossing with the Cassaro stands the church of **san Giuseppe dei teatini**, whose tall campanile serves as an observation post and sniper's nest in the novel.

Piazza Pretoria, the seat of the city government, is is located just across via Maqueda from the Quattro Canti and is centered on its great sixteenth-century Florentine fountain. The palace of the Municipio is also known as **palazzo delle Aquile.** The **teatro Carolino**, the site of another important scene in the novel, is located in behind piazza Pretoria. The **Fieravecchia** to the east of the Quattro Canti in the Kalsa mandamento is marked by a statue of the Genius of Palermo, recently restored. The site of an ancient market, it had been a focus of revolutionary expression in previous uprisings.

The **via Alloro**, the site of the Cortada palace, runs parallel to the Cassaro from piazza Pretoria to the foro Italico. A decaying aristocratic street wedged between the plebeian districts of the Steri and the Kalsa, via Alloro is the site of many notable palaces, several of them damaged in WW II, such as the gothic palazzo Abbatellis, now the Galleria Regionale, and the ruined palazzo Bonagia with its superb Baroque double staircase. The enormous Franciscan church of santa Maria della Gancia boasts the 'buca della salvezza,' the hole through which two imprisoned patriots managed to tunnel an escape from the Bourbon forces in 1860.

Prisons: the Palazzo delle Finanze was built in 1844 on the site of the Spanish prison of the **Vicaria**, near the bay of the Cala at the edge of piazza Marina, centered on the giardino Garibaldi with its magnificent *ficus magnoliades*. The **Ucciardone,** which replaced the Vicaria, is located to the west of the Castelammare mandamento and was opened in 1842. The gothic **Steri**, the former palace and prison of the Inquisition, faces on piazza Marina.

The central portal of the façade of palazzo Filangeri di Cutò, a palace at the eastern end of via Maqueda, was known as the **arco di Cutò** and was used as a public passage. In Chapter III/8, Goffredo and his companions set out on foot from the western end of town, in the neighborhood of the ponte dell'Ammiraglio. They follow the Corso dei mille, momentarily blocked by a barricade at porta s. Antonino, then via Maqueda, passing under the arco di Cutò to piazza del Carmine, and on to their destination, a palace in via s. Chiara.

The lovely Spanish Gothic church of **s. Maria della Catena,** where don Assardi exercises his dubious pastoral ministrations, is located on the edge of the bay of the Cala, a short walk from the Cortada palace.

The convent of the **Cappuccini**, Franciscan Friars Minor, and its adjacent catacombs, which play a recurring role in *Sette e mezzo*, are located on the outskirts of Palermo (compass SW). Just as described in the novel, the church faces on a piazza featuring 'two plane trees and a rough and imposing wooden cross.' The catacombs still exist and remain a grim tourist attraction. Their contents have been estimated at some 8,000 corpses and 1,252 mummies. Either through a natural process of mummification or by more sophisticated means, the corpses in the catacombs remain more or less intact and recognizable. They are hung along the underground corridors variously arranged by gender, age, rank and profession, and are dressed in their original garments.

The marchesa Teodora Cortada is immured in the convent of the **Stimmate** where she dies mysteriously, perhaps a suicide, while stubbornly following the battle for Palermo from the nuns' balcony on the convent terrace (terraces and balconies which allowed nuns to observe without being seen were a regular feature of Sicilian convents). The church of san Francesco delle Stimmate and its monastery of the Clarisse urbaniste di Santa Chiara, called the Stimmate di San Francesco, were located on via Maqueda, at the western end of town near the barricade erected at porta Maqueda. During the sette e mezzo uprising the monastery was captured by the insurgent forces and employed as a fortress against the royal troops, its roof terrace a nest for snipers. With the defeat of the rebellion the nuns were expelled and the monastery was converted to secular uses. In 1875 it was demolished along with several other religious institutions to make room for the construction of the opera house, the pachydermic Teatro Massimo Vittorio Emanuele.

The **vicolo conte Cagliostro**, site of the café Indipendenza in Chapter III/7, is a small grungy street running from Benefratelli to piazzetta Ballaró in the Albergheria quarter. **Via Gioiamia**, the decrepit residence of the lecherous don Prospero, is tucked in behind the cathedral, running from via Matteo Bonelli to piazza s. Cosimo in the Capo. The spacious park of **villa d'Aumale**, used as a dueling ground in III/ii, is located just outside Porta nuova to the east.

Outside Palermo:

The royal park of **La Favorita** extends between the Colli and Monte Pellegrino with its gate at the porta Leoni. It is traversed by parallel rides dedicated to Diana, with a statue of the goddess, and Hercules, with a fountain. **Ficuzza**, where Garibaldi assembles his volunteer army for the march on Rome, is a former Bourbon hunting lodge and forest some 30 km. south of Palermo.

Some characters mentioned in the text:

Giuseppe Balia: a garrulous and opportunistic revolutionary who appears in III/viii

Gabriel Camozzi: head of the National Guard

Salvatore Maniscalco: in 1849 he was placed in control of the Bourbon police and became famous for cruelty and repression.

Giovanni Meli (1740-1815): poet in the Sicilian language. A somewhat critical view of his liberalism is taken in the novel.

Salvatore Miceli: double agent, mysteriously released from prison, hailed as a liberator of political prisoners.

Felice Pinna: head of the Palermo police under the Piedmontese.

Bettino Ricasoli (1809-80): a puritanical Florentine nobleman, succeeded Camillo Cavour as prime minister of Sardegna-Piedmont in 1861; he resigned office in 1862 and returned in 1866.

Marchese Rudinì (1839-1908) the twenty-seven-year-old mayor of Palermo.

Luigi Torelli (1810-87). Prefect of Palermo 1862-64, 1866. A more complex figure than the clown depicted in the novel: hero of the Five Days of Milan in 1848, holder of ministeries such as agriculture under the Piemontese, of whose government he was s strong supporter. The débacle of Palermo marred but did not end his later career.

The uprising

The Piedmontese considered the Sicilians to be sub-civilised barbarians worse than the Bedouins of Algeria and governed them accordingly. A forced military draft, a novelty in Sicily, was widely resented. The cancellation of the feast of santa Rosalia was an insult to Sicilian culture, as was the partial demolition of the fortress of Castellammare in Palermo. The confiscation of the Sicilian National Bank, whose resources surpassed those of Piedmont, was a simple act of theft. The expropriation of Church property in 1865 resulted in widespread misery and in the closing of religious schools, whose inadequate replacement by the State deliberately increased the spread of illiteracy and consequent political impotence. An epidemic of cholera resulted in some 4,000 victims. By 1866 civil order was disintegrating; the Piedmontese retained control of Sicily only through a massive presence of continental and foreign troops (Bavarian mercenaries), especially in the west of the island (now prime mafia territory).

This discontent created a patchwork coalition: disappointed partisans of Garibaldi's Mille after the defeat of Aspromonte, jobless functionaries of the Bourbon kingdom of the Two Sicilies, doctrinaire Bourbon monarchists, religious adherents protesting the confiscation of Church property, opponents of the annexation of Sicily to the new Italian state. Some diagnosed the uprising as a clerical-Bourbon plot, others as a republican conspiracy headed by Giuseppe Badia, a leader of the Palermo Workman's

Society and an advocate of Sicilian separatism. The insurgency was supported by the middle and lower classes of society, who were economically disproportionately affected by the expropriation of the religious houses: peasants, artisans, coachmen, builders, butchers, tailors, municipal employees, open market traders such as porters and carters.

In the night of 15-16 September 1866 a barricade was erected in the vicolo D'Alessi leading from piazza Bologni to via Maqueda. On 16 September the city was invaded just before dawn by bands from mafia-controlled Monreale and the surrounding settlements. At midday the Municipio was bombarded by the insurgents, prompting a momentarily successful sortie by the beleaguered civil authorities. They were fired on from the terrace of the Stimmate and fell back to the Palazzo Reale.

The insurgents assembled a principal barricade of the Cassaro from porta Nuova with a hinge at the Quattro Canti (piazza Vigliena) toward the barricade at porta Maqueda in order to to keep the besieging government forces assembled on the south outside the porta Nuova from combining with reinforcements disembarking from the sea at the north end of the Casssaro (porta Felice). The rebels aimed to cut communcations between the military command at the Palazzo Reale and the city government at the Municipio.

On Sept.17 the the government troops abandoned the Municipio and fell back to the Palazzo Reale. The mob, led by Salvatore Miceli, moved on to the prisons to free political prisoners. Miceli was a turncoat who had been an agent of Salvatore Maniscalco, the Bourbon chief of police. He then became the confidant of Felice Pinna, the Savoyard Palermo police chief. Miceli had been arrested for revolutionary activity but had been illegally released from prison by Pinna, who was suspected of favoring the uprising. The mob was fired on by the steam corvette *Tancredi* from the Cala and Miceli was killed.

By 18 September the rule of the mob was complete and the civil and military authorities were contemplating surrender.

On the morning of 22 September a government fleet with reinforcing troops was sighted and the battleship *Re di Portugallo* began the bombardment of the Palermo marina. A battalion of Bersaglieri advanced from porta Nuova, and the arriving forces moved up the Cassaro from the marina. The insurgents were caught between two fires, their main barricade was breached, and by early afternoon the uprising was finished, to be followed by fierce reprisals on the part of the government.

CPSIA information can be obtained
at www.ICGtesting.com
Printed in the USA
LVHW080456111022
730425LV00009B/354

9 781954 744721